Lord
of the
Libraries

TOR BOOKS BY MEL ODOM

The Rover
Hunters of the Dark Sea
The Destruction of the Books
Lord of the Libraries

Lord
of the
Libraries

mel odom

TOR®

A TOM DOHERTY ASSOCIATES BOOK
NEW YORK

This is a work of fiction. All the characters and events portrayed in this novel are either fictitious or are used fictitiously.

LORD OF THE LIBRARIES

This book is printed on acid-free paper.

Edited by Brian Thomsen

A Tor Book
Published by Tom Doherty Associates, LLC
175 Fifth Avenue
New York, NY 10010

www.tor.com

Tor® is a registered trademark of Tom Doherty Associates, LLC.

Library of Congress Cataloging-in-Publication Data

Odom, Mel.
    Lord of the libraries / Mel Odom.—1st U.S. ed.
       p.   cm.
    "A Tom Doherty Associates Book."
    ISBN 0-765-30724-3 (acid-free paper)
    EAN 978-0-765-30724-8
    1. Libraries—Fiction. 2. Librarians—Fiction.
    3. Apprentices— Fiction. 4. Older people—Fiction. 5. Book collecting—Fiction. I. Title.
    PS3565.D53L67   2005
    813'.54—dc22
                                       2004029202

First Edition: July 2005

Printed in the United States of America

0 9 8 7 6 5 4 3 2 1

Lord
of the
Libraries

Holding the Line

Novice Librarian Dockett Butterblender cowered in the shredded shadows left to the night. He had not managed to escape the vicious trap that had sprung in the Vault of All Known Knowledge as had many of the Librarians. All around him, goblinkin battled the dwarves who had sworn to shed their life's blood to protect the Great Library.

Firelight gleamed across the scaly green hides of the goblinkin. They shouted and snarled, their black hair in disarray. Some of them had smoking heads from the embers that burned in their hair. They waved their weapons and set ladders to scale the walls of the Vault of All Known Knowledge.

Not far from where Dockett hid and shivered in fear, a knot of archers with horned helms took up positions along a jutting shelf where the Library's wall had been breached. The archers resembled lizards, and the little dweller knew that they had to be beings summoned from some other place by the treacherous spell that had stricken the Library and filled the great halls with enemies for the first time in its long history.

As Dockett watched, goblinkin grabbed Librarians

and heaved them from the walls. Then dwarves rushed in—too late!—and cut down their vicious foes. Humans up from Greydawn Moors, the town at the foothills of the Knucklebones Mountains, arrived now, accompanied by elven warders and their animal companions.

But no dwellers accompanied them.

The fact hurt Dockett. *We're not warriors,* the Novice Librarian told himself. *The Old Ones didn't create the dwellers to be warriors. We were made to hide and to preserve ourselves.* He wanted desperately to hide even now.

However, he was training as a Librarian as well. Under one arm, he carried a bundle of books wrapped in a wall mural he'd rescued from one of the burning rooms. If he had truly wished to save his own hide, he would have abandoned his efforts at rescuing anything from the Library. He knew his da would reprimand him for ever taking the chance that he did if he found out. His da ran a tavern down in Greydawn Moors and was loath to give up a son as a Librarian to the Vault of All Known Knowledge. Most dwellers resented losing their children (their free labor!) to the Great Library as had been the arrangement since the beginning.

So many other Librarians fled. Dockett saw them running hither and thither, screaming for help, for someone to rescue them. None of them would blame him for dumping the load he carried and seeing to his own escape.

Ah, but you would be going back on your word that you gave to the Grandmagister, wouldn't you? a voice chided Dockett at the back of his mind. *You swore that you would cherish and defend the Library.*

In the hallways, Dockett had seen Grandmagister Edgewick Lamplighter doing all that he could do to save the Library's inventory. And, as ever, First Librarian Juhg had been at the Grandmagister's heels.

Dockett pressed himself against the stone wall and wished for a path that he might follow to safety. And he wished that the wizard Craugh would appear. The wizard was powerful, a force even the army that lay siege to the Vault of All Known Knowledge would fear.

Except that someone had told Dockett that Craugh was down in the basement levels of the mountain where the lowest rooms were. Some said that he was dead, slain by the spell that had broken the Library and released the raiders that now slew everyone they found in their path.

Elven warders set themselves at the walls across from the lizard archers. In the space of a heartbeat, the elves bent their bows and loosed arrows at their enemies. Several of the shafts pierced the lizards and sent them tumbling from the walls.

Despite his fear, Dockett saw the courage and the skill of the elven warders. Their race produced legendary bowmen the way oak trees produced acorns. He had read accounts of the elven bowmen in books among the Library's holdings, but he had never before seen them in action. It was savage and beautiful at the same time.

Without warning, an explosion ripped into the rooftop behind the elves, filling the night with roiling yellow flames. Rocks shot high into the air, bowling over the dwarven warriors guarding a few of the surviving Librarians. The blast temporarily deafened Dockett.

He took advantage of the distraction to creep farther along the narrow stone shelf that he'd climbed out onto when he'd had to abandon the room where he'd been hiding. Goblinkin had very nearly gotten him then. Thankfully, the shelf was generous with space even though it didn't allow him to reach the ground nearly fifty feet below.

As he watched the bloody battle, Dockett remembered several accounts he'd read of wars and skirmishes. He'd always wondered how the historians and writers had managed to detail the events while standing in the middle of those things. Then he realized that if they had not, battles such as the one waged by the elven archers against the lizard archers might not ever be recorded.

9

Were they this scared? Dockett wondered. *Could they possibly have been as frightened as I am and still manage to write accounts of all the terrible and brave things they had seen?*

He knew it had to be true.

Having nowhere to go, mesmerized by the battle before him, Dockett placed his bundle of books on the ledge beside him. He took out his personal journal, the one the Grandmagister encouraged all Librarians to carry everywhere (because the Grandmagister had learned firsthand the value of keeping a journal with him after being kidnapped by dwarven pirates from the Blood-Soaked Sea), and sat down. He took a stick of charcoal from his bag of inks, quills, and charcoal.

With dexterity and confidence, Dockett attacked the page. The Grandmagister had impressed upon him the value of Librarians, and of the

Vault of All Known Knowledge. He couldn't sit by and do nothing. He had a calling. The Grandmagister had seen it in him, and had told him that one day Dockett would know what that calling was.

Now, with the charcoal in hand, with the page clean and blank before him, along with the vision of the battle and the warriors, Dockett knew what that calling was. The fear vanished as he was consumed by his work.

And the battle raged on around him.

Weeks Later . . .

Death sculled silently across the coastal waters of the Blood-Soaked Sea. It came in small longboats equipped with black sails and was divided among dozens of goblinkin armed with swords, axes, and bows. Some of them pulled at oars and the oarlocks creaked with the strain. The northerly wind brought in great rolling heaps of gray fog as well as the invaders.

Varrowyn Forgeborn ran through the forest along the coastline to meet them. His heart sang with the anticipation of the coming battle. He carried naked steel in his hands, and his intent was to ambush the goblinkin and kill them all. The act would be a warning to others, but it would also be vengeance for the attack the goblinkin and their allies had made on the place and the city that he had sworn his life and blood to protect.

Occasionally, the cold tide still brought in the bodies of the dead— elves, dwarves, humans, dwellers, goblins, and sometimes things that could not be so easily identified—that had not been eaten outright and only munched on by the (only lately) overfed monsters that lived in the wine-dark sea. Those bodies that had belonged to Greydawn Moors—the elves, dwarves, humans, and the dwellers—were seen to and buried as they arrived. At least, as much of them as could be recovered was buried.

Goblinkin and other *things* were thrown back into the sea with the outgoing tide for the monsters to have another go at. Of late, there had been less killing so the numbers of the dead had decreased. The defenders of Greydawn Moors had proven the taking of the island costly, and goblinkin were never known for bravery. Their savagery, however, was phenomenal. The goblin ships out in the Blood-Soaked Sea awaited reinforcements from the mainland, but evidently some of the commanders grew impatient.

Or mayhap they only intended to test the strength of the chosen victims.

Varrowyn intended to fill the outgoing tide with the bloodied bodies of his enemies.

Tonight, with the absence of true moonlight, with Jhurjan the Swift and Bold only a pale crimson thumbnail in the cloudy sky and Gesa the Fair and Lovely only a dim silver twinkle, the goblinkin thought to send a raiding party from the ships they used to blockade the island.

Those blasted beasties are gonna have themselves a surprise or two, though. Varrowyn's thoughts were grim and determined as he paused to listen. He put out a hand and brought the warriors behind him to a halt. They obeyed in the space of a heartbeat. He was a captain of the surviving dwarves who had pledged their lives to defend the Vault of All Known Knowledge.

Generations of his family had served before him, but none of them had ever been called upon to shed blood as he had. Several of the warriors he'd trained, battle-ready though not battle-hardened, had died during the vicious attack that had left the Great Library in ruins less than a month before. He had seen to their burials and mourned them. He still missed them.

Ears straining, Varrowyn heard the sound of cautious oars moving in oarlocks. The goblinkin weren't far out now. He pulled at his beard and smiled in anticipation, then once more trotted through the darkness along the shelf of thickly forested land that butted out into the sea.

Clad in full armor, Varrowyn carried his battle-axe in both mailed hands. The rest of his gear was padded so it would not make a sound, colored with lampblack so it would not reflect even the wan moonlight. The goblinkin would not know he or the island's other defenders were among them until the first of them had been shorn of their lives.

Halting again, Varrowyn looked through the darkness and spied Farady, one of the elven warders who had sworn to watch over the islands.

"Do ye see them?" Varrowyn asked quietly. The elf's vision was, at times, keener than his.

Farady Shellon was slender and bronzed by the sun. He wore a hooded cloak that hid his pointed ears and his alabaster hair but not his faintly luminous amethyst eyes. As a warder, he cared for the ecology of the island, keeping the wild things—animal and vegetation—balanced and in good health. He held a longbow in his hand and carried a longsword in a scabbard between his shoulders.

In the combined darkness of the hood and the moonless night, the elven warder's eyes glowed a little brighter. "Yes. They cannot hide from Whisperwing." He stretched his gloved left hand up into the sky.

Soundlessly, a great horned owl dropped out of the darkness, furled its wings, and clasped its black claws around Farady's gloved hand. Varrowyn knew even the leather glove wouldn't have protected the elf's hand if the owl wished him harm. The bird was huge, with a wingspread nearly eight feet across. The elven warder looked too slender to support the large creature, though he did so with apparent ease.

"There are four boatloads." Farady took a morsel from a pouch on a leather strap looped around his neck. "Twenty to a boat. Eighty warriors."

Varrowyn knew his elven friend had peered at their enemies through his animal companion's eyes. Whisperwing could do many things, but the great horned owl could not count. Varrowyn spat in disgust.

"Call them eighty in number," Varrowyn admonished. "Don't dignify them goblinkin by callin' 'em warriors." He hefted his axe. "We got warriors here that are standin' tall against them toad-faces."

A faint smile touched Farady's lips. "Still. Eighty of them. And only thirty of us."

"I know, I know. Ain't hardly worth the time nor the trouble of gettin' up outta bed." Varrowyn turned and scented the air. He thought he scented a faint, acrid goblin stench. "There's others gonna be upset we didn't wake 'em to share." He spoke bravely, but he knew that Farady was aware they'd been pressed for time when they'd assembled the group he led. "Take me to 'em."

Throwing the owl once more into the night, the elven warder took the lead.

Varrowyn followed, knowing Farady moved in the direction he'd seen through his animal companion's eyes. They were thirty strong from Greydawn Moors. That thirty was a mixed bag, though, of elves, dwarves, and humans. All of them warriors who had volunteered to stay on the island even though they knew a goblinkin army would come for them.

Since the destruction last month of the Great Library, Greydawn Moors—the city that lay at the bottom of the Knucklebones Mountains under the brutal twists of the ridges called the Ogre's Fingers—had remained in a state of panic. (Of course, that was primarily because dwellers—the race of small people given the custodial responsibility of the Library by the Builders—were in the greatest numbers in the city.) Only a month ago, an army of Dread Riders and Blazebulls, accompanied by other creatures and enemies, had arrived at the Library through a spell of trickery.

During the battle that ensued, the Vault of All Known Knowledge had been all but destroyed, all but razed to the ground. Most of the collections of books were eradicated as they had been by the Goblin Horde under the command of Lord Kharrion so many years ago. The Unity, the armies made up of dwarves, elves, and humans, had sought to protect the libraries that they could. The rich farmland of Teldane's Bounty was no more there, and monsters roamed the wreckage of the coastline.

Were it not for Craugh the wizard, one of the oldest friends of the Library, Varrowyn was certain that not only the Vault of All Known Knowledge would have been destroyed, but every living person in Greydawn Moors would have been slain and the city burned to the ground.

Varrowyn's head was filled with bitter thoughts. It irritated him because he knew he needed to be focused on the coming battle. Outnumbered almost three to one, his group would have a hard time of it. He couldn't imagine being beaten. His pride wouldn't even allow him to admit that possibility existed.

Farady halted at the edge of a scrap of rocky land that peered out over the Blood-Soaked Sea. He had his bow to hand and an arrow nocked.

The incoming tide lapped the broken rocks twenty feet below. If the goblinkin intended to make their landing there, they would find the going treacherous and slippery.

Without turning, Varrowyn lifted his left hand and waved the warriors behind him into hiding. Sea spray from the tide that slapped the rocks lining the coast mixed with the rolling fog and the night. Except for the port at Greydawn Moors, the island was a cold and inhospitable place. The Builders had planned it that way. The only easy access to the island was through the harbor at Greydawn Moors where undersea monsters patrolled the waters.

Goblinkin weren't by nature sailors, but after Lord Kharrion's final battle, when the Goblin Lord had been killed, the goblins still outnumbered the other races of the world. It had taken time, but the goblinkin had gradually ventured out on the sea in captured ships, drawn by greed and by bloodlust. However, they had never learned to build vessels, using only those vessels they took from others.

Crouching, his battle-axe comfortably in both hands, Varrowyn stared out at the fog swirling above the black sea. Dirty silver foam rode the curlers into the harsh shoreline where rocks waited like a mouthful of broken fangs.

The dwarf couldn't see his enemy, but he knew they were there. He heard the creaking oarlocks and smelled the goblinkin stench plainly now.

A twig snapped behind him.

Instantly, Varrowyn turned and trotted back through the ranks. "Who was that?" he whispered. "What lead-footed numbskull wasn't watchin' where he was steppin'?"

A chorus of "not-mes" sprang up. The offender didn't step forward.

Varrowyn wasn't used to having to ask twice. Fouling up earned a sharp rebuke, but not immediately taking responsibility for fouling up when he asked earned a quick knot on the head when he caught the perpetrator. And he always caught them. The dwarven captain also wasn't used to anyone in his command making such a mistake, but there were humans among the elves and dwarves tonight.

"Wasn't us, Varrowyn," Anell said quietly. He was a young dwarf, but he'd been blooded in the battle for the Vault of All Known Knowledge.

Over the last month, Varrowyn had seen the young warrior age years. The quick and good fun of youth was gone, replaced by a haunted soberness.

"Then who?" Varrowyn demanded. "I got goblinkin lookin' to make a landin'. I ain't got time for somebody to be blamin' forest creatures. I know they's been settled down by the warders." He scowled at the humans, who didn't always come graceful to woodcraft.

"Was these two," a voice in the back stated.

A slender elven warder in a hooded cloak pushed two small figures forward.

"Please," one of them whispered. "We meant no harm. We only wanted to see."

Surprise drew a curse from Varrowyn, who seldom cursed except during the heat of battle, as he studied the two the elven warder had rousted from the forest. They were barely three feet tall, dressed in gray robes, and cowered with their heads tucked down into their shoulders like they were second cousins to turtles or baby chicks trying to hide their heads under their own wings.

"Dwellers," one of the humans snarled in derision.

Varrowyn knew that many among the elves, dwarves, and humans didn't have respect for the dwellers. Slight of stature and prodigious of appetite, egotistical and stingy (all of this through a combination of birth and upbringing), dwellers were cowards at heart.

The Old Ones' magic had brought the dwellers into the world and given them the responsibility of caring for the Vault of All Known Knowledge. As the books had been destroyed under Lord Kharrion's orders, the world had fallen into dim and cold ignorance. Reading and writing vanished, along with histories and scientific knowledge. Nothing was spared. Oral traditions could only keep so many things alive. On the island, the dwellers of Greydawn Moors taught their children to read so they could serve in the Great Library.

Unfortunately, over the years and the generations, the dwellers in Greydawn Moors had come to resent the human Grandmagisters who had orchestrated the cataloguing and restoration of the books that the Unity had successfully transported to the island. The dwellers had chosen to step away from their duties and concentrate instead on mealtimes and finding ways to fill their coin purses through secret trade with the mainland. They sent fewer children to the Library, and those children spent less time there as well.

As a result, the dwellers earned only derision and scorn from the dwarves, elves, and humans who lived on the island. All of them still gave everything they had to offer.

Some of the dwarves had sworn their lives and the lives of their children for generations to the protection of the Great Library. The elves had sworn on as warders to care for the island and the creatures that roamed it. Because they were so drawn to the sea, humans had agreed to operate the navy and pirate fleets that protected the island.

Other warriors made derisive comments as well.

The two dwellers stood tight against each other, fidgeting and nervous. The small hands of each caught at the robe of the other. One of them carried a book and a Librarian's bag containing writing utensils and inks.

Children, Varrowyn realized. He quieted the warriors with a terse command.

The silence fell immediately, broken only by the sweep of the oars out over the water.

"What are ye two doin' here?" Varrowyn made his voice gruff. "An' ye'll not be talkin' loud, ye won't."

The tallest one, though only by two inches, struggled to answer and finally got it out. "We-we-we had to c-c-come."

"Ye had to." Varrowyn pulled irritably at his beard. "If'n I asked yer ma, would she say ye had to come here tonight?"

"No, Varrowyn," the dweller replied. He was dark haired and fair, with the leanness of youth on him that a life of largesse hadn't yet blunted. "My ma would have my da to thrash me good."

"Well, out here in the dark, what with goblins in them waters, ye deserve a thrashin', ye do. If yer ma was to find yer beds empty, she'd be worried sick, she would." Varrowyn had such a mother still yet to this day.

"I know," the dweller lad said. "But we knew the goblinkin were coming and that you were going to fight them."

"How did ye come to know that?"

16

"Our d-d-da owns the Sea Breeze T-t-tavern. Rutak and I d-d-do kitchen chores there sometimes. My n-n-name is Dockett Butterblender. We w-w-were there when you came c-c-calling for warriors tonight." The young dweller looked glum. "When we get b-b-back, I expect our d-d-da to w-w-whip us anyway."

"An' still ye came." Varrowyn shook his head. That wasn't ordinary behavior for dwellers. They never risked unless there was something to be gained and they felt certain about the outcome.

"Hopin' to see some blood spilt," one of the dwarves said. His white grin split the night. "That's not such a bad thing, Varrowyn."

"W-w-wasn't to come s-s-see blood spilled," Dockett Butterblender said. "I c-c-came to do the t-t-task Grandmagister Lamplighter wanted us to do. We h-h-heard about the t-t-talk he gave at the town m-m-meeting before the goblinkin attacked." He shook his head. "Until t-t-the attack, I'd never seen b-b-battle."

Most of you hadn't, Varrowyn thought. He felt bad that children had been forced to bear witness to such atrocities. Not only that, but many of them had been victims of the flaming catapult loads of pitchblende and rock that goblinkin ships had hurled into the city from the harbor. None of the dwellers living on the island had ever been exposed to war.

For hundreds of years, Greydawn Moors had gone long forgotten and never again found. Sailors plied the sea for trade with the mainland, and all the crews were sworn to secrecy about the existence of the Vault of All Known Knowledge and the Librarians that kept all the books in the world. All of them kept that secret because they had family on the island who would be exposed to the untender mercies of the vengeful goblinkin.

The oars creaked out on the sea, sounding closer now.

"Ye lads shouldn't be here," Varrowyn said. "Hurry on now an' get back to bed. A beatin' from yer pap, why it'd be safer than stayin' here."

"I can't," Dockett said. He held up the book he carried. "I learned to read and write from Grandmagister Lamplighter and First Librarian Juhg. They are the only two dwellers I know that have been off this island. I read accounts they wrote of their travels and adventures."

"Lad," Varrowyn said, "I ain't got the time nor the patience to be dealin' with ye. Now ye just get on—"

"No." The young dweller's answer was bold and strong. (Except for when his voice cracked in the middle.) But he folded his arms stubbornly like he hadn't noticed. "My place is here. I'm staying."

"It ain't yer pap ye'd best be afraid of," Varrowyn promised. "I bet my hand's a lot more callused than yer pap's, an' I'll last longer at whelpin' ye than he will, I wager."

"My place is here," the young dweller pleaded. He held forth the book again. "Grandmagister Lamplighter said one of a Librarian's greatest responsibilities is to write about things he learns and sees. First Level Librarian Juhg always maintained that any writing you do should be important, otherwise you were simply practicing words you'd learned."

Varrowyn's attention was split between the young dwellers and the approaching goblinkin longboats. "I'm sure the Gran'magister, he meant well, but this is not the time nor the place to—"

"We have lost so much," Dockett interrupted. "All those books. The Librarians. All that knowledge is gone. We have to start getting some of it back. And future generations need to know what happened here during this time."

High up on the Knucklebones, where the Great Library had once stood, flames flickered in the earth. Some of the caverns in the underground section of the Vault of All Known Knowledge still burned. On dark nights like tonight, the flames could be seen as orange flickers against the underbelly of the perpetual fog.

Varrowyn kept his tone deliberately harsh. "Ye should go."

The young dweller shook his head sorrowfully. "I have to do my duty here."

"What duty?" Varrowyn asked, exasperated.

"I have to record this battle." Dockett opened the book he carried.

A brief bit of moonlight skated across the pages, but it was strong enough and long enough to show the sketches. Varrowyn recognized Farady and two of the dwarves featured in the drawing. They were seated at a table in the Sea Breeze Tavern.

"I started recording this at the Library," Dockett said. "Where it all began. I'm trying to do what the Grandmagister charged us all with. I—"

"Varrowyn!"

Farady's call galvanized Varrowyn into action. He pointed at the forest. "Ye two get over there. Now! I'll not have fightin' men trippin' over ye whilst they're battlin' for their lives." There was no time and no way he could see them safely home, and the forest was going to quickly fill up with goblinkin that wouldn't think anything of slitting the throats of a couple of dweller children.

The young dwellers turned and scampered for the tree line.

Taking up his battle-axe in both hands again, Varrowyn joined the elven warder at the shoreline. Farady pointed into the boiling fog.

Squinting his eyes against the stinging salt spray that whipped up over the small cliff, Varrowyn wiped his face and stared into the darkness. In the distance, he made out the first of the three longboats less than a bow shot away. Goblinkin shadows sat hunkered in the boat, pulling oars.

"Do we take them in the water?" Farady asked. He lifted his bow meaningfully.

"No," Varrowyn answered, shaking his shaggy head. "On the land. Here. These ones will be a warnin' to the others. I don't want to kill some of 'em or maybe even most of 'em. I want 'em *all* dead. When none of these come back, them goblinkin commanders of them ships out in the harbor will have to think about that. It'll be harder for 'em to assemble another group of raiders."

"Very well." Farady pulled back, staying low so he wouldn't be detected against the skyline by the ships from below. He nocked a dark-fletched arrow to his bowstring and never turned from the approach of their enemies.

Varrowyn pulled his troops to the tree line, allowing the arriving goblinkin room to climb on shore.

Minutes later, the longboats smacked hollowly against the jagged rocks below. Goblins cursed in their harsh tongues and the sound of flesh striking flesh carried to Varrowyn's ears. Commanders ordered the goblins to keep silent.

The beasties are tense, the dwarven captain thought, smiling to himself. Even as much as he anticipated the battle, part of him dreaded it. The chances of all the warriors he'd gathered emerging from the engagement unscathed was near nonexistent. But a message needed to be sent to the goblinkin waiting out in the monster-infested sea.

The first of the goblins came into view slowly. He shoved his head over the edge of land cautiously, ducked down so his ill-fitting helm slid down his face. If Varrowyn hadn't known blood was in the offing, he might have laughed at the sight. There were a few blacksmiths who made armor among the goblinkin, but they were seldom seen. Most of the armor the goblins wore came from the spoils of war, dragged from the bodies of humans and dwarves.

Come on now. Don't back away none. Just us trees in the forest a-waitin' on ye. Ye're safe enough here. Varrowyn took a fresh grip on his battle-axe.

Almost as tall as humans and loutish looking, the goblins possessed triangular, wedge-shaped heads filled with wide mouths and big, crooked teeth. Spiky black hair sprouted from their heads, chins, and out their flaring ears. Most of them were broad-shouldered, but either tended to be overweight or undernourished looking. A goblin's diet and metabolism either made for feast or famine, with few left between, so they either ran fat or they ran skinny. Ugly, gray-green, splotchy skin covered them and marked them instantly.

All of them wore armor tonight, but few had taken care to work in a layer of lampblack so the metal wouldn't shine. At least, if the armor were clean it would have shined. As it was now, the metal surfaces only reflected a dulled sheen, but it was still visible. They carried axes, swords, and cudgels.

Finally, the goblins were all ashore. They clustered together along the shoreline.

Stupid beasties, Varrowyn thought. If he'd been in charge, he'd have ordered four separate landings at minimum that were properly spaced apart so they couldn't all be taken at once but would still be able to help each other.

He rose with a yell. "Archers!"

Instantly, the eight elven warders among the group loosed shafts. Arrows hissed through the air and sank into the goblinkin, piercing their chests, throats, and eyes. At least twenty of the enemy died in that onslaught, their bodies falling at the feet of their comrades and over the side of the drop-off to the foaming water below.

"Again!" Varrowyn yelled.

Arrows took flight again. This time the goblinkin lifted their shields and most of the shafts broke against them. Crying out in fear and rage, the goblinkin rushed the tree line.

"Set anvils!" Varrowyn roared. He stepped out of the darkness and into step with his shield mates.

Dividing into four-man groups, the dwarves set anvils, their chosen defensive posture. Two by two, with the front two men carrying large shields and hand axes, maces, or morning stars, the dwarves met the goblinkin attack and held them. The thunder of metal-on-metal filled the forest. The two dwarves in the back carried battle-axes and waited for the cry to go out for—

"Axes!" Varrowyn commanded.

As the goblinkin reeled back from the dwarven shields, the dwarves rotated into axes, forming the offensive groups in a diamond shape, or a two-by-two square turned on edge. One of the warriors carrying a battle-axe stepped to the forefront and was flanked by two others so no one could intercept them without braving a deadly net of flashing steel. They became wedges that drove into the midst of their opponents.

The humans moved in to confront their enemies one-on-one without the concerted effort of the dwarves. The elven warders, accompanied by their animal companions consisting of birds, badgers, and bears, fought as well, staying on the outside of the battle and picking off their opponents.

But it was the dwarves who ripped the heart out of the massed goblinkin, driving deeply into them again and again and leaving a twisted trail of bodies behind.

Varrowyn sang a dwarven fighting song, timed perfectly so that the cadence matched a warrior's natural weapon swing. His fellow dwarves joined in, and their voices reverberated throughout the forest and across the crashing surf.

He blocked a spear thrust to the side with his axe, then swung the iron-bound haft up into the goblin's face, breaking teeth and sending the foul creature stumbling back to take down yet another. Sidestepping a blow, the dwarven captain brought the battle-axe down and cleaved through an iron helm and the goblin head that wore it. The death screams of goblins mixed in with the dwarven war song.

The battle lasted only minutes. The execution, for that was what the action truly was, only stopped when the defenders of Greydawn Moors ran out of goblinkin to kill.

Breathing hard and bloodied, fire skating along his ribs from a spear wound, Varrowyn shook the blood from his battle-axe. Amid the carnage left of the goblinkin, bodies of a handful of dwarves, humans, and also elves lay.

"Varrowyn," broad-faced Kummel called. The warrior sat on his knees holding the hand of young Anell.

Heart heavy with dread, Varrowyn joined them. The young dwarf's parents had already lost one son to the goblinkin. Anell lay bleeding from a wound to the throat. Kummel was attempting to stanch the flow with a compress made of his own tunic, but experience told Varrowyn the effort was in vain.

The young dwarven warrior was dying and there was naught any of them could do.

Varrowyn took the young dwarf's hand. "Ye fought well, Anell. Ye did. I saw ye, glimpsed ye from the corner of me eye, I did. Ye are ever' inch a brawler."

A faint smile tugged at Anell's bloody lips. His beard was scarce thick enough to mask his chin. "The dweller," he gasped. "I would speak . . . with the dweller lad."

Varrowyn sent the order and Dockett was brought forward. Despite the horrors of the attack on Greydawn Moors last month, the dweller hadn't hardened to the ways of war. His eyes rounded in fear and filled with tears, and he stood on shaking legs.

"Me," Anell said to the dweller as he took hold of the other's shirt. "I am Anell, son of Morag Thur, of the . . . the Unrelenting Hammer Clan. I died here tonight fightin' . . . against the goblinkin to save the Library. As I swore to the Old Ones an' my father . . . that I would. Make them . . . remember . . . me." He swallowed. "Please. Do not let . . . them forget."

"I-I-I will," Dockett promised. Tears leaked from his eyes and ran down his dirty cheeks. "The world will know you forever, Anell. I swear by the Old Ones that they will."

With a final exhalation, Anell passed. His sightless eyes rolled up and his lifeless body relaxed on the bloodied earth.

Kummel cursed. Pain and rage cracked his broad face and tightened his voice. "He was just a young 'un, Varrowyn. It ain't right. Wasn't his time to die. I don't want to tell his ma. Her heart's already broken."

Varrowyn sat quietly. Kummel and Anell had been shield mates for years.

"I am sorry for your loss," the young dweller whispered.

Uncoiling, Kummel put a big hand on the young dweller's chest and shoved him away. Dockett rolled a half dozen times and sprawled. Hesitantly, obviously expecting further attack, he pushed himself up.

22

The other survivors of the attack gathered around. All of them had lost someone they knew.

"Don't ye be apologizin' to me!" Kummel roared. "An' that promise ye made to Anell? That was worthless, was what it was!" He took a step toward the dweller.

Fearing that Kummel was out of control in his grief, Varrowyn stepped forward and intercepted the dwarven warrior. "Stand down," the dwarven captain ordered.

Kummel stopped, but the thought flashed through his eyes that maybe he wouldn't. "We're dyin' here, Varrowyn. Dyin' one by one for these dwellers that don't know how to fight for themselves an' wouldn't even if they did because they're all cowards."

"This one left the safety of his da's tavern," Varrowyn said, "an' is sure to get a thumpin' when he gets back for sneakin' along with us as he did."

He spoke loud enough so that all could hear. "An' he made his way through the dark forest at night." He paused. "Do ye know why he did that?"

No one answered.

Varrowyn knew that only a few of his comrades felt as Kummel did. Most accepted their lot to defend the island even though the goblinkin had found out where it was and would work together to destroy it.

"He came out here to tell our story," Varrowyn said. He reached back and caught Dockett by the shoulder, hauling him forward to stand at his side. The youth flinched but Varrowyn held him protectively. "Ye all heard him say that. An' he gave Anell his word that he would make certain people remembered him."

"Won't do Anell no good," Kummel argued. "When he's cold an' lifeless in the ground—"

"People will still remember him," Varrowyn cut in. "They will remember what he did here tonight. These Librarians have the power to do that."

"Pity they ain't much better fighters."

"An' it's a pity ye can't write nor read," Varrowyn said. He raked his gaze across those assembled around him. "Let me tell ye what ye're fightin' for here. There was a time when dwarves could read, an' they could write. I've seen some of the stone tablets inside the Library. They wrote of their histories an' the way they forged metals or mined for gems. Some of ye standin' here, mayhap ye've taken a lesson or three from the Grandmagister or First Librarian Juhg or one of the others what ain't so selfish with what they know."

Some of the dwarves had paid closer attention to the books that they guarded, forming, if not friendships, then acquaintanceships among the Librarians.

"We lost all that durin' the Cataclysm when Lord Kharrion assembled the goblinkin tribes an' tried to take over everything," Varrowyn said. "No tellin' what all was lost because we have no way of knowin'." He looked back in the direction of the Knucklebones Mountains where the firelight flickered against the dark underbelly of clouds. "An' we lost more a month ago."

"We lost a lot of warriors that night," Kummel said. "An' in the time that followed. Savin' books ain't gonna make up for that."

"No," Varrowyn agreed. "But through the Librarians, we're gonna have histories of what happened. We're gonna know who stood their ground an' died there. A thousand years from now, as long as books exist, dwarves will still know about the good that was done here."

Silence hung over the crowd.

Varrowyn's voice softened. "We lost Anell tonight. That's true. But we're gonna keep him with us. An' through this young dweller, through his skills as a Librarian, we're gonna keep Anell with us forever. My children will know of him. An' their children after them. An' all the dwarven children yet to come." He looked around. "That's what ye warriors are layin' yer lives down for."

Kummel hung his head. Tears still ran down his broad face. "There are stories about Anell that must be told," he whispered. "There are things that must not be forgotten."

Dockett stepped forward. "I will listen to them, Kummel. And I will record them faithfully. I swear to you that I will not let him be forgotten."

"I thank ye," Kummel said. Then he returned to Anell and began preparing him for burial.

After a moment's hesitation, Dockett sat cross-legged on the ground. He took out a stick of charcoal and drew on the page, quickly blocking out the image of Kummel tending to poor, dead Anell. The other dweller youth joined the first, taking out a bag of inks and quills and burned charcoal sticks, laying them out for his brother.

No, Varrowyn thought with fierce pride as he watched the dweller lad, *that one's pap isn't gonna lay a hand on him. I'll not stand for it, I won't.* He turned away and walked back to the ledge to peer out at the black sea.

Farady joined him, lifting his arm to accept Whisperwing again. "You did well back there. The situation could have deteriorated radically."

"They just forgot, is all. Them's good warriors. By the Old Ones, ye can't take that away from 'em. It's hard bein' here, knowin' them goblinkin are gettin' reinforcements whilst we're dyin' with no help in sight. It would have been better had Gran'magister Lamplighter an' Juhg not been captured as they was. The Gran'magister, he could have helped us hold the line."

All throughout Greydawn Moors, the story was still told of how dragonets had carried away the Grandmagister and his chosen apprentice from the mystical Shrikra's Tower the day of the attack. Many feared that the Grandmagister was dead, having already been cut up and tossed into a goblinkin stew.

"Well," Farady said with soft conviction, "the Grandmagister is not here. We will simply have to make do until his return. This is not over."

Varrowyn blew out his breath. "I know. But I can't help thinkin' maybe it would be better if it was over. One way or the other. Waitin' wears on a body."

" 'One way or the other'?" Farady repeated. "I thought you told me we were going to win this."

"We are." Varrowyn wiped blood from his face. "Just soon or late is what I was referrin' to. I just hate all this dyin' what lies in between." And in his heart, he was sure they had a lot of that left to face.

1

"They're *Our* Monsters!"

One-Eyed Peggie lurched hard over to starboard and a horrendous scraping noise drawn out like a banshee's wail filled the ship's waist from prow to stern.

Only quick reflexes, a determination not to mar pages, and years of experience aboard a sailing vessel allowed Juhg to keep the freshly dipped quill from the paper before he could render a mistaken stroke. His other hand slapped at the papers, pinning them in place and managing to hang on to the inkwell.

Then the fear set in as he, like all the dwarves gathered in the galley, waited expectantly for the sound to be repeated. Or for someone to scream that the ship's hull had been ruptured and she was sinking.

He sat alone at a table in the pirate ship's galley working on the journal. Lanterns filled the area with golden light. He was the only dweller among the group seated at the tables. Brown breeches and a maroon shirt, his clothing marked him as different from the others as much as his smaller stature. His fair hair and light-complexioned skin spoke of a life spent mostly indoors with some time outside. He was also, despite a month of travel aboard the vessel, cleaner than most of the crew.

One-Eyed Peggie was a pirate ship, one of those given the duty of patrolling the Blood-Soaked Sea so that no ships from the mainland sailed out to discover Greydawn Moors and the Vault of All Known Knowledge hidden there. Juhg had sailed aboard her before, but never with such grim purpose as he did now.

"That weren't just me, were it?" a dwarven pirate asked in the tense silence that followed the noise. *One-Eyed Peggie* still rocked as she leveled out again. "I mean, I've had a little grog to drink, but I didn't think I just imagined that kind of cauterwaulin'—"

"We've run aground," another dwarven pirate cried out in a trembling voice. "We've been skirtin' too near the coast. I knew this was gonna happen. There's too much broken rock and reefs there. The cap'n knew that, too. He knew he orter be more careful."

"I didn't think that were just me," the first one replied. He finished his cup of grog and glanced anxiously around.

"Stow that bilge," another pirate growled. His name was Starrit and he'd been with *One-Eyed Peggie* under the old captain as well. Most of his life had been spent tending the pirate ship. "Cap'n Hallekk knows whereat he's a doin'. I'll not suffer ye to be a-talkin' behind his back."

The accuser glared at the other pirate, but said nothing more.

Captain Hallekk, Juhg knew, had the respect of his crew.

The other pirates got up from their meals, automatically picking up their plates and cups so they wouldn't slide around unattended if the ship should hit again. Gradually, the ship righted herself, pulled back into position by the ballast she carried.

Juhg allowed himself a deep breath as he waited, as every pirate in the galley did, for the fear-filled cry that *One-Eyed Peggie* had been holed. He'd spent enough time aboard ships while journeying with Grandmagister Lamplighter on errands for the Vault of All Known Knowledge that he felt certain he'd know if the vessel had been damaged and was now taking on water. In years past, he'd gone down in both ships and boats while adventuring with the Grandmagister.

I know this ship, Juhg told himself nervously. *I've sailed on her many times. If she weren't all right, I'd know.*

In fact, the Grandmagister had gotten shanghaied aboard *One-Eyed Peggie* all those years ago and set upon the path that had led him to his destiny. Edgewick Lamplighter had learned to wash dishes and peel potatoes in this very galley, something only cooks did at the Vault of All Known Knowledge.

Juhg had seen dozens of drawings and sketches of the galley in the books that the Grandmagister had written that detailed his adventures with the pirates then and later. A lot of time at sea the galley had been a place where councils of war met, where wounds were tended, and where the pirates came for safe harbor during fierce storms or lulls in hot seas.

"Wasn't a sandbar or a reef," another pirate said. "Woulda hit again if'n it was."

"Unless we just got lucky," said a third.

Without warning, *One-Eyed Peggie* lurched again, turning even harder to port than she had to starboard. All of the dwarves who had been standing ended up on the floor, squalling and hollering.

"Topside!" a raucous voice screeched from the companionway leading to the deck. "Topside! Topside, ye scurvy dogs! Cap'n's orders! Squawk!"

In the next instant, one of the ugliest and most malignant birds Juhg had ever seen flapped into the kitchen. The bird was a crimson horned rhowdor, intelligent as any being, some said. Of course, Critter, the bird, maintained that he was more intelligent than most.

The bird's harsh hatchet face, bearing its cruelly curved beak, looked merciless. The features matched their owner's disposition perfectly. Bright pink horns, one of them broken off midway, thrust up four inches, each of them curled. He only had one bright emerald eye. The other was covered with a fierce black leather eyepatch that featured a skull made up of shiny brass studs. A gold earring dangled from one feathered eartuft.

With a graceful flap of wings, Critter landed on the table where Juhg worked. That was impressive considering that *One-Eyed Peggie* still lurched back and forth. The effort was doubly impressive because the rhowdor had only one leg. The other was a wooden fork carefully whittled to size and fitted to his leg stump.

Whatever we hit, Juhg thought as he held on to the table, *or whatever hit us, was huge.* The pirate vessel was large and wide-bodied to handle a lot of cargo and men.

"Avast there, ye miserable flea-biters!" Critter screamed, flapping his wings menacingly and limping on the fork as he walked across the table.

"Get yer fannies to movin', ye goldbrickers! Cap'n's orders! *Peggie*'s takin' on water, she is, an' I'll have everyone of ye topside fer orders or I'll keel-hauls ye meself!"

The dwarven pirates scrambled up and made for the door immediately. Despite the fact that he was a bird, Critter enjoyed all the rank and privileges of a member of the crew. Currently he served as Third Mate under Captain Hallekk.

Critter turned his one-eyed attention to Juhg. "Squawk! Ye get movin', too, ye mangy cur!" The rhowdor had few true friends on this ship, but he was a fine Third Mate, proving himself both irascible and unyielding. "Cap'n needs ever' hand. Ever' able body he can get. We're even takin' dwellers."

Juhg capped his inkwell, placed his quill into the box of writing instruments he had, closed his book and tied it shut, then shoved everything into the waterproof rucksack hanging from the back of his chair with his traveling cloak. He pulled on the cloak, then hoisted the rucksack over his shoulder.

"Ye think ye remember how to handle yerself?" the rhowdor challenged.

"Yes," Juhg answered, loath to get into an argument with the mean-spirited bird. "It hasn't been overlong since I was aboard this ship."

"Then why are ye here a-jabberin' to me when ye should be topside?"

Exasperated, tense, and fatigued from not sleeping well and worrying about the Grandmagister's whereabouts for the last month, Juhg stared at the short-tempered and unkind bird. He was tired of getting pushed around. For the last month, Craugh the wizard had kept Juhg with his nose buried in work, penning one book and making copies of it. The wizard had also ducked every question regarding how the Grandmagister had ended up in the hands of their enemies at the battle for Greydawn Moors.

More to the point, Juhg was tired of carrying around the guilt that he was more to blame for the Grandmagister's predicament than any of the others. Perhaps Edgewick Lamplighter and Craugh had schemed together to put the Grandmagister in a position of vulnerability, but Juhg had cost the Grandmagister his way out by getting captured and needing rescue himself. The Grandmagister hadn't hesitated and had immediately given Juhg the potion that had gotten him free of the goblinkin ship. *One-Eyed Peggie* had swooped in and picked him up from the sea almost immediately.

But the Grandmagister had been left trapped with his foes. The three ships had made straightaway for the mainland, toward the South where the goblinkin forces were strongest. Alone and in dangerous waters, *One-Eyed Peggie* and her crew of dwarven pirates hadn't been able to effect the Grandmagister's rescue.

Then again, with Craugh not talking to him much over the past month, Juhg wasn't even sure that was the plan.

"What are ye a-starin' at?" the rhowdor demanded.

Juhg didn't know what to say. The bird didn't deserve all the rancor he felt compelled to unleash on him.

"Keep it up," Critter threatened, "just keep it up an' I'll peck yer eyes out for ye, I will."

Ignoring the bird, knowing that he could never win an argument with Critter—or, if he did, that the bird would never admit it—Juhg headed for the door.

One-Eyed Peggie lurched again, and this time the sound of a timber cracking shot through the waist. The report was enough to cause a sailing man's stomach to knot.

Caught off-balance, Juhg flailed for the table. The table, like the benches around it, was secured to the floor by trunnels. The wooden nails made certain the furniture would not move. He fell across the table hard enough to knock the wind from his lungs.

Critter narrowly avoided being flattened. He ran awkwardly across the table on his mismatched legs, flapping his wings and cursing the whole way. His fork pegleg slipped out from under him suddenly and he fell in a rolling tangle of feathers. Crimson and yellow down puffed out around him. He flared his wings at the last second and took to the air.

The ship lurched back the other way as she was hammered once more. Critter banged into the wall and went down with an undignified plop. He cursed terribly and got himself up once more. He rubbed a wing on his head and his good eye squinted in pain.

"What's going on?" Juhg demanded as he righted himself. The ship wasn't striking something. He knew that now. *Something* was striking the pirate ship.

"Ye'll find out, dweller." The rhowdor flapped for the doorway. "Just ye hurry topside. There's things to be done, an' scribblin' in them books ain't gonna much help keep ol' *Peggie* afloat."

The ship lurched again, twisting violently as she fought the water, the wind, and whatever was hitting her. Critter sailed into a wall, struck his head on a lantern, and cursed in a manner that would have made even the most callous dwarven pirate aboard the ship blush.

With the rucksack hanging over his shoulder, Juhg made his way through the hallway to the ladder leading up to the deck. Dwarven pirates ran through the waist, already carrying out Captain Hallekk's orders.

Has it come to this, then? Juhg wondered. *Have we come all this way only to be sunk in unfriendly waters by the mainland?*

He tried to put the bitter and depressing thoughts out of his mind. But he couldn't. He knew that back in Greydawn Moors people died every day while defending their island home and the remnant of the Great Library from the goblinkin ships that remained lurking in the Blood-Soaked Sea.

And all he'd done was make three copies of a book no one might see. If he hadn't been trapped aboard *One-Eyed Peggie* and hadn't felt so responsible for the Grandmagister's current situation, he wouldn't have stayed. The feeling of futility filling him was one of the reasons he'd tried to leave the Vault of All Known Knowledge and his life as a First Level Librarian. Only the book he'd found with Ertonomous Dron had pulled him back to the island.

All those lives wasted, Juhg thought bitterly, thinking of the sailors aboard *Windchaser* who had died to acquire that book, *only to deliver a trap into the Library.*

It was too much to live with during the time he worked on the books. All while they helplessly pursued the goblinkin ship that had taken the Grandmagister captive during the battle for Greydawn Moors. So far, the three goblinkin ships had remained together, too strong for the dwarven pirates to take, but neither did the goblin captains know that they were followed by the mystic eyeball that gave *One-Eyed Peggie* her name. The monster's eyeball, taken by Peggie herself (who had been one-legged), had the power of watching over every sailor who crewed aboardship.

"Are we holed?" Juhg asked one of the passing pirates who hurried toward the hold that led to the cargo area with an armful of tools.

"She's cracked," the pirate admitted. He was scarred and thick, a sailing man who'd seen more than his share of rough seas and ill luck. "We're takin' on water, but we'll get her shipshape again soon enough. Long as that beastie don't find a way to smash us to pieces first."

"What beast?" Juhg asked. The Blood-Soaked Sea was filled with all manner of creatures.

The pirate waved him off, then dropped down the hold.

Feeling the impulse to go see for himself how bad the damage was, then reconsidering because he didn't know enough to help and because he really didn't want to know how bad things were if they were bad, Juhg pulled himself up the simple wooden ladder.

Rain splashed his face before he reached the deck. The world was dark gray overhead and dull gray all around him. Dwarven pirates ran along *One-Eyed Peggie*'s deck wearing hooded rain slickers and carrying harpoons.

When had it started raining? Juhg didn't know. He'd been committed to writing down everything he could remember about Imarish, the city where the Grandmagister had left something, he'd said, for Juhg to find.

Craugh the wizard had insisted that be done so others could perhaps find the something the Grandmagister had left there for him in case he got killed along the way. The statement, especially while on a sea full of monsters frenzied by blood, hadn't offered Juhg any comfort. But Craugh, as always, was a rocky shoal of pragmatism.

"All hands keep a sharp lookout!" Critter crowed from the mid 'yards. "Stick 'im in the eye if ye gets the chance! That thrice-blasted beast won't like that none, I'll warrant!"

Juhg gazed toward the stern bridge, thinking he would see Hallekk or Craugh there. Instead, only the helmsman stood at the great wheel. A dozen dwarven pirates flanked him, all of them peering down into the swirling gray-green water that surrounded them.

Thick fog pressed upon them, flitting in layers across *One-Eyed Peggie*'s rain-slick deck. Juhg could scarcely see either end of the ship. Lanterns were lit fore and aft so that she might be seen by other ships. However, getting seen was one of the last things anyone aboard the pirate ship wished for. They were in dangerous waters. Goblinkin in their stolen vessels and true human pirates sailed these seas, always searching for the valuable trade shipments the south mainland made with the north.

"Dreezil," a familiar voice barked, "do ye see anythin'? Anythin' at all?"

"No, Cap'n Hallekk. I see water boilin', but no hide nor hair of no creature." Dreezil stood watch in the crow's nest high above the deck. He was lost in the thick fog, and Juhg didn't think the young dwarf could even see the deck from where he was.

Another blow struck *One-Eyed Peggie,* rolling her over to starboard. Again, the impact came from below the waterline. Juhg thought about the crew down in the hold working to repair the cracked timber. How fast were they taking on water? He remembered the three times he'd tramped through rising water to help seal a puncture in the cargo hold of a ship. None of those experiences had been pleasant. Twice the ship had gone down despite their best efforts, and Juhg had never gone down once himself.

"Well," Cap'n Hallekk bawled in frustration, "it ain't gone away, now has it? It's still knockin' us about like we was a child's toy. There's a monster down there, an' I want it found."

Holding on to the railing, getting more soaked by the minute, Juhg made his way forward. The ship rolled slowly from side to side as she recovered her balance.

On the forward deck, Hallekk stood braced and ready with a harpoon in one massive hand. The dwarven captain was nearly as broad as he was tall, carrying massive shoulders and standing a few inches taller than most dwarves, though still shorter than most humans or elves. His fierce beard trailed down to his belly, woven with bits of yellowed ivory carved into the shapes of fish and other sea creatures. Gold hoops hung from his ears. Scars marked his face and arms, testifying to the long and violent years he had put in as a Blood-Soaked Sea pirate. The pirates' reputations were often earned with a weapon and bravery.

When the Builders had first caused the island to be raised from the sea floor so they could hide the Great Library there, they'd also set up lines of defense to prevent its eventual discovery. The first and most fearsome had been the monsters they'd loosed in the waters, and the second had been the volunteers who had taken up lives and battles under the skull and crossbones. Mainland ships stayed away from the heart of the Blood-Soaked Sea.

Pirates were plentiful after the Cataclysm. During Lord Kharrion's time, goblinkin had captured ships and harried rescue efforts transporting

34

books from the mainland. But those efforts had been few because the Unity Army had known leaving the mainland to the goblin forces would have meant Darkness had prevailed. In the end, they'd managed to stand and bring the Goblin Lord down.

Mostly, the volunteers from Greydawn Moors had been humans. Their natures, short-lived and determined ever to be wanderers and conquerors, suited the humans for the sea and the promise of combat. It helped that not a few of them gained substantial wealth from their efforts.

Still, a few dwarves and elves had taken to ship occasionally. Generally they tended more toward joining ships for a time. Dwarves liked to go a-roving for gems and chances to work metal in different smithies, and brought back news of the mainland. Elven warders brought back new stock—plants and animals—to keep the island's plant life and wildlife healthy and hardy. None of them talked about the island or the Great Library while they were about. All of them had families there who would be forfeit the first time they let slip the secret they protected. Strangers were seldom welcome at Greydawn Moors because strangers didn't have much investment in the city or the people who lived there.

But there had been exceptions. Juhg had been born on the mainland, had never known about the Great Library until Grandmagister Lamplighter had freed him from slavery at a goblinkin gem mine.

One-Eyed Peggie was unique, the only ship in all of the Blood-Soaked Sea under a dwarven captain. Captain Hallekk had taken over the ship after Captain Farok had died in the Grandmagister's arms during their escape from the undersea port of Callidell after tracking down and stealing the fabled Gem of Umatura. Callidell had been located in the dead heart of a volcano. The carved facets of the Gem of Umatura, once identified and translated, had unlocked a dead language in books long forgotten that had set the Grandmagister off on another whirlwind quest through the history and dangers of the mainland.

Lurching with the motion of the rolling ship, feeling the dreaded heaviness to her now that told she was taking on water, Juhg went up the stairs to the forward deck. The task was made even harder because *One-Eyed Peggie* bucked and twisted instead of cleanly cutting through the sea. He gazed around, struggling to make sense of the sky and the sea since they insisted on being very nearly the same color.

"There!" a pirate shouted, pointing to port.

Juhg turned at once, staring out at the gray-green sea. At first he saw nothing, then his keen vision tracked the underwater movement despite the rain pinpricking his eyes and peppering the rolling mountains of the ocean.

An undulating mass of deep purple and red scales moved beneath the sea. The mass was gone, disappearing under the ocean surface, almost as quickly as he'd spied it.

"What was it?" Hallekk demanded.

"A monster," someone replied.

"What kind of monster?"

"Big."

Hallekk growled a curse as he prowled the prow. "Big? I knowed it was big. From the way it was a-smashin' up *Peggie,* why I didn't need to see it to know it was big. What I need to know is how we're a-gonna deal with it."

"We can throw meat in the water. Maybe the beastie will chase the meat to the bottom an' leave us alone."

Juhg stood at the back of the bridge, leaving Hallekk plenty of room to pace. The big dwarf kept the harpoon at the ready.

"Meat won't help," a calm voice said. "That's a bearded hoar-worm. You can throw every morsel of meat aboard this ship into the water and that creature won't go break away from us. It feeds on live prey, and it lives to hunt."

Moving forward to peer around the triangular jib sails straining in the strong winds, Juhg spotted Craugh the wizard on the other side of the bridge.

Six and a half feet tall and skinny as a rake handle, Craugh was nevertheless an imposing figure even among the colorful members of a dwarven pirate crew. His pointed hat defied natural laws by staying atop his head in the gale winds. Of course, Craugh—by virtue (and yes, there was some argument about that word being associated with the wizard as well) of being a wizard—would have argued that magic was as natural as the seasons.

His long gray beard hung down to his belt and his hair past his shoulders. Of late, his face looked more haggard than usual, but his piercing green eyes blazed with the eldritch forces he commanded. His face was long and narrow, seeming to surface from a sea of iron-gray hair and beard, and appeared fierce enough to chop stone. His nose was prominent and he used it as a weapon to look imperious or to show derision.

He wore simple homespun breeches and a white shirt, covered by a russet colored traveling cloak. He carried a gnarled wooden staff thick as his forearm that was even longer than he and his hat stood together. The end of the staff curved into a hook.

"I've never seen a bearded hoar-worm," Hallekk said.

Craugh joined the ship's captain at the prow railing. His voice was strong and somber, carrying to all of the crew in the immediate vicinity despite the wind and the snapping sailcloth overhead. "You will today."

"I heard tell of them, but I thought they was a myth." Hallekk took a fresh grip on the harpoon he carried.

"No. They're most definitely not a myth."

"No one's ever seen one that I can recollect."

Juhg stopped behind them, feeling awkward about eavesdropping. But he also knew that Craugh hadn't told him anything more than what he'd wanted him to know even since the attack that had leveled the Vault of All Known Knowledge. Resentment had filled Juhg but he hadn't confronted the wizard about it. No matter what, Craugh was as interested as Juhg was in rescuing the Grandmagister.

And irritating Craugh meant running the risk of being turned into a toad. A toad, Juhg was certain, wouldn't be much help to the Grandmagister.

The sea remained chaotic and rough. Waves crashed all across the horizon, matching the stormy movements of the gray clouds in the sky. But to one who knew the sea as Juhg did, there were unnatural movements even in the chaos. Huge ripples warred with the natural tide and movement of the ocean, warning of the large creature that prowled below the waves.

Evidently, Juhg decided with some growing apprehension, *the pictures of bearded hoar-worms in the bestiary books don't do the creature justice when it comes to size.*

"Monsters in these waters," a pirate complained, "why, they ain't supposed to attack us none. They're our monsters."

"Not these," Craugh answered.

"An' why ain't they?"

"When the island was first constructed so that the Library could be built there in the Knucklebones Mountains," Craugh said, "a number of bearded hoar-worms lived in the waters there. That past history of ships lost at sea to them was one of the reasons that area was picked as the location of the Great Library. Lord Kharrion would never believe that anyone had gone there."

Another ripple started to the port side. Just as Juhg turned to observe the movement, he caught a glimpse of dark purple scales.

"The other gargantuan creatures living there," Craugh went on, "the giant squids and the other things, were all able to be charmed so they would recognize the spells carved into the bottom hulls of the island ships and leave them alone."

The wave created by the creature slapped into *One-Eyed Peggie*. A salty sheet of cold spray lashed over the side and drenched Juhg. He was chilled to the bone instantly.

"But the bearded hoar-worms couldn't be charmed," Craugh said. "So the Builders chose to put them to sleep. It took considerable doing, you know, because the bearded hoar-worms were not at all amenable. Since that time, they have lain at the bottom of the Blood-Soaked Sea, unmoving and unchanging."

" 'Cept this 'un," Hallekk growled.

"Yes," Craugh said. "Except this one."

"Which has decided it fancies an interest in us. So why ain't it sleepin'?"

"Because," Craugh replied ominously, "someone woke it."

A thousand questions immediately flew into Juhg's mind. *Who had waked the creature? Why? Just to set it on us? How had that been managed? And if this one was awake, were there others awake in the harbor at the Yondering Docks in Greydawn Moors?*

Before he could frame the questions, or weigh the wisdom of letting Craugh know he was there, Juhg saw the creature rise from the ocean.

"Look out!" Dreezil yelled from the crow's nest. "It's coming fer us! To starboard! To starboard!"

Hallekk roared orders to the helmsman, instructing him to take what evasive action he could, but fighting against the wind and the waves of the storm had limited his ability. The captain bolted past Juhg, carrying the harpoon over his shoulder as he ran to the starboard side.

Craugh turned and saw Juhg. The wizard's eyes narrowed and he frowned. "You shouldn't be up here," the wizard said. "This place is too dangerous."

"In case you haven't noticed," Juhg shot back, "not only are we under attack, but the ship is sinking. Belowdecks is hardly the place I want to be right now."

"You would be better protected there. I do not want to lose you to your impetuosity."

Juhg didn't bother to answer. The argument would have been pointless. There was no way he was going belowdecks. He'd gotten tired of not being in a position to take control of his own life this past month. Maybe he couldn't get off the ship, but he could choose where he stood on it. He turned and sprinted after Hallekk.

The bearded hoar-worm raised its head clear of the brine. Massively huge, the head carried the wedge shape of a serpent, but had the depth of forehead of a bear. Mottled olive skin covered the face, stretching out to the cheeks and chin where it mixed with a darker color of purple than was on the thing's body. Dark red underscored the big eyes and the flaring nostrils. Mottled, ice-blue tendrils trailed down from the creature's broad chin to its neck, giving it the appearance of streams that had frozen there.

Behind the creature, a wake of eighty- and ninety-foot waves suddenly rose up from the ocean. They stayed close to the creature as if it had summoned them.

Hallekk set himself to throw the harpoon, but the creature came too fast. By the time the dwarven captain hauled his arm back to throw and loosed the weapon, the bearded hoar-worm had glided back under the water. The harpoon pierced the sea where it had been, but Juhg was certain the throw had missed.

"Get set!" Hallekk yelled, reaching for the nearest ratline. "It's gonna ram—"

The bearded hoar-worm slammed into *One-Eyed Peggie*'s stern so hard the aft section lifted clear of the water and swapped around so fast that for a moment Juhg was certain the stern was going to overtake the prow. The pirate ship reeled, then was immediately caught by the oncoming waves that had trailed the huge monster. *One-Eyed Peggie* rode up on the first wave sideways, listing hard to port. The successive wave came on, lifting the pirate ship higher and higher, turning her over more and more.

Juhg couldn't help wondering if the thunderous power of the waves was going to smash *One-Eyed Peggie*'s fractured side in. Instead, the ship kept climbing the ninety-foot waves. The water came on so fast and so strong that *One-Eyed Peggie* was helpless, snared in their grip. Incredibly, as she neared the apex of the moving wall of water, the pirate ship rolled over so that it was perpendicular to the ocean and showing signs of rolling all the way over. Her 'yards on that side dipped into the water suddenly as she came over ninety degrees.

Feeling the familiar symptoms of nausea in the pit of his stomach as he achieved momentary weightlessness, Juhg lunged for a fistful of ratlines. His hands caught in the rough rope and he held on tight. His body floated free, caught only by his fingers. In disbelief, he clung to the ratlines and stared down at the swirling water a hundred feet below him.

Nearly all of the pirates had secured holds in the rigging and on the masts and railing. They hung, dangling over the ocean, then three of them lost their holds and they fell.

The screams of the falling men cut through even the sound of the storm and the winds and the ship's sails ripping free. Juhg watched helplessly as the dwarven pirates flailed until they dropped into the sea.

They're dead, Juhg knew. *We'll never be able to find them in all of this.* Moreover, very few of the pirate crew knew how to swim. He clung fearfully to the ratlines.

Hallekk's ratline snapped without warning. The big dwarf shot downward as the rope burned through his hands. He struck the mainmast's topgallant, which luffed in the strong winds, and slid slowly across the sailcloth. He flailed his arms, trying in vain to get a grip on the elusive sail.

Almost as soon as the idea hit his mind, because dwellers were so quick thinking occurred at almost the same time as doing, Juhg released his hold on the ratline and dropped. Usually, though, those quick responses came about purely in the act of self-preservation, not what Juhg intended.

One-Eyed Peggie continued scaling the tall wave, only now near the peak of it. Once the ship crested the wave, Juhg knew she'd whip away from the pirate captain and leave him to drop into the deadly sea.

Juhg pulled his arms in as he fell, plummeting the way a hawk did when it swooped from the sky to take a field mouse. He saw Craugh holding on to the railing, standing erect despite the ship's position. The wizard saw him, too.

"Nooooo!" Craugh yelled.

Even if I live, Juhg thought, *I'm a toad for sure.*

When he hit the topgallant, the sailcloth burned Juhg as it whisked under him. He spread his hands out like a child playing in a snowfield, keeping his balance as he shot under the rigging across the rough material. He focused on Hallekk as the big dwarf neared the end of the topgallant.

Hallekk saw Juhg then. The pirate captain's eyes rounded in disbelief. In the next moment, he was over the edge, beginning the long fall to the ocean. Below, the bearded hoar-worm broke the surface and seemed to be waiting in anticipation.

Juhg concentrated on the topgallant's rigging at the edge of the sailcloth. He reached for Hallekk and stuck both feet into the space between the topgallant and the rigging.

Catching hold of the pirate captain's coat, Juhg fisted his hands in the material. Then the tops of his feet caught the rigging, which slid back and chewed against his shins above his boots. At the end of his reach, Hallekk came to a stop. Juhg felt as though his arms were tearing free of his shoulders.

"I can't hold you!" Juhg shouted. He wasn't strong enough. Hallekk outweighed him at least four times. The pirate captain grabbed hold of Juhg with both hands and began climbing along him. Juhg felt like he was about to be pulled apart. The pain was incredible.

Hallekk reached the topgallant rigging and found a new hold.

Once released from the captain's weight, Juhg tried to turn back on his own body. He bent at the waist in time to see that *One-Eyed Peggie* had finally crested the immense wave. All of his weight left him as the pirate ship suddenly flipped sideways and started down the wave it had climbed.

Before he could get a grip, Juhg was flung away from the topgallant as if from a slingshot. Hallekk reached for him, managing to touch his leg, but couldn't get a grip. Juhg hurtled through the air away from the ship.

Then he fell toward the raging sea.

2

Craugh's Challenge

aaaaayyyyyyy!" Juhg didn't want to scream in fear. He recognized it as a waste of time, but it wasn't like he was going to have a lot of time to waste anyway. *"Aaaaaaayyyyyyy!"*

At the time, screaming in fear seemed the most natural thing to do. But even as he screamed, he was thinking. *They are foolish thoughts!* part of his mind yelled at him. *You're going to die, so just scream and get that out of your system! When you scream, dying won't hurt as much!*

Juhg fell through the air, turning end over end. The roiling sea grew closer and closer. And still he couldn't quite get over the notion that he was going to manage to survive. He could swim. It was just possible he could stay above even these storm-tossed waters. It was even possible that *One-Eyed Peggie,* only now making her way down the other side of the colossal wave, could find him.

All those years spent in the goblinkin gem mines had taught him that he could survive. Such an experience made hollow people of those who had been through it, but Juhg had learned under the Grandmagister's tutelage that he was of a different sort of dweller. Where the Grandmagister had been raised in the safety and comfort of the Vault of All Known Knowledge then learned about the evils in the world (or at least along the mainland), Juhg had grown up in the midst of them.

You have strength, the Grandmagister had told Juhg on more than one occasion. *You have an inner resolve that I have seen in only a few.*

The memory flitted through Juhg's mind and he felt the guilt that rushed through afterward. He and the Grandmagister had not parted on good terms before the Grandmagister's capture by the goblinkin and Aldhran Khempus. The brief meeting aboard the goblinkin ship hadn't counted because the Grandmagister had been too busy providing instruction and helping Juhg escape.

Scream! the voice inside his head commanded. *Scream! It is almost over!*

Staring at the sea, which now filled all of his vision, Juhg realized that the voice wasn't his. He wondered where it was coming from. He stopped screaming and worked on taking one last good breath before plunging into the ocean. *You can find your way back up,* he told himself. *Natural buoyancy will bring you up.*

Something bit into his right leg.

Startled, Juhg looked at his leg, seeing the rope that coiled around his calf twice more then pulled taut. He stopped in midfall, hanging less than twenty feet above the heaving ocean.

Gazing along the rope that held him, Juhg saw that it led back to *One-Eyed Peggie*. At the other end of it, Craugh stood pulling the rope back in. Small green sparks, like flying embers from a cook fire, danced through the twisted hemp of the rope.

One-Eyed Peggie turned her prow more into the lee side of the wave. The rope moved accordingly, and the wizard ran, still hauling on the rope, like he was bringing in a large fish.

The sea below Juhg exploded. A maelstrom of salt spray drenched him as the bearded hoar-worm rose up from the depths.

You're not a fish, the voice told him. *You're a tantalizing little piece of bait. Scream before you die.*

The monster opened its huge maw. Juhg saw himself reflected in the enormous black eyes that were bigger than he was. Fangs taller even than Craugh with his hat on filled the cavernous mouth. The creature's breath was horrible, so strong that it burned Juhg's eyes.

Tasty morsel.

Juhg put his hands out before him and grabbed the bearded hoar-worm's upper lip.

You dare put your hands on me!

It isn't like I have any choice, Juhg thought.

I heard that. Like a dog trained to do a trick, the monster flicked its head and knocked Juhg end over end into the air, then readied itself to catch him in its teeth when he came back down.

Juhg reached for the monster's lip again, hoping to save himself, but he couldn't span the distance. He dropped—and just as suddenly rose into the air.

The bearded hoar-worm's fangs gnashed together without their prize. Glowering at Juhg as he flew backward through the air, the monster dived beneath the ocean and disappeared again.

Flailing and struggling, feeling the rope chafing his leg terribly, Juhg tried to bend up and grab the rope so he could lessen some of the pull. Unfortunately, he couldn't. Hallekk and a handful of dwarven pirates reeled him up toward the ship as it dropped into the trough at the bottom.

Juhg hit *One-Eyed Peggie*'s brine-soaked deck and sprawled inelegantly. He hurt all over and the wind was knocked from his lungs. Before he could recover, Hallekk had jerked him to his feet.

"Are ye all right then, Juhg?" the pirate captain asked anxiously.

Juhg tried to answer but couldn't. He didn't have his wind back.

Hallekk beat him vigorously on the back, nearly knocking him to his knees. "Stop. Please."

Grinning mightily, Hallekk stepped back. "He's all right, Craugh. Just some'at shook up."

Juhg nodded, hoping he would be left alone.

"By the Old Ones," Hallekk said, chucking Juhg under the chin, "ye are a brave one, aren't ye?"

Just then, *One-Eyed Peggie* hit the bottom of the wave trough. Brine splashed over her, drenching her deck and everyone one on her.

"Gotta see if I can save this ship," Hallekk muttered. "Thanks fer savin' me life." Then he was gone in a whirlwind of bluster and orders, marching across the heaving deck.

Juhg started working on the rope around his ankle, certain that the leg had stretched dramatically and he would walk lopsided the rest of his days.

Craugh snapped his fingers.

Like a live thing, the rope untangled itself and slid away from Juhg. He looked up at the wizard, knowing Craugh was surely about to toadify him.

"You," the wizard said imperiously, looking down his blade of a nose, "have a job to do. You have no business being brave."

Juhg's anger flamed to the forefront. As many times as he'd seen Craugh put his life on the line for the Grandmagister, he couldn't believe the wizard would have the audacity to chastise him for saving Hallekk's life. He tried to stand, intending to take umbrage for all the mean things Craugh had said and done lately, and the way he had basically ignored him the last month while they were aboard the pirate ship, but his leg wouldn't hold his weight. It buckled beneath him and dropped him to the deck.

Craugh turned away from Juhg, obviously dismissing him as he searched the sea.

One-Eyed Peggie fought the wind and the sea. Her sails were a shambles, several of them flopping free at the end of broken rigging or unsupported by snapped 'yards. Hallekk ordered men into the rigging to deal with the damage.

"Get up there with ye!" Hallekk bawled through his cupped hands as he walked beneath the sails. "Get that canvas furled some'at! We can't give *Peggie* her head in this here wind unless she's evened out!"

Several of the dwarven pirates climbed the rigging, furling sails with difficulty. Handling the amount of damage the ship had been dealt even in calm winds would have proven a daunting task. As things stood now, managing the canvas was almost impossible. Still, they were dwarves and not used to giving up or backing away from a challenge, and they would surely die if they lost the ship, so they fought the sails.

"Lean her out!" Hallekk ordered. He stomped beneath the three masts, calling out individual orders.

Memory of the dwarven pirates falling from the ship wouldn't leave Juhg's mind. He grabbed the rope that had been wrapped around his ankle and pulled it into a coil while he raced for the railing. There was a chance one of the three dwarves might yet live.

"Apprentice," Craugh yelled from the forward deck, addressing Juhg as he always did. From the rank of novice and even when he'd earned the position of First Level Librarian, the wizard had insisted on calling him by that title. Out of all the dwellers that the Grandmagister had trained as Librarians over the years, Juhg was the only one that Craugh had addressed in such a manner. If the wizard's tone hadn't been usually disparaging, or if he'd used the title during times of praise instead of remonstration, it might have sounded good.

Juhg hesitated just a moment. The weight of the rope was on his arm. He wondered if the wizard would simply have the rope truss him to the nearest railing.

"I would not have you throw your life away after I worked so hard to safeguard it," Craugh warned with a glare. "I would be most displeased."

Juhg spared the wizard only a glance. "Thank you for your concern, but we lost others overboard. There may still be a chance to save them." He peered into the thrashing sea.

"They're gone, Apprentice. Lost to us."

Anger and sorrow warred within Juhg. He hated the way Craugh seemed so able to accept the loss of the dwarves. However, Craugh was always that way. The only time Juhg had seen the wizard get emotional over anyone, it had been over the Grandmagister.

Stubbornly, Juhg kept his attention on the sea. If he saw one of the pirates who'd fallen overboard, he intended to attempt a rescue. But the bearded hoar-worm remained at large also. His heart thundered in his chest and the rope burn around his ankle throbbed with it. He was also tired of following Craugh's instructions blindly.

Hallekk continued bellowing orders, bringing discipline back to the fearful crew. Critter, for all that everyone despised the rhowdor, performed admirably, calling out commands as well.

The ship lurched again, once more struck by its attacker. Before the crew could recover, the monster raised its broad head from the depths. The prow pointed right at the bearded hoar-worm. Malignant intelligence gleamed in the creature's black eyes. The massive jaws opened and sea froth poured forth. It towered twenty feet above the main mast.

One-Eyed Peggie slammed into the creature, shuddering, then sliding past, gliding along the slick scales. The bearded hoar-worm lunged forward, swooping toward the dwarves clinging in the rigging. Before it could close its terrible jaws, Craugh stepped forward and raised a hand.

Green lightning gathered around the wizard's hand. Harsh, sibilant words cracked over the low growl of the wind.

The bearded hoar-worm's attack halted a few feet distant from the dwarves, who had panicked and dropped from the rigging. An invisible wall held the monster back as it lashed out again and again. Then it lunged forward again, attacking from the side and striking Craugh.

Propelled by the creature's immense strength, the wizard vanished over the ship's side. Juhg couldn't believe what he'd seen.

"Attack!" Hallekk bellowed. "Attack this cursed thing!"

The pirates massed with weapons, drawing cutlasses and battle-axes. Juhg drew his knife, though he knew it would hardly make a dent in the monster.

When the bearded hoar-worm launched itself again, the pirates scattered. But this time they also struck back, swinging their weapons with all the might they could muster. Unfortunately, the weapons had little or no effect against the rigid scales that plated the monster.

Attacking yet again, the creature seized a dwarf in his mouth and bit him in two. As it swung its great head about, the monster struck the mainmast and snapped it in half only a few feet from the deck. Shorn of its support, the mast fell to the starboard side. Two pirates went down under the rigging and sails, and *One-Eyed Peggie* tilted dangerously.

Juhg took a tighter grip on his knife, but he knew it was useless. *We're going to die. Either the monster will kill us or destroy the ship and we'll perish in the water. Even if we survive that, we'll be helpless in these waters, and we won't find any friends here.*

 Still, even as he resigned himself to his fate, Juhg's main concern was for the Grandmagister. Since he was taken from his own family by the goblinkin slavers, Juhg had never really been close to anyone. Until the Grandmagister had taken him in, cared for him, and taught him everything he knew. Now he was going to die and there would be no one to rescue the Grandmagister from the hands of the goblinkin.

Even faced with an opponent they could not vanquish, the pirates girded themselves for battle. Juhg ran to join their ranks. There was no other place for him.

"ENOUGH!" Craugh's voice split the howling wind.

Completely surprised, thinking that if the wizard wasn't dead they had surely left him behind because *One-Eyed Peggie* still ran before the wind, Juhg turned toward the starboard side. Even the monster gave pause.

Amazingly, Craugh rose on a swell of ocean that acted independently of the swirling sea. Wild green fire tinted the water, glowing and shifting within it like coals on a brazier.

Drenched by the sea, the wizard stood wide-legged on the tide. He'd lost his hat and his gray hair and beard hung in matted clumps. With the cloak wet and sticking to him, he looked like a drenched cat, somehow shorn of its size. If he hadn't been riding the sea, obviously in control of at least that part of it, he would have looked like an old man about to meet his doom.

But Juhg knew the wizard, and knew what Craugh was capable of. The air popped and cracked with the power the wizard called to him and gathered.

"By the Old Ones," Craugh roared, "this ship and these people are under my protection! *My* protection! I am *Craugh*! You know me! And I will not allow this!"

Incredibly, the bearded hoar-worm paused. Then it laughed, throwing its head back and howling with mirth like a madman. The whole time, the monster kept pace with the pirate ship just as the wizard and the magicked wave did. When it finished laughing, the creature looked at the wizard and cocked its head to one side.

"Do not forget your place, *Craugh*. O mighty wizard." The monster's voice came out thunderous and insulting and hoarse, like the watery wind whipped through a tidal cave. "These petty beings are forfeit. They are *mine*. Because *I* wish it so."

"No," the wizard returned. "I will not allow it."

The huge face scowled. "You cannot stop me."

"I can," Craugh declared forcefully. "And I will."

"You and the others put me and my kind to sleep at the bottom of the ocean for years," the monster accused.

"You worked at cross purposes to us."

Juhg listened to the exchange. Little had been written about the bearded hoar-worms. Most of what he had read in the Vault of All Known Knowledge had been speculation and myth. But to learn that Craugh had known them, had interacted with them—that one of them actually knew Craugh!—was astounding. So much of the wizard's long life was unknown. Even the Grandmagister talked little of Craugh's background.

"You are no friend of mine," the monster said.

"I never was," Craugh agreed. "Who awakened you, Methoss?"

The monster laughed again. "So inquisitive. All these years, Craugh, and you have not changed." The big eyes blinked. "Except, I see, to finally get old and frail."

Craugh glowered at the creature and lifted his nose ever so little. "Believing that would be a mistake on your part. You should have left as soon as you recognized me."

"Why? You, even with those others of the Round, could not kill us. You only succeeded in enchanting us."

"That was a long time ago," Craugh warned. "I have learned things since those days that I did not know then."

"I do not fear you, Craugh."

The wizard stood straight and tall, a reed that would not bend in the howling wind. "Then you will surely die."

Juhg didn't know if Craugh was bluffing or not. Craugh was powerful. Juhg had seen the wizard do amazing things over the years. Turning annoying people into toads was a hobby, nothing more. A parlor trick, Craugh claimed, though his victims lived out long, sad lives filled with flies.

But the creature that swam in the sea before him? Juhg had never seen Craugh face anything like that.

"Your time is over, Craugh," the bearded hoar-worm snarled. "You are not as good a man as you would have yourself to believe. You still battle the darkness that is within you."

"Perhaps. But I win. And every day I find more reasons to fight against it."

"You should have sided with us when you were given the chance."

"I would rather die."

"Then you shall." Without any preliminary flicker of movement to betray its intent, the monster popped its head forward and gulped Craugh down whole.

One moment the wizard stood there on the small shelf of water he'd controlled, and the next he was gone.

The bearded hoar-worm laughed uproariously, as if at the best joke that it had ever heard. Then it turned its attention back to the pirate crew. "Now, where was I?" It smiled. "Oh yes. Now that you've lost your would-be defender, you should be absolutely filled with fear and—*aaaccckkk!*"

Aaaccckkk? That didn't sound like part of a gloating speech to Juhg. And the monster was surely in a position to gloat.

Then the giant creature loosed a howl of pain. In the next moment, it coiled in on itself as if in agony, whipping back and forth like a snake that had been run over by a wagon wheel.

Mesmerized by what he was seeing, Juhg walked forward, stopping at the railing, then running back toward the stern as the bearded hoar-worm stopped pacing *One-Eyed Peggie* and fell by the wayside. Juhg halted behind the helmsman, unable to go any farther.

"The monster's sinkin'," Hallekk said as he stood beside Juhg. "Craugh killed it."

In the distance, the bearded hoar-worm began slowly drifting under the sea.

"But it's taking Craugh down with it," Juhg said as he saw the coils of the monster sinking beneath the ocean surface. Grief filled him. Although the wizard had always treated Juhg as if he were a child with straw for brains, Craugh had been a part of Juhg's life almost as much as the Grandmagister.

"He's done fer," Hallekk said, patting Juhg sympathetically on the shoulder.

"No. He may still yet live." Juhg ran for one of the longboats hanging from davits on *One-Eyed Peggie*'s starboard side.

"Ye can't hope to put a longboat out in that water," Hallekk protested. "Not an' stay afloat."

"I've got to try." Juhg reached for the rope that held the longboat tied up.

"Wait," one of the pirates cried. "The monster ain't dead yet! Craugh didn't get it killed!"

Impossibly, Juhg watched as the bearded hoar-worm surfaced, then struck out for *One-Eyed Peggie*, overtaking her in short order. The creature came up on the starboard side, away from the tangle of rigging and sails the broken mainmast had caused. The dwarven pirates trotted alongside, watching the creature and cursing it to the best of their abilities, which were quite extensive and improved by the fear the monster had put into them.

Despite the fact that the monster moved beside them, Juhg noticed the dead way its eyes simply stared.

A moment later, the creature's mouth opened and smoke boiled out of it, bringing the stench of rot and burned meat. When the smoke cleared, Craugh stood in the bearded hoar-worm's open mouth. Seawater lapped up over the broken fangs and swirled around the wizard's boots.

Craugh looked haggard and worn. Smoke clung to his hair and clothing. He held his staff and gazed up at the crew.

"Well," Craugh demanded in a disgusted tone, "am I going to have to crawl up the side of the ship to get back aboard?"

A mighty cheer went up from the pirates. Despite the losses of their comrades in arms, the wizard's survival cheered the pirates' hearts. Also, the dead monster floating beside the ship spoke volumes about their increased chances of getting out of their current situation alive if the wizard was with them.

Hallekk gave the orders and a net was quickly put over *One-Eyed Peggie*'s side.

Craugh grabbed hold of the net and waited a moment. "Hallekk," he called up.

"Aye," Hallekk responded.

"You'll need to tie this carcass to the ship."

"Whatever for?"

"So we can bring it along with us for a while."

"An' why should we want to do that?"

"Because I need to harvest some of the things Methoss has eaten over the years." Craugh started up the net, moving slowly, like a man near exhaustion. "I'll want its heart, too."

Juhg helped Craugh onto the ship. He felt how shaky the old wizard was although Craugh gave no indication of it as he peered at the destruction made by the fallen mast.

"It's made a proper mess of your ship," Craugh commented.

"Aye." Hallekk scratched his beard. "We're gonna be some'at shorthanded now, an' definitely gonna fall behind them goblinkin ships."

"We'll do the best that we may," Craugh told him. "As for reinforcements and supplies, there is that ship of reinforcements I asked for."

Seventeen days ago, Craugh had pulled a dove out of his hat, tied a message to its leg requesting additional supplies and men, and put it into the air to fly to Greydawn Moors. There had been no answer. When Juhg had asked the wizard how he expected another ship to find them even though they didn't know where they were, Craugh had pointed out that the other ship would know where they would be.

During the few minutes he'd gotten to talk to the Grandmagister aboard the goblinkin ship right after the battle for Greydawn Moors had begun, the Grandmagister had told Juhg that he'd left something for him in Imarish, also known as the City of Canals. So far, the goblinkin ships were heading for Imarish as well.

The fact had filled Juhg with some trepidation. Despite the fact that he believed the Grandmagister could do anything, Juhg couldn't help feeling that Aldhran Khempus—the man who had captured the Grandmagister in Greydawn Moors—might have tortured the information out of Edgewick Lamplighter.

And if Aldhran had, was *One-Eyed Peggie* sailing into a trap? The possibility was unsettling. Then Juhg realized that Craugh was talking to him.

"Yes?" Juhg replied, looking up at the wizard.

"I said that you and I have a task to accomplish once Hallekk and his men have the bearded hoar-worm tied up alongside."

"What task?" Juhg felt instantly rebellious.

"We're going to cut the heart out of that monster."

Juhg gawped. He couldn't help it. "Not me."

"Yes, *you*," Craugh thundered. "By the Old Ones, I find this rebellious nature you've suddenly sprouted to be totally insufferable."

"I am *not* going to do that," Juhg said. He couldn't put up with the wizard ordering him around any more.

The crew drew back from Juhg, obviously afraid that they might get turned into toads by the fallout of the spell Craugh was undoubtedly going to blast the object of his irritation with.

Craugh glared at Juhg.

Juhg stubbornly held his ground. At least, he liked to think that he was stubbornly holding his ground. The truth was that after his outburst, after realizing what was likely to happen, he was frozen to that very spot.

Green sparks leapt from the crooked end of Craugh's staff.

"Uh," Hallekk said quietly. "Mayhap I can get one of the crew to do that, Craugh. It's a mite dirty work. Not fit fer a proper Librarian at all, much less a First Level Librarian like Juhg. I mean, there's gonna be blood involved. I could get Cook to have a go at it, because he's used to bleedin' things an'—"

"Captain Hallekk," Craugh interrupted.

Hallekk blinked and took a half step back. "Aye."

"I want this ship fixed. You'll need everyone of your crew to do that."

After a brief pause, Hallekk said, "Aye."

"You do want to rescue the Grandmagister, don't you?" Craugh asked.

"Aye." There was no hesitation at all.

"Then see to those repairs."

"Aye." Hallekk turned and yelled orders at the crew.

Juhg stood there, alone as anything, as the dwarven pirates jumped to do their assignments. They weren't abandoning Juhg, after all, they were tending to the rescue of the Grandmagister.

"What about you?" Craugh demanded.

Juhg swallowed hard and hoped that he wouldn't stammer. "Me?"

"Yes you. Do you want to rescue the Grandmagister?"

Juhg licked his lips. He'd been asked trick questions before. Was this a trick question? "Yes."

"Then get a knife. A really sharp knife." Craugh turned away from him and went to the railing where Hallekk had crew throwing out ropes to bind the bearded hoar-worm's body to *One-Eyed Peggie*.

Juhg stood there on the rolling ship's deck. He'd wanted to ask how getting a knife would help save the Grandmagister, but he knew that Craugh had said all he would say on the matter. He also felt certain the wizard was speaking the truth. Getting the knife would—somehow—help save the Grandmagister.

After a moment, he took a breath, only then realizing he'd stopped breathing. Then he blinked. After that, he went to get the knife.

Walking barefoot across the belly of the dead monster wasn't the most unpleasant thing Juhg had ever done. Certainly carrying around the severed leg of a fellow dweller who had died from overwork and beatings down in the goblinkin gem mines had been horrible. The slaves had to bring up the leg to prove that the dweller had died rather than escaped, and dragging a corpse around all day hadn't been possible. They'd had to stay down in the mines till they filled their carts.

There were other worse things, but Juhg knew he'd have to think for a long time to come up with them.

In death, the bearded hoar-worm's flesh was loose, and walking across its belly was like walking through a swamp.

The storm had abated. The fog remained, but the lashing waves had gone wherever it was they'd been headed when they'd overtaken the pirate ship. The sea was like that, always moving, always restless.

The monster's body bobbed in the water, occasionally bumping into *One-Eyed Peggie* because the ropes that tied the carcass to the ship were short. Gulls landed on the enormous body, tearing at the meat and eating their fill. Dark shapes under the water kept bumping up against the monster like nursing pups, but Juhg knew they were sharks drawn by the creature's blood. They, too, feasted on the monster.

Juhg felt a little sorry for the bearded hoar-worm. That surprised him, but he supposed it was because he had known it could think. Somehow that made watching it being eaten worse.

"Here."

Turning, Juhg found Craugh behind him. Surprisingly, the wizard had followed him onto the monster's body. Juhg had felt certain Craugh would leave him to tend to the ghoulish task on his own.

"You're sure?" Juhg asked.

Craugh tapped the bottom of his staff against the body. He held an oil lantern in his other hand. "Here," he repeated. Then he sat down, crossing his legs with his staff across his knees. He put the lantern to one side.

Juhg hunkered down and took a fresh grip on the flensing knife he'd borrowed from Cook. He smoothed the monster's flesh with his other hand, testing it. His mouth dried and his stomach turned over as he readied himself to carry out his instructions.

"Go ahead!" a raucous voice shouted. "Go ahead an' stick 'im! Give 'im a good 'un fer me!"

Looking up, Juhg spotted Critter perched on the ship's railing. The bird sat lopsidedly due to the fork pegleg.

"Apprentice," Craugh said in a low voice, "we're going to lose the light."

Already, the sun was setting in the westering sky. Pinks, purples, and reds tinted the clouds.

Red sky at night, sailor's delight. Juhg remembered the odd bit but couldn't remember where he'd gotten it from. The Grandmagister would know, of course. And that turned his thoughts back to the chore Craugh had assigned him.

He no longer felt that Craugh could have done the task himself. The fight with the bearded hoar-worm had all but done him in. Craugh would not have admitted it, Juhg was sure, but it was the truth. The wizard was not sure-footed crossing the monster's body.

"The creature is well beyond feeling any pain you may think you're causing," Craugh said.

"I know." Juhg thrust the knife into the dead flesh and started cutting. He found out at once that he hadn't cut deeply enough and the task would be more arduous than he'd believed. Still, the knife was sharp and he was determined. After all, this was supposed to help save the Grandmagister. He didn't know if he hoped to help or prove the wizard wrong. Craugh couldn't be right all the time.

Gradually, just as dusk had started to swell in the eastern sky, Juhg sliced through the skin and into the stomach beyond. When that happened, a little more energy seemed to spark in Craugh, but the wizard appeared a trifle more apprehensive as well.

At Craugh's urging, Juhg sliced into the stomach. The stench was horrible.

"Make the hole larger," Craugh said, leaning forward and peering inside. "We're going to have to enter."

"Enter?" The thought horrified Juhg.

"Of course," Craugh snapped. "This is a sizeable monster, after all. The stomach is a cavern inside this thing."

"You never said anything about entering the corpse."

"I'm saying it now. Cut."

Having no choice, Juhg enlarged the hole.

When he had the hole big enough, Craugh lit the lantern, then his pipe. He handed the lantern to Juhg. "Go, apprentice."

Staring at the large wound he'd created, Juhg asked, "This will help the Grandmagister?"

"Didn't I say that it would?"

Juhg took a handkerchief from his pocket and tied it around his face, hoping that it would block some of the noxious stench. After adjusting the lantern wick to glow more brightly, he clambered down inside the dead body.

The footing was treacherous and slippery. Gore covered him, fouling him at once. Inside the belly of the beast, he lifted the lantern high and gazed around. Fluid several inches deep ran over his toes.

Craugh crawled down after him.

"These are stomach fluids," Juhg said. "Won't they hurt me?"

"No. I've already tended to that." Craugh puffed on his pipe and the scent of the pipeweed seemed to overcome the stomach stink. He gazed in all directions.

Juhg waited, totally amazed. The inside of the bearded hoar-worm was larger than *One-Eyed Peggie*'s belowdecks. Then he remembered the creature's body was long, and there would be a lot of room.

Craugh drew a symbol in the air that caught fire and burned with a green flame. He blew smoke at the symbol and it floated forward.

"Come on," Craugh said. "That marks our way."

Without a word, Juhg held forth the lantern and started after the glowing symbol. He tramped through stomach fluid and then piles of ancient armor he recognized from books at the Vault of All Known Knowledge. Many of the civilizations that had constructed the armor had disappeared even before Lord Kharrion had called the goblinkin tribes together.

Questions ran rampant through Juhg's mind. *How long had the bearded hoar-worm lived? How had it known Craugh? What had it meant when it had accused Craugh of having a darkness within him? When had it—not it,* Juhg amended, *Methoss—when had Methoss and its comrades offered Craugh a spot among them?*

They walked for at least fifty yards. The darkness inside the monster's stomach was complete except for the lantern and the hole Juhg had cut into it. The hole was dimming as the sun went down. For a moment, Juhg worried that they might not be able to find the way out.

Then the glowing symbol stopped.

"There," Craugh breathed in a smoky whisper. His eyes narrowed and he moved his staff in front of him.

Staring into the darkness, Juhg crept forward. The lantern light invaded the innards of the beast, chasing the darkness back.

A multifaceted blood-red gem the size of a horse's head sat in the stomach amid a pile of human bones. Some of the bones spilled over the gem, arm bones and leg bones, like they were clinging to the gem.

"Well," Craugh said, "she's fed lately." He didn't look happy.

Drawn by the sight of the gem's elegant beauty, Juhg knelt down, scarcely paying attention to the fluids and the skeletons and partially decomposing bodies. He brushed away an arm bone. Then he realized what Craugh had said.

"*She?*" Juhg repeated. "Don't you mean that *he* has fed lately?"

"No," Craugh said. "I mean that *she* has."

Before Juhg could ask the question that immediately came to mind, the gem dawned with an inner light of its own. Crimson bathed the immediate area, stronger than the lantern light.

Something stirred within the depths of the gem. It whirled and flipped, like a cloud turning in on itself.

"No, apprentice," Craugh said. "You're too close."

Juhg barely registered the words, then a woman's face formed inside the gem. She was graced with elven beauty, her ears pointed and her nose slightly upturned. Her eyes warred with the crimson light, but they were purest amethyst. Her skin was dark, the color of old pecan. Her smile revealed fangs that spoke at once of a predator.

"Hello, Craugh," she said. Then she laughed and reached through the gem walls to grab Juhg around the head.

58

3

A Secret Past

uhg dropped the lantern and tried to escape the woman's clutches. Her strength proved too much and he couldn't. Her laughter echoed the length of the monster's belly and came back over them.

She cackled with glee as Juhg's struggles helped pull her free of the gem. She was almost as tall as Craugh. Obsidian black armor covered her and she wore an obsidian black blade at her side. She had seven fingers on each hand, and they were much longer than anything human, dwarven, elven, or dweller. Her long fingernails were razor sharp. Short red hair was plastered tightly against her head.

Most surprising of all, she had a tail. It looked like a lizard's. Juhg saw the appendage first when it whipped forward and closed around his neck, choking off whatever attempt he might have made at speaking.

"Ladamae," Craugh said in an even voice. He didn't move a muscle. "Don't kill him."

The woman took her hands from Juhg's head. Her tail held him off the ground easily. She drew her obsidian blade as she turned her full attention to the wizard.

"Don't kill him?" she repeated. "You killed Methoss."

"Methoss would not listen to me," Craugh said. "He chose to ignore my warning."

"He had been sent after that ship," Ladamae said. "He did not know that you were aboard."

"And if he had known that I was aboard?"

The woman grinned and waved the obsidian blade. "He would still have tried to killed you. You know how Methoss was, Craugh. He was always jealous of you." She smiled, but to Juhg the expression was like watching a cat unsheathe her claws.

Craugh said nothing.

Dangling from the woman's tail, Juhg struggled to breathe. Her tail around his throat was incredibly tight.

Ladamae maintained her stance between Craugh and the red gem. "I knew about Methoss's death, of course. How could I not? I am here, aren't I? I have been with him for centuries, Craugh. When he slept at the bottom of the sea, where you and your friends spelled him, I did not sleep. Did you know that?"

"No," Craugh answered.

Juhg watched the woman, wondering what she was. In all the books that he had read, he'd never seen anything like her.

60

"But you knew that I was inside Methoss," Ladamae accused. "You remember how he swallowed me whole after he was changed. He couldn't bear the thought of me being with anyone else. And he hated you for the time that I spent with you."

Craugh said nothing, keeping his arms spread to offer no threat.

"You cut your way into the corpse to kill me, didn't you?" Ladamae asked in a shrill voice.

Juhg feared that Craugh was going to say yes. He felt certain as soon as he did the woman would snap his neck with her tail. He kicked valiantly but couldn't escape.

"No," Craugh said. "I didn't come here to kill you, Ladamae."

The woman hesitated a little, watching him carefully. "You lie."

"No." Craugh regarded her, seemingly totally at ease.

"I had resigned myself to sitting at the bottom of the ocean till Methoss's body rotted into pieces," Ladamae said. "I didn't know how I was going to get the gem to the surface again, but the water here is shallow enough. I had hopes of a fisherman finding me one day." She smiled sadly.

"If it weren't for that cursed gem, I could go anywhere that I wanted to. I could have anything I wanted."

"But that's not how it is, is it?" Craugh's tone wasn't unkind, but his words were.

"You turned away from me all those years ago. Just turned and walked away and forgot about me."

"I didn't forget about you."

The woman laughed and the sound carried a hint of madness.

Juhg didn't blame her. He couldn't imagine how it would be to lie at the bottom of the Blood-Soaked Sea for hundreds of years. Still, the last place at the moment that he wanted to be was in her clutches.

The woman cursed and pointed her blade at Craugh's head. "Once you thought I was pretty."

"A long time ago," Craugh agreed. "I was foolish. Now I am not."

Listening to the conversation and the flat way the wizard responded, Juhg knew that if he lived he was going to recommend *The Language of Love* by Rugahr Dahalson. Of course, he wasn't going to mention that Rugahr had been poisoned while writing the sequel, *Keeping Happiness in Your Harem*.

"Now you are even more foolish," Ladamae said. "Perhaps even pathetic." She shook her head. "You should not have cut your way inside Methoss."

"I had to see you."

"Better that you had not."

"Coming to see you seemed better than letting you simply drop to the bottom of the sea and lie there forever."

"Many things can change," Ladamae said. "When you can live forever."

"Methoss," Craugh said with a grim smile, "thought he could live forever. He couldn't." He paused. "Neither can you. Without protection."

Ladamae paused to think. Juhg watched her watching Craugh with her amethyst eyes. She was cunning and savage. Juhg saw that at once.

"Why *did* you come here?" she asked finally.

"To strike a bargain," Craugh said.

"Bargains are hard things, Craugh. You know that. Most times you give away more than you get, even though you think it will be the other way around or at least balance. We all took on burdens to bear when we sought after *The Book of Time*."

Craugh hunted for The Book of Time? Juhg couldn't believe his ears.

"We were all foolish then," Craugh said.

"No," she said. "Just greedy. In the end, we weren't clever enough, were we? Methoss became a bearded hoar-worm like some of the others. I got trapped in that gem. We both got immortality, of course, but the cost was far more than we thought." She looked at the wizard. "And how is it you're still alive, Craugh? After all these years?"

"We all," Craugh said, "had a price to pay for our part in the evil that was done when *The Book of Time* was brought into this world."

If Juhg hadn't been hanging from the woman's lizardlike tail and fighting for every breath he took, he knew he would have been listening with bated breath. What were the secrets that Craugh had been hiding? He'd never mentioned how he'd achieved the longevity he enjoyed.

"Are you paying a price, Craugh? Truly?" The woman's tone mocked him.

"What do you think?" Craugh asked.

"Methoss was told you had aligned yourself with the dwellers. With that precious Library of theirs. I thought that was unbelievable even though I knew you had a hand in its building. I thought you served your own purposes. Yet, here you stand. And you are searching for *The Book of Time* to aid the Grandmagister."

"Who woke Methoss?" Craugh asked.

"It's a pity you can't ask him."

"I'm asking you."

"Maybe I'll tell you." Ladamae smiled. "And maybe I won't."

"Do you know a man named Aldhran Khempus?"

"Yes."

"He doesn't have the power required to have wakened Methoss."

The woman shook her head. At the end of her tail, Juhg shook even more violently.

"So someone else wakened Methoss," Craugh concluded.

"Yes."

"Who?" Craugh demanded.

"What do I get if I tell you?"

Indecision showed on Craugh's bearded face. "Letting you go free from this place would be a horrible thing, Ladamae." He nodded toward the pile of bones surrounding the crimson gem. "You feast on men. I see Methoss kept you fed."

She smiled as though embarrassed. "Methoss only caught me a few morsels now and again."

"Tell me who woke Methoss."

"And if I don't?"

Craugh eyed her levelly. Inside the body of the monster, his whisper was cold and filled with threat. "Then I will kill you."

Ladamae laughed, sounding more insane than ever. "I don't believe you, Craugh. Not even after all that we once meant to each other—or if we only thought we meant that to each other—you wouldn't allow me to leave this place. You can't. Despite all the wicked things you did with us before you joined the Round and tried to forget you were ever anything but a protector of the world, you were never truly as evil as we were. You just wanted to know if you could defeat the Guardians of Time and steal their precious book. It was more a challenge to you than anything else."

"Don't do this," Craugh said in a soft voice.

"If you didn't want it to end this way," Ladamae said, "then you would have never cut Methoss's body open and found me."

The tail around Juhg's neck tightened. He would have sworn he felt his neck separating from his shoulders.

Then Craugh attacked faster than Juhg would have believed possible, swinging the staff into the woman's tail. Juhg felt the vibration of the blow throughout his body, then the tail loosened about his neck. Using his inherent dweller's quickness and the instinct for self-preservation, he pulled his head from inside the coil of tail and dropped to the beast's stomach. He threw himself forward in a dive at once, sliding through the horrid fluids and striving not to think about what they were or that the woman was going to plant her sword between his shoulders at any moment.

Ladamae screamed in anger and the sound echoed and re-echoed the length of the monster's stomach.

Juhg rolled to his feet and picked up a short sword lying nearby. He turned, ready to defend himself, expecting to see Craugh dead or dying.

Instead, the wizard battled his opponent with skill and quickness that Juhg would not have believed even if Craugh hadn't been dead tired from fighting the bearded hoar-worm earlier.

Ladamae swung her obsidian blade like a warrior born to the craft of swordplay. But Craugh met her at every turn with the staff, and each time the wood met the obsidian blade, green sparks showered the air.

Lord of the Libraries

Juhg started to go to the wizard's aid. He pushed himself to his feet.

"Stay back, apprentice!" Craugh roared, blocking the sword again. "This is my fight!"

And when you fall, Juhg wondered, *whose fight will it be then?* The way back to the hole he'd cut in the belly of the beast was far. He doubted he'd make it before the woman overtook him. Then he saw the woman pull a knife from her boot with her tail.

Ladamae brought the blade up behind her, cleverly concealing the weapon from Craugh. The wizard blocked her sword, then swapped ends with the staff to aim a blow at her head. She ducked, calling him vile names, and her tail whipped forward with the knife.

Craugh blocked the knife at the last moment, then lifted the staff and halted the sword. Still holding both blades away from him, he sidestepped and pushed, throwing the woman off-balance. She whirled, wasting no time to get turned back around to once more face the wizard.

But there was no time. With a short step, Craugh swung the staff once more, this time driving it into the gem.

The gem exploded into a huge ball of crimson light at once, blinding Juhg with its intensity. He cried out at the pain and fought to get his eyes opened again to see if Craugh still lived. He blinked in amazement as his vision returned and he saw Craugh standing where the gem had been.

 Ladamae stood in front of the wizard. Disbelief, followed quickly by fear, twisted her features. "Craugh," she whispered. "What have you done? By the Old Ones, what have you done to me?"

As Juhg watched, Ladamae's boots turned white, and the whiteness spread upward, taking her legs and her hips and her upper body.

"Nooo," she whispered, and the sound was as plaintive as a child's. She went rigid as the whiteness enveloped her head. She stood there only a moment more, then dropped into a powdery pile.

Stunned but curious, Juhg approached. He gazed down at the pile of powder, then bent to poke his finger into it.

"Salt," Craugh said.

Juhg looked up at the wizard.

Craugh cleared his throat. "It's salt. When I destroyed the gem, she turned into salt. She's dead." A lone tear trickled down his face. "One thing—" His voice broke. "One thing you must know, apprentice, if you ever write about this." His eyes would not meet Juhg's. "Ladamae was not always an evil creature. She was once . . . a beautiful young woman. She was corrupted." He took a deep breath. "*I* corrupted her."

Juhg stared in openmouthed wonder. There were so many things inside his mind, questions that needed answering, emotions he needed to vent. "You—*you*—helped steal *The Book of Time* from the Guardians?"

Craugh's face grew stern. "We won't talk of this, apprentice."

"Does the Grandmagister know?"

"I said *enough*, apprentice." Craugh stood straight and tall and threatening. "Do not press me on this matter."

Juhg understood then. "The Grandmagister *doesn't* know. How could you not tell him?"

Green flame blazed in the wizard's eyes above the single tear.

At that moment, Juhg knew that his hold on life was as thin as a cat's whisker.

"We leave this place," Craugh said. "We leave this place now and don't you dare ever speak to me of this subject again!" He turned and walked away.

Juhg watched the wizard go. He didn't know what he was supposed to do. Even if he told everyone aboard *One-Eyed Peggie,* even if he could get Hallekk and the others to believe him even though they had been Craugh's friends for years, the lives of the captain and crew would be forfeit.

"Apprentice," Craugh said, "I'll not call you twice."

Reluctantly, with much confusion and pain, Juhg picked up the lantern he'd brought inside the dead monster and trudged along in the wizard's wake. He took a last, lingering glance back at the pile of salt that had been the woman. In a short time, the darkness claimed her and hid her from sight.

Once more aboard *One-Eyed Peggie,* Juhg stood and looked out over the dead monster lashed to the ship's side. Full dark had descended upon the sea, but the crew worked by lantern light and the pale quarter-moon to repair the damage done to the vessel.

"Didn't find anything?" Hallekk asked, walking over to Juhg.

"Nothing of import," Craugh answered in a neutral voice. There was no indication at all that he was lying.

And why would there be? Juhg asked himself. *He's a good liar. He's lied for years.*

"But it's dead, ain't it?" the pirate captain asked.

"It's dead," Craugh assured him. The wizard glanced at Juhg.

Juhg pretended he didn't see the look, but he had no intention of telling anyone aboard the ship. Maybe later when they had a chance to run for their lives.

Or maybe it will be too late then and Craugh will have already killed you. Juhg didn't like thinking like that, but it couldn't be helped. He'd grown up in a goblinkin mine. He knew a lot about how evil the world could be. What surprised him most was how he could be surprised by who was evil.

Is Craugh evil? Is he truly helping to find the Grandmagister because the Grandmagister is his friend? Or is he interested in finding The Book of Time *for his own purposes?* Juhg didn't know.

Craugh pointed his staff at the ropes holding the dead bearded hoar-worm to the ship. At a single command, a small green fireball darted from the staff and burned through the ropes. Released from the dead weight, *One-Eyed Peggie* righted herself, coming up from the leaning position she'd been in. The monster's body sank out of sight.

"What do ye think ye're doin'?" a pirate bellowed. "Don't ye know rope's in short supply right now?"

Craugh turned back toward the pirates working in the rigging.

High above in the rigging, three dwarves quickly scattered from a fourth. They were barely visible by the light of the moon and the lantern hanging from a 'yard.

Juhg held his breath, waiting for the wizard to blast the dwarf from the rigging.

Instead, Craugh turned from them all. "I'm going to bed. If you need me, wake me. Carefully."

Juhg watched the wizard go, torn by his own feelings for the man and what he had learned in the belly of the monster.

"Looks all done in, don't he?" Hallekk asked.

"Yes," Juhg replied.

"Let's hope we don't need him," the pirate captain said. "We got a fair mess to deal with here, an' we're fallin' behind the Grandmagister even further."

"How long do you think we'll be laid up?" Juhg asked.

Hallekk scratched his beard. "Two, mayhap three days."

"They'll be in Imarish by then," Juhg said. If Aldhran Khempus had tortured the Grandmagister into talking and he'd revealed the hiding place of whatever it was that was hidden in the city, there would be no way to stop it.

Hallekk clapped him on the shoulder. "I know. I know. But there's nothin' to be done for it. We'll do what we can. An' don't you be givin' up on ol' Wick. He's a canny one, he is. I got stories about things he's done that I still ain't told you yet."

Juhg worked with the dwarves all through the night. He couldn't sleep. His mind was too filled with questions and brimming up to his eyeballs with fear about what would happen in Imarish or with Craugh.

He tramped through the sodden hold, helped rescue cargo that could be salvaged, and helped man the pumps to keep the water from filling the hold till repairs could be effected. Then he worked on the rigging, sorting out the rope and sail that could be saved from that which could not.

The work was as strenuous as he remembered. He'd crewed aboard ships before with the Grandmagister, but he'd never worked on a vessel that had been as sorely stricken as *One-Eyed Peggie* that had survived.

Near dawn, when he found his flesh weak but his mind unflagging, he took his journal and his box of inks and charcoals from the protective rucksack and set to work in one of the longboats tied to *One-Eyed Peggie's* side. He let his mind free, knowing he was tired and that true focus would evade him time and again if he tried to force it. Instead, he let his mind and hand shape the images that caught his attention.

For a while, he worked with the charcoal, blocking out images that he wanted to remember. The bearded hoar-worm went on the pages several times, followed by the woman he and Craugh had confronted. He rendered the huge gem as well, then an image of the woman turning into salt in front of his eyes.

Craugh figured into the visual mix as well. Sometimes the wizard took on heroic proportions, as when he'd ridden the magicked ocean wave to battle the monster. But there were other times, like when he'd been steeped in the shadows in the monster's belly and when he'd talked with Ladamae that he was the very essence of the villain.

So which is he? Juhg asked himself as he worked. *Hero or villain?*

He didn't know. Every time he tried to deal with the problem his mind seemed wrapped in confusion and fear. He didn't know that much about Craugh. The wizard was tight-lipped about his past life, as well as his life when he was away from Greydawn Moors, which was most of the time.

Juhg grew uncomfortably aware that it was all too easy to see Craugh in the role of the villain. *Why did he make such a friendship with the Grand-magister?* Suddenly, even those motives were suspect.

Could the Grandmagister be fooled? Juhg struggled hard with that one. Edgewick Lamplighter was the smartest person Juhg knew. But even with that said, Juhg also knew the Grandmagister wasn't very worldly. The Grandmagister couldn't help that, of course. It was just the way he was. But he couldn't be fooled, either.

Except, perhaps, by a friend.

Juhg sighed with frustration as he listened to the dwarven pirates singing off-color sea shanties as they went about their labors. Later in the day they would put out the longboats and haul *One-Eyed Peggie* over so they could repair the cracked timbers below the waterline. Thankfully, Hallekk— just as Farok did before him—kept a surplus of wood and sailcloth aboard the ship.

The journal Juhg carried for his private thoughts was an old one. A number of images that he'd experimented with first before putting in a fin-ished form were on the pages. Some of the images were from the last quest he'd gone on with the Grandmagister. Before Juhg's frustration with the Library's continued hiding had rankled him and he could no longer deal with it. Before the trap had been sprung at the Vault of All Known Knowledge and the Library had come tumbling down around their ears.

Craugh had been with them on that trip as well. There were sketches of Craugh and the Grandmagister around the cook fire out in the wilder-ness of the Forest of Fangs and Shadows. Then again in the tavern of the Blistered Boots when they'd had to set a trap for the thieves who had taken the Tinker's Egg, which could have destroyed the whole town of Hanged Elf's Point if the Grandmagister and Craugh hadn't intercepted it in time.

Later images showed Craugh battling Dread Riders and Blazebulls and Grymmlings. Juhg had wanted to capture the sheer power and bravery of those moments for the book the Grandmagister had entreated him to write about the Library's calamitous fall.

The night gave way to the dawn. Pink clouds filled the eastern sky.

Juhg studied the horizon for a moment, then captured the image on the journal page. The sketch felt right, cool and clean, and went down on the paper with no hesitation. He loved the feel of putting the lines together. It felt . . . right.

He sipped soured pricklepear tea from the galley. Cook had made a lot of it, hoping to keep up the strength of the dwarven pirates. His stomach rumbled, reminding him he hadn't eaten, but he didn't have the interest for a meal.

He flipped through the pages as the fog filled the morning, promising another dreary day. The only good thing was that they wouldn't easily be seen by other ships, which would—doubtlessly—be enemies.

Feeling the chill bite into him more now that he was still, Juhg reached into the storage compartment aboard the longboat and took out a blanket that was mostly dry. There were hardtack biscuits in there as well, but he knew he couldn't stomach them. Those were meant to be softened with water or tea before they were eaten, and even then to be eaten only under the most dire circumstances.

He pulled the blanket over himself and studied the pictures he'd drawn of Craugh. The influence he'd been under during the times those drawings had been made were palpable. No historian he'd ever read, no artist he'd ever studied, had been totally neutral about their subject. They'd either hated them or loved them. Even the ones who hadn't cared about what they were doing had left telltale imprints on their work.

So which is it? Juhg asked himself. *Hero or villain?*

Friend or enemy?

Somewhere in there, with the fog-shrouded sun on his face warming his skin, he fell asleep. And in his sleep, nightmares came for him out of the darkness.

"Apprentice?"

Covered in sweat from his exertions, Juhg looked up from the tangle of rigging and sails to see Craugh standing only a few feet behind him. Sudden fear filled Juhg. He hoped it didn't show.

"Feeling better?" Juhg asked because he didn't know what else to say.

Since coming aboard after the incident inside the monster, Craugh had retired to his cabin and slept almost forty-nine hours. Full night lay upon

One-Eyed Peggie and the darkness had turned the fog a pale gray that bobbed and moved and looked like things were alive out in the distance. Hallekk had posted double guards and the rest of the crew worked on repairing the damage the monster had caused.

"I am," Craugh agreed. He looked a little better, but he still didn't look well enough to be up and around. Evidently all the magic he'd used against the bearded hoar-worm had left him hollow of energy. His shoulders were still stooped from hard use. "You shouldn't be out here working on this mess."

A few of the nearby pirates looked over at Craugh with some irritation.

"Sorting the rigging and the canvas after a disaster like this is hard work." Juhg kept his hands busy. They had most of the yards replaced and the canvas repaired. The rigging came next.

"You already have a task." Craugh shook his head. "I thought that was made plain enough to you."

"The books are nearly done." Juhg shook loose another tangled knot and continued working the line of rigging he was sorting. He felt the resentment toward Craugh banging at his temples. He still didn't know if he wanted to trust the man.

"But your task—"

Juhg hardened his voice, letting the pain of his confusion speak for him. "The work out here is more important now. We're not going anywhere until *Peggie* is seaworthy again. Right now we're just a plump goose sitting in the water." As he knelt there, he felt his heart beating in his chest. He knew he should shut up and not goad the wizard, but he couldn't help himself. Was he helping Craugh, whom the Grandmagister had entrusted his life to, only to be helping the very person who would turn around and betray him?

Craugh put his hands behind his back, holding on to his staff as if he had to restrain himself. He took in a short breath and let it out. "This work is best left to those who are good at it."

"I am good at it."

A dark flush fired under Craugh's pale cheeks. "By the Old Ones, you're pigheaded."

"I prefer to think of it as being practical," Juhg replied. "Valdos always maintained in his book, *The Sharing of Work,* that communities benefited from working together on common goals for the common good.

Right now, stranded out here on the open sea in enemy territory, we are a community."

"I don't need to be schooled, apprentice." Craugh frowned.

"And I don't need to be told how to conduct my work or use my time." Juhg's fingers encountered a knot but simply weren't knowledgeable enough to untie it. Frustration filled him and spilled over. He flung the knot from him and wrapped his arms around his upper body as he continued to sit hunkered down. He didn't know how he was supposed to act or what he was supposed to do under the circumstances.

Silence stretched for a moment as everyone in the immediate vicinity grew quiet. *They're all expecting me to be turned into a great big toad,* Juhg thought.

"You could use a break, apprentice," Craugh said gently. "Walk with me."

"No."

Craugh sighed. "Don't be churlish."

"I'm not."

"Then what name would you give to your behavior?"

Juhg refused to answer.

"Have you eaten tonight?"

After a brief hesitation, Juhg decided he was being too churlish to stand himself. He sighed. "No."

"I am hungry. I smelled chowder from the galley when I went in looking for you. Join me." Craugh turned and walked away.

Out of sheer stubbornness, Juhg held his ground and studied the twisted skeins of the rigging lying before him. It was just like the wizard to walk off imperiously and act like everyone else should fall in line with what he wanted.

"Juhg," Deldar said.

Knowing he couldn't be inhospitable to someone who didn't have it coming—because he was for certain that much better than some wizards he could name—Juhg looked at the dwarven pirate working across from him.

Deldar was one of the older hands aboard *One-Eyed Peggie*. He'd sailed with the Grandmagister on a number of occasions. He was a kind man, with a family back in Greydawn Moors. Thankfully, none of them had been killed, though he had a son who was injured and a brother who had been crippled.

"Ye should go with 'im," Deldar said quietly.

"Why?"

"Because he asked ye."

"He didn't ask. He told me to report to dinner."

"He come as close to askin' as I've ever seen with anyone outside of Wick." Deldar shook his head. "Social amenities, they ain't easy for such a one as Craugh. He's always been apart from most folks." He shrugged. "An' with us chasin' after the Gran'magister an' can't quite catch up to 'im, that's got to be weighin' heavy on his mind. Besides that, he saved all of us three days ago."

Juhg didn't speak. They just didn't know what the wizard was capable of. He still dreamed of Ladamae turning into salt before his very eyes. Sometimes it had been the Grandmagister who had turned to salt in front of Craugh, and the wizard had held *The Book of Time* just out of the Grandmagister's reach and laughed and laughed. Juhg had come up screaming from those dreams and the crew had gentled him, thinking he was only remembering the monster's attacks or that he was worried about the Grandmagister.

"Look," Deldar said, "I've sailed with ye on more'n one occasion. Been through some adventures with the Grandmagister meownself. This here? When all's said an' done, it'll likely be another."

If you live through it, Juhg couldn't help but think. *If Craugh doesn't betray us all.*

The crew had said their good-byes to the members they'd lost days ago in a short service that Hallekk had conducted, then they'd gotten on with the repairs to the ship. The ship's cooper had already seen to squaring off the broken mast, both ends, and was hopeful that most of it could be saved. Getting it repaired and set back into place was going to be a hardship. For the night, they were continuing to pump out the cargo hold. In the morning they'd have to see to replacing the cracked planks that were leaking.

"All I'm sayin'," Deldar said gently, "is that I don't think ye're the onliest one what's scared right now. Craugh, he can't turn to none of us. Can't talk to a one of us about them worries traveling through his head."

Realizing that the pirate was making perfect sense and that to turn Craugh's invitation down would be suspicious not only to the wizard but the crew as well, Juhg nodded. "All right." He didn't want the crew asking him questions about Craugh that he wasn't prepared to answer, and for the moment he wasn't prepared to answer any.

"An' if things go badly," Deldar said, holding up a length of rope, "these knots'll be here a-waitin' on ye." He smiled, but the effort was worn and tired.

"Thank you." Juhg stood.

Deldar nodded. "Weren't nothin'. But ye could do me a favor. If ye still feel beholdin' after ye sup with the wizard, maybe ye could see yer way clear to bringin' me one of them biscuits. Cook outdid hisself tonight, he did."

Juhg trudged toward the galley, not knowing what to expect. For all he knew, Craugh had been surprised he hadn't informed the crew and—wanting to make the most of his good fortune—had decided to shove Juhg over the side of the ship when no one was looking.

73

4

The Wizard's Tale

As it turned out, Craugh didn't want to eat down in the galley. He wanted to eat outside on the ship's deck, saying that two days of sleeping in the small cabin had made him feel too closed up for too long.

That choice made Juhg immediately nervous. In the dark, shoving someone over the side would be even easier. A number of rigging lines fouled the deck, providing a ready-made excuse for an accident. It was also known that Juhg wasn't sleeping well. His stomach puckered into a knot as he told the wizard eating out on the deck would be fine.

Craugh dipped up two heaping bowls of chowder, filled two plates with biscuits, and poured two tall glasses of razalistynberry wine. Craugh had to ask for the wine, and it wasn't a particularly good fit for the meal, but Juhg didn't object.

Cook thought about objecting. Juhg saw it in the man's harsh eyes above the mask he wore to hide his lower face. But Cook hadn't objected. Instead, he'd opened the wine and poured. Without a word of thanks, Craugh took the bottle.

Then the wizard led the way back up onto the main

deck and to the prow. On the way up the ladder, he asked, "What's wrong with Cook's face?"

"Critter bit his nose off," Juhg explained.

"Why?"

"Because he cut off Critter's leg. That's why Critter has a peg for a leg."

"This all has a starting point, I presume. Most things do."

When the pirate crew had told Juhg the story, they'd provided a number of colorful anecdotes. Juhg pared the story down to the bone. He didn't feel like sharing anecdotes with Craugh.

"They were down in the galley, Cook and Critter, playing cards for the last piece of firepear pie. One of them was cheating, though Hallekk tells me it was more than likely that both of them were cheating, and probably not very well. They do cheat. That's why no one else aboardship will play with them."

"They disfigured each other over cheating at cards?"

"No. They got tired of arguing over who was cheating, or who was cheating most, or however that went. So they started drinking." Juhg couldn't believe he was telling the story so nonchalantly when part of him was convinced the wizard was walking him to his doom.

"Drinking?" Craugh asked, as though he were truly interested in the story.

"Yes. After a while, when they were well into their cups, they started bickering over the cheating again. This time it came to violence. Cook cut off one of Critter's legs, and Critter gave Cook a nose he can't show in public."

Craugh snorted. "That's asinine."

"Yes. But now they're the best of friends. When they're in port, they go off drinking together."

"Strange, isn't it? How circumstances make traveling companions of people that shouldn't be together?"

"I've often thought so," Juhg answered. *And certainly never thought that more so than now.*

Two pirates watched over the prow. Craugh waved them away, promising that he and Juhg would keep watch while they ate. The dwarves departed, leaving their lantern at hand.

"Sit," Craugh said, waving to the deck as he bent and sat on the bare wood. Over the years, Juhg had noticed that Craugh was equally at home with the bare necessities as he was with a king's court. The wizard started in on his meal without saying another word. He kept his staff nearby.

Although he was filled to bursting with anger and questions, primarily why Craugh thought they should eat together, Juhg refrained from speaking as well. He'd learned patience and other survival skills while swinging a pickaxe in the goblinkin mines.

He devoted himself to his meal, something that wasn't a surprise since he was a dweller, but his motivation was incredibly different. As a slave, meals hadn't always been on time, or even always there. For years, he'd passed out on a thin blanket on a cavern floor without being fed more times than he'd care to ever remember.

At the moment Craugh wasn't going anywhere. They were stuck in the ocean, far from any goodwill or friends.

The chowder was thick and good. The warmth of it staved off the slight chill that had arrived with the night. The biscuits were light and fluffy. And the razalistynberry wine—

"This wine is Wick's favorite, you know," Craugh said, holding up the glass in his hand. The moonslight, unhampered at the moment by the near perpetual fog, lent a glitter to the dark liquid.

"I know," Juhg said, and he felt the resentment take shape between them again. He had a secret the wizard had never told the Grandmagister, and he was expected not to tell it. In addition to the friction over what should be done with the Library—*what survives of the Library,* Juhg amended—he also had to deal with the wall keeping Craugh's secret would compel.

"Wick is still alive," Craugh said. "I visited with Hallekk before I came to find you. He consulted the monster's eye. Given their course and their present rate of speed, the goblinkin ships will be at Imarish tomorrow."

Juhg hadn't known that for certain, but he believed that Craugh would have told him if the Grandmagister had been killed. The declaration reignited his anger, though, and he lost his appetite.

"You're not eating," Craugh said.

"No."

"Why?"

"I'm not hungry."

"Nonsense. Of course you are. You've been working every waking hour on those books and this ship for days."

"Yes."

"And there have been other . . . distractions."

Learning that someone you thought was your friend could be an enemy is a dis-traction? Juhg sipped his breath. "Yes."

"You know that Wick and I did not foresee this eventuality," Craugh said. "Him getting kidnapped at Greydawn Moors, I mean. We planned on him getting kidnapped, of course. Just not there. That had to happen at some point so we could get the information we needed from Aldhran Khempus. So when Aldhran Khempus showed up with the goblinkin after the trap in the Library was sprung, we took best advantage of it as we could." He paused. "Not that we could have truly forestalled the kidnap-ping. Aldhran Khempus was going to have Wick one way or another."

"You should have told me."

Craugh mopped his bowl with the last biscuit and ate it. "We couldn't tell you what we had planned."

For the first time, Juhg looked fully at Craugh. After the Grandmagis-ter's kidnapping at Greydawn Moors a month ago, Juhg had immediately asked how the Grandmagister had known an attempt would be made to take him. Craugh had brushed away the questions, telling him they needed to concentrate on what needed doing instead of what had already been done.

"Why couldn't you tell me?" Juhg asked.

"You were leaving Greydawn Moors, apprentice. For the second time." Craugh frowned. "Or don't you remember it that way?"

"Of course I remember it that way." Juhg hadn't been able to stay on the island. The Library and the outlying town had grown too small when he'd felt certain the books needed to be released out into the world again, and the Grandmagister would have none of that.

That place had grown even smaller after the Library and most of the books had been destroyed because he had brought the trap there. The guilt had been overwhelming. Even though he knew the Grandmagister was busy with saving what he could of the books, and with all the internal problems of some of the dwellers revolting against responsibility they owed to the Grandmagister, Juhg had still felt that the Grandmagister pointedly stayed away from him. He had been more than ready to leave. In fact, he'd been aboardship when he'd found out about the Grandmagister's Council meeting.

"Good," Craugh said. "At least we won't have that to argue about."

"If I had known the Grandmagister had something like this planned—"

"Would you have stayed?" Craugh looked at Juhg reproachfully. "It seems to me that you were only too happy to leave the island even after the Dread Riders, Blazebulls, and Grymmlings had leveled the library."

"That's not fair."

Craugh studied Juhg. "Would you have let Aldhran Khempus—or anyone like him, for that matter—abscond with Wick?"

"No." *And that's only one of the differences between us, Craugh. I don't trust villains. And I suspect you convinced the Grandmagister to risk his life with your clever words.* Still, Juhg felt a stab of guilt over his belief, though at this juncture it was unavoidable.

"That's exactly my point."

"Why did the Grandmagister have to allow himself to be captured? To suit some purpose of yours?"

"Not mine alone," Craugh said, looking irritated. "It was Wick's idea and I went along with it. So that we could learn what Aldhran and the others know."

Perhaps it was the Grandmagister's idea, Juhg thought sourly. *But I'll believe that when I see cows fly.* "You mean, to find out what they knew about *The Book of Time?*"

"Yes."

"You said, 'Aldhran and others.' What others?"

"We're not sure yet. That was one of the key reasons we concocted this plan. I agreed to the plan—with great reluctance, I might add—because we needed to do something. I had hoped the Grandmagister might come to his senses, or that we might establish another lead as to who our foes were."

Juhg scowled. "Getting the Grandmagister kidnapped isn't much of a plan."

"On the contrary. It was all that we were left with. That's how desperate we had become. Aldhran and his cohorts . . . well, they're very cunning, very dangerous." Craugh set his bowl and plate aside. "And letting Wick get kidnapped wasn't our first plan."

"That makes me so relieved."

"We are far more clever than you think. You forget, we knew we had the eye of the monster aboard *One-Eyed Peggie.* We knew we could use the eye to track Aldhran and his gang of cutthroats."

"You could have used your powers."

Craugh shook his head. "If I'd used my powers, Aldhran would have known. He would have sensed magic like the kind that I use. The monster's mystic powers are more elemental than mine, more a part of the earth, of the air that we breathe. Aldhran has no way of detecting the link the monster's eye has to Wick as a member of this pirate crew."

"Then the fact that the Grandmagister arrives at Imarish tomorrow morning doesn't surprise you? Because you and the Grandmagister planned this?"

Craugh blew out a disgusted breath. "Twaddle."

"Twaddle?" Juhg couldn't believe it. "*Twaddle?* You know that the Grandmagister told me to come to Imarish to pick up the package he left for me. Don't you think there's every possibility that he told Aldhran Khempus as well? Because he was being tortured? I mean, surely with all this planning going on, you and the Grandmagister had to have considered that he would be tortured."

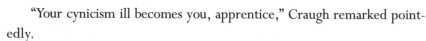

"Your cynicism ill becomes you, apprentice," Craugh remarked pointedly.

Refusing to be dissuaded, Juhg said, "If I had known what was going on, maybe I could have handled things differently."

"What things?" Craugh raised an arched, accusing eyebrow.

Juhg didn't answer.

"Do you really think you handled the matter of your abandonment of the Grandmagister after the Library and so many of the books were destroyed so well?"

Juhg started to get up.

"Oh, do sit down," Craugh said, exasperated. "You tiptoe around everything but what you want to ask. I only brought it up to show you that I do understand."

"I wasn't there when the Grandmagister needed me," Juhg said in a small, quiet voice. He was afraid of the wizard's wrath, but he also wanted some of the blame placed squarely where it belonged. "But I also wasn't the one chasing after *The Book of Time* years ago. I wasn't one of the people responsible for setting *The Book of Time* free in this world."

Craugh sighed. "Ah, I miss the certainty of youth. Truly I do. Those were the times when you could simply look at any question and know that the answer you have for it is the correct one. Never a doubt. Never a fear."

Juhg's anger finally slipped loose its chains. He stared harshly at the wizard. "I don't wish to talk to you."

"Well, you have to," Craugh snapped. "We're in this together, you and I. And the Grandmagister could well die because you and I can't get along at the moment."

"There's a reason for that."

"For Wick to die?" Craugh's voice was harsh.

Taking a deep breath, Juhg shook his head. The possibility banked his anger, though it could not extinguish the righteous heat of conviction. "Not that. Never that."

Craugh took out his pipe and lit it. He puffed for a moment or two. Juhg didn't move because he knew he hadn't been excused. He also hadn't gotten answers to the questions he had.

"We need to find a way to work together," Craugh stated. "What will that take?"

Juhg answered honestly. "I don't know."

"What do you want to ask me?" Craugh asked finally. "Do you want to know *why* I went after *The Book of Time* all those years ago?"

Juhg studied Craugh, striving to see through the wizard's seeming willingness to try to find a common ground. Craugh, even if he hadn't been a wizard, would have been a cunning master of artifice. But because he was a wizard, Craugh had even more reason to develop duplicitous skills.

"To begin with," Juhg said, "yes, I would like to know how you came by *The Book of Time*."

Craugh hesitated, then he turned his green eyes to Juhg. "Let me see your journal." He held out a hand.

Hesitating, Juhg searched the wizard's face. *Does he just want to make sure he gets rid of all the evidence of what I've learned?* He knew that Craugh was aware he wrote in his journal every day, just as the Grandmagister had trained him to do.

"Please," Craugh added. His hand shook a little.

Surprised that there was no surliness and no threats, and also—ultimately—no choice if he wanted cooperation, Juhg reached into his rucksack and took out the handmade book. He hesitated only a little before handing it over.

Flipping through the book almost casually, Craugh found the recent pages Juhg had filled. Mostly there were the images. Juhg hadn't known what to say about the turn of events. He hadn't yet found words to interpret everything he'd seen and felt.

The wizard smoked calmly. "Well, you've definitely stated your case in these. And you've gone on to your own style of drawing. Wick has every right to be as proud of you as he is."

Surprised, Juhg thought he detected a hurt tone in Craugh's voice. Without another comment, the wizard passed the book back, then sat and smoked for a bit.

"Perhaps," Craugh said in a thick voice after a few minutes, "this talk is just going to be a waste of time. I think you're already predisposed in the matter."

Relief flooded through Juhg. Had Craugh just released him? He started to get up and the wizard made no move or suggestion to stop him. Instead, surprisingly, he stopped himself and sat back down.

Craugh's eyebrows lifted in surprise. "Well then."

"Don't get me wrong," Juhg said, "I still don't trust you. I won't lie to you about that, and even if I did lie I think you would know. But I do want to hear your side of things."

"Why?"

Juhg thought for a moment. "To be fair?"

Craugh scowled and pulled irritably at his beard. "You're as bad as Wick. Both of you think the world is a fair place."

"No," Juhg said in a cold voice. "I don't think the world is a fair place. I grew up in a goblinkin gem mine, Craugh. I have learned to think the world will eat you the first day you take your eye off of it."

"Then we share that view."

"But *I* want to be fair," Juhg went on. He held the wizard's gaze with difficulty, feeling fear razor up his spine. Instead of swapping hard looks with Craugh, Juhg wanted to run for his life. "The world may not be a fair place, but I want to be a fair person." His voice caught with the sadness he'd been feeling and he made himself go on. "I've always respected you, Craugh. Maybe I haven't always liked you or liked the things that you did or liked what you said or how you said your piece, but I always respected you."

"Until today?"

Juhg made no answer.

Emotion flickered in the wizard's eyes but he quickly walled it away by staring at his next breath of smoke. He held his silence till it grew uncomfortable for them both.

"I am unwilling to simply throw that respect away," Juhg stated, knowing that the wizard could never bring himself to break the strain between them. "The Grandmagister is the wisest person I know. He believes in you. So, honoring his wisdom, I am forced to believe in you as well."

"Even after the *monster* knew my name and so many secrets came spilling out?"

"And the way that you killed the woman, Ladamae? Yes, even after that."

"She had to be killed. She would never have let you go."

"You freed me."

"She would have taken you again, and then she would have killed you. Or she would have run amuck among the dwarves here on this ship. I couldn't very well have that, now could I?"

"If that was going to be the case, no."

Craugh hitched himself up and resettled. "Despite your . . . honorable intentions, apprentice, once you hear me out you may distrust me even more than you wish to honor your mentor's belief in me."

"I can bear it," Juhg said, "if you can."

"All right then. But I'm going to have to ask you some questions as well."

Juhg waited.

"Do you remember what you told me about the disagreement you never bothered to have with Wick that led you to leave the Vault of All Known Knowledge?"

The memory stung Juhg and made him feel guilty. *Is that the tack the wizard is going to take? That we have both let the Grandmagister down?* He centered himself and denied the guilt. "Yes, of course I do."

"You left, *twice,* and you never once told Wick why."

"It was no use. He would never have understood. I thought the time had come for the books to be handed back into the world. The Library was supposed to keep them until the threat posed by the goblinkin was over. That threat is over. As over as it's going to be until the humans, dwarves, elves—and even dwellers—learn to unite again. And the only way they're going to do that is to communicate again. *Through books*. Crossing the distance involved in a quick fashion and talking face-to-face is out of the question. It's going to take common knowledge and a lot of years. They will all have to see that we have dreams in common. The Grandmagister wouldn't have seen it that way." Juhg had told Craugh that shortly after the Library had been destroyed.

Craugh nodded. "Wick wouldn't have. I told you that you were right about that. He loved the Library too much. He persists in loving the Library despite its destruction. But you still could have told him the truth. He could have known why you were leaving. Again."

"Like you told him the truth about *The Book of Time?*" Juhg asked.

Craugh leaned back against the railing and stared up at the sky. "When I was very young, an impossibly long time ago as I sit here and think of that period now, I wanted power." He stopped and shook his head. "No, that's not right. I *craved* power. I lived for it, and I killed for it." He flicked his green eyes to Juhg for just a moment and gave him a sad smile. "I was not overly concerned about others. Or what their dreams were. If I could scare them or beat them, or, failing either of those, kill them, they didn't matter. I guess you could say I was not a very good person. Perhaps even evil, if you want. But I was young and I was powerful. That is a very heady mix." He tamped his pipe bowl down and his voice softened. "And there was a girl. A very, very beautiful girl."

"Ladamae," Juhg said before he could stop himself. Still, he wanted all the facts and he wanted them right.

"Yes," Craugh agreed. "Ladamae. But she wasn't mine. In those days, she belonged to Methoss. I only wished she were mine." He sucked on the pipe, bringing it back to life. "She and I met by seeking some of the same things, again and again. Till finally we got past the distrust and forged a friendship. Methoss came to be my friend as part of that. Not a very good one, mind you, but a friend all the same. As the very young count their friends. Based on similar interests, ambitions, and strength."

"And two days ago, you killed them both."

"True, but in those days it was a friendship. There were others that we found interests in common with, and eventually there got to be a great lot of us." Craugh shook his head. "I think then we could have been called evil. There were too many of us, you see, to stop. We were too many and we were too powerful."

"All of you were wizards?"

"Not all of us. Most of us, though. Others were shape-changers, were-beings, and mercenaries. We took over empires, scattered troops with our magic, and killed with impunity any who dared stand against us. I was determined to learn all I could of magic. The others, well, most of them only wanted to take over empires, destroy armies, and kill people they decided they didn't like or people who unwisely made known that they didn't care for them." He paused and made a fist, like he was grasping something. Magical sparks flickered between his fingers. "But I wanted the very *heart* of magic."

Listening to the raptness in Craugh's voice, Juhg knew that ambition was not far from the wizard's mind even now. "This was before the Cataclysm."

"This," Craugh whispered, "was before Lord Kharrion. And we'll talk about him and his part in this as we go along. After years of roaming the world together, we found out about *The Book of Time*. You see, we had been gathering magic items the whole time. Some we stole and others we destroyed. But *The Book of Time* was special. Even the name was enough to spark our interest. It sounded like a name that could conjure great magic." He drew on the pipe and released a slow cloud of rolling smoke. "Do you even know what *The Book of Time* can do, apprentice?"

Watching the wizard's face in the shadows, Juhg could see the excitement, and he could hear it in Craugh's voice. Part of the wizard had not come far from those days. Sometimes—in fact, maybe most of the time—when Craugh had accompanied the Grandmagister on his quests for lost books and knowledge, the wizard had his own agenda.

"No," Juhg whispered. "I don't know what it can do."

"Once you gain possession of *The Book of Time* and learn its secrets," Craugh said, "you can alter the very fabric of time. You can go backward and forward in time. You can pick out a moment in time and save or take a life. You can change one incident and affect a future. You could affect a single man, or control the destiny of a nation. The man who controlled *The Book of Time,* why, he'd be the most powerful man in the world." He smiled.

"You wanted to be that man," Juhg said.

The wizard's smile faded. "Yes. More than anything in the world." He held out a bony hand. "Can you imagine what it must be like? To hold so much in the palm of your hand?"

"No. I would never want that kind of responsibility."

"Ah, but you're looking at it wrong, apprentice. I didn't see possession of *The Book of Time* as responsibility. I saw it only as opportunity." Craugh took his pipe from his mouth and aimed the stem at Juhg. "Just as you saw the chance to give back to the masses the books in the Library as opportunity."

"How do you think I meant them to benefit me?" Juhg was incensed.

"Perhaps to assuage your guilt over the fact that you lived through the goblinkin slave mines and your family did not," Craugh suggested.

"You lie!"

"A guess, apprentice, that is all that I offer. And possibly you wanted to be the one to give the books back to the world so that you could be an important person."

"You're wrong."

Craugh nodded. "I know that I am. I know you, apprentice. And I heard your impassioned speech by the ruins of the Vault of All Known Knowledge. You wanted only to free the books once more so that all of the world could benefit from them."

Juhg's cheeks burned. Saying it out loud like that, or maybe it was just because it came from Craugh, made him sound foolish.

"Don't be embarrassed," Craugh said quietly. "That's a noble dream. Wick hasn't yet experienced that one. He's been protecting the books far, far too long. Until the Library was destroyed, he could conceive of the books being in no one else's hands. They were his responsibility."

"They still are." Juhg didn't like the way Craugh's interpretation made it sound like the Grandmagister was no longer going to be able to care for the surviving books.

Waves lapped at the ship sitting idle in the ocean. The wind had changed direction again and the cold spray carried now and again across the ship's bow. The darkness surrounding them made the chill seem colder.

"Where did you learn about *The Book of Time?*" Juhg asked.

"From the Gatekeeper," Craugh said.

87

5

Blood of Bad Blood

he Gatekeeper?" Juhg echoed. "The Gatekeeper of the In-Betweenness? But surely that is a myth."

"After everything you've seen, apprentice, do you yet believe there are myths that don't at least have a root or two in truth?" Craugh shook his head. His gray hair blew. Far off, lightning flared out over the coast hidden by the night and the fog, and the sudden light flickered in his green eyes. "The Gatekeeper is real. To an extent."

"And he truly separates the world of the living from the world of the dead?" Juhg asked.

"Yes. Just as he separates the past from the present, and allows the future to trickle through in small doses rather than a deluge. His power is the only thing that separates *now* and *then*. *The Book of Time* was an aid he built to help him manage those things." Craugh shrugged. "And perhaps the book was a conceit as well."

"A conceit?"

Craugh smiled sadly. "Do you truly think a being as powerful as the Gatekeeper needs a book to help him keep his hand on the tiller?" He shook his head. "No, he only created the book because he wished the possibility to exist that one day someone might read it and know everything he had done. The Gatekeeper is vain."

Juhg thought about that. Many writers of the histories, sciences, and other discussions—including even the romances in Hralbomm's Wing that the Grandmagister had so enjoyed—were propelled by ego rather than a true desire to inform or entertain. The books were indulgences, made by people who created time in their lives to write them. Still, so many great things came out of their efforts.

"Unfortunately, being the Gatekeeper," Craugh went on, "he wrote *The Book of Time* showing the past, the present, and the future. All of them. He lives in a place between life and death, between past and future, and outside of present."

"Even now?"

"Yes. Even now. He tried to stop us from taking the book. We tried to kill him. Neither side was successful." Craugh relit his pipe and smoke plumed above his head. He carefully avoided Juhg's gaze.

Almost unconsciously, Juhg slipped his journal into his lap, took out a fresh charcoal, and began capturing the wizard's image to the page. His hands moved slowly, long strokes that brought the image to life.

"We found the Gatekeeper through careful searching as well as happenstance," Craugh went on. "We'd searched for years. Some of us had died during that time. Some from old age or sickness. Some at the swords of enemies." He paused, lost in memories. "And some of us died at each others' hands. None of us knew true loyalty. Some would say I have never learned it and that is why I am so often found alone."

Remembering how quickly the wizard had dispatched his old "friends," Juhg agreed. "Where was the Gatekeeper?"

"High up in the windswept peaks in the Iron Needles. At least, that was where we found the door that led us to him."

Juhg moved on from Craugh's image and began sketching the Iron Needles, the mountains that crawled up from Bajoram's Pots of Flaming Pain. There were books—*had been books,* Juhg told himself—of explorers who had gone up into the Iron Needles, but not many of them had survived. The air couldn't be breathed and ferocious birds and creatures that hunted each other—when humans, elves, and dwarves weren't handy— lived all over the mountains.

"How did you know he was there?"

"A spell was made that tracked the Gatekeeper. We followed it up the mountain. More than half of us died in the ascent, from the lack of air, from monsters, and from greed that intensified when we thought we were near our goal. Once we encamped on top of the highest peak, it still took more than a year to find a way in to the Gatekeeper. More of us died from the bad air and the creatures that lived among the mountains. We were about to give up when Jazzal found a way into the place between worlds and time."

"Who was Jazzal?"

Craugh's voice thickened and he spoke with effort. "For a while I thought I loved her. But I was mistaken, of course. Or maybe I was only mistaken in thinking she loved me."

Curiosity, stupid and dangerous curiosity, niggled at the corner of Juhg's mind, insisting that he ask questions about the woman who had captured the wizard's heart. Just as he was about to give in to the urge to ask, Craugh continued speaking.

"She was elven. Her hair was unruly and long, pale blue. Her eyes were smoky gray, depthless. She was more sensitive in her magic. It was she who found the crack that led us to the doorway of the Gatekeeper." Craugh shook his head. "I could spend hours telling you of the years we spent in the In-Betweenness that lies between the worlds and time. Suffice to say that we saw things no one has ever seen before or since. We some- times fought and killed things in one instant only to see them born in the next. Some of us were killed in those places, only to finish the journey with us and die once again upon re-entering the world that we had come from. Time had no meaning there. Nor did place. We often went to sleep in one area only to awaken in another. We could not tell how long day or night lasted. We sometimes passed through a year full of season, in any kind of order, between meals. We were often older and younger in the morning than we were when we went to bed."

Juhg sat quietly, awed by the tale. He hadn't studied the legends of the Gatekeeper often, but he knew about some of the details Craugh gave him.

"Time never exactly moved the way it was supposed to for any of us after we got out of the In-Betweenness," Craugh admitted. "At least, not for those of us that made it out or didn't die."

"How did you find out about *The Book of Time*?"

Craugh shook his head. "No one then even knew the book existed. We went there to lay claim to the In-Betweenness. We had reasoned that such a place had to exist, and we wanted only to conquer that region and explore the potential for power there. Then, when we found the Gatekeeper, we found the book."

"What did the Gatekeeper think of you?"

"Oh"—Craugh waved a hand—"he thought we were aberrations, of course. We existed on a level he was totally unaccustomed to. For a long time, he didn't know what to do with us. Ultimately, I think that was the only thing that saved us for however long we were there."

"Why didn't he know what to do with you?"

"Because we were bound by time even though the worlds around us were not. That fact alone caused the Gatekeeper great consternation. He lives for balance, a . . . fairness, if you will. From what I saw, he never takes sides, he never influences. He merely . . . observes."

"And keeps the worlds and time separate."

"Yes."

"What did he look like?"

Craugh shook his head. "Everyone that you ask, apprentice, who lived through that ordeal would have a different answer. To me, he was a strong warrior, a young man in his prime, but who had ageless eyes. To me, he always comported himself with grace and dignity, though Jazzal found him to be feminine and raucous."

"Not even the gender could be agreed upon?" Juhg was surprised. He was also surprised at how much the wizard's tale had pulled him into its thrall. The events were beyond his ken to a degree, but he found images flying from his mind to his fingers, defined by swift strokes of the charcoal across the pages of his journal.

"No."

"How did you find out about *The Book of Time?*"

"I don't know. That remains a mystery, you see."

"I don't understand."

"After we met the Gatekeeper, maybe even before, or maybe by the time we came to recognize *The Book of Time* for what it is, it was as though we'd always known about it. The power, however, was surprising."

"Why would the Gatekeeper put the power to affect all of time and the distance between worlds into a book?"

"I don't believe he meant to. It was just something that happened because of the nature of the book. Sometimes, apprentice, magic enters into an object unintentionally. Places tend to have magic all their own, but objects acquire it through exposure or intent. *The Book of Time* is part of the Gatekeeper. As much as the eye that Hallekk keeps in his captain's quarters is still a part of the monster that took Captain Peggie's leg."

"You and your friends stole *The Book of Time?*"

Craugh nodded toward Juhg's journal. "*Friends* is not a word you should use when you write about this, apprentice. Call them acquaintances. Better yet, call them accomplices, for that was all we truly were for each other in the end." He paused to take a sip of wine. "And yes, we took *The Book of Time.* For all I know, we would have stayed there with the Gatekeeper for all of eternity. Every occasion we talked with him, he showed no sign of noticing that time had passed. I think that we went a little insane then, too."

"Why?"

"We must have. Even though the world around us was mercurial, our minds were not. At times, we could go out into the Gatekeeper's garden and watch flowers blossom. They would open into the sun in a matter of heartbeats, then die and drop off before you could touch one of them. At other times, they blossomed backward, the flowers furling and twisting themselves back into buds. Still others seemed frozen into a single moment, never changing. A year's worth of seasons vanished in the space of a drawn breath. Staying there was out of the question. We were tempting madness. We took the book and ran."

"How did you get the book?"

"We took it from his study."

"While he was away? The Gatekeeper left the book unguarded?"

Leaning back against the ship's railing, Craugh sighed. "There are so many inconsistencies with what you just said, apprentice."

"What inconsistencies?"

"First of all, the Gatekeeper was never away. Yet, at the same time, he was always gone."

"I don't understand." Juhg felt thickheaded and perplexed.

"When time and place don't exist, all things are possible and impossible at once."

"If he was never gone, how did you steal the book?"

"Because he was always gone as well."

Lord of the Libraries

This line of thinking made Juhg's head hurt.

"Think upon this, apprentice. You see the stars in the sky." Craugh pointed upward.

Struggling to understand, Juhg looked up and glimpsed the stars between the masts, sails, and rigging.

"Those stars occupy a place outside this world. But where does that place end? Or does it not end?"

"Tupulok wrote about the vastness of the Starry Expanse in his philosophies, *Away from the Mortal Coils of Flesh, or Unleashing the Power of Thought*. You're familiar with him?"

"Of course. Mathematician, scholar, and king."

"Tupulok believed that the Starry Expanse was somehow twisted, so that it met itself, and so that the inside was the outside and vice versa."

"What do you think?"

"I don't know. I know that if the Starry Expanse ends somewhere, then there must be something that exists outside of it. Then, reaching the end of that, something else must then occupy the space beyond."

"And on and on again."

Juhg blew out a breath. He hated thinking about the Starry Expanse and what it could mean. Too much was uncertain, and the whole existence of the idea of limitless area was almost impossible to think about.

96

"With that before you," Craugh said patiently, "then you can imagine that the Gatekeeper was there and not there at the same time. Just as we escaped and didn't escape all at once. We fled, those of us that could, and we managed to escape back into this world."

"With *The Book of Time*?"

"Yes."

"Did the Gatekeeper come after you?"

"He tried, but in the end he could not."

"Why?"

"Because he can't exist beyond the In-Betweenness. If he left that place, he would die. Or never be born. We were never sure how that worked. He tried to come after us, but he could not span the barrier."

"But you had *The Book of Time*."

"We did. And even though we were near death and madness, or perhaps because of it, we fought. Finally, after days of battle with magic as well as weapons, nine of us stumbled from the Iron Needles." Craugh paused. "One of them was my son."

"Your *son?*"

Craugh's voice tightened. "Born to Jazzal while we were exploring the In-Betweenness."

"How could a baby survive such a thing?"

"He didn't. He walked from the In-Betweenness as we did, and he was a fully grown man when he did it." Craugh looked at Juhg. "Time flowed differently over there, as I have said. He grew up with us, and he grew up without us. To remain alive and sane, he concentrated only on himself, coming to believe that he was the center of all that was." The wizard was silent for a time. "Perhaps he was. None of us had time or wanted to take time to care for a child. Jazzal named him Chrion."

Juhg's mind reeled. One impossibility followed another. "That's a Laurel Tree elven name. It means 'middle child.' "

Craugh nodded. "Usually it is reserved for the middle son in a family. Jazzal thought it was appropriate in Chrion's case, given his birthplace."

Thoughts flew through Juhg's mind. "No one ever mentioned you had a son."

A hint of sadness surfaced in Craugh's green eyes for a moment then faded away, like an ember that had caught a fresh breath of air that caused it to burn itself out. "No one," he stated heavily, "has ever before known. The last two people who knew died two days ago."

"What of Jazzal?"

"Chrion killed her."

Juhg's stomach turned sickeningly. The flat tone with which Craugh delivered the shocking news caught him off guard.

"Why would he kill his mother?" Juhg, who had barely known his own mother, could not believe such a thing could happen outside of the goblinkin.

"Because he was blood of bad blood," Craugh whispered. "It was my son who stole *The Book of Time* from us. Jazzal worked to decipher the book while the rest of us went forth to secure our places among the empires of the mainland. She was the one most gifted with reading the confusing text that changed on every page. We went to trained sages at the time—elven, dwarven, and human—and showed them *The Book of Time*. Some of them killed themselves because they saw their own destinies writ out before them. Some of them went mad because they could not comprehend everything that was written. Others couldn't understand anything that was there."

The mournful cry of a seagull sounded off in the distance. Critter screeched an obscenity at the bird from high up in the rigging.

"What did you do to Chrion?" Juhg asked.

"We went after him, those of us that lived," Craugh said. "If we had caught him, we would have killed him. But he was too clever for us for many years. Eventually, though, we caught up with him. During the battle that raged, his goblinkin forces against the armies of the empires that we all ruled, *The Book of Time* was lost to him. And to us."

"Chrion took up with the goblinkin?"

"Yes. Haven't you ever noticed the goblinkin don't speak of history?"

"They do upon occasion."

"That's because they were changed during the war that purged the books from the mainland. They learned what they fought against, and even though they had no real use for it, they came to learn about history because they questioned the warriors they fought against. Have you ever read much about goblinkin before the Cataclysm?"

"Only a little. They weren't written about much. Mostly the human, elven, and dwarven books only mentioned them as monsters. There was no real description of their culture, only that they were savage and bestial and ate their enemies."

"In the early years, goblinkin had no concept of time. That was why Chrion felt so at home with them. They didn't strive under the weight of the past or look with disfavor toward the burden of the future. They only lived in the now, locked in the events that surrounded them."

"As Chrion had grown up with."

"Yes." Craugh put his pipe away. "We trapped Chrion and decimated his armies. And we earned forever the enmity of the goblinkin."

"But *The Book of Time* was lost."

"Yes. We questioned Chrion for months, employing some of the best torturers we could buy. At the end of that time, he was put to death."

Juhg's breath caught at the back of his throat. "You had your own son executed?"

"There was nothing to be done about it." Craugh looked away. "I know that some think that I am evil, that I am too forceful in my ways."

Juhg silently agreed. He'd been among mainland towns and villages where the wizard was feared, though he did not know why that was so.

"I have earned that reputation over the years, and that is the curse of having a long life." Craugh paused. "Nothing you've ever done—nothing evil—is ever truly forgotten. It lies ever waiting to spring forth and call attention to itself again. Nothing lasts so long as the evil that people do to each other in the name of whatever they choose to make their excuse." He cleared his throat because it had gotten tight. "For every bit of evil that I was, and perhaps still am, Chrion was ever more."

"But you did look for the book?"

"Of course we looked for the book, apprentice. We searched for it for centuries. All to no avail. But the worst was yet to come. Chrion was not dead as we believed."

Juhg scarcely drew a breath. Pieces fell together in his mind. "He rose once more, didn't he? And he again united the goblinkin."

Craugh looked at him and nodded. "So you have figured it out, then."

"Chrion went by another name. Or maybe it was only a name adulterated by the goblinkin tongue." Juhg couldn't believe what he was about to say. "Your son was Lord Kharrion."

"Yes." Craugh's voice was the thinnest whisper.

97

"How did he live?"

"As I told you, after our exposure to the In-Betweenness, none of us lived normal lives. Years no longer seemed to matter. None of us that went to that place and returned ever died of old age. It was as though we were somehow placed outside of time. Only violence or sickness—or suicide as when Capul could no longer take the strain of living on past his loved ones over the centuries—could end our long lives."

"Why did Chrion, Kharrion, seek to destroy the books?"

"Because *The Book of Time* can't be destroyed by fire. Its magical nature prevents that. Perhaps something can destroy it, but we never learned what that might be."

"Kharrion had no clue where the book was?"

"Obviously not. He destroyed nearly every library on the mainland." Craugh looked hesitant. "Though his body rose again centuries later, not all of his mind was there. He'd become a loathsome creature, filled with hate and a desire for vengeance."

"So the goblinkin didn't destroy all those books out of jealousy against the dwarves, elves, and humans."

"Oh, they destroyed them for those reasons, too. But primarily they searched for *The Book of Time*. During the Cataclysm, the Unity armies heard whispers about the 'book that would not burn.' "

"I've never read anything about it."

"We didn't allow that to be written about," Craugh said. "It was dangerous enough that Kharrion knew about *The Book of Time*."

And that you did, Juhg thought, but decided to keep still his tongue.

"We decided that the fewer who knew about *The Book of Time,* the better," Craugh said.

"But the myths persisted."

"Of course. They always do."

"How did the Grandmagister find out *The Book of Time* was real?"

"Because there were others that searched for it," Craugh answered. "He learned of Aldhran Khempus and the others who searched for the book."

"What others?"

Craugh shook his head. "I don't know. Perhaps Wick knows more about them than he has told me."

"He was keeping secrets from you?"

Craugh's green gaze turned misty with sadness. "It appears that he had uncovered enough of my secrets that he chose to play his own game."

Cold understanding dawned inside Juhg. "That was why you shamed me and told me I should stay with him. You thought that whatever burden the Grandmagister carries he might share with me. And that I could be persuaded or bullied into telling you."

"It," Craugh said softly, "was a plan."

"And you admit this to me?"

Craugh stared at him. "Would it help my case if I were to lie?"

"No."

"I could have tried to lie now. I could have tried to persuade you or bully you, but I didn't."

Juhg pushed himself up and started to walk away. His mind was dizzy with suspicious and questions. He wanted to walk away. By the Old Ones, he *should* have walked away.

But he couldn't. In the end, the Grandmagister was in the hands of goblinkin and Aldhran Khempus, and Juhg knew that Craugh's power would probably be needed to set the Grandmagister free.

If he chooses to help anyone other than himself, Juhg warned himself. He turned back to the wizard, trembling and more scared than he could remember being in years. The danger surrounding the Grandmagister seemed to have intensified during the last few hours.

"So you have told me the truth?" Juhg challenged.

"Yes."

"*All* of the truth?"

"I have." Craugh sat quietly, looking defeated, an appearance that Juhg had never before seen on the wizard.

"I can't bear any more lies or half-truths," Juhg said. "Your power can't be discounted in this struggle to free the Grandmagister, Craugh, but I'll not wish to leave myself or anyone else open to the dark side of that power."

"I want to save my friend," Craugh said. "The only true friend I've known in all these years. And I want to set right those things that I did wrong all those years ago."

Juhg paced the deck. *One-Eyed Peggie*'s crew watched the encounter, but none of them could hear from as far away as they were.

"There is something else you must know, apprentice," Craugh said.

Juhg waited, fearing what was going to be said.

"If you are correct and *The Book of Time* lies within Imarish as Wick told you, you must be very wary of it."

"I already am." *And should I get it, that book will never leave my hand and you will never lay eyes on it.*

"If you open that book and so much as peek at one page—" Craugh paused. "You may be lost forever."

A ghostly chill threaded up Juhg's spine.

"When I found out Wick was pursuing *The Book of Time* some years ago—"

"'Some years ago'?" Juhg echoed in disbelief. *Has the Grandmagister truly been searching for* The Book of Time *that long?*

"You didn't know either."

"No. Not until we were on the goblinkin ship together."

"Then Wick hid his secret from both of us."

Juhg shook his head. "No, back in Greydawn Moors you intimated that you knew the enemies that faced the Grandmagister."

"I knew of Aldhran Khempus and a few of the people that followed him. They are united as well."

"United how?"

"They also have a library that survived the Cataclysm."

Juhg's mind reeled. "That can't be."

"But it is, apprentice. Aldhran Khempus is only a vassal for Quhrag."

"Quhrag the Black?" Juhg remembered all the old stories of the wizard. From all accounts, Quhrag was evil beyond comparison. He had served with Lord Kharrion during the Cataclysm.

"Yes."

"I thought he was dead."

"He cheats death," Craugh said. "He lives, but not really. There is only a spark of life within him, but no true flame. He has been hiding for years. Until I saw Aldhran Khempus on Greydawn Moors, I thought Quhrag was dead. There has always been a being that has called himself Aldhran Khempus who has carried Quhrag the Black's mark. I didn't want Wick captured at that point. I tried to prevent it. I couldn't. And Wick would not have let me if I'd been able."

"Quhrag wants *The Book of Time?*"

Craugh nodded. "There can be no other prize that would interest him. Quhrag knows I have lived far past what I should have, and he knows I have been interested in *The Book of Time*. He believes that it has been the source of my long years."

"What about the other library?" Juhg asked. "Where is it? Why didn't anyone know about it?"

"I don't know where it is," Craugh admitted. "I don't know that Wick knows, though—as we have both come to recognize—he has kept his secrets from me."

"Why was a second library built?"

Craugh shook his head. "Evil built the second library. As the Unity armies raced through the town just ahead of the goblinkin hordes, books were found that were filled with evil. We discovered evil men that held them and wanted to pay us to rescue their personal libraries."

"Some of the books in the Vault of All Known Knowledge were filled with despicable and dangerous things. Poisons, torturers' skills, and traps are all there for the reader to discover. I have read several of them. With all the places I have gone with the Grandmagister, I had to know about those things."

"There are things much worse than those. Magic is neutral on its own, but humankind and most of the rest of the world found the power was much easier to manipulate when it was used for darkness. Magic often thrives on pain, whether from the wielder or from those it is used against. Haven't you ever noticed how spells for killing dozens of enemies are so much simpler than healing spells?"

Juhg had noticed, but since magic wasn't his purview, he'd had no real experience in those matters.

"The other library," Craugh said, "preserved the worst of the lot that the Unity forces chose to discard."

"But that was stupid," Juhg said. "As Dhon Korli Ohn says in his treatise *The Art of the Offer Others Cannot Refuse,* you have to understand everything you can about who or what you are dealing with. By discarding those books, the Librarians have been seriously disadvantaged in learning how to deal with whatever evil they contained."

"We could not save all the books," Craugh said. "We failed to save a great many of them. But we hoped to save what was the best, the books that would promise a better future for those that survived the Cataclysm."

Struggling to deal with all that he had learned—that it was Craugh's son who had become Lord Kharrion, that the Grandmagister had not fully trusted the wizard, that *The Book of Time* truly existed, and that another library existed somewhere out there filled only with evil things—Juhg walked to the railing and peered through the misty fog that surrounded *One-Eyed Peggie.* Somewhere out there lay the mainland and all the dangers it held.

"There is a further problem, apprentice."

Juhg shook his head. "Only one? With the list you've given me, I can't believe there would be only one."

"I didn't know Wick knew *The Book of Time* existed years ago," Craugh went on. "Now that he does, I worry about the consequences of that knowledge. You know how curious he is. I fear that if he were left to his own devices with the book, he would peer into it."

Dread filled Juhg because he knew Craugh spoke the truth. There had never been a book that the Grandmagister could pass up. Even if he never read the book, he always took time to get the feel of it. The mystic tome the Grandmagister sought could only offer mesmerizing passages.

"We have to get to *The Book of Time* before Wick gets it," Craugh said. "I fear what he might unleash if left to his own devices and not knowing the true history of the book."

" 'We'?" Juhg turned around to face the wizard.

Slowly, Craugh hauled himself to his feet. He brought his staff up with him. Green embers flared from the end of the staff. "Would you want to face the unpredictable nature of *The Book of Time* on your own?"

Juhg thought about that long and hard. The wind shot across *One-Eyed Peggie*'s deck and rattled the loose rigging.

"Those are the stakes, apprentice," Craugh said softly. "We have to save Wick, and we must save what's left of this world."

"The goblinkin ship is rendezvousing at Imarish tomorrow morning," Juhg said. "For all that you know the Grandmagister has told Aldhran Khempus where to find the prize they seek."

"No. Not even on pain of death," Craugh said. "Wick has the ability to hold his secrets, apprentice." He paused. "Or don't you think that keeping silent to us about what he knew and what he suspected wasn't painful to him?"

The knowledge settled heavily onto Juhg. *How did the Grandmagister hold up under all those secrets?* He looked at the wizard, loathing trusting Craugh and feeling shamed about that reaction at the same time.

"Well, apprentice?" Craugh asked.

"You want to come with me to Imarish?"

"Yes." Craugh waited. The slow wind pulled at his robe, sweeping the frayed hem across the scarred deck.

"Do we attempt to take the Grandmagister from the goblinkin?"

"Not before we secure *The Book of Time*."

Juhg started to argue.

"Think, apprentice," the wizard challenged. "Wick told you the book was there. He intended for you to safeguard it. He also intended that he not come into contact with the book."

"I don't want the Grandmagister to remain in goblinkin hands."

"Nor do I."

"Then we should trust that *The Book of Time* will remain hidden till after we free the Grandmagister."

"And if you are killed or captured, apprentice? What then?"

Juhg had no ready answer. "I can only hope that does not happen."

"That's a fool's hope and you know it," Craugh snapped. "Wick tasked you a mission. If you would honor him, then you will tend to that first."

Juhg barely held back a hot-tempered response. He took a deep breath and let it out. "And if I choose to see to the Grandmagister's rescue first?"

"Then the Old Ones protect you," Craugh replied, "for your mule-headedness may well have doomed the world." Without another word, the wizard turned and left.

Torchlight shone against the dark water surrounding the pirate ship, reminding Juhg how far he was from any place that might be called safe. *My mule-headedness may doom the world now, Craugh, but your greed and desire for power brought the means of that doom into this world.*

Reluctantly, he turned away from the wizard's departing back and stared out to sea.

6

A Hard Decision

uhg."

Lying abed in a gently swinging hammock, Juhg felt rough hands upon him. He woke from a fever-hot dream that was filled with nightmare images and screams of the dead and dying. He didn't know if the sights and sounds came from the night the Vault of All Known Knowledge had fallen or if they were from what he feared might lie in the future.

"Juhg, c'mon now. Get a move on. Cap'n Hallekk, he wants to see ye, he does. It's about Wick."

Hearing that, Juhg forced himself up, expertly grabbing the hammock's edge and flipping himself over. He kept his fingers knotted in the edge for a moment until his brain stopped spinning. He was tired from days of hard work and doubt and worry.

Deldar stood before him with a nervous look.

"Has something happened to the Grandmagister?" Juhg asked.

"He's alive, he is. But it seems as though Aldhran Khempus ain't stoppin' in Imarish after all. Cap'n Hallekk, he wants to see ye right away."

"Where's Craugh?" Juhg adjusted his clothing on the

run. Habits from the Vault of All Known Knowledge died hard. The Grandmagister had never put up with slovenly appearances from his Librarians and Novices.

"With the cap'n."

Juhg ran through the waist and climbed the stairs leading to the deck, then raced to the captain's quarters under the stern castle. He knocked on the door.

"Come in," Hallekk boomed in his big voice.

Juhg tried the door and found it unlocked. Entering the room, he saw Craugh and Captain Hallekk peering into the glass gallon bottle that held the monster's eyeball.

The eyeball was a tight fit inside the bottle. Red and purple veined, the dark olive eye watched intently as Juhg came closer. It was half the size of a human's head and always carried malignant intent. Due to its magical nature, the eyeball was capable of independent movement. The large cork that had been pounded into the bottle was covered with thick, melted yellow wax to make an airtight seal.

Though he had seen the eyeball before, Juhg never failed to gaze on it in wonderment. What manner of beast had the eyeball's owner been? None of the pirate crew who had been with Peggie, the ship's builder and first master, still lived. Old Captain Farok had been the last of those. With his passing, a bit of *One-Eyed Peggie*'s history had slipped away as well. Thankfully, the Grandmagister had traveled with the old captain one summer during a particularly nasty season of pirates and gotten all of Farok's story down. Juhg just didn't know if the book had survived the destruction that had swept over the Vault of All Known Knowledge.

Even though all of the original crew was dead and gone, the savage beast whose eye Peggie had plucked remained awaiting vengeance.

"Has something happened to the Grandmagister?" Juhg asked.

Hallekk shook his big head and looked unhappy. "No, but things has taken an interestin' turn, they has."

"We have a decision to make, apprentice," Craugh said. This morning he was once more cold and aloof, wrapped in a fresh, clean robe and looking clear-eyed and determined.

Do you regret telling me everything you did? Juhg wondered. *Or are you walling yourself off from your own fears about my reaction and the Grandmagister's?*

"What decision?" Juhg was instantly suspicious.

"Which course to foller," Hallekk growled. He looked at the wizard and at Craugh. "Heard tell the two of ye stayed up half the night a-talkin' amongst yerselves. Now ain't neither of ye worth a-talkin' to this mornin', ye ain't. Craugh seems to have the same hearin' problems as ye."

Craugh folded his arms over his chest and said nothing.

Feeling the weight of Hallekk's bold gaze, Juhg said, "I just woke up."

"Ain't no excuse. Ye both neither had no business a-stayin' up the way ye did so that neither of ye is worth the havin'. I ain't gonna ask ye what ye was a-talkin' about, unless it comes to makin' some kind of decision of me own about what to do." Hallekk slammed a big fist onto the table. The jar containing the monster's eyeball jumped and the huge orb inside swirled, flipping end over end for a moment. "But I'll not be takin' chances with Wick's life. He's stood by me through thick an' thin, he has, an' by the Old Ones I'll not be careless with his life."

"What decision?" Juhg asked.

"Gimme yer hand," Hallekk ordered.

Reluctantly, Juhg offered his hand. He knew what was coming, had been subjected to the process before, and he didn't like it.

Hallekk took Juhg's hand and held it to the bottle. Immediately, a thick miasma swarmed over Juhg and glued his palm to the glass.

Know, O beastie what breathes the deep water,
the unfound water,

Hallekk intoned in the old litany that Captain Peggie had bequeathed to Captain Farok and him to Hallekk when he took up the captain's post aboard the pirate ship. Juhg still didn't know if there was magic in the words or if they only served to irritate the monster's eye.

That yer vengeance ain't gonna be complete,
Never complete,
'Lessen ye have us all
At yer black mercy.
So then show me where me mates be.
Show me that ye can't lose 'em

Lord of the Libraries

'Cross the briny sea.
Use yer powers to strike fear
Into the heart o' me.

Hallekk took in a deep breath and let it out, concentrating on the bottle containing the eye.

No one understood the magic that bound the ship's captain to the eye and then to the creature. And no one knew how the creature could know the whereabouts of every pirate that had been sworn into service aboard *One-Eyed Peggie*. It was magic, just as Craugh had claimed. An older and more primitive magic.

A purple nimbus flared to life inside the bottle, then spread outward.

For a time, Juhg saw only the monster's eye floating in the colorless liquid inside the bottle. Then it disappeared, lost in the purple nimbus. When Juhg next blinked, he peered into the world in another place.

The panorama of the view was outstanding. To the left—*to the east,* Juhg reminded himself, knowing that the mainland was east of their position a good half day's sailing—the canal city of Imarish lay spread across the coastline. The gray-green waters of the Ravening Sea (called so even though it was connected to the Blood-Soaked Sea—though not burgundy colored as the waters were around Greydawn Moors—because it insisted on drinking down one of the tiny islands that made up Imarish every so often) leaked curved claws between the dozens of islands.

Several of the larger islands had ports that opened to the Ravening Sea, but most of the travel between the islands of the interior of the mass was by canal boats. All of the islands bore tall stone columns that plunged into the water at the dockyards or the small boat landings that held sculpted sea creatures. The sea creatures announced the political affiliation among the merchant classes that ruled the islands.

Some of the islands, usually the larger ones with a number of buildings but some of them were tiny islands with only two or three houses, had tall buildings made from the stone and shells taken from the sea. Some of the rock had been transported from the mainland, from quarries cut deep into the Shattered Coast by dwarven clans.

Most of the populace of Imarish were humans, though elves and dwarves could often be found there plying their trades or merely passing through while speculating on trade goods. A number of the islands were dedicated to one trade or another, ranging from houses that made tea, spun silk, and made candles to dwarven smithies that hammered weapons as well as farm tools, to mercenaries that trained on islands that were no more than barren outcroppings of rock where houses might be built, and some were outposts of elven bands dedicated to a deeper understanding of the sea and the creatures that lived within deep bodies of water.

Magic was stronger and more uncertain on the islands as well. Few wizards ever lived in the islands, and none of those had ever stayed unless they were unfortunate enough to be killed before they could leave.

Lord Kharrion had unleashed a spell that had destroyed the mainland here after the Unity armies had holed up and tried to last through the winter. Horrible forces had riven the land, breaking it and creating upheavals that had even freed the ocean floor to rise to the surface in places. Imarish was located at the northernmost point of the Shattered Coast, as Teldane's Bounty had come to be called over the years.

"Closer, O beastie," Hallekk murmured in a taunting lilt. "I ain't seen nothin' yet to be a-feared of."

The view changed, gliding in toward the cluster of islands as if on the wings of a seahawk. In the space of a drawn breath, the viewpoint hung over the coastline, showing the stone buildings and tall towers that had been constructed there over the years. Nausea rippled through Juhg's stomach as the view lurched to one side. Then it focused on one particular ship and closed in again.

Edgewick Lamplighter, Grandmagister of the Vault of All Known Knowledge—at least, Grandmagister of all that remained of the Library—stood in chains in the ship's stern. He was dirty and unkempt, standing in the same clothes he'd had on when Greydawn Moors had been attacked. Bruises darkened his face.

"No," Juhg whispered before he knew he was even speaking.

Slowly, the great sails that propelled the goblinkin ship filled as the goblinkin sailors turned them to the wind. The ship came about and sailed once more to the south, heading for the open sea away from the islands. Two other ships flanked the first, all of them filled with goblinkin warriors.

Aldhran Khempus came up from amidship to stand at the Grandmagister's side. The human spoke with the Grandmagister, but the Grandmagister said nothing. Without warning, Aldhran struck the Grandmagister with the back of his hand. Trapped by the chains that bound him hand and foot, the Grandmagister sprawled onto the deck, then raised his arms over his head as best as he could to protect himself.

The human gestured toward the fallen dweller. Four of the goblinkin came forward and picked the Grandmagister up. For a moment, Juhg was afraid that they were going to toss their prisoner over the ship's side and let him drown. Instead, they marched back to the hold and dropped the Grandmagister down.

"Enough," Hallekk whispered hoarsely.

The scene vanished. In the large glass bottle, the eyeball blinked and looked royally perturbed.

Juhg's own eyes burned from the strain of the ensorcelment that bound the monster's eye to the crew of the pirate ship.

"Wick didn't stay at Imarish," Hallekk said. "Means we're gonna have to make a decision." He grabbed the bottle containing the monster's eye and slid it under the bed built into one side of the room.

The captain's quarters had remained as meager as Captain Farok had ever kept them. There was scarcely room to turn around and personal belongings were kept to a minimum. Most of them were things that Farok himself had kept over the years. Hallekk wasn't one for sentiment when it came to things instead of people.

Hallekk used his foot to push the bottle farther under the bed. Then he dropped the bedding low so it hung to the wooden floor. No one liked talking in front of the eyeball.

"We have to go after the Grandmagister," Juhg said. *And what of* The Book of Time? He knew that question was going to come up from the look on Craugh's face.

Craugh said nothing.

Hallekk pulled at his beard and looked uncomfortable. "We *will* go after Wick," he said. "But that isn't your place, Juhg."

Angry immediately, Juhg glared at the wizard. "He put you up to this."

"No," Hallekk said in a clear voice that brooked no argument. "I'm captain of this here ship, an' no one tells me what to think or do. Been thinkin' for meownself an' fer the crew since Cap'n Farok passed on." He paused. "Yer place is here, Juhg, a-doin' what Wick bade ye to do. What I needs to know—"

"We don't even know if what we seek is here," Juhg argued.

"Wick," Hallekk stated slowly, "he told ye that it were here. He wouldn't a-told ye that if'n it weren't here. This thing, this *Book o' Time Craugh* mentioned, why I hear tell it's a powerful piece o' magic. Can wreck the world if'n it's in the wrong hands. That's why Wick trusted this job to ye."

"You can send other crew to look for the book," Juhg protested.

Hallekk shook his head. "Most of 'em, why they wouldn't know all forms a book takes the way ye can, Juhg. Wick knew that. That's why he up an' set ye free from them goblinkin what had ye. He counted on ye a-finishin' what he'd started."

Juhg opened his mouth to argue but couldn't find the words to get it done. His shoulders slumped.

"Ye ain't no warrior neither," Hallekk said. "Ye can't stand up in no fight."

"I have fought," Juhg said in a voice that carried more pleading than conviction.

"I knowed that ye has," Hallekk said. "I seen ye with me own eyes. But that ain't yer callin'." He paused. "I think we both knows that."

Juhg wanted to argue more, but he couldn't. Not without calling Hallekk a liar, and that would have been a lie itself.

"What I needs to know, as I were about to ask ye, is if ye needs *One-Eyed Peggie* to stay here with ye," Hallekk said.

Suddenly, Juhg understood. "You would stay here? And let the Grandmagister be taken away by Aldhran Khempus and his goblinkin ships?"

"If'n it meant keepin' ye safe," Hallekk returned, "aye. Wick, why he'd chew me ears off was I to leave ye here not a-knowin' if ye'd be all right."

Thinking quickly, realizing that he was fearful of leaving the Grandmagister stranded among enemies without help, Juhg said, "We need to go after the Grandmagister."

Hallekk shook his head. "We needs to finish Wick's mission. That's what he'd want us to do. Me, I been with him through good times an' bad times enough that I know what he'd want us to tend to. If'n that book is as dangerous as everybody's a-puttin' on, why I'd be foolish to go a-harin' off after Wick when they's more important business here to take care of."

"So if I choose to go after the Grandmagister—"

"We'll stay here an' tend to what you should be a-doin'," Hallekk said. "An' probably not with very much success."

"I need a ship to go after the Grandmagister."

"Aye," the big dwarf agreed. "That ye do. But I don't have an extry one in me pocket what I can give to ye. If'n we stay here, we gots to have a means o' escapin'."

"But if I choose to stay, and I tell you that you can go on——"

Hallekk smiled. "Why, we'll have no choice but to put to sail as soon as we can to go after Wick. We can find him right away with the monster's eye, but I prefers to stay close to him."

Exhaling loudly, irritated beyond belief, Juhg said, "That's blackmail."

Thinking for a moment, Hallekk grimly nodded. "Aye. I suppose ye might reckon that it is. But that's the wind that's a-blowin', an' ye can go with her or agin her. Ye set yer own tiller in the matter."

Finally, Craugh put in, "We all have our responsibilities, apprentice. You appear to be the one with all the control."

Angrily, Juhg tried to express how he truly felt about the situation. His hands clawed the air before him, but his voice was strangled. At length, shaking, he asked, "How soon before we sail?"

As he'd approached the captain's quarters he'd noticed that most of the rigging was back in place. The mainmast had been reset, bridged mightily with new timbers.

"Before midday," Hallekk said. "I'll give ye me word on that."

"Then put me ashore in Imarish," Juhg said shortly. "And you will go after the Grandmagister."

Grinning broadly, Hallekk reached out and clapped Juhg on the shoulder. "Fairly called, Juhg. Break your fast an' make ready. Won't be long now."

Juhg turned and trudged from the room.

Hours later, Juhg stood at the starboard railing as *One-Eyed Peggie* came sharply about in Imarish's Garment District docks. Canvas cracked overhead and the repaired rigging held up to the strain. As always, he enjoyed watching the rapid movement of the dwarven pirates as Critter set them about their paces. The pirate ship was a sharp vessel.

The stench of lye and ash and dye pots tickled Juhg's nose. Several buildings spewed noxious black and colored smoke streamers into the clear blue sky. Lines filled with brightly dyed cloth swelled and fell in the gentle breezeways between buildings as they dried.

Other ships lined the large docks. Cargo handlers ferried raw goods from some vessels to warehouses and transported finished goods from warehouses, sometimes to the same vessels. The workers sang as they labored, all of them passing the time they spent in physical drudge.

Children ran through the cobbled streets pestering sailors and merchants, begging for small coins. Here and there, a few horses waited at hitching posts or pulled small wagons. Hawkers stood in front of small pushcarts calling out their goods, or in front of inns and taverns bawling out the bills of fare and what there was to drink.

"Ye been here afore?"

The dwarven pirate captain's voice rumbling near his ear scared Juhg. His hand almost darted down to the small knife at his waist. Glancing over his shoulder, he looked at Hallekk. Juhg still hadn't decided whether to be mad at the ship's captain or not. Hallekk had made a good case, but Juhg didn't care for the way he'd been made responsible for all the decisions no matter what he decided.

"I've been here twice before. With the Grandmagister," Juhg replied.

Hallekk shaded his eyes with a hand. "They's got free halfers here. Ye shouldn't be bothered overmuch with folks wantin' to tell ye what to do. An' slavers fight clear of this place for the most part."

"I know." Irritation grew inside Juhg. *Don't sound like you're worried about me when it was your idea that I abandon the chase for the Grandmagister.*

113

"We'll work our cover here for a few hours," Hallekk said. "We've got gold enough to make some wise purchases that we can sell farther down the mainland."

The statement made Juhg remember the last voyage aboard *Windchaser* when he and Raisho had left Greydawn Moors together. He'd copied information he'd written about during earlier travels from Greydawn Moors and built a list of potential investments for them to pursue. Until they'd discovered the book in goblinkin hands in Kelloch's Harbor, they'd done quite well for themselves.

Posing as a merchant ship was *One-Eyed Peggie*'s first line of defense.

"We'll be in port for a few hours at most," Hallekk said. "Staying any longer is problematic. We're not from around here. An' we don't wanna give Aldhran Khempus too big of a lead."

Juhg leaned down and picked up his bedroll. He had a change of clothes, his writing utensils, the latest journal he was working on and a blank one, a compass, and a few journeycakes. He carried coins and a few small gems in a pouch around his neck to pay his way.

Turning, he extended his hand to Hallekk. "May the winds treat you fairly, captain."

Hallekk's hand swallowed Juhg's. "An' ye, me friend. Do yer mentor proud, an' us of ol' *Peggie* as well. We brung ye this far. See that we made good use of our time."

"Take care of the Grandmagister when you find him."

"I will. An' soon's we can, we'll come for ye." Hallekk winked. "Remember, we got our eye on ye now."

Only that morning, Hallekk had sworn Juhg in as a pirate. Now the same curse that linked the eye to the crew watched over him as well.

Juhg said his good-byes to the crew. Critter even flew down to rest on his shoulder for a moment, then tossed off a few choice insults about dwellers in general and Juhg in particular, and flew away to remonstrate the crew.

As Juhg marched down the gangplank the crew had run out to the docks, studying the unfamiliar faces before him, he felt a new and awkward vibration settle into the thick boards beneath his feet. He stopped and turned around, seeing Craugh walking after him.

Suddenly seething and scared at the same time, Juhg walked back to the wizard. "What do you think you're doing?"

Craugh crossed his arms over his bony chest. He wore a bedroll over his shoulders as well. His staff was in his right hand. "What does it look like I'm doing, apprentice?"

"No," Juhg said. "You're not coming with me."

"And why not?"

Juhg was grimly aware that his confrontation with the wizard was bringing on a few interested stares. "You need to stay with the ship."

"Whatever for?"

"So you can help save the Grandmagister."

Craugh frowned. "And who will save you?"

"I'll save myself."

Craugh shook his head. "I'm going with you, apprentice. Wick is safe enough for the time. Aldhran Khempus won't dare do anything to threaten Wick's life until he has *The Book of Time* in his hands. You and I both know that ship is headed away from here and away from the book." He paused. "You can trust me to—"

"No," Juhg snapped. "I can't. For all I know, you're still wanting power just as much as you did all those years ago. *The Book of Time* is much too tempting."

Slowly, Craugh leaned down. He was close enough that his large brimmed hat shadowed Juhg's upturned face as well as his own. "Apprentice," the wizard said in a low, cold voice.

Juhg stood his ground but his knees felt weak.

"Would you rather trust me as a dweller," Craugh asked, "or as a toad?"

Juhg swallowed hard. "If I am a toad—"

"I'll make sure you retain your wits," Craugh promised. "I can do that, you know."

Actually, Juhg didn't know that for sure. He'd never met any of the people Craugh had turned into toads over the years. For all he knew, they could talk and hawk an alesman's goods in three-part harmony.

"So," Craugh said, straightening the line of Juhg's jacket the way he might that of a child, "your choice is in whether you dine on real food or flies as we travel."

"I don't trust you," Juhg announced in a hoarse whisper, "and I don't like you very much either."

Craugh's left eye twitched. Juhg fully expected to plop to the gangplank on a brand-new, warty behind.

"Well," Craugh said, straightening, "we don't have to like each other if we're going to save the world." He adjusted his hat and stamped his staff on the gangplank. "Lead on, apprentice."

Grumbling to himself, Juhg resettled his bedroll and continued down the gangplank. He was grateful that he could walk instead of hop. In Hralbomm's Wing while perusing some of the romances the Grandmagister had put on his required reading list, Juhg had read tales of heroes who had been turned into snakes and fish and birds who had still managed to rescue those they had been sent after or had retrieved magical objects they were supposed to get. Those tales had suggested such an endeavor was possible, but he didn't want a book written about his part of the adventure—if it even turned out to be significant—to be of him hopping along like a toad.

Besides that, toads didn't seem to fare well when confronted by cats or dogs, let alone goblinkin.

7

Imarish

he Garment District island was a large, rambling affair, a maze of warehouses and textile mills. Cotton came in from the agriculture islands by ship and by boat, then was processed by huge looms powered by waterwheels turned by the incoming and outgoing tides. All of the mills possessed two waterwheels, one set on either side of the building, and the drive axle was shifted between the two as the tide changed from incoming to outgoing. That way crews could work all day and all night if necessary to meet demand. As a result, the Garment District creaked night and day.

"I don't know how anyone could put up with such racket," Craugh griped. "It's enough to make your ears burst."

Juhg had to walk fiercely to keep slightly ahead of the wizard. Craugh didn't know where they were going, but it didn't stop him from trying to lead all the same. Several times, the wizard had gone on ahead in the wrong direction in the twisting maze of streets that bore no name. When he'd found he was going in the wrong direction, after Juhg had had to call him back, Craugh's mood had darkened. Juhg had felt compelled to remind the wizard that a toad would be even slower, and that even if he could talk as a toad, a talking toad would surely call attention from everyone that passed by.

As if we don't call attention to ourselves enough already, Juhg reminded himself grimly. There were few dwellers on the island and very few humans as old or as shabby in appearance as Craugh. And none of them were in the company of each another.

"Are we almost there yet?" Craugh groused.

"Almost." Juhg sighed.

"As far as we've come, we might as well have rented one of the canal boats."

"I'm not sure I would have found the way. The Grandmagister and I seldom used the boats to get around here."

"Wick never mentioned coming to this place."

"Maybe he had a reason."

"Hrrummph."

Glancing over his shoulder, Juhg studied the wizard's reflection in the plate-glass window of the seamstress's shop they were passing. Seamstresses weren't needed by anyone who lived on the island because everyone there sewed or knew someone who did. But the sailors who put into port did hire their services, and merchants who wanted their personal finery handmade came into the shops.

Craugh's head turned constantly, surveying the sprawling town around him. Stone buildings rose three and four stories tall on either side of them, festooned with clothing because even the mill workers and loom handlers often created clothes and bedding and curtains they hoped to sell as unique items. The wizard wasn't as at ease as he tried to project.

The *cloppity-clop-clop* of even a dray mare drawing a wagon always caught the wizard's ear and gave him pause. Screams from children dashing through the neighborhood ululated between the confines of the narrow, twisting alleys, often sparking more such screaming as if the sounds fed off each other. They dashed and ran like dervishes, most of them human, but there were a few dwarves and elves among them. A group of them played tag, one of them using the wizard as a means of defense for a moment by circling Craugh's legs. Then, with a shrill yell of triumph, he was off again, leading the pack of screaming opponents.

"And there should be a place for all of these idle children to go,"

Craugh growled as he brushed at his robe to straighten the folds out. "That way they wouldn't be underfoot so."

Personally, Juhg enjoyed watching the children at play. Human children were especially inventive, never at rest, never satisfied. And they could make games of the simplest things. The Grandmagister had often said if a group of human children were given a stick or a crate, their imaginations would allow them to think of the sticks as magic wands or swords, to believe—at least for a while—that the crate was a boat or a cave.

Elven children weren't so free with their ways because they were tied into nature, constantly distracted by scents and animal trails, even in cities. An elven child paid attention to the wild things that inhabited forests or plains or deserts, and the meeker subset that dwelled in urban areas. Given time and attention, an elven child could mimic and understand the creatures found there.

Dwarven children, on the other hand, tended to be taught the craft of smithing or gem hunting from the time they could walk and lift the full weight of a hammer or a pick. They were slow to play, preferring to learn the warrior's skills at axes and anvils as soon as they could.

"I suppose they could get work at the mills or the looms," Juhg said with thinly veiled sarcasm. "Of course, children seem to bear the brunt of accidents in industry when they start so young."

Craugh scowled. "That's not what I meant."

"Or perhaps they could be sent out on ships and travel to dangerous places where goblinkin could conceivably capture them and sell them in awful places like Hanged Elf's Point."

"You annoy me, apprentice."

They traveled in silence for a while, steadily climbing the cobblestone road that led up to the hill near the center of the island. A dray pulling a milk wagon with the latest shipment of milk from one of the other islands rolled past them on ironbound wheels.

"I have never seen so many children in one place," Craugh commented.

"Nor have I," Juhg said. "The people here are blessed, truly. They are unafraid to have children, and they seldom lose them to disease or violence. Here they are loved and given freedom, then trained in the ways of their parents."

"I've never been here," Craugh said. "I'd always heard it was crowded. It is."

Unable to stop his thought, Juhg said, "Do you know what these islands need?"

"Need?" Craugh shook his head. "They don't *need* anything, apprentice. I've never seen a more successful place. Not everyone appears to have wealth and privilege, but they are well-to-do."

Taking a quick step, Juhg stepped in front of Craugh, bringing the wizard to a stop. "What they need," Juhg said in a low voice, "is a library and a school to teach the young. And the old that are willing."

Craugh looked at him.

Juhg hurried on before the wizard cut him off or complained. "As I thought about how best to start releasing the books from the Vault of All Known Knowledge back into the world, I realized that Imarish would be one of the best places to begin."

"We're wasting time here."

"No," Juhg said firmly, "we're not. You're here now, Craugh. You bullied your way into being with me, so while you are here at my sufferance, I'll share my secret with you."

"You're exhausting my patience, apprentice," Craugh warned.

"I don't care," Juhg declared, and felt a twinge of fear. "Don't you see what Imarish offers?"

"What?" Craugh snapped.

"Safety and room and wealth."

"And none of those things they would be willing to share."

"That's the environment it takes to educate a population," Juhg said. "Take children and give them those three things, and you can show them the world. But it is hard to enjoin a child to be grateful about receiving an education when he's threatened or has no room to be himself or lacks enough to make himself comfortable with himself and his friends. You could not teach children in slave camps. Their minds would be locked in on merely surviving the day. Nor could you teach the children of a starving people. Even if they could shut out the rumblings of their empty bellies, they would still be haunted by the arguments of their scared and frustrated parents."

Craugh only listened.

"You knew that," Juhg said. "When you and the other Builders raised the ocean floor from the bottom of the Blood-Soaked Sea to become

Greydawn Moors, you designed the island so it held game and fruits and could grow grains and vegetables. Monsters were set free in the Blood-Soaked Sea to patrol the waters and keep our coasts clear. There are no creature enemies on the island that the elven warders can't tame or eliminate, and we have a dwarven army standing guard there. The humans keep the trade flowing by crewing ships and protecting the waters against any who might be curious or foolhardy enough to brave the monsters."

Craugh shook his head. "We need to be moving."

"We will." Juhg waved to the Garment District. "Don't you see that the same things are offered here? Peace and prosperity. All that is missing is a school or a Library to provide education. Can you imagine what these people, and people like them, would do with an education?"

"No, I can't." But Craugh was peering around that the Garment District with a little more interest.

"Imagine it, Craugh. A Library. Schools. Here." Juhg gestured with his hand. "This place entertains a huge amount of trade. People would come and go. Once teachers were trained, they could accompany ships, educate the crew to read. Some of them would go other places and teach still others. Once a proper Library is set up here, it won't be long before a new industry could be established among these islands as well. Books could be copied and made according to a buyer's wishes."

"By Librarians?"

"At first. Then by others skilled solely in copying books. They used to do that, you know, before the Cataclysm. I've read about those times."

Craugh closed his eyes. "I remember."

"It could happen again," Juhg said, feeling the old excitement as he gave in to his vision. "It could happen here."

"Perhaps."

"Why did you and the Builders elect to populate Greydawn Moors with dwellers and make them the custodians of the Vault of All Known Knowledge?" Juhg watched the wizard closely, thinking perhaps for just a moment he saw uneasiness in him.

"Dwellers have quick minds," Craugh said. "And their first inclination is to save their own necks. Both of those traits serve a Library in good stead."

"Dwellers also take pride in their laziness as a general rule," Juhg stated baldly. "They lack ambition. They do only what they have to do to get by. I have seen it over the years. And when the Grandmagister faced the Council before the attack on Greydawn Moors, I saw all of those things again. During this trip, after the Grandmagister's kidnapping when so many dwarves and elves gave their lives to protect Greydawn Moors in the battle that raged across Yondering Docks while most of the dwellers ran and hid, I remembered all of that. It makes me sick that such a responsibility as the Vault of All Known Knowledge would ever have been entrusted to dwellers."

A lump swelled up inside Juhg's chest. He hated talking so badly of his own people.

Craugh looked at him, for the first time entertaining the idea of the conversation. "Who else do you think we should have given such a responsibility to?"

"Anyone would have been better."

"Do you think so?"

"Yes."

"Tell me then, apprentice, you talk highly of the humans here in Imarish becoming teachers and Librarians. Do you think they could do that?"

"Yes."

"Of what, do you suppose?"

"Of anything."

"That caught their fancy, I suppose. But humans have a short attention span for things that don't interest or concern them. Have you ever realized that, even as long-lived as I am, you know more about histories and literature than I do? Hasn't that ever struck you before?"

Juhg thought about that, remembering that time after time—unless it was an event or a place that the wizard had passed through—Craugh seldom had knowledge of those things.

"I am a powerful wizard," Craugh said, "and sometimes people attribute all-knowing in the same breath as all-powerful. Most wizards would never dissuade someone from that point of view. But I am not all-knowing. Wick—and you, apprentice—know far more than I do about the whole of the world. I just have no patience for the parts of it that don't interest me. Dwellers have long lives and prodigious amounts of patience, and more than average intelligence for the most part."

A small fingerling of pride moved within Juhg. He had so harshly discounted his people that Craugh's views were uplifting. Especially since they were also valid.

"Remember," Craugh said, "all the libraries of the mainland were shipped to Greydawn Moors and dumped there. No rhyme, no reason. Just dumped. Can you imagine what humans would have done if faced with the generations-long chore of assembling those books into some cohesive whole that made sense?"

"It would not have been done," Juhg admitted. "Humans lack the patience to have done something like that."

"Yes. I seldom visited the Library in the early days. It was just too hard to find something. Wallowing through all of those books, building shelves, organizing and copying—" Craugh shook his head. "I could not have done it. Even going there to search for books at later dates frustrated me." He pulled at his chin whiskers. "For a time, though the Librarians of the day were loath to admit it, the Vault of All Known Knowledge was filled with toads and positively vibrated with plaintive croaking. Until I relented and turned them back into dwellers."

Is that a threat again? Juhg wondered. Then he decided Craugh was being honest with him.

"And elves?" Craugh sighed. "Old Ones grace me, but do you imagine what elves would have done if someone suggested a large number of them stayed inside and worked so books could be protected from the elements?" The wizard snorted. "Impossible. We would have had a war on our hands."

Juhg knew that was true. "But some of the elves at Greydawn Moors have taught themselves to read." That had come out at the Grand Council and shocked nearly everyone there.

"They read some things," Craugh admitted. "But do you think they took the time to learn as many written and oral languages as the dwellers learn?"

"I don't know."

"No. That was just a threat the elves brought forward that day while they were supporting Wick's argument. And have you yet given any thought to what the dwarves' first response would have been had they been placed in charge of the books?"

It only took Juhg a moment to see the problem behind that line of logic. "Their first task would have been to build a better book. One that wasn't so perishable."

"Then they would have transferred all the old texts into a uniform *book*," Craugh agreed. "Copies would have been made with hammer and chisels instead of a quill and ink. Do you know how long it would have taken to make a copy of a book under those circumstances?"

Too long, Juhg realized. *And how would a book have been that wasn't made of paper? All the beautiful laminated manuscripts would not exist.* Dwarven books were works of art in their own right, but dwarves would never have used paper for their tomes.

"No, apprentice," Craugh said, "choosing dwellers to be Librarians was the right thing to do."

"It helped that they could be so easily subjugated, though, didn't it?"

"Not subjugation," Craugh said. "They exchanged safety and well-being for task." He gazed out at the Garment District. "These people have done that as well."

"Tasks of their own choosing," Juhg countered.

"The dwellers were never held back from being warriors or warders or pirates," Craugh said. "Several of them back in Greydawn Moors have either gone into business for themselves or work for others. It's no differ-ent than working for the Library. They just perceive it so."

Juhg studied the wizard, suddenly understanding. "We would have never come this far if each race didn't contribute, would we?"

"No."

"And still it didn't keep us from the darkness. The Vault of All Known Knowledge was destroyed all the same."

Craugh was silent for a moment. "No, no it didn't, apprentice. There was too much evil let loose in the world all those years ago." He smiled a little. "But you are right about this place. Should we survive the undertaking we now follow, this would be an exemplary place for a school. I will do what I can to help you make that happen. Wick has seldom been able to withstand both of us, and never when we were right."

Juhg considered the offer. *Is he only offering lip service to get me moving again, or is he sincere?* He didn't know. But he chose to feel generous because they might not even live through the coming ordeal.

Taking the lead once more, Juhg struck out again.

Less than an hour later, very near to their goal, a group of men attacked Juhg and Craugh.

Juhg had only a moment's warning, hissed through Craugh's teeth. The warning was apparently brought about by the sudden appearance of a winged crimson gecko that dropped down into the alley where Juhg was leading the way.

At Craugh's warning, Juhg froze immediately. His quick eyes darted around, seeing only the gecko clinging to the side of the wall. The thing was barely the length of his hand. Unless it carried poison, the creature possessed no real threat.

Then hooded men filled both ends of the short, narrow alley. They carried naked blades in their scarred fists. Armor showed in places beneath their traveling cloaks. Other men stood back of them with drawn bows, arrow fletchings touching their jawline. Hard eyes watched them beneath hooded cowls.

"Hold still," one of the men ordered, "and you may yet live through this."

Craugh shifted like a cornered wildcat, flattening against one wall so he could peer back and forth. The curving wall offered a little defense from the far end of the alley. He snaked out a hand and caught the back of Juhg's jacket, pulling him in close.

"Fools," Craugh snarled contemptuously, "do you know who it is you face?"

"A dead man by the looks of it," the leader said, grinning a little. "You'll be quieter after I've slit your gullet for you."

"Faugh!" Craugh growled.

"We were told only to find this dweller," the man said. He was tall and fair, with a jutting chin and a long nose. "The old man doesn't matter. Kill him."

Two of the archers standing behind their leader released their holds. Their arrows jumped across the distance, well over Juhg's head and straight for Craugh's skinny chest.

With incredible quickness, Craugh swung his staff around and shattered the arrows in midflight. The broken pieces fell down to the cobblestones at his boots.

The archers looked surprised, but fitted new arrows to bowstring automatically. Five more took aim as well.

"Kill him," the leader said again.

The archers loosed their shafts again. One of them shattered against the stone wall over Juhg's head. Craugh managed to break four of the arrows, but two of them got through. Both of the arrows lodged in Craugh's clothing, though, and didn't find flesh.

"Again," the leader called out.

This time archers at both ends took aim.

At that moment, Craugh's body started glowing green. He moved quickly, stepping into the wall behind him and vanishing.

Juhg waited expectantly. He'd seen Craugh perform this bit of magic before. The last time had been back in the Vault of All Known Knowledge. The wizard had prevented his death then. Instead, Juhg remained alone in the alley.

The archers looked as confused as Juhg felt.

"He's a powerful wizard," Juhg called out, hoping to scare the men away. *It probably would have helped if your voice wasn't quavering,* he chided himself. "And he's very vengeful. If I were you, I'd run." He pressed back against the alley wall, hoping that Craugh would tug him on through to safety.

"Take him," the leader called out, and pointed to Juhg.

The other men advanced slowly with their swords and their bows. "Wizard," one armed man whispered.

"Or he has a spelled charm," another man said.

Juhg stood his ground, not knowing what to do.

Before the men reached him, Craugh walked out from the wall. His voice echoed strong and loud through the alley, speaking in words that Juhg didn't recognize. The wizard slammed the butt of his staff against the cobblestones. Green flames suddenly wreathed the top of the staff.

Before the men could charge or flee—from the looks on their faces Juhg knew both impulses had occurred to them—the cobblestones rose up in a tower nearly ten feet tall and two feet thick. They whirled as if caught up in a hurricane, and the alley filled with the angry whir of their passing.

Two of the archers fired their bows again. The arrows never made it through the rocks.

With another word from Craugh and a gesture of the staff, the cobblestones shot toward the men. The rocks broke bone and tore flesh despite the armor they wore. Their clothing turned to tatters. Loud clanking filled the alley, followed instantly by the screams of pain from the survivors.

The glowing green nimbus of light around Craugh deepened as his magic took a firmer hold. "I am *Craugh*," he roared. "I will fear no man. And I will not be taken by such as you."

For a moment, Juhg thought the men would go away. Then someone said, "It's just one wizard," and both groups rushed toward the middle of the alley.

Without hesitation, Juhg drew his boot knife and stood back to back with the wizard as their enemies approached. Even though he thought he was going to die almost immediately, he couldn't help wondering how the men had come to be there. Someone had set them upon their trail. Or his at least, because they didn't seem familiar at all with Craugh.

Juhg stood his ground, slipping into a knife-fighting stance he'd learned while reading books. Boloy Trasker's *Ribbons of Shining Steel* had provided numerous illustrations that showed the moves. Still, even Boloy Trasker, who had been a human of incredible skill and prowess, couldn't have stood up to twenty armed men. Even though he hadn't been able to count all the men, Juhg was sure they didn't fall short of that number by much. He stood with his left hand and left foot forward, his right hand holding his blade point outward with his hand above his head. If he got lucky, he'd be able to menace the first man's chin before he went down under their numbers.

Then a familiar war cry ripped through the alley.

"Wah-hoooooo!"

At almost the same instant, the twenty men in front of Juhg tumbled like stacked tiles, plunging face forward as they were barreled over from behind. The closest man went down at Juhg's feet. His sword clanked against the cobblestones.

A dwarf hauled himself up from the pile of scattered men. He was in full armor. Although not as tall as Hallekk, the warrior was—almost impossibly—broader through the shoulder. Scars marked the cheeks of his face. His graying beard hung to his massive chest. He lifted a double-bitted war axe that gleamed in the afternoon sun that crept over the edge of the building and into the alley.

"Hello, Juhg," the dwarf said with a grin. "I see you went and saved a few for me."

"Cobner?" Juhg said, recognizing the dwarf from the adventures they'd had along the mainland with the Grandmagister.

Cobner had been one of Brandt's band of thieves back when the Grandmagister had arrived in slaver's chains at Hanged Elf's Point. At that time, Brandt had been lawless, still unable to return to his ancestral lands and claim the title that was his by birth and later his by might and cunning. Brandt had bought the Grandmagister at a slave auction because he'd seen the Grandmagister writing in his journal.

Drawn to the goblinkin-infested city by tales of indescribable wealth, Brandt had put the Grandmagister to the task of solving a riddle that had allowed them to plunder the loot. During that night in the all but forgotten graveyard where a wizard had left his fortune, and when the Grandmagister had found the first four books hidden in ruins on the mainland, the Grandmagister had also risked his life to save Cobner's. The dwarven warrior had always insisted that the Grandmagister had the most interesting scar for saving his life. They had become the deepest of friends in the years that had followed.

"Aye," Cobner growled, grinning wider still. "Surprised to see me?" He lifted his battle-axe and drove the ironclad hilt hard against one of his opponent's helmets, knocking the man unconscious almost effortlessly.

 128

"Very," Juhg admitted. The man in front of him had regained his senses enough to reach for his sword. Juhg stomped on his fingers, then kicked him in the head, knocking him out against the cobblestones.

"Hah!" Cobner growled with pride. "I see you haven't forgot all that ol' Cobner taught you. Was Wick that taught me halfers might be small but they had the hearts of warriors."

Several of the humans got to their feet and took up arms.

"I'll be talking to you soon," Cobner promised. "Just stay alive. Wick told me what he had to do here was going to be interesting." He slammed shut the faceplate of his helmet. "I'm looking forward to it." He took up his battle-axe in both hands and started battling ferociously.

One of the men got up and started for Juhg. The man drew his sword back and Juhg had no doubt that the man intended to kill him.

The man stopped suddenly and looked down at his chest. An arrowhead protruded through his armor where his heart would be. He tottered forward another step, then fell on his face. The arrow that had entered through his back and pierced him all the way through stood upright between his shoulder blades. The fletchings were a unique violet and blue pattern.

Looking back past the dead man and past Cobner driving two men backward against a wall with his battle-axe haft shoved against their throats, Juhg spotted the young elven maid at the end of the alley calmly putting another arrow to string as if killing a man were something she did every day.

She was lissome and lovely. Her bronze hair gleamed in the sunlight, tied back in a queue that left her pointed ears revealed for all to see. High warder's boots rose to her knees. She wore a violet jacket over white breeches. A longsword hung at her hip.

She lifted her chin in greeting, then put a shaft through the eye of an opponent who drew back his own bow. Before the dead man fell, she'd reached over her shoulder and pulled out another arrow.

Her name was Jassamyn. She was the daughter of Tseralyn, the elven woman mercenary the Grandmagister had freed from a giant spider's web near the Broken Forge Mountains. Although her mother had settled down to a overland trade kingdom she'd carved out of the wilderness herself, Jassamyn maintained some of the same wanderlust that had fired her beautiful mother.

The Grandmagister, Juhg couldn't help thinking. *He called them here. He must have.* Hope sprang in his heart. Whatever he faced, whatever they faced, there could surely be no more stouthearted companions for whatever dangers lay ahead.

A glittering jewel swooped down from the sky, almost straight as one of Jassamyn's arrows. At the last second, the tiny draca unfurled its batwings and swung its claws forward, slashing the face of another of the armed men. The draca whipped its wings immediately, seeking yet another target.

Turning to make certain of Craugh's well-being, Juhg watched as the wizard unleashed a fiery blast from the staff that hurled three opponents into the street at the other end of the alley. The others came at Craugh with swords, axes, and knives, driving him backward.

Juhg dashed forward, trusting his faster speed in tight areas to keep him safe. He ducked below a man's sword, then stomped on the side of his knee. Bone cracked and he went down.

Ellgot's Tips and Tricks to Dirty Fighting, Juhg thought. *Lesson number eighteen.* Then he fought alongside Craugh, turning the sword blades away with his long knife and keeping the men bunched into one group so they couldn't work as effectively. They had picked a poor battleground considering how many of them there were. If Craugh and he had simply given up, there would have been no problem, but now their numbers worked against them.

Craugh slammed his staff forward again, striking a man squarely in his armor-plated chest. The next instant the man sailed backward as though hit by a gigantic fist.

Struggling to stay alive and help Craugh at the same time, Juhg didn't see the corpse beneath his feet until he had tripped over it and was falling. The man before him brought his sword down in a glittering arc, his face a mask of bloodthirsty rage. Juhg had no doubt that his head was about to be split into pieces.

"No!" Craugh yelled, turning to aid him, but too late as well.

130

8

The Grandmagister's
Puzzling Journal

hen a cutlass intercepted the attacker's blade and turned it aside.

Startled, not daring to believe he was still alive, Juhg stared up at the man who had saved him. He recognized him at once. *Raisho.*

Juhg had met the young sailor little more than a year previously. They had formed a fast friendship and spent time together when Juhg was free from his duties at the Library. Juhg had told Raisho tales and histories, and Raisho had told him of the things he had seen on the mainland while serving as a pirate protecting Greydawn Moors from anyone interested in crossing the Blood-Soaked Sea. Later, when Juhg had decided the Vault of All Known Knowledge no longer held a future for him, he had forged a friendship with the young sailor and they had gone into business together as traders.

Before the attacker had the chance to pull his blade back to defend himself, Raisho disemboweled him and kicked him backward. Raisho was tall and fierce looking. Sunlight glinted from the silver hoops in his ears. His black skin marked him as a human from the south. A red leather band with osprey feathers held his long, unruly hair back from his face. He was twenty and an orphan. Eight years of his life had been spent at sea, all of them at hard labor either tending cargo or pulling oars. Indigo blue good luck tattoos on his arms, legs, and chest stood out against his skin. Like Juhg, the young sailor had been raised as an orphan until *Windchaser*'s captain had taken him in.

"Are ye all right then, scribbler?" Raisho asked with much concern. Worry darkened his warm brown eyes.

"Yes," Juhg croaked, but he believed his heart was going to explode.

"I thought I'd done gone an' arrived too late, I did," Raisho admitted. A wide white smile split his lips. He reached out a hand, catching Juhg's hand, and helped him to his feet.

For a short time, the attackers tried to continue their assault, bunching in small knots and attempting to overpower one of Juhg's defenders. Instead, the men were killed or repeatedly driven back. Bodies littered the alley floor, but Craugh, Cobner, Jessamyn, Raisho, and Juhg stayed alive.

"Cobner," Craugh said, breathing hard. He whipped his tall hat against his leg to knock the dust off. "It's good to see you."

"And you," the dwarf replied as he shook the blood from his battle-axe. "I don't suppose you know who these would-be ruffians are?"

"No." The wizard clapped his hat back on his head. "But they knew Juhg. They didn't know me."

Cobner grinned mirthlessly. "I guess they know you now."

Craugh smiled back, the expression equally devoid of warmth. Over the years, Juhg had noted that the dwarven warrior and the wizard shared the same bloodthirstiness when it came to battle.

"Mayhap we should ask one of 'em a question or two," Cobner suggested. He sorted through the fallen men with the haft of his battle-axe, striking each one in turn till he found one that groaned. He kicked the man over onto his back, then grabbed a fistful of the man's shirt and lifted him as if he weren't full grown at all but a small child. He spun and smacked the man up against the alley wall. Then he pressed the head of the battle-axe against the man's throat so that the man had to hang onto the axe or drop a handful of inches to the ground.

The man gripped the axe head tightly and held on. His eyes rolled white with fear.

"I'll be after having your name," Cobner threatened. "Elsewise I'll do for you and leave your body for the alley strays to care for in their ungentle manner."

"Mullock," the man cried. He held his wounded shoulder with his good hand. He made no move for the knife belted at his waist.

"What were you doing here, Mullock?" Cobner asked.

"Came for the halfer."

"How'd you know he would be here?"

The man hesitated. Showing more than a little irritation, Cobner shook the man and slammed him against the stone wall. "I can check to see of one of your mates is alive, but if'n I do and I find one, I got no more use for you."

"Aldhran Khempus," Mullock said.

Cobner squinted at the man doubtfully. "Aldhran shipped this morning. If'n he knew my friend was gonna be here, why didn't Aldhran stay here himself?"

"I don't know."

Cobner drew the man away from the wall and prepared to slam him back again.

"No, I swear. I swear I don't know."

Cobner hesitated, his doubting look clearly showing he was torn in his beliefs.

"No, Cobner," Craugh said. "I believe he speaks the truth."

Juhg believed him, too. Cobner in his full wrath was a frightful thing to behold.

"What were you supposed to do?" Cobner demanded.

"Capture the halfer. We weren't going to hurt him."

"But anyone else you were gonna massacre."

"We were told to."

Cobner shook the man, making his prisoner's teeth clack together. "And if you'd captured my friend, what were you supposed to do with him?"

"Take him to Aldhran Khempus." The man gritted his teeth together in pain.

"Where were you supposed to meet Aldhran Khempus?"

"At the Buzzard's Neck."

"In the Haze Mountains?"

Mullock nodded.

"What is Aldhran Khempus doing there?"

"I don't know. By the Old Ones, I swear to you that I don't. We were only told to find a halfer fitting this one's description if he showed up, then take him to the Haze Mountains."

Juhg took the information in. The Haze Mountains, so named for the perpetual fogs that surrounded the mountain range's top half, which was thousands of feet above sea level, were located far into the interior of the mainland. Some said the fogs were created by the spirits of those who had been slain in the Valley of the Dead below, that the ghosts couldn't go on to their final rest until their business in the earth was finished.

Even though he had seen a number of strange things, Juhg didn't believe the stories. However, as a result of the legends, few people ever traveled there, and fewer still returned. Legends persisted that hunters sometimes wandered into the Haze Mountains seeking game only to return years older with a head full of madness. Others came back with fabulous treasures, the like of which had never been seen or had not been seen in centuries.

"Craugh?" Cobner asked.

"We're done with him," the wizard replied.

A look of wild-eyed terror filled the man's face as Cobner plucked him from the wall, still holding his weight one-handed, then slammed him against the wall so that his head hit with a meaty *thunk*. He slumped unconscious, then Cobner opened his fist and let the man drop bonelessly to the ground.

Cobner turned and surveyed the dead and injured men. There were over two dozen dead and unconscious at his feet. "Gonna be right interesting while we're here," he commented. Then he looked at Craugh. "Got any idea how long that might be?"

Craugh pointed his chin at Juhg. "He has all the answers at this point."

Shouldering his battle-axe, Cobner looked at Juhg. "Well, if you got no more business with these men, I suggest we get back to whatever it is you were doing here. We're a threat here to these men, and they're not going to wait around till it's convenient for us to fight them for our lives. And there's Peacekeepers. Getting stuffed into a jail here on the island now wouldn't be a pleasing prospect."

"I know," Juhg said.

"If you've got a place for us to be, let's be getting there."

Silently, Juhg agreed. He took the lead and trotted out of the alley with Raisho at his back.

"*Windchaser* caught up with *One-Eyed Peggie* out in the harbor," Raisho said as he followed Juhg through the Garment District.

In terse sentences, he told how Captain Attikus had rendezvoused with the pirate ship and quickly talked with Captain Hallekk to find out that Juhg and Craugh had been set ashore. Raisho had quickly secured permission to be set ashore and had spotted Juhg and Craugh only a short time before Cobner and Jassamyn had staged their rescue bid. Captain Attikus and *Windchaser* took up the hunt for the Grandmagister with *One-Eyed Peggie*.

The elven archer quickly recounted how she and Cobner had come to the Garment District fully expecting to meet up with the Grandmagister, as was prearranged by a note the Grandmagister had sent by pigeon months ago. The Grandmagister had asked them to be there, and had mentioned that Juhg might be with him.

The fact that the Grandmagister wasn't at Imarish's Garment District was news to them. Still, they had recognized Juhg and Craugh, and noticed immediately that they were being followed. By more than Mullock and his buddies, as it turned out. They'd caught and questioned Raisho while holding a knife blade to his throat. Once they'd found out they were all on the same side, Cobner had told the young sailor to follow their lead.

Several minutes later, Juhg led them deep into the warrens that made up the Garment District. The shrill pipes of the Peacekeepers sounded now and again.

"Ye know these alleys as well as any thief, scribbler," Raisho grumbled. "Unless ye've up an' got us all lost."

"We're not lost," Juhg told them, suspecting they all thought that. After the rush of adrenaline had flooded through him, he felt tired. Carrying Craugh's secrets, suspecting that the wizard accompanied him out of his own dark desires and fearful over the Grandmagister's fate had kept Juhg up worrying most of the night. "There is a friend not far from here."

"Why go there?" Craugh asked.

"Because he's the only man in this town that I know the Grandmagister would leave anything with," Juhg said. He led them on.

Sharz's Beadworks was located in a small two-story building nestled between a tavern and a dye-maker. With dusk closing in over the city and some of the shifts ending at the looms and the mills, the tavern was starting to fill. Carriages and wagons trundled across the cobblestones, carrying passengers and cargoes.

The shop was narrow with a hard-weathered wooden face. A sign out front held only the name BEADWORKS pieced together of multicolored beads. Windows on either side of the door held samples of Sharz's craft on jackets and pants.

Juhg led the way into the buildings. Shelves contained hundreds of small boxes filled with beads of different colors, sizes, textures, and even scents. Some were carved, some were poured from molds, and some were found in the wild, like the honeyseeds of the pearl ants. The smell of fruits and trees mixed inside the shop much as they did in a candlemaker's shop.

The wall to the left held a thousand more boxes of beads in built-in shelves. A long counter occupied the wall to the right. Sharz's personal workspace—used while he minded the store and not while he worked on special orders because he did those upstairs without interruption—filled the rear third of the shop, made up of small tables surrounded by simple straight-backed chairs where he taught his craft to others who wanted to learn as well as did a half dozen projects at any one time.

A customer stood at the counter haggling over the price of a jacket.

When Sharz spotted Juhg, he settled for the amount the customer wished, wrapped the jacket in colorful paper, and sent the man happily from his shop. Following the man to the door, Sharz shot the bolt and lowered the curtains in the windows so that everyone would know he had retired for the evening.

He was one of the smallest adult male humans Juhg had ever seen. Standing scarcely a foot taller than Juhg, Sharz was thin as a rake. His bushy brown hair curled tightly, making it look like he was horned. He wore a leather apron over his simple breeches and a shirt with the sleeves rolled up to his elbows. Needles glinted at his left wrist, embedded in the special sponge he wore on a band there to hold them.

"Juhg," Sharz greeted warmly. "It is so good to see you again."

"Sharz, it is good to be here," Juhg replied, then introduced his companions.

"It has been far too long, my friend," Sharz said, waving them to the back of the shop where stairs led up to the second floor. "Have you eaten?"

"Not for hours," Juhg admitted. Craugh had sampled sweets and meat pies from pushcarts along the way. Over the years, Juhg had never seen how the wizard had stayed so skinny because he had a sweet tooth and a prodigious appetite.

"Then you must be my guests. If I had known you were coming I would have been able to set a better table." Sharz took off up the stairs, raising his voice to call for his wife.

Juhg followed his friend up the stairs, feeling suddenly guilty about bringing so many to Sharz's humble home.

"Has Wick come with you then?" Sharz asked.

"Not this time," Juhg answered.

"Pity." Sharz shrugged. "Nyia loves the puppet show he always puts on for her."

"I remember."

At the top of the stairs, Sharz called out again to his family, alerting them to the fact they had company. Nyia, his daughter, was a six-year-old who looked like her mother, Teeyar. Both of them had blond hair and bright blue eyes. Teeyar was no taller than her husband, though a little bit heavier than his rawboned state.

Flustered at the unexpected prospect of company—*and so much of it!*—Teeyar began at once to be anxious over what to prepare. She clattered through pots and plates in the open kitchen, checking vegetables and salted meat. Her distress was obvious.

Craugh doffed his tall hat and smiled at the woman. "Please, madam," the wizard said in his best voice, "we didn't travel all this way to beggar at your table. Let us help out with the provisions for the evening fare."

Uncertain, Teeyar glanced at her husband.

"We came with no warning," Juhg said, knowing Sharz was a proud man and would not take well to the request if it hit him wrong. He had always provided for his family and anyone he invited to his table. "Please allow us. It is the least we can do. And we had not planned to dine at your table when there are so many taverns in town."

"Nonsense," Sharz said. "You'll not be eating in one of those places as long as I have a warm hearth."

"But no chickens, husband," Teeyar said in a meek voice. "At least, we don't have enough chickens for the company we have now." She looked pointedly at Cobner and Raisho.

Reluctantly, Sharz agreed to accept Craugh's generosity. The wizard dropped coins into the woman's hands, enough so that Teeyar's eyes opened in surprise. She closed her fist around them, then got Nyia by the hand and set off downstairs to acquire the needed provisions.

"Would you lay a fire?" Sharz asked Juhg. "I will see about opening some wine."

Grateful for something to do, Juhg quickly laid the wood and searched the mantle for the tinderbox.

"Let me, Apprentice," Craugh said.

Backing away from the hearth, Juhg watched as the wizard blew into his hand. In response, green flames slithered between his fingers, leapt across the intervening space, and bit into the dry wood. In just heartbeats, a cheery fire had sprung up in the fireplace.

Sharz glanced askance at the wizard. Wariness flickered through the beadmaster's eyes. He'd never entertained a wizard in his home before, evidently. Possibly he hadn't even seen one.

Jassamyn walked toward Sharz's personal workspace at the back of the open area. The kitchen, dining area, living area, and workspace were all located in the room that took up over half of the top floor. Only the two bedrooms and the privy were locked behind doors.

Beaded canvases hung on the wall behind the workspace. Juhg watched happily as Jassamyn was enthralled by the images portrayed in beads on thick sheets of framed canvas. All of the beads were carefully sewn on with tiny stitches.

Two of the images were of Nyia. One of them showed her as a baby and the other was more recent, revealing the striking difference between the little girl and the baby. Juhg knew from his friendship with the man that he made a portrait of the girl every year. He only chose to show these.

"By the Old Ones," Jassamyn whispered, her voice barely covering the popping and spitting of the dry wood, "these are . . . *beautiful*." Drawn by the beauty of the beadwork, she ran her fingers over the images.

"They are." Juhg joined her, glancing over the canvas displays. "They are from Sharz's personal collection, but this is only a fragment of what he has finished. He keeps the others safely locked away."

"I saw some of what he had downstairs," Jassamyn said. "The style in these is so much stronger."

"That's because I don't have to attract anyone's eyes but my own." Sharz climbed the stairs and entered the room carrying four dark wine bottles. "I have learned that most people don't share my taste. The majority of them want something bright and shiny, something that at once sets them apart from others and unites them with their friends."

He took glasses down in the kitchen area and poured drinks for everyone. Removing a wheel of goat's milk cheese leavened with chives from the larder, he removed the cloth and cut chunks for the taking, leaving them on the cutting board. A small wooden barrel to one side provided a half dozen bright red apples, which he also cut up. He invited his guests to indulge until Teeyar returned and was able to get a meal on the table.

Walking into his personal work area, Sharz regarded the canvases. "I taught myself something far more than mere decorative beading. At least, that's what Wick tells me." He paused for a moment, touching the recent picture of his daughter. "He thinks I have found art."

"You did," Juhg said. "Art disappeared along with the books during the Cataclysm under Lord Kharrion's effort. Few practice any of the arts now, though I have seen glassblowers, metalsmiths, and others who wield their skills with an eye toward passion at times rather than profit."

"You can never take your eye from the profit margin," the beader lamented. "That fact is bedrock among craftsmen. I have talked to millers and loomers who have designs and patterns they have fallen in love with but are reluctant to put into production. Lands away from Imarish are hard pressed for mere survival." He paused. "Sometimes I forget how fortunate we are here among these islands, how we have flourished when others have faltered or fallen."

"There are a great many here in the south that have struggled all their lives," Cobner commented.

Juhg couldn't help but think of the goblinkin mines the Grandmagister has rescued him from. Although he sometimes fostered hopes, he knew there was little chance that his family had escaped from those. More than likely, they had died harsh deaths, broken and scared, before the Grandmagister had ever found him.

"Sometimes I think the prosperity we have found here has doomed us," Sharz said. "Everyone knows of Imarish."

"Why would you be worried?" Jassamyn asked. "Pirates don't dare attack here. They have tried in the past but have always been repulsed."

"I know, but times are changing. The goblinkin in the south are reuniting again. I have heard that the tribes once more prepare for war. That has been the rumor up and down the Shattered Coast for more than a season."

Juhg knew that was true. Even when he'd been in Kelloch's Harbor he had heard the rumors. No one knew for sure what the cause was.

"There's a lot of water between these islands and the mainland," Cobner said.

"Not enough. A number of small islands, some of them no more than stone spurs thrust up above the waterline, exist in those open places. And reefs as well. Those hazards that have saved us from ships for so much of our past now threaten to doom us. The goblinkin have become organized and have begun to build bridges over them."

"The goblinkin are building?" Juhg couldn't believe it.

"Not them," Sharz corrected. "They force the slaves to build the bridges."

"But where did goblinkin learn the technology to build bridges?" Craugh asked. He sat in one of the hand-carved chairs before the fire. His staff lay across his lap. A one-eared black cat had joined him. He stroked the cat's fur and the animal purred in contentment, keeping one eye on the small jeweled draca perched on Jassamyn's shoulder.

Sharz shook his head. "No one knows. But spies from the islands have seen the bridges being built. In another five years or so, given the present rate at which they are progressing, the goblinkin will reach an outlying island large enough to support and stage an attack."

"What can be done?" Raisho asked.

"Nothing. We have no army or navy to draw upon. We have always been protected by the sea. Now we are betrayed."

"You could raise an army," Cobner suggested.

"Where?"

"From the mainland."

"They are jealous of us there," Sharz said. "Jealous of our successes. They buy our goods, but they would shed no tears if the goblinkin were to overwhelm us."

"Have they not realized that were Imarish to be destroyed much of the clothing and bedding and goods they buy so readily will go away as well?" Jassamyn asked.

"Lady," the beader said. "I know not what is in their heads. Perhaps most of them have not thought that far."

"Warriors could be hired," Cobner suggested.

"To fight what would probably be an unending war against the hordes of goblinkin?"

"The goblinkin bridges could be destroyed."

"Mercenary chiefs have been there to look," Sharz said. "None of them want to take on the task. The goblinkin are too firmly entrenched, and the slaves would have to be killed. The goblinkin chain the slaves to the bridges so they are forced to work." He took a deep breath. "They say that the goblinkin decorate the bridges with the bodies of the slaves who have died there, that carrion birds feast on the corpses and leave only skeletons clattering in the breeze."

The image filled Juhg's head and he shuddered.

"What will Imarish do?" Cobner asked.

"When the time comes that we can no longer hold them back, we will abandon Imarish and seek our fortunes elsewhere."

Juhg could not imagine the great mills and looms of the islands shutting down. Every time he thought of Imarish, he thought of the creaking waterwheels turning with the tides, how the sound seemed to permeate everything on the major manufacturing islands. No longer would happy children run rampant throughout the districts.

And in the same instance, he knew that his plans for establishing the first of the schools spawned by the Vault of All Known Knowledge were in danger as well. If he couldn't help found a school in Imarish, where commerce and travel met so readily in a healthy environment, where else could he put one?

Sadness and frustration gripped him. So many things were spiraling out of control. Abruptly, he realized that Sharz was talking to him and that an answer was expected. He apologized for his inattention.

Sharz waved the apology away. "I was just asking about the other beaders. You have seen their work?"

"Yes. Several times." In fact, after seeing the work Sharz did, Juhg had read a few books about the craft. He'd discovered designs and methods that the beader had not yet discovered for himself. But he had never told Sharz about them because the Grandmagister had suggested that the Imarish beader be allowed to continue the pursuit of his craft on his own because he was so unique.

Sharz looked wistful. "I wish I could see their works."

"Maybe some day you can," Juhg said, hoping that at least some of those books and examples still existed after the destruction of the Library.

"In its own right," Sharz admitted ruefully, "my personal work doesn't sell well. Except now and again I'll find someone captured by a design or color scheme."

Juhg looked at the current work-in-progress on the table. It showed a canal boat, the fish head on the tall prow prominent in the foreground, slipping through a canal as the sun went down. Shadows of night had already closed in and stretched across the canal water. The boat mate stood in the rear with the long pole he used for navigation firmly in his hands. The gray-green beads in the canal caught the color of the ocean, as the white ones caught the color of the man's shirt.

"I've never seen anything like this," Jassamyn whispered. "What prompted you to do this kind of craft?"

"I don't know," Sharz said. "I see something that I think is moving or beautiful. Maybe days or months later, sometimes a year in a few instances, and my hands find ways to bring those images to life in beads on canvas."

"You don't work from drawings?"

Juhg knew that Jassamyn had an interest in art. Her mother's talent had turned to music. The Grandmagister had taught Tseralyn how to write down her music years ago. Music and mathematics had been the keystones to interpreting so many unknown languages that Librarians had encountered in the jumble of books in the Vault of All Known Knowledge.

"No." Sharz touched the partially completed image. "The images I capture on the canvas come from things I have seen. Sometimes people bring me images of things they wanted rendered, but for my own pieces, I always work from memory."

"You have a beautiful memory."

An embarrassed smile twisted Sharz's lips. "Thank you, Lady."

"Sharz," Juhg said, feeling bad that he had to switch over to a more serious topic, "we didn't come here for a social visit."

"I know." The beader sighed. "You and the Grandmagister, you have never come to my home just to visit, though I have often wished you would."

"I was sent here by the Grandmagister," Juhg said. "I hope to find a package he left for me."

"A package." Sharz nodded. "Yes, he did indeed leave a package. He said he might be back for it. Or you. When he left Imarish the last time only a few months ago, he seemed quite agitated. He had recently found some books that had brought him a great deal of anxiety."

Years ago, on one of the early trips to Imarish, the Grandmagister had met the beader and taken him into his confidence while having to hide from a powerful wizard whose books he'd stolen. Sharz had been a dependable friend, and he'd been interested in the Grandmagister's ability to read and write. The secret was still closely guarded from anyone along the mainland, but there had been a few taken into confidence along the way.

"Didn't you come with Wick on his last visit to Imarish?" Craugh asked. The cat remained content to sit in the wizard's lap. It winked sleepily.

"No," Juhg answered. "The Grandmagister had sent me to Shadowmire to investigate a ship that had washed up from the sea that had been rumored to have been sunk during the Cataclysm."

"Was it?"

"Yes. The Grandmagister had thought some record of the ship's mission or what the captain had witnessed might have been in the salvageable goods. There was nothing but the picked-over bones of a broken ship when I arrived. Very little had survived the battle, the fire, or all the long years resting at the bottom of the Blood-Soaked Sea until the underwater quake tossed it up into the tides that brought it to land."

Sharz walked to the back of the room, pulled a chair over, and climbed on top of it. He reached up to the ceiling, pressed against a timber that looked solidly in place, and reached inside to withdraw a rectangular object covered in oilskin.

Juhg's heart sped up and he was moving before he knew it. *Is this* The Book of Time? *Can finding it have been so easy?*

But he knew that couldn't have been the answer. If the Grandmagister were to have gotten *The Book of Time* in his grasp, he surely wouldn't have left it behind. That made no sense.

Sharz handed the package down.

With dweller-quick fingers, knowing and canny, Juhg stripped the oil-skin from the book. Cobner, Jassalyn, and Raisho crowded in around Juhg, peering over his shoulders, which was simple since he was so much shorter than they were.

Craugh maintained his seat by the fireplace and absently stroked the cat.

With the oilskin free of the book, Juhg stared down to see the thin, courtly letters writ in the Grandmagister's hand, which was easily recognizable by the beautiful Qs he made. No Librarian had ever made Qs so easily and so artfully as the Grandmagister.

"An' what do ye have there?" Raisho asked.

"A journal," Jassalyn said, folding her arms. She frowned. The tiny draca shifted irritably on her shoulder, then scratched at its face with one clawed foot. "Wick's, if I'm any judge of the handwriting."

The Grandmagister had taught the elven maid to read when she was very young. With her mother's blessing, she'd sometimes accompanied the Grandmagister on his adventures through the Forest of Fangs and Shadows, honing her woodcraft with the warriors Tseralyn had sent with them as well as learning from the Grandmagister.

"It is the Grandmagister's hand." Juhg opened the book and a piece of paper floated free. Quick as a wink, he snatched the paper from the air, beating Raisho by a lot. No human's was as quick as a dweller's covetous hand. That was a saying that existed on the mainland as well as Greydawn Moors.

146

Looking at the first page, all neatly written in the Grandmagister's best effort, Juhg realized he could not read the book.

"Is somethin' wrong?" Sharz asked.

"The book is written in code," Juhg said. He frowned at the lines of script.

"Code?" Raisho asked.

"Wick masked the writing," Jassalyn said.

Cobner rubbed his lower face with a massive hand, shook his head, then went to stand by the fire to warm his backside. The dwarf liked the warmth of the interior of the mainland. The coolness along the coastal waters had never agreed with him.

"Why would 'e do that?" the young sailor asked.

"To prevent prying eyes from knowing what he wrote in that book," Cobner said. "I've seen Wick do that a number of times. He has always been a crafty one. I taught him everything he knows."

"But 'e left the book for you," Raisho protested.

"Wick didn't know who might try to fetch it," Sharz said. "He told me to care for it until he came for it." He nodded toward Juhg. "Or until he came for it."

Juhg looked at the note, finding the Grandmagister's hand there as well. He read aloud for everyone. "Rest your head, go jump after."

"Go jump after what?" Cobner growled. "Resting your head? That don't make no sense."

No, Juhg thought gloomily, *it doesn't.* He stared at the letter, thinking that perhaps he had missed something.

"And one thing ol' Wick was always about," Cobner went on, "he was about making sense, he was. I remember when I first met him and Brandt gave Wick that Keldarian elf gem puzzle to figure out. Of course, we had no idea it was a puzzle. Just thought it was some interestingly cut gems." The dwarven warrior shook his head. "But Wick, he knowed right away it was a puzzle. Lead us to that wizard's hideout in the cemetery in Hanged Elf's Point."

Looking up from the piece of paper in his hand, Juhg saw that everyone in the room was looking at him as if to ask, *So where are* you *leading us?*

147

9

Code-Breaker

The repast filled the large room with delicious scents. Using the wizard's gold, Teeyar had spent with a vengeance, purchasing fish and chickens, fresh fruits and vegetables, and spices.

During the hour and a half after she'd gotten home, Teeyar had put the chickens in the stovepipe oven with loaves of fresh bread—pickleberry and tomato basil with a green persimmon glaze—fried the fish, made two casseroles with the vegetables that she breaded with crushed walnuts, and made six pies. Raisho and Jassamyn had volunteered their services, adding a few things of their own, while Nyia got out the good plates.

Craugh and Sharz had smoked their pipes near the fireplace and talked, getting to know each other and sharing stories about the Grandmagister. Cobner, without being obvious about it, kept watch over the building with frequent trips to the windows till it got dark. Then he took to rambling downstairs to the darkened shop and stayed away from the windows where he could easily be seen by someone keeping watch from outside.

So far, there had been no indication that the men

Aldhran Khempus had left behind in the Garment District had any idea where they were.

Seated at Sharz's personal work table, with all the small containers of beads safely out of the way, Juhg worked on the journal the Grandmagister had left behind. One thing he did know, the number in the upper right hand corner of the first page—3/5—indicated that four other copies of the book existed, all of them exact duplicates. The numbering sequence was one used by the Librarians at the Vault of All Known Knowledge for generations to indicate what copy a book was of how many.

With four others in existence, Juhg had to wonder what happened to them. And who might have possession of them. The thought wasn't pleasant and he fretted over it.

He read the message on the piece of paper several times, and had finally started to believe that it was merely a note the Grandmagister had made for himself.

But why such a strange note? Why would the Grandmagister feel the need to remind himself to rest his head? When they were on the mainland, they rested whenever they felt the need when they were in a safe place. There was no need to remind himself to do that. Their adventures along the mainland had always been fraught with peril.

Grandmagister, Juhg thought wearily, *why did you send me here? My place was on* One-Eyed Peggie. *At least there I could have tried to help you.*

Every now and again, Juhg looked up and saw Craugh puffing contentedly on his pipe, still absently stroking the cat in his lap. A few times, Juhg had caught the wizard staring at him. He felt like Craugh was weighing and measuring him.

Or did he have something more sinister in mind?

On those occasions, a cold breeze blew up Juhg's back that the warmth of the fireplace couldn't take away. He remembered how Craugh had fought in the alley, but all of their lives had been on the line then.

Rest your head, go jump after.

The words on the paper held a cadence to them that niggled at something at the back of Juhg's mind. Every time he reached for it, though, the stray thought scurried away like a mouse scared of its own shadow. There was something . . . something about the cadence. He could almost hear the Grandmagister's voice. He closed his eyes, stopped breathing, and reached for it—

mel odom

"It's time to eat," Teeyar called, sounding tired but happy.

Gone. Juhg released his pent-up breath, feeling strangled by frustration.

"I'm sorry," Teeyar apologized. "Did I wake you?"

"No," Juhg replied, hoping to keep his frustration from his voice. "I've got a small headache."

"I've got some healing powders you can use if you like."

"Thank you," Juhg said graciously. "Perhaps I will."

Nyia took great pride in showing everyone to their chairs around the table. Even though the table had an addition and two drop leaves, seating seven adults and a child around it was difficult. Raisho and Sharz had brought chairs up from the shop.

"Teeyar, you set a magnificent table," Craugh boomed as they took their places after Sharz's wife had called them to sup.

"Thank you, Master Craugh." Teeyar blushed a little. She quickly filled bowls with chowder from the big pot hanging above the fire in the fireplace.

Try as he might, and with all the delicious smells tickling his nose, Juhg couldn't find much of an appetite. He ate the chowder and mopped it up with a piece of pickleberry bread, and he took his time about that.

Raisho and Cobner dug in with gusto, putting away slabs of pecan-covered fish and honey-glazed chicken with melon dressing. The vegetable casseroles and mushrooms sautéed in lemon butter fell victim as well. All of it led up to firepear pie slathered in fresh cream that Teeyar had whipped and left to sit on the ice-filled box that kept the vegetables crisp. With the fast ships coming down from the north, ice was a delicacy that Imarish was wealthy enough to afford. There were also a rhubarb pie, pecan pie, peach pie, blackberry pie, and even a salty sweet spoon-cactus pie made from the exotic meat of the sea cacti that drifted in from the open ocean.

But even after all the damage the dwarven warrior and the young sailor could do, Craugh outdid them all. When Cobner was loosening his belt and Raisho was leaning back in his chair to make room, the wizard sat hunched over and drank hot tea as if he had plenty of room to spare and no discomfort at all.

Nyia was in awe of how much they could eat, and her mother shushed her, embarrassed at her daughter's incorrigible nature.

"You think I eat a lot, do you?" Craugh asked the little girl. He sat with his pointed hat on the chair back behind him.

"You eat a *lot,*" Nyia told him. Her eyes rounded with amazement.

Craugh poked his fork at her. "I believe I've yet room for a morsel or two. Tell me, are you tender?"

The little girl squealed in delight and hid in her mother's embrace in mock fright. Everyone at the table laughed at Nyia's antics.

Except Juhg. He couldn't forget how easily Craugh had slain Methoss and turned Ladamae to salt. And he couldn't forget all the atrocities the wizard said he'd committed while looking for *The Book of Time.*

"Is nothing to your liking, Master Juhg?" Teeyar asked, looking at the dweller's nearly untouched plate.

"Forgive me," Juhg said. "Your table is fine. It's my stomach and my head that are off." He excused himself and left the table.

Rest your head, go jump after.

The cadence contained in those words rolled sickeningly through Juhg's head, like a tillerless ship caught out on the open sea during a sudden summer squall. His head ached in pain for real now.

He sat at Sharz's table and continued working by the light of a single candle. Smoke from the candle kept drawing to him, burning his nostrils and his eyes. He turned page after page in the book, thinking he might somehow break the code. He'd done that before, transcribing secret political books whose authors had died a thousand years and more ago. All the ambitions and betrayals lay moldering in the ground, but the secrets had survived.

Usually, one of the first things a code-breaker looked for were repeated single-letter words. Such as *a* or *I.* When those were located, then two-letter and three-letter words were sought out. Such as *to* or *too,* or *an* and *and* and *the.* After those words were deciphered, the others came faster. Those words often unlocked single-letter, double-letter, or even more-letter exchanges.

But the Grandmagister's journal wasn't giving up its secrets.

He forced himself up from the table. His back and legs ached, but only a little of that discomfort was from the battle earlier in the day. Most of it came from sitting for hours at the work table poring over the book.

At the tiny kitchen, he helped himself to another cup of cold tea. He was down to the dregs now and he knew he couldn't go much longer with what he had.

mel odom

The others had all gone to bed. Craugh, Raisho, and Cobner all slept downstairs in Sharz's shop on cots and tables. All of them were used to mean ways. Nyia slept with her parents so that Jassamyn could have a room to herself.

Juhg walked to the nearest window and peered out. He made sure he never stood in the line of the candle so he could be silhouetted against the window.

Most of the Garment District was to bed. Only the mills and the looms worked throughout the night. The creaking of the waterwheels echoed through the silent darkness. Here and there, groups of men walked the cobblestoned streets to jobs.

The island city was unlike so many places Juhg had been. In the south, the goblinkin ruled, gathering in ever-increasing numbers, pushing their boundaries northward again. In the far north, the ice crept over the small pockets of civilization that fought winter itself for survival. Between, villages of humans and dwarves plied the sea or carved an existence from the land, elves roamed the forests, and here and there small towns of dwellers sprang up, all of them still wearing fresh scars from the goblinkin slavers they'd escaped.

Nowhere else was like Imarish, with all its promise and prosperity. Despite the jealousy the other places had, most of them wished to be Imarish.

But the goblinkin are building bridges out there, aren't they? Going to crawl right over the sea and gobble up the islands one by one.

Juhg sighed. Nothing was going to matter. Not in the end. The Vault of All Known Knowledge was destroyed and the books were lost. At least, most of them were lost. And those living at Greydawn Moors would like nothing more than to go back to being lost from the rest of the world.

"You're going to make yourself sick if you keep this up."

Startled by Jassamyn's voice, Juhg almost jumped out of his skin. He whirled around, feeling his heart thudding in his chest.

"Sorry," she said, but she didn't look like she meant that as she leaned in the doorway of the small bedroom she'd been given. She wore her breeches and blouse, but had doffed her leather armor. Her bronze hair hung to her shoulders. The glow from the candle turned her skin to warm butter.

"I thought everyone was asleep," Juhg said.

"I was. I'm a light sleeper when I'm not in my mother's kingdom. You were up moving around."

"I didn't think that I would wake anyone."

Jassamyn shrugged. "You move well. Not heavy-footed. Probably most people wouldn't hear you moving around. But I'll bet Cobner has. And maybe Craugh as well, though I don't know how anyone could eat as much as he could and not lapse into a life-threatening coma." She smiled.

On another night, Juhg thought he might have found humor in the comment. But it wasn't there tonight.

"You're in a sour mood," Jassamyn commented.

Juhg didn't bother to try to deny it. Over the years he'd gotten to know Jassamyn well. For a time he'd even been jealous of the Grandmagister's attention to her. Jassamyn was an excellent student, but she wanted to learn about the world as well, more than could be learned from flipping through pages in musty books.

She'd traveled to Greydawn Moors and spent a month at the Vault of All Known Knowledge. At the end of that time, she and the Grandmagister were each frustrated with the other.

Juhg returned to the work table and sat. The candle smoke stubbornly insisted on following him.

Jassamyn pulled up a chair and sat on the other side of the table. She touched the candle and spoke a word that Juhg didn't understand. Abruptly, the candle smoke threaded in a lazy spiral to the ceiling and stayed away from him.

"A spell?" Juhg asked, surprised.

Smiling, Jassamyn said, "I'm learning new things. That's one thing you and I have in common, Juhg. Both of us like to learn new things."

"Is that what brought you here?"

"Wick's summons brought me here. Or rather, my friendship with him did." Jassamyn leaned back in the chair. At her mother's courts in front of elven nobility she would have never gotten away with such relaxed posture. "Besides, I enjoy Imarish. For a time. There are too many people here to suit me. I prefer the openness of the woods."

"I really have to tend to this." Juhg indicated the Grandmagister's journal.

"You can't."

The elven maid's casual dismissal of his skills angered Juhg. "Everyone else seems convinced I can."

"Are you convinced?"

Juhg sighed. It was time to quit fooling himself and the others. "No."

"Good." Jassamyn smiled.

Grudgingly, Juhg turned the opened pages of the journal toward her and moved the candle so that she might see it better.

Jassamyn didn't even glance at the pages. She shook her head. "That was not meant for me."

"But I thought you—"

She turned the journal back to him. "Juhg, listen to me. I am Wick's friend. I am your friend, too. We've shared good times and horrible times with each other chasing after one of Wick's missions. But he would never leave something like this for me. After all the years he's shared with Craugh, Wick wouldn't have left this book for him either. That's why Craugh hasn't demanded to look at the book himself." She tapped the journal. "This was meant for you. This is only part of what Wick intended for you to find when you got here."

Juhg ran his hands through his hair. "I can't decode it," he whispered. "I've tried. None of it makes any sense."

"It will all make sense," she replied. "I can't imagine Wick ever doing anything that doesn't make sense." She paused and studied him. "Your mind just isn't clear, that's all. You're overtired and you're overworried. Wick always taught me that when I was in such shape I could never be at my best."

"I can't sleep."

Jassamyn flicked his tea cup with her finger. "Not if you keep drinking tea."

Juhg blew out his breath and folded his arms. "You're not making this any easier."

"I know. I'm sorry." Jassamyn looked apologetic. "How bad was it in Greydawn Moors?"

Images flipped through Juhg's head with painful intensity. "It was horrible. The streets of the city were littered with dead. During the four days it took for *Windchaser* to get repaired enough that she could get underway, Raisho said they gathered dead in from the harbor. Some still washed in with the tide the day he left Greydawn Moors."

"I can't imagine it."

Juhg nodded. "I can't forget it."

"Some things should not be forgotten."

"I can't forget that the Grandmagister is somewhere out there in enemy hands," Juhg whispered.

"He's where he wanted to be. For whatever reason."

"You didn't know he was going to do this?"

"No. Cobner and I were told that he would be here. We arrived three days ago. We were also told that you might be with him."

"And Craugh? Was he supposed to be here as well?"

Jassamyn frowned. "No mention was made of Craugh accompanying him."

Why was that? Juhg wondered.

"Craugh didn't always come with Wick," Jassamyn said. "You know that. Why do the two of you have tension between you?"

"There's no tension," Juhg lied, and knew immediately that his effort had been poor and unsuccessful.

"Perhaps you'd like to try that one again," Jassamyn suggested. "I knew there was trouble immediately when Craugh didn't try to take the journal from you or start griping at you to figure out the riddle."

"We're having . . . problems."

"Well, get them sorted out. We're going to need all of us to be at our best to do whatever Wick has outlined in that book that must be done."

If the book can be decoded, Juhg thought.

154

She must have seen the doubt on his face. "You're forgetting one thing, Juhg. That book wasn't written for anyone else to understand. Whatever Wick has written in there, he wouldn't have needed a book. He would have remembered whatever he wrote. He made the book for you. No matter what else is going on in your mind, know that and trust it."

Juhg ran his hands over the book. He knew the paper and the binding, knew how all the stitches were put into place to hold it together. He had learned to make books with the Grandmagister.

"It will come," Jassamyn said. "In the meantime, you need to get some rest." She pushed up from the table. "I'll see you in the morning."

Juhg thanked her for her company and her kind words, and stared at the book a while longer.

"She's right, ye know. Ye ain't got much done tonight, an' ye're gonna get even less done tomorrow because ye don't know when to give it up an' rest. Ye're only flesh and blood."

Turning toward Raisho's voice, Juhg spotted the young sailor hunkered down in the shadows of the stairs. His cutlass rested across his knees.

"Is everyone up?" Juhg protested.

"Enough of us," Cobner growled from below. "If you can't sleep for yourself, sleep for us."

"She's a smart girl, that one," Raisho said. "Smart and pretty." His grin split the night.

Giving up, Juhg blew out the candle. Darkness plunged into the room, filling the space held by the candle flame instantly. He took up the blanket Teeyar had left for him, then crawled onto the pallet on the floor.

For a time, he lay on his back and stared up at the ceiling. His mind wouldn't stop buzzing. Dozens or hundreds of code-breaking tactics screamed through his thoughts. None of them were new to him that night. He'd tried everything he could think of. The Grandmagister's code was elaborate. How had the Grandmagister expected him to be able to decipher it?

Juhg didn't remember going to sleep, but he knew he must have because he recognized the dream. Part of him knew that he lay still on the pallet in Sharz's home, but he felt the gauzelike pull of the dream, like taffy stretching finally under its own weight. Having no strength to fight, he went with the dream that tugged him back into memory.

He and the Grandmagister rested, panting from their long run, in the Forest of Fangs and Shadows, only just come from the goblinkin mines that the Grandmagister had freed Juhg from after slipping his own chains. Traveling with Brandt had taught the Grandmagister the art of picking locks. The master thief made it a habit never to travel with lockpicks and other canny devices because a life of taking from others, especially those who could afford guards and clever traps, usually led to narrow escapes.

The Grandmagister had taken time to free the other dweller slaves in the tunnel he and Juhg had been assigned to. Most of the other dweller slaves had scattered in all directions, knowing the goblinkin followed with their fierce hunting lizards to sniff them from hiding.

The Grandmagister had coated Juhg in stinkweed so strongly that he could barely stand the smell of himself. With a few indigenous plants gathered along the way while they ran for their freedom and perhaps even their lives, the Grandmagister had made up a healing salve that made the sores around Juhg's wrists and ankles instantly feel better.

"How do you know so much?" Juhg had asked, feeling the cooling balm of the healing salve. He hadn't really expected an answer and didn't know much about the Grandmagister at the time. Back in the mines, though, the Grandmagister had been the only one who hadn't seemed distraught and near to giving up all hope. Somehow the Grandmagister had quietly waited till an opportune moment for the escape.

Juhg still hadn't known why he'd charged after the Grandmagister, other than the fact that the Grandmagister had been the only dweller who seemed to have a plan for getting away from the mines. And there was the fact that the Grandmagister had waited until he could free everyone in that tunnel instead of merely seeing to his own freedom.

"I know so much because I take the time to learn," the Grandmagister had answered. "I make a conscious effort to look past my own needs of the moment and learn what I can of anything. You never know what you truly need in your life. I've found it's often best to be prepared for anything you might envision." He'd grinned a little then, but the fear never left his eyes. The goblinkin lizards had screamed in the distance, challenging the night and looking forward to the task their loutish masters had set them to. "After everything I've seen, everything I've done, I can imagine quite a lot."

The dream had flashed forward then, moving ahead weeks after the escape from the mines. The Grandmagister had pursued the legend of an article that had turned out to be one of the forty-seven accounts of the Ruhrmish dwarves that had specialized in making iron boats along the Smoking Marshes to battle the goblinkin there for the iron mines. The account of their struggles had been hammered into a set of multifaceted iron balls that interlocked to give the whole story.

During the intervening time, Juhg had seen the Grandmagister drawing and writing in his journal. At first the Grandmagister had been reluctant about admitting what he was doing, pretending that he was an artist and nothing more. But Juhg hadn't been fooled. There had been too much similarity between the marks on the pages that hadn't been devoted to sketches. He'd recognized it as a pattern of some sort, and the shapes had called out to his naturally inquisitive mind.

When they had rested, Juhg had drawn some of the letters from memory on a bare patch of ground, not knowing what the letters were, but knowing they were important. He'd sought understanding of the letters by taking them into himself, thinking that pushing the letters from his mind and through his own hand might offer further elucidation.

Upon seeing the letters drawn crudely on the ground, the Grandmagister had quickly shuffled his feet over them to obliterate them. A look of true fear had tightened his face. Juhg had felt at once humbled, knowing he was working with something truly beyond his ken.

"Don't ever do that where someone can see you," the Grandmagister had whispered hoarsely.

Juhg had felt ashamed. He had still been young in those days, hardly more than a child even after years spent in the goblinkin mines. The Grandmagister's words of remonstration had scored him terribly.

After seeing the effect of his quick words, the Grandmagister had relented. Several hours later, he had revealed the truth to Juhg, stating that he was a First Level Librarian at the Vault of All Known Knowledge. Over the next few days, he had taught Juhg the letters of the language shared by most of the people, what he referred to as the common tongue, stating that many other diverse languages had existed before Lord Kharrion and the Cataclysm. The Grandmagister was conversant in most of them and was working to learn the others.

At first, Juhg had been afraid. Books and writing were to be avoided. Only wizards worked with that knowledge because they sought power they could control, and even they were plagued by goblinkin when they were discovered. All the dwellers knew that only bad things could happen if books and writing were involved. Thinking about a whole building full of books on an island somewhere out in a treacherous sea was unimaginable.

Then, a few days later, once he'd mastered all the alphabet, the Grandmagister had brought the journal to Juhg and shown him a brief line of writing. He'd patiently waited while Juhg had sounded the two words out, praising him for so quickly learning all that he had been taught, telling him that he'd never taught a grown dweller who had learned so fast before. The truth, of course, was that the Grandmagister had *never* taught a grown dweller before because on Greydawn Moors every dweller was taught to read as a child.

Finally, after a torturous session, Juhg had sounded the two words out. "Dearest Juhg," he read in a hesitant voice.

"Yes," the Grandmagister had responded. "Dearest Juhg. That's exactly right. Now, whenever I write you a note, I will always address you as 'Dearest Juhg.'"

In the time since those dark and fear-filled days fleeing for their lives, the Grandmagister had always addressed personal notes to Juhg in such a manner.

When Juhg opened his eyes again, it was early morning. Pale pink sunlight poured into the room through the eastern window.

Teeyar was making corncakes on the griddle and the sweet smell of the thick batter filled the large room. Nyia and Jassamyn helped her prepare breakfast, giggling and playing as they squeezed barbtail plums for morning juice. Craugh was already up, talking in a quiet voice with Sharz. Cobner stood post at the windows, ever watchful. Only Raisho was missing, and Juhg knew from his past association with the young sailor that Raisho only roused early morn when there was food or work or adventuring to do.

Keeping himself wrapped in the blanket he'd slept with against the chill of morning, Juhg stumbled over to the work table and sat. He took the Grandmagister's mysterious journal from his jacket pocket and opened it with fumbling hands. He knew he should have waited to wake up better before attempting the decoding, but he was too excited.

Now, whenever I write you a note, I will always address you as "Dearest Juhg."

Uncapping his inkwell, Juhg took up a fresh quill. He didn't question what he was doing, going with the instinct and with years of friendship with the Grandmagister.

Dearest Juhg.

He started with that.

"Apprentice," Craugh said softly.

Only then did Juhg realize the room had fallen silent in expectation. He hoped that he didn't let anyone down. His heart leapt when he found the letters were there.

Craugh got up from his chair by the fire and crossed the room.

Even though he didn't completely trust the wizard, Juhg didn't try to hide his work from him. The note was only the key. Even with the incomprehensible message deciphered, Craugh could not figure out the content of the book. The Grandmagister had left that for him to do.

"Do you have it then?" Craugh asked.

"I believe so," Juhg said. He looked up at Jassamyn, who held Nyia on one of her hips and gazed at him with congratulatory amusement. "You were right, Jassamyn."

"I was?" The elven maid raised an inquisitive eyebrow.

"You were. The Grandmagister left this message entirely for me." Juhg's wits and his quill gained speed. "On the surface, the message appears complete, but it is a hidden message."

"A clue?" Craugh asked. His interest grew. Wizards were curious people, almost as curious as dwellers.

"A clue made up of all its parts." Juhg wrote *Dearest Juhg* on a clean piece of paper under *Rest your head, go jump after*.

" '*Dearest Juhg,*' " Craugh read aloud.

"The Grandmagister always addressed me that way in any personal correspondence," Juhg said. "When it came to Library business, he addressed me by my title. First or Second or Third Librarian. Even Novice, but generally the notes at that level were always personal."

Working swiftly and carefully, Juhg marked through the letters in the mysterious message that made up the personal address.

R̶e̶s̶t̶ ̶y̶o̶u̶r̶ ̶h̶e̶a̶d̶, ̶g̶o̶ ̶j̶ump after.

That used up all the letters that made up *Dearest Juhg*. Being right about that much left him feeling hopeful, but those hopes were quickly dashed.

He was left with the letters R Y O O U M P A F T E R. He stared at them, but none of them made any sense. Frustration began creeping back in at him. He still didn't know what to do or what the message was supposed to be. He still had the word *after,* but that couldn't be what it was supposed to be, could it?

"What's wrong?" Craugh asked.

Juhg sighed. "I'm stumped."

"Nonsense. I think you're on to something, apprentice," the wizard stated. "You've made a good start and cut nearly half the letters."

After a long moment of staring at them, Juhg shook his head. "What is left makes no sense, Craugh." His mind ached with the impossibility he faced. "I'm just not as clever as the Grandmagister thought."

"No!" Craugh's voice swelled to feel the small room. Nyia darted in close to Jassamyn, hugging her tightly.

Fearful, Juhg looked into the wizard's hard green eyes. Emerald sparks swirled around the head of his staff. For a moment Juhg felt certain he'd hit the floor on webbed feet and covered with warts before his next heartbeat.

"Don't you dare underestimate your master, apprentice," Craugh thundered. "Not even by thinking that Wick somehow overestimated you. If anything, he underestimated your abilities and your vision."

"But I don't understand," Juhg whispered. He hadn't intended to whisper, but facing the wizard's wrath seemed to turn his throat to dry stone.

"You must." Craugh looked deeply into his eyes. "Wick would not have set this task before you if he had not thought you could accomplish it. Nor would he have allowed himself to be taken captive by Aldhran Khempus. Sacrifice doesn't come easily to a dweller. It's not supposed to." Craugh smiled, but the effort was coldly cruel. "But cleverness? Now there's something that a dweller embraces completely. Wick believed he was being clever in everything that he did. I'm convinced that some bit of cleverness is at the heart of everything we're doing here."

Juhg looked back at the incomprehensible line of letters. He was truly afraid that if he failed he would live out the rest of his life as a toad.

"Apprentice," Craugh said in a softer tone, "your master has put something before you—a task—that he fully believed you could perform. With the stakes that are against us, I know it's no easy task, but it can be done. You've come this far."

"Don't you see, Craugh? Even this can be wrong." At that moment, Juhg felt certain that the guess he'd made was wrong. It couldn't be right. Not if he was left with the letters that mocked him on the page.

Gracefully, the wizard sat across from Juhg. He maintained a steadfast gaze. "This isn't beyond your reach. Think about the letters that are left. Wick would have wanted to leave you a message that you would understand."

"I see the word *after,* but that is no help."

"That's a false word. The true meaning is still disguised. Look through that façade."

Juhg looked at the letters. Hot tears burned at the back of his eyes. *Why had the Grandmagister left such a message?* "The Grandmagister can't have known that I would even be alive at this point."

"He couldn't have thought you would be dead, apprentice," Craugh said softly. "He would never allow himself to think anything like that." The wizard tapped the paper. "This was prepared in the event of his death. He faced implacable enemies and he knew that."

He might even be dead now. Juhg didn't want that thought to enter his head, but now that it did, he couldn't get past it.

"Wick would have named something in there," Craugh went on. "Something that would have carried volumes of meaning for you. A reference to something else that you both would have known."

Juhg stared at the letters but nothing came.

"What about the word *book*?" Craugh asked. "Is it in there?"

"There is no *b*, no *k*," Juhg replied.

"Perhaps another language that spells book."

Juhg turned the letters around in his mind, sifting through the dozens of written languages he knew. Nothing. Nothing. Nothingnothingnothing-*nothing!*

"No. It's not there," he said.

"Another word then," Craugh persisted. "If not a book, then a tale, perhaps. A story. A monograph. A diatribe."

"Not in another language," Jassamyn said. "Wick is clever, but he liked to keep things simple. The more simple the bit of cleverness, the stronger the impact when the trick was revealed." She approached the work table. "He wouldn't have changed languages. But I think Craugh is correct, Juhg. I think you're looking for a body of work, perhaps an author's name, that would make a connection for you."

Frenzied now, feeling that he was near to bursting, Juhg studied the letters, moving them around in his mind, seeking words. By the Old Ones, he'd never really paid attention to how many words were his to lay claim to—even when he limited himself just to the common tongue. Then he saw it, and he couldn't believe that he hadn't seen it before.

He marked through the letters.

R Y Θ O U ̶M̶ ̶P̶ A F T E̶ R

Feeling more inspired, he wrote the new word down. *Poem.*

"A poem?" Craugh asked.

"Yes," Juhg said. "It has to be. You were right, Craugh. And Jassamyn must be right as well. The Grandmagister had to have left the name of a poem that I would remember."

"How many poems do you know?" the wizard asked.

"Thousands," Juhg answered. "And bits and pieces of thousands more."

"Then it'll be like searching for a grain of sand on an ocean beach," Cobnor grumbled. "No telling how long that will take."

"No," Craugh said. "Don't think that the task is impossible or even near to it. The poem Wick will have left will have double meaning, apprentice. It will serve as both the key to the coded journal and to some special occurrence between the two of you. What poem did you have in common?"

"Several," Juhg answered, trying not to give in to the knot of apprehension swelling within his belly. "Many of them are mnemonics designed to remember tables and charts and bodies of work."

"Then it won't be that," Craugh said. "Something simpler."

R   Y   O   U   A   F   T   R

Suddenly, the letters moved in Juhg's mind though they didn't move on the page. The answer was suddenly clear as Sambaanian crystal, and it was as simple as Craugh had suggested. The quill in his hand moved almost of its own volition.

F   O   R   T   Y   U   A   R

Juhg leaned back in his chair, trembling with relief.

"Fort Yuar?" Craugh read. The dark scowl on his face made it clear that he didn't understand the reference.

" 'Fort Yuar' is a dwarvish poem." Cobner grimaced. "Though you'll find no true-blooded dwarf that will term it so. What it actually is, it's a war song of the Ruhrmash dwarves of the Smoking Marshes." After being introduced to the Grandmagister and all the knowledge that the Grandmagister had known, the warrior had become something of a romantic when it came to dwarven histories. "They built iron ships and fought the goblinkin of the Smoking Marshes for the iron mines they needed to survive. They won, too. Until Lord Kharrion rose up and triggered the Cataclysm. I've been through there with the Grandmagister, and a few times later on my own. Those iron ships still sit at the bottom of the marshes. Few know about them."

"Why is that poem important?" Craugh asked.

Juhg smiled. "It was the first piece that the Grandmagister taught me. We were running from goblinkin after he freed me from the mines. I had caught him at his journal and he had given in and told me what he really was, and told me all about Greydawn Moors. When we came upon the Smoking Marshes, I was bitten by a thorn adder." Memory filled his head and he relived those days for a moment. "I thought I was going to die. I begged the Grandmagister to leave me because the goblinkin were all around us. I knew if they found us they would kill me out of hand rather than try to nurse me back to health, and the Grandmagister would be hauled back to the mines where he would not find a second escape so easily."

"But he didn't do that, did he?" Jassamyn asked, smiling.

"No."

"It's not in Wick's nature to desert a friend."

"Sometimes," Craugh said, "I think that the better part of a dweller's survival skills missed him."

"He's a warrior at heart, he is," Cobner affirmed. "I taught him everything he knows."

"I lay near to death," Juhg said, "burning up with fever, and the Grandmagister promised me he would teach me to write if I would follow him home to Greydawn Moors." He swallowed hard at the memory. "I had no home of my own. I don't know what would have happened to me if he hadn't taken me in."

"You would have died, of course," Cobner growled. "You weren't ready to take care of yourself."

"During my recovery, the Grandmagister taught me to recite 'Fort Yuar,' and to write it in his journal, and the history of the Ruhrmash dwarves' battles against the goblinkin. The poem was the first thing I ever wrote."

"But how does that help you with the journal Wick left?" Craugh asked. "It's still encoded."

Feeling slightly ebullient, Juhg opened the journal. "The poem detailing the victories of Fort Yuar holds a particular resonance and cadence. Knowing the code the Grandmagister used it is much easier to decipher. I can eliminate most of what's written in the journal because it's gibberish, just there to confuse the uninitiated. I'll recopy the journal using the cadence of the poem and do the translation from that."

Craugh nodded. "How soon, apprentice?"

"Soon," Juhg promised, and he eagerly got started.

10

The Drowned City

From the journal of Edgewick Lamplighter, current Grandmagister of the Vault of All Known Knowledge—"

Dearest Juhg,

See, I will always address you in such a manner for personal correspondence!

Salutations and my blessings.

Juhg's throat tightened a little as he read his transcription of the coded journal. He hurried on and hoped that no one else noticed.

They all sat around him in the small upstairs living room of Sharz's bead shop. Little Nyia sat on Jassamyn's knee and partially drowsed after the big breakfast her mother had prepared.

If you're reading this, then it means that I am not with you and we are separated by circumstances beyond our control. Not that I expect much control in this situation. I had planned to be with you, of course, because I wouldn't want you involved in the dangerous endeavor on your own. Alas, I've often found in my life as Grandmagister—and before!—that things all too often fall outside my ability to plan.

I have instructed Sharz to deliver this book into your hands or my own.

And not Craugh's? Juhg wondered. *Why was he excluded?* He stumbled a little while he was reading as the thought occurred to him, but he thought that the audience he read to would think only that he'd been overcome by emotion.

We're at a point when so many secrets are about to spill out. You've heard of The Book of Time. *I know that you have. I've mentioned it to you on occasion and I know that you seldom forget anything I've told you.*

So many people think that the book is only a myth. Who could possibly organize time, after all? But the book is real. I have read about it for these past months, and I've wanted to talk to you at length about everything I've discovered. Unfortunately, you seem to be caught up in your own life at the moment.

Juhg, I know you sometimes feel guilty about living when your parents did not. Thaskale wrote a number of works about "survivor's guilt" that I would like to recommend to you.

 166

The Grandmagister had, Juhg remembered, but he'd always found projects that kept him too busy to read most of them. Instead, he'd just drawn further into himself and begun preparing his departure from the Library to attempt a life as a merchant with Raisho aboard *Windchaser*.

I don't know your pain, of course. That would be egotistical and rude and presumptuous of me to even suggest that I do. But I've dealt with pains of my own. Over the years, I've lost a great many friends who have been with me through fierce adventures.

Captain Farok dying in my arms, so small and frail and afraid, after I had been terrified of him when he'd been One-Eyed Peggie's *master, stays with me. I miss Brandt fiercely as well, though his death was calm and peaceful because he was taken away by years and not by violence. So many, by the Old Ones, there have been so many that I have lost through the ages.*

Ah, and listen to me prattle across these pages like we had all the time in the world for this discourse. We don't, of course, because all the time in the world is exactly what we are after.

That is what our enemies are after, too. After all, The Book of Time, *is the single most powerful thing in existence, and—for the time at least—it is in our world and accessible to those who would use it for good and those who would use it for evil or simply their own power.*

Juhg couldn't help but glance at Craugh. Bright interest stirred in the wizard's green eyes.

I have found The Book of Time, *Juhg. Or rather, I have found where I believe it to be. All that reading I have done here in the Library has led me to it.*

Surprisingly, it was legends I encountered while indulging in the guilty pleasures of Hralbomm's Wing that turned the key. Perhaps, if previous Grandmagisters—or even Librarians, for that matter—had indulged in those selfsame guilty pleasures, The Book of Time *would have been found much sooner.*

I don't know.

Perhaps, as has been suggested in those legends that I read, The Book of Time *chooses its own moment of discovery. I admit that I am uncomfortable with that thought. But, if one were to believe—as Zakoth proclaimed to in his treatise* Time Shall Move Your Cheese—*that everything that ever was, ever is, and ever will be is written in* The Book of Time, *then perhaps the book even holds record of its discovery and the discoverer.*

I want to see it. I am so curious.

Can you even guess what it must be like, Juhg, to know everything? *I can't wait. Truly, I can't.*

However, the date of my death—especially the happenstance of it—is something I'd rather not know. Particularly if that death is violent or gruesome.

It strikes me that perhaps I am already dead as you read this. I hope not. For your sake. But probably more for my sake. I would hate to miss out on the best book that has been written, is being written, and will be written. I'm not exactly sure how that works out.

If I am, then read it over my grave to me. (Surely I will have a grave. I am Grandmagister, after all. Hmmm. Unless one of the monsters of the Blood-Soaked Sea or another like it has gulped me down while I was not looking. I do try to look. Cobner has always and forever been after me to be aware of where I am at all times.)

"That I have," Cobner commented. "He has the right of that. And he's gotten better, he has. Much, much better."

As I have been led to believe, the narrative and Juhg continued, *before the rise of Lord Kharrion and the time of the Cataclysm,* The Book of Time *entered our world from a place simply referred to as the In-Betweenness.*

I found the account in Hralbomm's Wing, as I has said, in a romance called Cockleburr's Beastiary and Other Tales. *Cockleburr was a traveling thief pre-Cataclysm who made money stealing as well as writing. He specialized in fictional accounts of monsters he'd met and outwitted. They were grand tales, too. I heartily recommend them because Cockleburr had an acerbic sense of humor that I found to be a delight.*

There was one story in the collection, though, that Cockleburr insisted was a true tale, not one he'd created of whole cloth or embellished mightily upon. During one of his adventures near Hargis's Crossing, that meeting place of oceans far to the South, Cockleburr had chanced upon a bearded hoar-worm that had claimed it had once been a human wizard named Methoss.

The hoar-worm insisted that—as a human—he had traveled to the In-Betweenness, confronted the Gatekeeper of Time, and helped steal The Book of Time. *The creature had gone on to claim that he had even helped kill—or attempt to kill—Lord Kharrion.*

The mention of Lord Kharrion was a conundrum, I tell you. Purely coincidence, I thought. For Cockleburr's account was written nearly nine hundred years before Lord Kharrion rose to prominence among the goblinkin tribes and began the Cataclysm.

Curious, naturally, because I know of no other mention of Lord Kharrion's name outside of the Goblin Lord, I researched the name Methoss, which is also not in much use. Certainly not in the time Cockleburr wrote of. Then I found out why.

As it turns out, Methoss was one of a group of bloodthirsty and power-mongering villains that ran rampant along the mainland. I read about those people, Juhg. They are the reason that children are no longer named Methoss or Ladamae or Zorrocks or Pean or Ybarris. There are other names, but there's no need to list them here.

The atrocities they committed will live in history forever. Some of them killed each other. Others, according to Methoss, were lost in the In-Betweenness. A few more simply vanished from record. I can only hope that they met with the harsh ending they all deserved and did not live out their lives in comfort and peace.

Across the room, Craugh pushed the cat from his lap and stood as if wanting to stretch. But he walked away from the others, stopping at the window to peer out.

Juhg alone knew how much the Grandmagister's words had to have hurt the wizard. For a moment, looking at Craugh's back and seeing the slump of his shoulders, Juhg's heart went out to Craugh.

The Grandmagister loved the wizard like a brother. They were close. But Craugh had managed to keep his other life from the Grandmagister. For the first time, Juhg had to wonder at the cost of that secrecy.

Was that why you were so often gone from the Grandmagister's side, Craugh? Because you felt ashamed? The Grandmagister is so good, so willing to share and to give of whatever he has. And you—you were a taker, a bandit, a thief, and a murderer. How did you think the Grandmagister would feel when he found out your secrets?

169

"Juhg," Jassamyn said, calling attention to the uncomfortable silence that had strung out.

"Sorry." Juhg reached for a glass of wine. "Parched throat. Didn't get much sleep last night." He sipped, then resumed the reading, conscious that Craugh never turned around to face them, to offer a conjecture, or to acknowledge them in any way.

My investigation has led me to believe that The Book of Time *was lost here in this world, separated into four pieces, four distinct divisions of Time itself.*

I can't help but wonder at that. Cockleburr's book, though he didn't know it at the time because—even though he traveled extensively—he

didn't travel the world over, was not complete. Methoss told him that—
while he was still a human wizard—he and the group of—

Here the Grandmagister broke off into a rather uncomplimentary description of Methoss and his companions. The vilification was quite uncommon for the Grandmagister.

Juhg choked on the passage and couldn't read it. Even if he couldn't trust Craugh, he couldn't hurt him either.

—he and the group . . . had confronted Kharrion and discovered The
Book of Time *had been divided into four portions, locked into underground vaults among four cities.*

One city was Seadevil's Roost, which was a southern sea empire of humankind.

"I've never 'eard of such a place," Raisho said. "An' I've traveled all along the coastline."

"This would have been a very long time ago," Jassamyn said.

"Pre-Cataclysm," Craugh said. "Actually, it was very near to this place."

Juhg continued with the narrative.

I performed a massive amount of research on my own, the journal continued. *I couldn't justify utilizing any of the Librarians on this task. For all I knew, my quest would turn out to be a wild trilik chase after all, despite the details Cockleburr provided.*

Still, I persevered.

I almost asked you to help me with this task, Juhg, but things between us just weren't . . . right somehow. For the first time, I began to suspect that asking you to do something like this would be an imposition.

Please accept my forgiveness for ever thinking this, but that is the only excuse I can offer. I would not willingly keep you from anything I did that I considered of merit.

Pain shot through Juhg's heart. His hands trembled, shaking the book and making his rapidly written transcription hard to read. *You weren't wrong,* he thought silently.

Both he and Craugh had much to bear from the Grandmagister's open-hearted ways.

I was surprised to learn that Seadevil's Roost, named for those obnoxious flying fish that Jassamyn seems to favor so when we're at sea, had actually existed at one time.

I found a map and set to the task of locating the city. Unfortunately, the city no longer existed. Not as a city, anyway. But I located its ruins.

From what Methoss told Cockleburr, placing the four pieces of The Book of Time *in the underground vaults beneath the cities had detrimental effects on those cities. All of them experienced violent deaths.*

Seadevil's Roost sank into the ocean after a tsunami ripped the sea floor to shreds for miles around it. Lord Kharrion's later attacks destroyed Teldane's Bounty and rendered the Shattered Coast.

In the Smokesmith dwarven community of the Molten Rock Forge, where the Smokesmith dwarves became the most successful armorers of their time, an underground river speared into the heart of the active volcano they used as a natural forge. The magic they used—a seldom seen thing among dwarves—to bind the volcano to their bidding agitated the natural explosiveness of the underground river mixing with the molten lava to the degree that all of them perished when the mountaintop blew. Those once proud mountains tumbled into rubble and became the Smoking Marshes.

By the Old Ones, Juhg, we were so close to one of the secrets back when you and I escaped the goblinkin mine all those years ago! If we had but known!

But we didn't.

And, as it turns out, it was a good thing we didn't know.

The four pieces of The Book of Time *have to be picked up in order. But I'll get to that in a moment.*

The third piece of the book is in the Drylands, at the Oasis of Bleached Bones. Before The Book of Time *destroyed it, the land was once filled with one of the most beautiful forests every warded by the Crown Canopy Elves. They had the tallest trees in the world, a quarter mile tall, by some accounts, and communities safely ensconced among the high branches, hidden away by magic and the camouflage of the leaves and branches they trained to grow in the manner they wished. The city was called Sweetdew, named for the gorgeous flowers that provided the elves drink so that they never had to touch the ground if they didn't wish.*

A horrible wind tore through that forest, climbing up from the bowels of the earth and ripping the trees from the earth and throwing them away for miles. When the wind finished, only bare earth was left for miles in any direction where once that verdant forest grew. Over the years, that place and the places around it became desert. Later, that place became known simply as the Drylands. Methoss believed that the Oasis of Bleached Bones offered a way down into the earth where the piece of The Book of Time *lays hidden.*

I believe the fourth piece is in the hands of the goblinkin somewhere in the Haze Mountains. I am working hard now to ascertain that. As you can plainly see, the next few pages of this journal are intentionally left blank. Other pages follow that detail the histories of the three places I have mentioned, but I am leaving space for whatever I may uncover regarding the location of the fourth piece.

"The Haze Mountains," Cobner rumbled. "Isn't that where Aldhran Khempus is supposed to be taking the Grandmagister?"

"Yes," Craugh said. He turned. With the bright sunshine coming through the window behind him, the shadows of his broad-brimmed had masked his face. "Wick has gone there after the fourth piece of *The Book of Time*."

"Ye think 'e figured out where it was, then?" Raisho asked.

"In the hands of the goblinkin," Craugh said irritably. "Surely the truth of that is as plain as the nose on your face. Wick has gone there in an attempt to abscond with the fourth piece of the book. Aldhran Khempus, with all his blustering, must have intimated to Wick that they had found the fourth piece there."

"That's a stretch, don't you think?" Jassamyn asked.

"Is it?" Craugh demanded. He stamped his staff, sending a shower of glowing emerald sparks dancing toward the floor.

Nyia *oohed* with the colorful display.

"Why else would Wick have allowed himself to be captured by his enemies? Why else would he have *planned* for that eventuality?"

Cobner ran his fingers through his thick gray beard. "It would be masterful strategy planning on his part, it would." He grinned. "In a way, he has 'em right where he wants 'em, doesn't he?"

Juhg held his place in his journal where he'd transcribed the hidden message he'd interpreted from the Grandmagister's journal. "The Grandmagister won't be able to get the fourth piece."

All of them looked at him.

"He mentioned it in the section that I've read to you," Juhg told them. "The four pieces must be gathered in order. First—if it truly is here—the one here. Then the one in the Smoking Marshes, followed by the one in the Drylands. Only then can the fourth piece be found."

"That might not be true."

"It *is* true," Juhg said. "I've read this much to you, but I've read most of the rest of the journal. I haven't quite finished deciphering it. A later section goes back to the story Methoss told Cockleburr." He looked at the wizard. "You remember Methoss, right? The bearded hoar-worm?"

Craugh regarded Juhg in stony silence.

"Methoss tried to get the four pieces of *The Book of Time*. He tried to get the piece from the goblinkin in the Haze Mountains first, then the one in the Drylands. He stated that he'd reached them, had even talked with the Slither there—"

"What Slither?" Jassamyn asked.

"Apparently there is a guardian that protects the four pieces," Juhg answered.

"Who does the Slither serve?"

Juhg shook his head. "The Grandmagister didn't know. Methoss talks about being frustrated by the Slither—"

"The *same* Slither?" Craugh asked.

"Again, the Grandmagister didn't know."

"Did he offer some clue as to the nature of the guardian?"

"No. Either Methoss or Cockleburr wasn't forthcoming with that information. Maybe it was simply lost. Or Cockleburr figured it was just a fanciful tale told by a talking sea monster and didn't give the story much credence." Juhg took a deep breath. "The point is, the Grandmagister believed that the proper order was to start here, then the Smoking Marshes, then the Drylands."

"Saving the Haze Mountains for last?" Cobner asked.

"Yes. As each piece of *The Book of Time* is acquired, it unlocks the others," Juhg said.

"An' 'ow does it do that?" Raisho asked.

"I don't know. According to the Grandmagister's notes, the first piece was given to the humans."

"Why?"

"I don't know. That's part of the mystery he hoped to uncover."

"Mayhap he did already," Cobner said. "Just had no way of telling anyone. Or it's in one of the books back there buried in the rubble of the Vault of All Known Knowledge."

"Why didn't he take the piece of the book here?" Craugh asked.

"He couldn't get to it."

"Where is it?" Jassamyn asked.

"Inside the Drowned City," Juhg said. "At the bottom of Skull Canal."

No one traversed Skull Canal at night if they could help it. Even the breeze seemed to scamper as lightly and as silently as it could across the dark water.

The canal was named for the fact that no fisherman in generations had ever dropped a net into the waters that he didn't draw up a skull or other bones. Usually there were several. Besides that, the sunken city offered too many underwater obstacles to fishing and the long vessels used by the Imarish boatmen.

Juhg sat in the prow of the boat. Jassamyn sat behind him, clad in leather armor and her longbow close to hand. Her small draca prowled the air above them, snatching luckless mosquitoes with its long, snapping tongue. Craugh sat in the middle. Raisho and Cobner manned the short oars that propelled the craft across the smooth water.

On either side of the canal, hints of the destruction that lay underwater ahead of them rode the stony ridges of rocky soil that had survived the tsunami all those years ago. Carrion beasts prowled the dark earth, rats and corpse beetles as long as Juhg's arms. Winged things fluttered through the air and flitted toward the draca then backed away at the last moment, causing the miniature dragonling to hiss at them.

The Garment District was three miles back, through a maze of canals that wended through the islands leading to the center of the city region. The lanterns at fore and aft on the canal boat swung as Cobner and Raisho paddled. With the light shining on it, the water looked black and lifeless. Fish and turtles broke the surface from time to time. Those incidences never failed to send a quaver of fear thrilling through Juhg.

"There's the bridge," Cobner said.

Staring hard through the darkness, Juhg spotted the broken bridge. Perhaps once it had jutted across a wide canal, connecting two islands. Now it was a broken boot of a shape, kicked straight upward with the toe where the bridge had broken off at a pronounced angle.

"Is that it?" Craugh asked.

All of them talked in low voices, aware of how easily sound traveled across flat water.

Juhg consulted the Grandmagister's journal. He hadn't yet had time to copy the maps to his own journal, though he had left blank pages in the proper places for that task. Tilting the book so the page could catch the light of the prow lantern, he consulted the map.

"I think so." Juhg looked around for other landmarks. A huge dome stuck out of the water, looking forty feet across but only a couple feet above the water line. He pointed. "That's on the map near the right bridge."

There were other bridges on either side of the canal. When Skydevil's Roost had first sunk, it hadn't gone completely beneath the sea. Sharz had told them stories of the city's leaders trying to save the palace and the other trade guild buildings where business was conducted.

Dwarven architects had been called in to reconstruct some of the sunken buildings and save as much of them as was possible. For a time the dwarves' efforts had worked. Bridges spanned the waters to the buildings, which were dried out and built on top of. But in the end, the sea floor had opened up again and pulled the new constructions below as well, shattering all the bridges.

"Then this is the place," Craugh said. "Pull the boat over."

A fish broke the surface near the boat and cold water splashed up on Juhg's face. He checked the Grandmagister's journal immediately, reminded at once how fragile paper and ink were. Closing the book, he slipped it back into the waterproof oilskin pouch and secured it inside a jacket pocket.

Cobner and Raisho handled the boat with expert precision, putting it into the muddy bank at the bottom of the broken bridge stump. Both of them got out and waded into the water to steady the craft. Cobner tossed Raisho the stern line, which Raisho attached to the large rusting iron chain hanging from the bridge.

Jassamyn leaped lithely from the boat with bow in hand and took up a crouching position in the bridge's shadow at the crest of the hillock. She held her bow across her knees with an arrow to the string and three others in her left hand.

"The man I talked to when I got this 'ere boat," Raisho whispered, "said no one come 'ere anymore 'cause the dead keep watch over this place. Said if'n ye come out 'ere sometimes, ye'll see 'em walkin' around."

"Do you believe that?" Cobner scoffed.

"I seen Boneblights in Greydawn Moors only a month ago," Raisho said, drawing his cutlass. "An' once I seen a ship full of dead men pass us in a fog out on the Blood-Soaked Sea." He glared at Cobner. "Ain't ye never seen the dead walk?"

"Seen 'em walk," Cobner declared, "seen 'em run and seen 'em come crawling after me when they had no legs to stand on. I've seen skeletons and zombies. You haven't been with Wick when he's been on one of his proper tears. You go on one of those, you're like to see all manner of things you ain't ever seen before."

"Dead things," Jassamyn said, "break and they burn. And I've never seen anything that was dead that could think well for itself." She shook her head. "The thing you still have to worry about the most? A scared or a skilled warrior with a clothyard length of steel to hand. A scared warrior will do the unpredictable, and the skilled one will take advantage of your mistakes."

Craugh stood in the darkness, wrapped in his cloak. He held his staff at his side.

During the hours it had taken them to get ready for the trip to the Drowned City, Juhg had felt the weight of the wizard's intentional distancing from him. It was as if a truce had been called, but it was an unfriendly one at best. Juhg didn't notice if the others had noticed. If they had, they weren't calling attention to it.

And if they haven't, Juhg thought, *I'm not sure if I care for any of them watching my back out here.*

They spread out and began searching around the hillock. It was near to sixty feet long and half that wide. The Grandmagister's journal had stated that he'd found an entrance beside one of the broken structures near the shattered bridge. There had even been an X on the map.

Unfortunately, Sharz said that sporadic undersea earthquakes still shivered through the area. While most of the islands suffered no damage, perhaps the loss of a waterwheel from a mill or loom in the Garment District, the Drowned City often succumbed to new damage. That fact was made plain when more skeletons washed up-canal to the islands on the other side of the ruins, or down-canal to the Garment District or one of the other islands there.

"Did Wick's journal say anything about the bridge being in the water?" Jassamyn asked.

"From his description," Juhg said as he walked around a square building that listed badly toward the water, "the bridge remnant sat well clear of the water."

The elven maid stared down at the brackish water lapping at the foot of the bridge. "That's no longer true."

"Either the water has risen or this bit of island had sunk more," Juhg said. The thought didn't sit well with him. If the pieces of *The Book of Time* had somehow conspired to sink the various cities where they had been stored, what was to say that the sinking was over? He kept having visions of all of them trooping down into one of the sunken buildings in search of the first piece of *The Book of Time* and getting drawn down into the wet sea floor only to be lost forever.

Hooking a finger inside his shirt collar, Juhg loosened it, feeling as though it was shutting his breath off. He had been buried alive before, in the goblinkin mines. Twice, in fact. And once with the Grandmagister when they'd gone in search of a small library of books rumored to exist under an old dwarven fort high up in the Knobblies in the frozen climes of the north. To this day, Juhg didn't know whether being buried alive in the crypt with the Grandmagister was the worst of that particular adventure, or whether it was the dragon they had faced.

A pained cry sounded in the distance.

Juhg ducked down, instinctively finding a hiding place up against the building. He waited, breathing shallowly. He couldn't see Jassamyn and guessed that she had gone to ground as well.

"Just me," Raisho called sheepishly. "Couldn't see where I was going in this miserable dark."

Taking a deep breath, feeling the knots in his stomach unclench, Juhg stood. The stench from the sluggish water filled his nostrils with the scent of wet earth. *Like an open grave,* he couldn't help thinking. He'd had first-hand experience with those.

"Why didn't Kharrion just gather up *The Book of Time* after he returned from his death?" Jassamyn asked.

"The Grandmagister brought up the same question in his journal," Juhg said as he continued around the building. "He had no answers. He also went on to state that there was no proof that the two Kharrions were the same person."

"How many could there be?"

Juhg silently agreed.

"Kharrion was damaged," Craugh said from a short distance away. "He was believed dead. He hid *The Book of Time* from his enemies."

"The rogues that originally stole the book from the Gatekeeper?" Jassamyn asked.

Craugh's answer was slow in coming. "Yes. Perhaps his mind was damaged enough so that he forgot what he did with the book."

"That's why he encouraged the goblinkin to burn the books," Jassamyn said. "If this book truly is indestructible—"

"Believed to be indestructible," Craugh corrected.

"All right. If it is, then it wouldn't have burned."

"Yes," Craugh said. "But Kharrion also hated everyone in this world. His hate was so strong in him that the goblinkin recognized him as one of their own even though he wasn't a goblin."

As Juhg listened to the exchange, he couldn't help wondering when all of Craugh's secrets would come spilling out. And what would the wizard do then?

Movement drew Juhg's attention. He crouched again and waited to see if the movement repeated. A moment later, he spotted a dark shape slipping along the roofline's shadow on the muddy ground.

Flattening himself against the tilted building, he glanced up in time to see a huge rat peering down at him. At least, on first impression the figure looked like a rat. Gray and black rat hair covered the figure, but the smudged, dirty face looked wholly human.

Fearfully, Juhg started to open his mouth to call for Craugh and Jassamyn, both of whom were out of sight on either side of the building. Then a dirty hand that smelled like old rot clamped tight over his mouth from behind. Someone roughly pulled him back through the empty window he'd stood in front of.

Since he was dweller-sized, half the size of a human, and his captors were at least human-sized if not human, they had no problem manhandling him. Dirty rat fur covered both of them.

Wan, ambient moonslight came in through the building's windows, allowing Juhg to see his captors as they shoved him down onto the muddy floor of the big room. Since the building was once one of the trade guilds, the space inside the room was large. Cracked stone pillars held up the sagging ceiling that had holes leading to the second and even the third floors. The floor had once been a marble checkerboard, black and white squares, or at least some light color that hadn't been black. Or maybe the black was blue.

The rat-things were actually men in rat hides. They smelled foul on their own, but the rat hides made the stench even worse. Wetness clung to the nasty coverings and mud matted the fur in places. Even their boots were made of rat hides.

One carried a short sword and the other carried a pair of hand axes. The one with the sword put a knife against Juhg's throat.

"Don't make a sound, halfer," the man whispered threateningly. "If you do, why, I'll slit your gizzard for you and leave you for the rats to feed on."

Now that his vision was starting to compensate for the darkness inside the tilted building, Juhg saw rats all along the inside of the building. They clustered in corners of the structure, and up on the second and third floors above. Others waited anxiously with tiny squeaks on the broad stairs leading up on one side of the building.

It was easy to see how the men had come by their rat garments.

The man removed his other hand from over Juhg's mouth. The knife stayed pressed where it was.

"How many?" the one holding the knife asked, looking up.

A dirty face separated a pool of hairy rats, sending them scuttling in all directions on the second floor. "Four others," the man above called down in a whisper. "Two warriors. A woman. And an old man. Nothing that we can't handle."

"We won't move against them," the knife wielder said. "Not until we talk to Gasparl about them." He turned his attention to Juhg. "Up. Easy."

Cautiously, feeling the sharp prick of the knife at his throat and the warm trickle of blood sliding down his skin, Juhg got to his feet. As if he could see in the dark, the man guided him to the rear of the building where water had collected. It looked like the building had sunk into the canal, filling up with the brackish water.

The other man waded into the water and shook out a fisherman's net.

"Hurry up," the knife wielder said. "I don't like being up here while they're wandering around."

"Just a—"

Feeling the sharp bite of the knife loosen at his throat, Juhg seized the opportunity and threw his right arm forward, popping his captor's arm loose and the knife from his neck. Then he ducked from his captor's smelly embrace and dropped to all fours. His hands were instantly in water, and he realized he hadn't known the man had walked him out into it.

The knife wielder cursed, but still kept his voice low.

Juhg ran, streaking for the door the rat-men had pulled him into the building through. He filled his lungs and yelled. *"Craugh!"*

He was surprised at how easily the wizard's name came to his mind when he was so full of suspicion. He ran, managing two more steps, and drew in his breath to yell again.

Then a murky shape flashed in front of him, came back at him, and wrapped around him. He tripped on the fisherman's net and went down, stopping short of falling on his face on the marble tile by inches. Stunned, his hands hooked clawlike into the net, he stared at the tilted floor. A moment later, the net gathered at his ankles, like a birder taking a prize, and he was yanked backward. The stone hammered at him as he skidded over it, softened only somewhat by the thick mud that covered it.

"Cra—!" Before he could get the wizard's name out again, Juhg was dragged into the water and pulled under. Dirty water entered his mouth, tasting foul and coating his teeth with grit. He floated a little, and tried at once to fight free but was unable to escape the net.

He held his breath, but he knew he wasn't going to be able to hold it long. He'd spent his last breath trying to scream. Struggling against the net, he was pulled deeper into the water, and that didn't make any sense because the water hadn't looked that deep.

Above him, though, the moonslight that barely illuminated the room faded and drew back. The net tightened around him as the man holding him pulled him even deeper.

11

Smugglers

ocked in the unforgiving embrace of the fisherman's net, Juhg fought to be free. The opening above
him grew steadily smaller. The man bearing him down
swam with an uneven stroke, jerking his prize deeper and
deeper.

Juhg wasn't sure that Craugh and the others had
heard him. Or that he hadn't called them to their doom.
In the darkness, he couldn't be certain they'd even known
where he was. He doubled up in the net, trying desperately to reach the knife sheathed at his ankle, but the net
stayed taut, closing on him like a sausage wrapper so that
he wasn't able to bend down and close his fingers on the
blade.

His lungs burned with the need for air. Still his captor dragged him down and down. The pressure on Juhg's
ears grew steadily stronger. The Grandmagister hadn't
mentioned how deep Skull Canal was in his journal.
Maybe he hadn't known and maybe it hadn't mattered.
The secret rooms the Grandmagister had finally reached
were well below the sea surface.

Black spots swam in front of Juhg's vision even
though he couldn't see. He tried to put a hand over his

mouth and nose to keep himself from breathing in but he couldn't reach.

Thankfully, the swimmer started upward, pulling him after (though Juhg still felt certain the man had a pair of gills and could breathe like a fish). Another light dawned above him. He chose to take heart in that, though he was just as sure that the man meant him no good. Any death except by drowning suddenly looked appealing, though.

Almost passed out by the time the man clambered onto a narrow shelf at the bottom of a huge rectangular room, Juhg hung limply in the net as he was hauled from the water. Two other men met the first, dressed in rat hides just like the first. Together, they tied a rope through the bottom of the net and flipped it over a long boom arm.

Coughing and wheezing, shuddering from the rapid beating of his heart against his chest, Juhg struggled weakly against the net as he was lifted up the rectangular shaft. He spun as he rose, and his dizzying view almost caused him to throw up.

From his new view, Juhg saw that the rectangular chamber had been a lower floor in a large building that had evidently once been a large entertainment area. The décor had been stripped, and what had been left had rotted away after centuries of flooding and hardship. Bubbling mold clung to the walls. Abandoned refuse, clothing, and armor and other detritus that couldn't be identified, as well as broken skeletons littered the floor.

Rats and spiders had made nests on the walls and on ledges between the spacious rooms. The presence of the rats and insects let Juhg know there was a way that fresh air got down into the structure, otherwise they would never have made the trip through the water.

Someone held up a lantern on the second floor. By the low light, held out at arm's reach, Juhg noted at least a dozen figures around the second floor opening.

"What have you got there, Civak?" a man's voice demanded.

"An intruder," the man who'd captured Juhg called back. He scrambled up the side of the building, following broken marble stairs for a time, then shifting over to a rope ladder to make the last leg of the climb.

"What makes you think he was an intruder?"

Juhg jerked with dizzying abandon at the end of the long pole as he was drawn up. He'd only just gotten his breath back, still couldn't reach the knife at his ankle, and was certain he was going to be sick.

"He was poking around outside the bridge," Civak answered. "Come up on the building where the secret entrance is like he knew it was there."

"Is that right, halfer?" the man with the lantern demanded. "Was you come looking for the entrance to this place?"

Juhg drew even with the man.

The man held the lantern close to Juhg, eyeing him with open speculation. He wore his long brown hair loose, but it mixed in effortlessly with the rat hides he wore. He was an ugly man, his face crusted with hard bone beneath sallow skin scarred by a bad case of the pox in his youth. Scars left proud flesh around his right eye, which had obviously suffered horribly because it was covered with a black leather patch adorned with a stylized silver rat done in beads.

Juhg couldn't help wondering if Sharz had done the beadwork. He was cold and miserable inside the net. The rough rope tore at his flesh with bruising force.

"Do you know me, halfer?" the man demanded, shining the lantern directly into Juhg's face.

"No," Juhg answered in a voice that cracked. Despite the bright light shining into his eyes, he saw that the men with the one-eyed man were equally clad and looked just as fearsome.

"You don't know who I am or what this place is?"

"No."

Behind the man, a fire burned under a spit filled with rat bodies. Sleeping pallets that looked like they'd been there a long time lay around the fire. Some of those pallets had rat bodies moving through them. Hammock webs containing large spiders with glowing eyes like embers hung in the corner of the roof above the pallets. Evidently the long-term camp had attracted an entourage.

The one-eyed man laughed. "Then how is it, halfer, you've come to the wrong place?"

"I'm new to Imarish," Juhg said. "My friends and I got lost."

Glancing over his shoulder, the one-eyed man asked, "How many friends, Civak?"

"Four. An elven maid, an old man, a dwarf, and a young black man, Dusen."

"Really?" Renewed interest and avarice gleamed in the single dark eye as Dusen returned his attention to Juhg. "And you're new to Imarish?"

"Yes," Juhg said. Helcun's *First Rule of Lying* advised lying small—*just enough to save your neck from the gallows, friends and neighbors! Or to put coins in your hat if your life has come to that!*—and staying with the lie.

"How new?"

"I arrived only yesterday."

"From a ship?"

"Yes."

"What ship?"

Juhg panicked. If he'd been on his toes, he would have noticed the other ships in harbor yesterday. He and the Grandmagister had developed that skill while on the mainland. But yesterday, with Craugh stalking him like some great bird of prey, Juhg hadn't even taken notice of the other ships.

"*One-Eyed Peggie.*" Juhg was fairly convinced that the name would mean nothing to Dusen.

"I don't know her."

"She's from the north," Juhg volunteered. "A trade ship." And part of the time, *One-Eyed Peggie* was exactly that.

"Where are you from?"

Keep it simple, Juhg warned himself. "Kelloch's Harbor. I worked as a cook."

"A cook?"

"Yes." Cooking was a skill that Juhg enjoyed, and one that could find him employment almost at once in any big town along the mainland.

"What brought you here?"

"I heard Imarish was a safe place to work."

Dusen grinned at him. "So your friends thought they'd come along to watch you work?"

Swallowing hard, realizing that Dusen was more intelligent than he'd given him credit for—*but who wouldn't underestimate someone wearing rat hides?*—Juhg remained silent.

Dusen handed the lantern off to one of his cronies. He placed a boot against Juhg inside the fisherman's net and shoved.

Juhg arced out over the empty expanse, then pendulumed back and forth. His stomach revolted and a sour bubble burst at the back of his throat.

Reaching out lazily, Dusen caught the net with one hand and halted the spinning. He turned the net so his face was presented to Juhg's.

"I smell lies, halfer," he growled. "It's a gift I've had since I was a child." He smiled. "Now I've heard two stories about a halfer coming to Imarish. The first was about a halfer, an old man, an elf, a dwarven warrior, and a young black warrior that got into a fight with another group of strangers in the Garment District. You wouldn't know anything about that, would you?"

Juhg didn't say anything. Helcun's *Second Rule of Lying* advised giving no lie at all when an audience—singular or many—didn't believe a word that was being said.

"The second story I heard was about a man named Valeithar who was willing to pay a dear price for a dweller answering your description. What do you think about that?"

"I don't know anyone named Valeithar," Juhg replied.

"He's a wizard. Like your friend in the pointy hat," Dusen said. "I've done business with him before. There was another halfer through here before my men and I seized this place as a base of operations. He was a red-headed dweller."

The Grandmagister, Juhg realized.

187

"Moog followed him down here," Dusen said, hooking his thumb over at a slightly built man with crooked teeth that matched his rat hide outer garments. "Found this secret passageway after that, and we've been using it for our smuggling operation ever since."

Juhg's head hurt from being suspended upside down. The men operating the boom arm showed no inclination to swing him around to put him on solid ground, or to turn him around upright.

"What," Dusen mused, "makes a dweller so important? And what brings you down here after the other halfer was here all that time ago?"

Juhg waited, wondering if he friends were all right. He wished that the Grandmagister's journal had warned about the smugglers, but if he hadn't run into them, there was no way any mention of them would have been made in the encoded journal.

Dusen pushed Juhg again, swinging him precariously out over the open expanse of the water some forty feet below. The rope creaked threateningly and Juhg had sudden worries about how old the rope was and whether it had been properly cared for. Given the surroundings and the fact that the men wore rat hides, he sincerely doubted that anyone had ever thought of caring for the rope.

"If he ain't gonna answer your questions, Dusen," one of the other men said, "there's no reason to keep him around here. Just be one more worthless mouth to feed." He pulled a long knife from a scabbard at his belt, then laid the blade's edge on the rope. A few of the strands parted.

Then the man's head jerked back suddenly. The violet-and-white-fletched arrow stood out sharply in the lantern light for a moment, jutting from the man's eye socket. Without a word, the dead man toppled over the edge of the second floor of the building toward the dark water below.

Jassamyn! Juhg thought. There could be no mistake about the arrow, not with those fletchings. Or about the archery. He tilted his head and looked down at the water.

Shadows moved there, and the bright green magic of Craugh's staff as well.

Two more arrows plucked smugglers from the wall, then they moved back, snarling and cursing their unseen foe.

"To arms!" Dusen roared. "Grab those rocks and that pitch! We've got invaders in our midst!"

Peering through the darkness, Juhg saw that bodies floated in the water. For a moment he was afraid that they might belong to his friends; then he saw Cobner break free of the water with a bull's roar of challenge and his battle-axe held high, somehow finding the strength to pull himself along a rope that had been anchored somewhere inside the room below. Clad in armor as he was, he would never have made the swim without the rope to guide and hasten him.

Following the line of the rope with his eyes, Juhg spotted Raisho racing up the decrepit marble stairs with his bare cutlass in one hand. A smuggler on the lower reaches struck from hiding. Raisho blocked the blade with his own, then attacked, blocking the smuggler's sword up over the man's head. Reaching in with his free hand, Raisho grabbed the smuggler by the shirt front, fell backward, and used his feet to propel the smuggler over the stair railing.

"Jassamyn!" Raisho yelled.

Smooth as a bead of perspiration on an icicle, the elven maid turned and released an arrow at the flailing smuggler falling toward her. The shaft pierced the man's neck and his corpse slammed limply into the water.

Cobner clanked up the stairway after Raisho.

"Cut the halfer free!" Dusen ordered. "Let his friends fend for him!"

Fear scratched at the back of Juhg's neck as he realized Jassamyn was aiming at him. Time slowed and he saw her release the shot. The arrow zipped through the air quicker than thought. Unable to move, Juhg watched as the broadhead closed on him, then it kissed the net near his right hand, loosening the weave of the net.

Her next three shafts buried themselves in the two smugglers that jumped to do their leader's bidding. One man fell from the second story landing, but the other pitched backward with an arrow in his belly, wounded mightily but not dead.

"Fire the pitch!" Dusen yelled.

A smuggler ran back to the campfire and picked up a flaming brand. With the angle he was at, he was safe from Jassamyn's bow. Crossing to the barrels of pitch that other smugglers held at the ready, the man fired the barrels. Yellow flames sprang up slowly, accompanied by thick black smoke that made the spiders scurry across the huge webs on the ceiling.

"Heave!" Dusen ordered.

Smugglers shoved four of the flaming barrels of pitch over the side. Spinning and twisting, the barrels plummeted toward the water below.

"Look out!" Juhg warned.

Jassamyn took one more shot, catching a smuggler who peeked over the side. Evidently the smuggler had thought he was safe . . . up until the moment the arrow plunged through his head and he dropped like a child's doll.

The flaming pitch hit the water and submerged for an instant. Even underwater, the fire refused to go completely out, feeding on the oil. Then, since it was lighter than water, the oil spread out across the flooded lower floor. In heartbeats, the whole surface of the water was ablaze.

Jassamyn raced for the stairs just ahead of the lake of flames that sped after her. She pulled herself onto the marble stairway just before the fire reached her.

Smoke boiled up at once, turning the area below murky. The acrid stink of it burned the back of Juhg's throat and made his eyes water. He shifted inside the net and found the weakness Jassamyn's shot had caused. Plunging his arm through, he got purchase and began turning his body, working his head and shoulders into the hole and hoping he didn't get stuck.

The water below was covered completely by fire. If he fell, there was a good chance he'd never survive without inhaling flames when he came up for air. And he doubted that he could swim underwater in all the confusion to reach the marble stairway where the others were. Getting back topside in the dark without knowing the way didn't seem like a safe bet even if he could find the rope Raisho had evidently guided the others with.

Even if Juhg succeeded in his escape attempt, the first piece of *The Book of Time* was in this building. He'd have to return.

The smugglers threw large rocks and pieces of mortar from piles that had been stored there for that purpose. Raisho was able to avoid most of them with his quickness, but Cobner used his shield to block them away with thunderous claps.

Once his head and shoulders were through the opening Jassamyn's arrow had made in the net, Juhg shot through the net like an eel through a mud pit, falling toward the hot flames below. He twisted and threw out a hand, just managing to hook his fingers into the net. His weight hit the end of his arm and nearly pulled him loose. Then he swung his other hand up and secured a hold.

Just as he took a deep breath, a crossbow bolt whizzed by his head, missing killing or blinding him by inches. Galvanized into action, he climbed the net like he would rigging back on *One-Eyed Peggie* or *Windchaser*. By the time he reached the boom arm, stretching tall to get it, Dusen had spotted his escape attempt.

"Kill the halfer!" the smuggler leader shouted.

The crossbowman raised his weapon again, took aim, and fired. The quarrel thunked solidly into the beam, skidding along the wood and ripping a long splinter free. Either the wood or the quarrel kissed Juhg's cheek and he felt warm blood running down the side of his face.

The crossbowman worked to restring his weapon, but before he could complete the task, one of Jassamyn's arrows found a home in his heart. He crumpled, dropping the weapon on the ledge where it hit and spun out over the ledge to drop into the flames.

"Throw the boom over!" the smuggler leader ordered.

Other smugglers hurried to get more pitch barrels while their comrades threw rocks down on the four hurrying up the stairs. Raisho was already swinging up the rope ladder. Jassamyn covered him, putting arrows into any that dared advance on the young sailor while Cobner protected her with a shield he'd picked up from the litter scattered around the room. Behind them, Craugh chanted and emerald embers whirled around him while the fire coming from his staff grew brighter. Finally, the wizard thrust the staff forward. A green fireball spat from the staff and slammed into the smugglers awaiting the torch to light their barrels of pitch.

The fireball hit the pitch barrels and blew them backward, dousing the smugglers with oil and setting them alight. Screams of dying men filled the empty hollow of the building. They ran across the second floor landing till they dropped or ran off the edge to plummet to their deaths below, or were mercifully killed by their comrades.

Clinging to the end of the boom arm, Juhg watched in horror as one of the smugglers slid across the floor. At the base of the boom arm, the smuggler levered his sword into it, then twisted viciously upward.

The boom arm shuddered and went up, dipping at the end where Juhg desperately clung. He saw then that the boom arm wasn't bolted on, just sat onto a support beam so it could freely turn. Weight at the end of the beam normally kept it wedged tight so nothing slipped. With sword blade worked in between, everything slipped incredibly easily.

The smuggler levered his blade again, scooting the beam up another inch or two. At the end of the beam, Juhg dropped another foot, till the incline was drastic and it became harder to hold on.

"You're gonna die, halfer," the smuggler chortled.

Pulling himself up, grateful now that he was a dweller and was so small and quick and agile, Juhg rolled forward, tucking his head into his chin, and came up to a standing position on the beam. His large feet overlapped the narrow beam on either side. Evidently the smugglers had been in the habit of winching up small loads.

The smuggler redoubled his efforts to loosen the beam.

Juhg ran forward. Only fifteen feet long, the beam wasn't an impossible distance to span. However, three steps into it, some eight feet short of his goal, the beam fell away from underfoot. Even as he fell, Juhg threw himself forward, arms outstretched to cover precious inches.

His hands slapped against the ledge, slipped for an instant, then held.

The smuggler cursed in surprise and swung his sword at Juhg's left hand. Letting go with the hand that was menaced, Juhg dangled from his other hand, swinging wildly. The smuggler drew back and swung at the other hand by that time. Juhg transferred hands again, barely avoiding the terrible blade. The beam plunged into the fire-covered water below.

Quick as a monkey, Juhg swung along the ledge with the smuggler chopping the ledge in his wake. When he had enough clearance, he pulled with both arms and threw a leg over the ledge, trying desperately to scramble up.

"Oh, and you're a quick one, ain't you?" the smuggler accused as he crawled rapidly on his hands and knees to reach Juhg.

Just as the man chopped at him, Juhg dropped back over the ledge, then scampered along like a monkey through the trees till he got behind the smuggler. In position there, Juhg hung by one hand and grabbed one of the smuggler's feet with the other. He pulled with all his strength.

The smuggler had time for a surprised look as he slid across the loose gravel on the ledge. In the next moment, he lunged for a hold on the ledge . . . and missed. Knowing he was falling to his doom, he screamed until he hit the flaming water and disappeared.

Hating the grisly death he'd pulled the man to, Juhg hardened his heart. After growing up in a goblinkin mine and watching dwellers die harsh deaths around him every day, he'd learned to put his own survival ahead of those who would strip him of his life. He still couldn't have dealt out the harsh deaths his companions could, but he could fight to live.

Swinging along the ledge, hoping that he didn't get a poor grip and slip, Juhg reached the far wall away from the smugglers. Arms aching, fear sour in his belly, he pulled himself up to peer over the ledge.

The smugglers hadn't noticed him, no doubt thinking he had fallen with their comrade. Instead, they'd turned their malicious attentions to Juhg's friends, holding them trapped along the stairway and unable to employ the rope ladder.

Cobner raged, calling out fierce dwarven curses and challenging his enemies to meet him on common ground. High up on the rope ladder, Raisho clashed swords with a smuggler attempting to slice through the strands. Standing his ground, his pointy hat pierced by a crossbow quarrel, Craugh raised his staff and spoke words of power again.

A green blaze whipped from the staff as Craugh waved his weapon.

Eldritch flames snaked along the ledge, temporarily breaking the smugglers' defense. Jassamyn took advantage of the wizard's attack to put a shaft though another smuggler.

Fewer than twenty smugglers remained, but Juhg couldn't be certain of the exact number due to the shifting shadows along the second floor. The lower floor was brightly lit by the flaming oil. Unfortunately, the smoke from the burning pitch was pooling in a great cloud against the building's third floor ceiling, growing thicker and creeping down.

The air already burned Juhg's lungs and nose to breathe, and his eyes burned and blurred with tears. If his friends simply left, provided they could find a way through the flames and into the water below without having the pitch stick to them and kill them or at least hamper them, they could wait till the smoke overcame the smugglers.

But they won't leave me, Juhg realized, and he felt partially responsible for their plight. If he'd taken more care he wouldn't have gotten captured. Desperate, knowing that the smugglers' efforts to crush his friends with the rocks would succeed sooner than later, he hauled himself over the ledge.

Movement scurried along the ceiling above him. He gazed up, seeing the spiders crawling through the massive hammock webs. Their eyes glowed in the darkness, either from an inner light or from the flames burning below. Smoke collected in the webs, causing them to sag in places.

A smuggler turning to grab a rock spotted Juhg standing on the ledge. "Over here! The halfer is over here!" He dropped the rock and freed the short sword at his hip, lurching forward with teary eyes caused by the smoke.

Swiftly, his mind concocting the plan on the spot, Juhg bent and picked up a short sword, preferring that weapon's length over the knife at his ankle. He ran back from the man, running toward the crates against the back wall of the room. Evidently the smugglers had brought stolen provisions into their hiding place. Some of the crates were broken up for use as kindling.

Another of Craugh's magic fireballs detonated in the ranks of the smugglers, scattering a half dozen men in different directions. Two smoldering bodies did not get up to return to the fray.

Juhg leapt up onto the crates, narrowly avoiding the smuggler's sword blow as the man closed the distance between them. Lifting the sword as he gained the top of the stack with another jump, he slashed along the wall, reaching as far as he could. The hammock webs parted as easily as the smoke pillowed against the room.

The effort, immersed as he was in the thicker smoke atop the line of crates, brought on a coughing fit that made Juhg feel as though his head was going to explode. He jumped to another crate, leaping over the smuggler's keen blade as he slashed at Juhg's feet.

All along the wall, Juhg continued cutting the hammock webs, freeing them from their moorings. The webs shook and vibrated from his blows, and it was evident that the strands were weighing more and more from the gathering smoke. Before he reached the back wall, still staying ahead of the smuggler who had pursued him from the beginning and another that had joined in the first's efforts, the spider-laden web tore free and swung toward the knot of surviving smugglers.

"Look out . . . below!" Juhg managed before the smoke triggered a coughing fit that took him to his knees.

The hammock webs struck the smugglers squarely, falling around them like a heavy drape. Frightened by the unaccustomed smoke and noise, the spiders attacked the men beneath them immediately. Their glowing eyes made them appear even more fierce.

Hoarse, fearful shouts ripped free of the smugglers. Abandoning their attack, they concentrated on their own problems, striving to dust the fist-sized spiders from their faces, arms, and bodies.

Unable to take another step, Juhg hunkered down on the crate. He tore a length from the bottom of his wet shirt and tied it around his head over his mouth and nose. The wet cloth served to filter a lot of the smoke, though it was still hard to breathe.

With no one guarding the rope ladder, Raisho easily made the ascent and stood guard as Cobner threw down his shield and climbed up after the young sailor. Craugh followed next while Jassamyn kept watch with her bow until finally it was her turn.

Beneath the hammock webs, the smugglers quickly stopped struggling. Evidently the spiders carried some sort of venom, though Juhg didn't know if it was lethal or merely toxic enough to cause paralysis. He found he really didn't care. Either would have been fine.

Only three of the smugglers hadn't fallen to the spiders' venom. They made the mistake of attacking Raisho and Cobner. Cobner killed one of them almost offhandedly with his battle-axe and the two survivors quickly surrendered, though they pleaded to be allowed to move away from the webs where their comrades lay conquered.

Cobner allowed the surrender but stood over them with his weapon ready.

Jassamyn alighted on the ledge as well. She plucked a scarf from somewhere in her clothing and knotted it around her face.

"Scribbler!" Raisho called.

"Here," Juhg called from atop the crates. The two smugglers coughed and wheezed below him. The hammock webs had missed them.

Raisho started forward at once, walking around the outer edge of the hammock webs where the frenzied spiders still crawled. Firelight skated along his blade, though it was dulled because of the matte finish he preferred for night work. He halted a few feet from the smugglers, spotting Juhg atop the crates.

Lifting his cutlass meaningfully to the two smugglers by Juhg, Raisho said, "Ye have a choice: surrender or die. Makes me no nevermind." He struggled not to cough but was overcome all the same.

Neither of the smugglers felt compelled to fight. They threw their blades down and lay on the ground at Raisho's direction.

As if untouched by the smoke, Craugh walked to the middle of the ledge. He took off his pointy hat and pulled the crossbow quarrel from it. With the hat back on his head, he glared at the smoke. He spoke arcane words in a guttural voice thickened by the smoke, then lifted his staff. Emerald embers swirled around the end of his staff, then darted out into the center of the smoke mass gathered at the ceiling.

Coughing and struggling to breathe, Juhg clambered down from the crates. His lungs felt like they were on fire, and it seemed like coals burned in his eyes.

Slowly at first, but with gathering speed, the emerald embers began a circular motion. As the speed increased, a funnel formed and the smoke was sucked up toward the opening in the third floor.

Moving so that he could see better, Juhg watched as the smoke slid up through vents in the third floor ceiling.

Craugh turned his attention to the flaming pitch still burning across the surface of the water below. The funnel elongated, reaching over the ledge and snaking down to the flames, then pulled them up through the third floor ceiling as well.

As the fire left the building, the room grew steadily darker.

"Apprentice," Craugh said. "There are lanterns in those crates. It might be an idea if you lit some of them before we end up in the dark."

His lungs and eyes already feeling better, though he'd just noticed that he'd abraded his fingers with all his clever scampering along the ledge, Juhg went to get the lanterns.

 196

12

Dead End

s it turned out, the spiders' venom wasn't lethal, but it did deliver a long-lasting paralysis.

In the lantern light, Juhg examined one of the spiders killed by the fire as he listened to Craugh's interrogation of the smuggler leader, Dusen. He thought the spiders might have been kin to the strider spiders that commonly lived in the area in pools of water. Or perhaps they were kin to the coffin spiders that lived in the woods along the mainland and sometimes ended up floating in spider eggs into Imarish.

Only strider spiders weren't as big as his fist like these were, and coffin spiders were known to kill a grown person with a single bite. Glancing at the swelling on the smuggler leader's scarred face, Juhg judged that the bites were necrotic and would probably leave cherry-sized pits in the flesh that might never heal properly. The effect was not going to improve Dusen's already ragged features.

Dusen kept his story simple, but Juhg felt certain the man was in a lot of pain and not all that interested in lying. He lay paralyzed and helpless, and he said the bites felt like coals dug in tight against his flesh. Several of the other smugglers had groaned and moaned terribly, until

Craugh—finally tiring of the caterwauling—put them all to sleep with a spell.

"I'm the son of a merchant," Dusen insisted. "I've just fallen upon hard times. I don't deserve to be treated like this." He managed to throw his head around a little.

Unimpressed, Craugh peered down at his captive. "You're a thief."

"Through no fault or intention of my own," Dusen said. "My father was a guildsman, a man of considerable wealth. The other guildsmen grew jealous of him, though. They started taking their business elsewhere. Soon my father fell upon hard times."

Silently, and perhaps a little pessimistically, Juhg guessed that the apple didn't fall far from the tree in Dusen's case. Probably his father was a bad thief as well. Or an overly greedy one.

"It wasn't long before my father lost his fleet of trading vessels," Dusen said. "He hanged himself from the clock tower in the Metalworks District. It was a terrible thing. I was ordered up to cut him down." His eyes turned down and crocodile tears poured down his cheeks. "It was the . . . hardest . . . thing I've ever had to do."

Raisho rolled his eyes.

"After my father's death, after my mother was thrown from our house and we were left to fend for ourselves in the street," Dusen went on, "I started stealing from the guildsmen that had broken my father. I only saw fit to take back what they had stolen from my father."

"What of your mother?" Jassamyn asked in a voice that offered only cold rebuke. "Did you leave her to fend for herself as well?"

Dusen thought quickly. "Of course not!" It was hard acting haughty when he didn't have body language to use. "I took care of her until she died . . . from . . . from a broken heart. It was terrible, I tell you. Just watching her wither away. My wife tried to help but—b—"

"Wife?" Cobner growled.

"Yes," Dusen said. "Didn't I tell you? I have a wife and son. A wonderful woman, actually, and hardly deserving of the cruel life fate has thrust upon her when I lost my inheritance. And my son, truly a wonderful lad. Smart as a whip, too."

"A wife and son?" Cobner shook his head, then stuck his finger down his throat and made retching noises.

Dusen's eyebrows leaped. "You don't believe me?"

"No," Cobner said. "I think ye're wastin' our time."

"It's true!" Dusen said. "Everything I have told you is true!"

Settled on his haunches and looking totally comfortable with unconscious, spiderwebbed smugglers lying strewn all around him, Craugh looked at the smuggler leader. "Enough!"

Dusen started in again, pointing out that he should be shown forgiveness. After all, it was dark and he couldn't be sure that he hadn't been under attack by the Imarish Peacekeepers, who had helped his father hang himself as it turned out. And the Peacekeepers only wanted him dead, Dusen insisted, because they didn't like the competition he brought to their own efforts to steal the city blind.

Craugh gestured with a forefinger. A single green spark sailed from his forefinger to touch one of the spiders, which still crawled over the inert bodies of the smugglers. He had laid out a small spell that kept the spiders from coming among them.

Summoned by the wizard's magic, one of the fattest and ugliest spiders Juhg had ever seen scuttled across the gravel-covered expanse of the ledge. Jassamyn stepped back from the horrid thing.

It would take an elven warder to find love in his heart for such a thing, Juhg decided.

"No!" Dusen cried. "Make it go away! Don't let it near me!" With the paralysis, he couldn't do anything but watch the spider's dedicated approach with his single, wide-open eye.

The spider caught hold of the smuggler leader's hair and climbed up on top of his head. Stopping on Dusen's eyepatch, the spider rocked back onto its hindmost legs and prepared to strike.

Dusen screamed. The tortured sound ululated through the empty building.

"Now," Craugh said calmly and coldly, "you will speak only when I ask you to. Otherwise the spider will bite your eye and that sight will be the last thing you ever see because the poison will rot your flesh. Do you understand?"

Nausea stirred in Juhg's stomach. He knew from past experience that Craugh could be hard and merciless, but he had never seen the wizard take such advantage of a helpless foe.

Is this what he was like when he went in search of The Book of Time? Juhg couldn't help but wonder. *And if it is, does this mean that he's reverting to that older self now that the prize is almost in his hand?* He swallowed hard, filled with the fear of what was about to happen to the smuggler leader as well as the rest of their little group. He hoped that Hallekk had—or would—at least rescued the Grandmagister. If Craugh truly let his evil nature show, Juhg could only hope that the Grandmagister was clever enough to stop him.

"I . . . understand," Dusen whispered, staring in hypnotic fascination at the spider's poised legs.

"Good." Craugh laid his staff across his knees and gave every appearance of being totally comfortable. "Tell me how you found this place."

Talking slowly and with care, Dusen relayed how Moog—one of the smugglers who was now dead and whose body now floated in the dark water below—had followed the little redhaired dweller out of curiosity to the building near the broken bridge. The building had not been nearly as sunken then as it was now. Afterward Moog had shown the building to Dusen, shown how the windows had been filled in against the flooding that occurred when the island it had been built on had sunk beneath the waves.

"Why do you think this building was so preserved?" Craugh asked.

"There was supposed to be a treasure here from the time before Lord Kharrion raised up the goblinkin hordes and nearly took over the world. That has always been the rumor."

200

"Was there a treasure?"

"Perhaps. But it was long gone from this place."

"But enough people believed in it that the building was preserved," Craugh pointed out.

"I had the story from one of the taletellers in the Quarry District, where the dwarves cut stone from the heart of the earth to construct buildings with. He told me that the dwarves a long time ago spent years sealing up this building and others around it, then pumping it dry."

"And no treasure was found?"

"A few things. Gold coins. A scattering of gems. Enough so that people knew a treasure had once been held here. Either it was taken when the underwater quakes reaved the island or shortly thereafter, before the sinking became so extensive."

"Did anyone ever say why only this place was affected?"

According to the story Dusen had heard, the buildings had once been part of the palace courts of Skydevil's Roost, but the smuggler leader wasn't sure that place actually existed or was only a tale that had been told so long it had become like truth.

"It was part of the mainland in those days," Dusen said. "Not an island. That didn't happen till the Cataclysm when Lord Kharrion destroyed Teldane's Bounty farther to the south when the Unity armies tried to hold the goblinkin back so they could evacuate people caught between them and the sea. There weren't enough ships to get all those people to safety. That's why there are so many bones in this area. They didn't just come from the people who died here during the sinking of this city. You'll find a lot of goblinkin bones around here, too."

Juhg remembered the stories of the battle fought at Teldane's Bounty. The Unity armies had held as long as they could, staving off the goblinkin hordes while ships ferried the women and children to safer places north and south of the confrontation. Even then, they hadn't succeeded in saving all of them. Several innocents perished when Lord Kharrion used the spell that broke the mainland and created the Shattered Coast, reaching for miles in all directions from the epicenter. It was the single largest display of magic ever known to have been unleashed. The dwarven warriors, humans, and elves had died in the destruction or the slaughter that took place shortly after.

Then, when it seemed no more evil could be done, Lord Kharrion had strode among the fields of dead and—under a moonless sky—raised dead goblinkin warriors up, used his magic to wed their decayed flesh and the special clay he had made up with the fear and suffering of the innocents who had been slaughtered. He had called them Boneblights, and everyone who opposed him learned to fear them.

Juhg had seen the loathsome creatures in Greydawn Moors. Nightmares still haunted him, though they had grown smaller in light of everything else he had learned.

"Seadevil's Roost was destroyed before then," Craugh said.

"Mayhap. You hear stories both ways."

"Do you know what Wi—" Craugh caught himself before he spoke the Grandmagister's name. "What the dweller was searching for?"

Dusen hesitated.

The spider flexed its legs and leaned in closer.

"I don't know," Dusen said. "Moog followed the dweller down into the building, but he didn't follow him into the lower levels."

"The floor down there isn't the lowest level?" Craugh asked.

"No. There are two floors beneath it."

"Flooded?"

"No."

Juhg knew there had to have been from the description in the Grandmagister's journal, but he hadn't had time to take everything in. Still, the lower floor didn't look like the one the Grandmagister had talked about in the coded journal.

"Those rooms are walled up and protected," Dusen went on. "When Moog followed the dweller's path later, he found where the dweller's wet footprints went to a false wall."

Juhg's pulse raced. The Grandmagister had written about the false wall.

"Later, after Moog had told me about this place, I realized we could use it as a hideout. You only had to swim a little ways back then. Now, this whole building lies beneath the sea. Copper pipes run to the surface to bring fresh air into this place. They are so low now that when the water is bestirred they sometimes let in the sea. Soon, we will either have to add onto the pipes or abandon this place."

"Did the dweller leave with anything?" Craugh asked.

"Not that Moog could see. We went in search of him later but he was already gone."

"Why did you go after him?"

"Because of the thing I found. I didn't understand it, but I know it must be worth something. If it is even real."

"What thing?" Craugh asked.

Following Dusen's direction, Juhg stopped at the blank eastern wall in the fourth room to the north from the main room. He'd used his compass to find his way. Marks from tools, axes and swords and crowbars, dented the wall in several places.

"Here," he announced.

The room had once been the private quarters of the baron of Seadevil's Roost. Remnants of an iron bed and other furniture lay scattered around the room. There were also the bones of the dead, all gathered in a heap where they had evidently rolled after the building had tilted during one of the subsequent settlings.

Here and there, bits of gilt glinted on the woodwork, but for the most part the room was filled with mold and mildew and the wood was rotted and eaten by worms. Small fish and crabs lived in the ankle-deep water that covered the floor.

According to the Grandmagister's notes in the latter half of his journal, Seadevil's Roost had once been governed by a human named Gaultanot who had convinced neighboring human communities to pool their resources together—including their ships—till they became a strong trade guild. Gaultanot had ruled as baron of Seadevil's Roost, and by all accounts he had been a good man.

How then, Juhg couldn't help wondering again, *did Kharrion tempt the baron into holding one of the sections of* The Book of Time? *And why break up such a thing of power? Was it truly just to outwit Craugh and the others who pursued him? Or was there another reason that couldn't yet be seen?* He sighed. One of the frustrations of having a mind trained to think and consider possibilities was that it couldn't simply be stopped once engaged.

"Well," Cobner asked impatiently, "are you gonna open that door or stare a hole in it? I'm thinking that you're not gonna be able to stare a hole in it. And even if you do, I don't think you're going to be able to stare open a hole big enough to let me through."

Moving his lantern, Juhg glanced down at the waterline. The door wasn't watertight. Seepage showed on both sides of the hidden entrance.

He knelt and studied the water in front of the door. Even with the lantern trained on the area, he couldn't see anything.

"What are ye doin'?" Raisho asked.

"The Grandmagister mentioned that the hallway leading down to the vault room where the section of *The Book of Time* is held is filled with traps." Extending his hand along the floor under the water, Juhg concentrated on feeling for suction. If the hidden door was leaking, then the trapdoor had to be leaking as well.

"After all these years?" Jassamyn asked. "Juhg, it's been a *really* long time."

"Most of the traps are already sprung," Juhg said. "But not this one." *A-ha!* He felt the suction he was suspecting, though it was slight and feathery soft, and traced the rectangle with his fingertips. His palm slid across a layer of mud and he felt the straight edges of the trapdoor mirrored in the sediment. "Someone has gone through this one literally. Perhaps one of Dusen's people."

"Kind of him not to mention the trap," Cobner rumbled. "Mayhap I'll have a brief visit with him on the way out. Leave him a knot on his melon to remember me by."

Juhg stood, carefully marking the trapdoor in his mind. He was glad the Grandmagister was so thorough. In all eventuality, though, he would have checked the door before going through. The life he'd led exploring legends and myths with the Grandmagister along the mainland had trained him to be careful.

He turned to Jassamyn and held out the lantern. "Can you manage this?"

The elven maid took the lantern and held it steady on the door as she pulled her bow over her shoulder and freed her longsword. The smugglers showed no sign of recovering from the paralysis any time soon, but there was every chance of other things shambling around in the dark.

"The trapdoor once dropped an unwary person down onto a clutch of sharpened stakes," Juhg said. "The corpses were taken out down in the basement and burned in the fireplace that heated the building." He straddled the trapdoor. "The hidden door here is spring-loaded." Placing his hands on the door, he set himself, then shoved.

The door slid back slowly and Juhg had to lean into it harder. Before he could get it to lock back in position, the trapdoor between his feet popped open and a dead man floated up out of the dark recesses.

Frightened, repulsed by the agony and fear branded onto the dead man's rat-gnawed face, Juhg cried out and shoved himself backward. He heard the hidden door click into place even as he fell on his rump and the dead man floated up out of the hole.

"Easy there, scribbler," Raisho said. "Ain't nothin' about that one gonna 'urt ye none."

Jassamyn had kept the lantern trained on the dead man, stepping slightly in front of Juhg to defend him if necessary.

"Evidently," Craugh said, "he didn't know about the trapdoor."

"Came to a dead end, 'e did," Raisho commented.

The dead man wore regular clothing and not rat hides. Most of the flesh remained on his bones, but it was going fast.

"'E's not been dead long." Raisho stepped forward and picked up an abandoned crowbar covered in wet rust. He hooked the body with the crowbar and pulled it free of the trap. As soon as the obstruction cleared the deadly shaft, the trapdoor closed behind it. Whoever the architects were that had built the trap, they had built it to last. Counterweights grinded in the wall.

Two dead rats floated free of the corpse as it came out of the water.

"Well," Craugh said, kicking one of the rodents with a big boot and causing it to plop into a nest of its brethren on the other side of the room, "there's two that didn't get a free meal."

"Them being there, drowned like that," Jassamyn said, "and that dead man being a fairly recent victim, means that the water is new to this part of the building. Could mean the lower two floors are flooded."

Raisho used the crowbar to loot the dead man. A pouch at his waist held a handful of gold and silver coins.

Grinning at the coins, Raisho said, "'E wasn't wealthy by any means. The next time we stop at an inn, I'll be buyin'."

"Let me see those coins," Craugh said.

A hurt look filled Raisho's dark face. "I don't mind sharin', but it was me what took the time to loot this man."

"The coins." Imperiously, Craugh held out his hand. "By the Old Ones, give you eyes to see and still you are blind."

Grimacing, Raisho dropped the coins into the wizard's outstretched hand. "I don't think there's enough there to change yer life," the young sailor stated truculently.

Craugh held the coins up to study them under his lantern. Then he looked at Juhg, who had gotten to his feet, nearly as soaked as he had been after the fierce swim underwater.

"Have a look at these, apprentice."

Juhg cupped both hands and caught the coins. A quick inspection of them revealed what Craugh had spotted. "They're Torvassiran coins. Not Imarish."

Each of the communities along the mainland struck their own coins. Sometimes a successful trade guild or a ship owner with a small fleet did the same. There was no standard between the nations and the cities of the mainland. Gold and silver were minted, and they were all checked for weight on the scales of every marketplace where they were spent.

"Exactly." Craugh glared at the dead man. "This man came a long way to die."

Torvassir lay to the east, far inland where the trade caravans met. It wasn't too unusual to think that the man had come from Torvassir, but since he had few other coins mixed in, he'd come from there almost straightaway and hadn't mixed much with the locals. That kind of behavior was curious.

During his travels with the Grandmagister, Juhg had twice been through Torvassir, finding the city a comfortable place to be. A consortium of merchants ran Torvassir and provided for the city's defense. Several of them had interests in history, as Juhg had found out while journeying with the Grandmagister. During that time, the Grandmagister had searched for two books that one of the merchants had purchased. Fleeing Torvassir later, after they'd successfully stolen the books with Brandt's help, they had been pursued for days before finally eluding them.

"I 'ave something else as well," Raisho announced. He ripped open the dead man's inside coat pocket and took out a waterproof oilskin pouch.

The familiar rectangular shape set Juhg's heart to pounding at once. The shape could have belonged to anything, but he only imagined one. He crossed over to the young sailor and offered the coins in exchange for the oilskin pouch.

Raisho gratefully made the exchange, dumping the coins into his own coin pouch, then tucking it away inside his shirt.

Excitedly, no longer paying much attention to the dead man, Juhg opened the oilskin pouch. Inside was a handmade book.

He took the book from the pouch. It was smooth and clean and unadorned, obviously something that had been well cared for. But the pages swelled with writing, having to be tied shut with a bright blue ribbon.

Opening the book, Juhg found a simple declaration: *The Journal of Liggon Phares, Being an Account of My Travels and Discoveries*. Hypnotized by the find, still not believing what he was looking at, Juhg flipped through the pages.

"What have you got there, apprentice?" Craugh asked.

"A journal," Juhg whispered in awe. The pages revealed a good writing hand and several diagrams that he quickly recognized as Skull Canal and the building they were currently in. *The Book of Time* was mentioned (and heavily underlined) on a number of pages. The language was one of the human ones, and one that Juhg could read, though not without considerable effort.

"A journal?" Craugh stepped closer.

"Yes," Juhg replied. "This man's journal. He came here looking for *The Book of Time* as well."

Arms folded over his chest, Cobner glared down at the dead man. "Mayhap this quest ain't any too healthy."

"He came here alone?" Craugh asked.

"I don't know." Halfway through the book, Juhg came to an end of the narrative. It was dated, as the Kashaller human traders counted days, no more than three ten-days ago.

Cobner suggested they open up the trapdoor and look for the dead man's companions. No one took him up on it.

"A mystery better saved for a more convenient time, apprentice," Craugh said. "For the moment, let's turn our attentions to the matter at hand."

Regretfully, Juhg closed the book and replaced it into the oilskin pouch, which he tied tightly. He shoved the book inside his jacket where he carried his own journal and the Grandmagister's coded one. *If this keeps up,* he thought wryly, *I will soon be carrying a Library around with me.*

Returning his attentions to the hidden door, he once more straddled the trapdoor and placed his hands on the surface of the door. Knowing the door had clicked back into the secondary ready position, he shoved it sideways. At first he didn't think he was going to be strong enough to move it, then the door grudgingly got underway.

The light from the lantern Jassamyn held speared into the dark throat of the hallway on the other side of the door.

Juhg had expected the water swirling around his ankles to slide down the long hallway ahead of him. Instead, it splashed a little, but stayed level.

The hallway was flooded with sea water.

Jassamyn pressed forward. The draca on her shoulder hissed and spat, obviously afraid that she was contemplating entering the water.

The lantern light penetrated the hallway, following the curving descent till the sea filled it. Fifteen feet down, the stairway was completely submerged.

"Everything below is filled with water," the elven maid said. "Whatever is down there must be ruined."

"Not *The Book of Time*," Craugh said. "It's magical. The elements can't harm it. Only another, more powerful spell can unweave it. And since it came from the In-Betweenness, magic to do that might not exist in this place." He took a deep breath in through his nose and let it out. "If it's down there, it's in one piece."

"Might as well be on one of the moons, for all the good that does us," Raisho said. "It would take a team of dwarven engineers days to dry dock that tunnel. An' then, they wouldn't be able to do it because this room might not be big enough to hold all the water what's down there."

"Maybe there's an air pocket down there." Juhg was loath to turn away from the chance to find the piece of *The Book of Time*. The Grandmagister had given him the task and he didn't want to let go of it.

"Did the diagrams you looked at show any upward turn in the hallway leading down?" Jassamyn asked.

"No."

"Then there's no air pocket down there," she said. "That area is filled with water. No one can hold their breath long enough to go down there and back. And you said the Grandmagister couldn't free the fragment from whatever was holding it."

"Get to the other side of the room," Craugh ordered as he stepped forward, stopping short of the trapdoor, and held the staff on the ground before him in both hands.

208

Juhg and the others quickly cleared the area as the emerald sparks around the end of Craugh's staff whipped themselves into a frenzy. In a powerful voice, the wizard spoke in the language of magic.

Immediately, a whirling waterspout rose from the water in front of Craugh. It stood nearly four feet tall, moving so violently that spray spattered Juhg on the other side of the room.

More harsh words followed.

In response, the waterspout skated from inside the hallway, spitting up even more of the brackish water as it shot toward the big room where they had entered below the waterline. A moment later, the water inside the hallway rushed out, spilling into the room where they all stood and running in the direction the waterspout had taken.

"The waterspout is a construct," Craugh said. His brows knitted in concentration. "An artificial thing. It's very hard to maintain, and it takes a lot of power." He glanced at Juhg. "We'll have to be quick about this."

Hesitantly, Juhg walked to the wizard's side and peered down the hall-way in disbelief as the water continued to run uphill and evacuate the bottom two floors. The gurgling noise of the water rushing by echoed within the room, sounding like the ocean.

Long moments passed. Juhg didn't know how many thousands of gallons of water Craugh caused to relocate, but he knew he was witnessing something few wizards could master. He remembered again how Craugh had wrought the healing spell to mend his own broken leg down in the basement levels of the Vault of All Known Knowledge.

Magic that healed or changed things without destroying them was hard to work. Generally only very strong wizards could work such spells, and most of them didn't because it took too much from them. Craugh had sworn Juhg to secrecy, not wanting him to tell anyone about the incident. He hadn't wanted anyone to know that he handled "good" magic.

For a moment, Juhg felt guilty about being suspicious of Craugh's intentions. The wizard had done a great deal for the Library and for the Grandmagister.

But he's got a lot to atone for, Juhg told himself in rebuttal. *Unleashing* The Book of Time *into this world. Fathering Lord Kharrion. All those untold people he put to death and the empires he overturned. Besides that, although he doesn't destroy them so the spell is supposed to be inherently good because of that, turning someone into a toad is* not *a good thing.*

"Hey!" Dusen squalled from the other room. "You're floodin' the buildin'! Hey! Can you hear me!"

Craugh gestured and a single green spark tore through the rooms, heading back toward the smuggler.

Dusen cried out in true alarm, sounding panicked. "Okay! Okay! I'll shut up! Just make the spider go away again!"

Just when Juhg could see all the way to the bottom of the stairs, though water still rushed from the downstairs area, a terrific crunching sound came up from the bottom of the building. The floor listed underfoot, increasing the angle the building was already sitting at.

Craugh put out a hand and the water stopped coming up the stairs for a moment.

"Taking all the water out of there has affected the way the building's sitting on the sea floor," Jassamyn whispered. "It's already not sitting flat, but the water changing places is affecting it."

Gradually, the crunching sound stopped and the building seemed once more anchored in the mire of the sea.

Lord of the Libraries

Peering down into the hallway, Craugh said, "We've got to continue. I've not taken out enough water yet."

Eventually, puddles followed the deluge. After a time, no more water came up the stairs.

"All right, apprentice," Craugh said in a strained voice, "let's see if we can find *The Book of Time*."

Raisho took the lead, walking boldly down into the hallway with his cutlass in one hand and a lantern in the other. Cobner followed him, both hands on his battle-axe.

Juhg looked down at the water that was now up to his waist. He wasn't happy. A *lot* of water had been moved, and if Craugh lost control of his spell, a lot of it would rush back down into the hallway. He followed Craugh, stepping through the water and past the invisible wall that held it back from the hallway.

He held the lantern high as he walked down the narrow curving stairs. Steep anyway, and wet now, the stairs were made even harder to negotiate because the building leaned in their direction. Juhg experienced a touch of vertigo as he went down because he was leaning so far forward.

They passed a number of sprung traps and bones of what were probably victims of those traps. Juhg had to step over cruel spears that jutted out of the walls in two places, duck through the legs of a skeleton that had its head pinned to the ceiling, and negotiate a section of the stairs that had gone flat as a result of a trick step that caused twenty steps to fold downward. There were also four open pits where more skeletons were wrapped around jagged spears of glass.

At the second floor, Raisho and Cobner split off to search the rooms.

Craugh looked back over his shoulder at Juhg. "Our destination is down farther still, isn't it, Apprentice?"

"Yes," Juhg replied.

And they were off, leaving Cobner and Raisho exploring. The dwarven warrior and the young sailor caught up with them before the others reached the second floor.

The bottom of the stairs let out into an immense circular room.

Craugh walked into the middle of it. His face was ashen and his hand holding a lantern shook a little.

"Are you all right?" Juhg asked.

"It is a *lot* of water, apprentice," the wizard snapped. "Don't waste what time we have. Find the hiding place Wick wrote of."

Getting his bearings in the room, barely able to see the lines of the sundial marked on the floor, Juhg walked to the wall to the right. Skeletons littered the floor. Several of them wore different uniforms and carried weapons showing diverse craftsmanship. Juhg's practiced eye told him they were of separate cultures and disparate times.

When it was first built, the room was probably an entertainment room for the Baron of Seadevil's Roost and his most important guests. Remnants of broken furniture lay all around the room, mixing with the skeletons and shattered stonework. Maybe there had once been a fortune in fine goods, in gold-rimmed glasses or beaten copper mugs bearing the baron's crest, but now there was only moldering garbage.

And, perhaps, a final secret still.

Another quaver ran through the building, causing everyone to glance up apprehensively.

"Apprentice," Craugh said hoarsely.

Turning his attention to the wall, Juhg searched for the hidden door. Water droplets gathered on the stone surface and ran down through the grooves. A preternatural chill filled the room, so cold with him in wet clothes that his bones ached.

Holding his lantern up high, Juhg wiped his free hand across the wall until he found four circular patterns that looked like the rest of the design. Satisfied that he'd found what he was looking for and that the design matched the description in the Grandmagister's book, he depressed the top upper left pattern, the bottom right, pressed down and turned the upper right counterclockwise, and pressed down and turned the lower left clockwise. Then he pressed at the block in the center, causing it to sink back three inches till it locked.

Rumbling echoed through the big, cold room.

Listening for the sound, Juhg turned to the center of the room. A circle four feet across unlocked in the room's center, then it dropped down the height of a human man and revealed a recess in the stone.

Something glowed a deep sea-blue inside.

"I've got it," Raisho said, dropping over the edge and starting for the object.

Walking closer, glad the young sailor had volunteered, Juhg watched with interest. The blue glow radiated from two gemstones floating inside the space. The gemstones possessed square bases that flared up to cube-shaped points that were flat on top. They looked like short mesas on broad bases.

No, Juhg thought. *That can't be right. That isn't a book.*

But he knew that it had to be because the pieces matched the description the Grandmagister had given in his journal. The Voldorvian elves wrote on handmade amber jewels they grew layer by layer and then laid spells upon so the book within could be read in the mind of the person who held the gems. They were some of the hardest books Juhg had ever had to read because they took such a high level of concentration. Most of the First Level Librarians at the Vault of All Known Knowledge hadn't been able to read them. The Grandmagister had been able to read them as easily as he might read by trailing a finger along a line of script. Juhg had heard rumors that some wizards carried spell books written by the Voldorvian elves, although that craft had been lost back during the Cataclysm.

Tentatively, as if realizing that he had put himself directly into the path of danger, Raisho reached into the space with a knife. Without warning, he dropped to his knees as the knife fell from his hand.

"It *burned* me," Raisho exclaimed.

212

Wanting to make certain his friend was all right, and to tend to his wounds if he wasn't, Juhg dropped inside the recessed place as well. A quick examination of the young sailor's hand showed no injury.

"Well," Raisho said sheepishly, "it *felt* like it burned me."

"The knife is iron," Craugh said. "Some of the old magic wars with iron."

Juhg remembered that then. Iron was a product wholly of the world, not of whatever place magic came from. That was why the magic swords in so many of the romances in Hralbomm's Wing didn't really exist. Iron and magic could seldom be bonded, and only then with simple spells and for not very long.

Well, if the gemstones reject iron, Juhg thought, *that's one argument for these being ancient pieces.*

"If you're just going to look at it," Craugh growled, "let me down there."

Hesitant, Raisho reached into the space for the two floating gemstones. His hand seemed to graze them because they suddenly tumbled end over end. But when Raisho closed his hand, it came out empty and the two gemstones continued to float and spin inside the space.

"I could have sworn I had them," the young sailor said. He tried again, but experienced the same results. Still, the gemstones spun differently, as if he'd made contact yet again.

Abruptly, the building shivered again. A sudden deluge sprayed down the stairwell and Juhg thought the wizard's spell holding the water back had slipped. But after the initial splash, no more water came.

"We need to hurry," Craugh said, sounding more strained than ever.

"The Grandmagister had the same problem retrieving the gemstones," Juhg said. "He came here and saw these gemstones, but he couldn't get hold of them."

When he'd decoded that passage in the Grandmagister's journal, Juhg hadn't known how that could be possible. Now he'd seen Raisho struggle with the same problem several times.

"Let me," Juhg asked, stepped around Raisho and reaching out to the gemstones. He felt them somehow slip through his fingers like cold mist up in the mountains. Repeating the action, he watched more closely and saw that he wasn't missing the gemstones, his fingers were actually passing *through* them like they were apparitions instead of the real thing.

"What's taking so long?" Craugh demanded.

"I can't close my hand on them," Juhg said. "I mean, I can close my hand on them, but they pass through my hand. I can feel them, feel how cold they are, but I can't get a grip on them."

"Maybe they're an illusion," Jassamyn offered. "There have been traps all along the way, thankfully much removed from this point in time, but who's to say if the gemstones are really the part of *The Book of Time* that is supposed to be here? They could be part of a trap that was left here all those years ago."

"No," Juhg said. "This is it. It has to be. The Grandmagister would not be wrong about something like this." He felt the chill of the gemstones pulse against his hand, like they were there one instant and gone the next. Concentrating on the pulses, he tried to time them, get a feel for when he could close his hand on the gems.

It's like a tumbler lock, he told himself. *You just have to feel your way through it. There. Almost. No, wait, wait. They have vibrations. Like music. To the* untrained and unknowing ear, music is just sound, but a mathematician recognizes the patterns and sequences and knows they have measure and form.

He felt for the measure and form, listening to the music of the gemstones. They grew more tangible in his hand, and the feeling of physical presence lasted longer and longer.

Unexpectedly, Craugh fell, obviously no longer able to hold onto his staff. Or hold the water back. In the next instant, Juhg heard the gurgling sea rushing pell-mell down the hallway.

And in that instant the contact he had with the spinning blue gemstones was at its strongest. There was an instant of jarring shocks and he went deaf. Then he was gone from the basement level of the Baron of Seadevil's Roost.

 214

13

"What Do You Know About the Nature of Time, Librarian?"

When Juhg reopened his eyes, he was on a narrow trail that wound around a mountain that vanished in the clouds before him. He looked everywhere, up the huge stone mountain to his left, over the steep side of the drop-off to his right, then up the trail he was apparently following in the direction he was headed, and back along the way he must have come to get here.

Where are Craugh, Raisho, Cobner, and Jassamyn? Juhg asked himself. *And why can't I remember climbing this mountain?*

Only a short distance from him in any direction that he looked, gray clouds obscured his vision. He couldn't tell how far he'd come up the mountain or how much farther he had yet to go.

"Craugh?" he called. He remembered how the water had started pouring down through the hallway, knowing that the wizard had overextended himself. He raised his voice. *"Craugh!"*

His voice was lost in the cloudy darkness. Not even an echo came back to him.

Think, Juhg. You can reason this out. You were trained to

use your mind at the Vault of All Known Knowledge, by the best Grandmagister who ever lived.

He glanced down at his clothing, discovering that he was dressed in First Level Librarian robes. Where had his clothes gone? He would never wear the Librarian robes outside of the Vault of All Known Knowledge or Greydawn Moors. Reaching up to his head, he was surprised to discover that his hair was no longer wet. In fact, he was dry all over.

How much time had passed since Craugh had fallen? Then a cold suspicion stared to creep in at the edges of Juhg's mind.

Am I dead? Is this what death is like?

"You're not dead, Librarian Juhg." The voice was quiet and pleasant.

Turning, Juhg discovered that there had been another traveler on the road after all, though he didn't know how he could have missed the fellow earlier. *He must have stepped out of the clouds. That's it. He just stepped out of the clouds while I had my back turned.* Unfortunately, he knew he hadn't had his back turned long enough for the other traveler to have climbed the mountain, not even the short distance he could see.

The figure was tall as a human but looked more like a praying mantis. Standing on its back four legs, the creature held the other two arms curled up under its chest. The body was sleek, covered in a bright green carapace with mottled purple brushed in. The creature was so thin that it looked fragile, but the chitinous hide looked like armor. The head was a rounded triangle with a carved mouth and two bulging black eyes. The antenna wriggled constantly, slight movements that tested the air.

216

"Who are you?" Juhg asked, stepping back from the fantastic creature till he teetered at the edge of the cliff. There was nowhere else he could go.

"Your guide."

"My guide?"

"Yes."

"My guide to where?"

"Wherever it is you wish to go, Librarian Juhg."

Juhg took heart in the fact that the thing hadn't tried to eat him. "Where are my friends?"

"Back at the building."

"I want to go back there."

"You're already there," the creature said.

"Nonsense," Juhg said, "as you can plainly see, I'm here. Wherever here is."

"And you're there." The reply was stated calmly and reasonably.

Juhg blinked his eyes, realizing he was suddenly back in the basement room watching Craugh still falling and the water rushing down the hallway to fill the room where they were. The two blue gems hung frozen in the secret space before him, and for the first time he realized the chill of contact with them was maintaining. He closed his hand on the gems only to feel them fade through his fingers again. When he blinked his eyes again, he was once more standing on top of the mountain with the praying mantis.

"Here," the creature said, "time is malleable and has no rules. Or rather, time here has every rule. You are here, and you are there."

"I don't understand."

"Of course you don't. That is why you are here now: so that you may understand in time."

In time? Juhg wondered how those two words were used. Was it meant that *given* time he would soon find some kind of understanding (though, personally, given present circumstance he very much doubted that)? Or did the creature mean that he was there to understand *in time* so that he could prevent some horrible occurrence (like the building basement flooding and drowning them all)?

He didn't know.

"I need to go back with my friends," Juhg said. "I can't just leave them. They're in a lot of trouble."

"Yes. But there will be time for that. That's what this is all about, isn't it? Time?"

"Can you send me back?"

"When I am ready. And I won't be ready until you are ready."

"I am ready." With the water rushing down the hallway, he had to be ready. He couldn't leave his friends to die.

"You are not," the praying mantis insisted.

"When will I be ready?"

"Once you understand some of what you came here to understand. You can't understand it all at once because your mind will only stretch so far. You're—too much a part of organized time. You lack the vision and skill it would take to absorb everything I could give you now. If I tried, the burden would destroy your mind."

"My friends will still be there when I get back?"

"No time is passing there now for you," the creature said. "You're standing outside of Time. You could watch time go by here if you wanted to, but I perceive that you wish to rejoin with your friends at the same moment that you left."

"Yes."

The creature shook its round head. "You may die."

Juhg thought about that. Things certainly did look bad back when he'd . . . when he'd . . . whatever it was he'd done to stand back in that room. "I can't leave them."

"I could save you."

"Can you save them?"

"Perhaps, but the effects of my intervention would cause ripples that could offer dire consequences at this juncture. It would be better to save them later."

"How can you save them later if they're dead?" Juhg felt frustration and anger building up. He didn't understand what was taking place.

"Your perceptions of time impair you, Librarian. For now accept that such a task is not beyond my ken."

Accept? Juhg couldn't do that. He struggled with understanding what was going on with him now. "Is this real? Or am I hallucinating from some side effect of those two gems?"

"This is real."

"You brought me here?"

"No. *The Book of Time* brought you here."

"You mean the two blue gems?"

"Yes. That is the portion of *The Book of Time* that Lord Kharrion left in the keeping of the Baron of Seadevil's Roost all those years ago."

"I can't get those two gems," Juhg said. "They keep slipping through my fingers."

"That's because you lack proper understanding. That's why you were brought here."

"Why wasn't Raisho brought? He touched the gems."

"He didn't see the resonance within the gems that you did. His mind only grasped the physical aspect represented by *The Book of Time*. You reached for the possibilities. In that instant, *The Book of Time* chose you. You are the one that was chosen, the one that is chosen, and the one that will be chosen. Always."

"Because I felt the pulsing of the gems?"

"Because your mind was open. As it was and is and will be."

Unable to grasp the meaning of what the praying mantis was talking about, Juhg decided to concentrate on easier to digest facts. "Who are you?"

"Your guide, as I have told you."

"Why do I need a guide?"

"Because, at this point, you don't know how to guide yourself. There is much that you don't know."

Juhg was growing frustrated and scared. Maybe he was lying under an ocean of water—*at least a bay,* he argued—drowning, and the discussion he was having with the giant praying mantis was only a distraction to spare him from the pain of death.

"You are not dead, Librarian Juhg."

"I know. You keep telling me that."

"What do you know about the nature of Time, Librarian Juhg?" the creature asked.

"It marks the passage of the day into night, of the night into day, and divides the seasons of the year."

The praying mantis thing frowned—which was a hard thing to do when there were so few facial features to work with, but Juhg clearly understood that it wasn't pleased. "Those are the artifices that those who live in your world choose in an attempt to make sense of the passage of Time. Do you know what Time is?"

"No," Juhg said, interested in spite of the dire circumstances he found himself in at both places where he was.

"Time is limitless, Librarian Juhg. Everyone works to hard to quantify it and pay special attention to the passage of it. Like Time is going somewhere." The creature laughed, and it was a very odd sound. "Time is as limitless as space. Also like space, it has no beginning and no end. It has always been, and it will always be."

"I knew that," Juhg said. "Herrah Snez wrote in his discourse on Time, 'Time can never be wasted nor saved. So approach each moment with an eye toward making it be the best moment you can.'"

"An excellent thought," the creature said, "but, sadly, incorrect. In true Time, there are no moments. All divisions made of Time were wrought by those of limited perception."

"Time passes," Juhg said. "Something that happens . . . an . . . an action—" He waved his hand. "—has a place in time. It's marked. It's finite."

"Is it?" The mantis smiled.

"Time passes," a voice said to Juhg's left.

He turned his head, wondering how yet another person had come upon the mountain without him knowing it, and he saw *himself* dressed in Librarian's robes.

"Something that happens . . . an . . . an action—" His other self waved his hand. "—has a place in time. It's marked. It's finite."

In disbelief, Juhg reached out to touch his other self. He felt the warmth of flesh and blood brush against his fingertips. Then his other self turned to face him, his face filled with surprise and a little fear.

A heartbeat later, someone touched Juhg's face. He whipped his head around and stared into the face of yet another self.

"This doesn't make sense," the self to his left said. And that was only a heartbeat before he heard those same words coming from him. Even then, he realized that another self was suddenly to the right of the self to his right, and the reaction to being touched by the self beyond him was taking place.

Suddenly, the mountain trail seemed filled with Juhgs all in a row. They were all touching and being touched, all of them just as surprised as he had been.

"I don't understand," his left self said, and Juhg agreed with himself only a moment later.

The mantis waved. All of Juhg's other selves vanished, leaving him standing on the trail facing the creature. Juhg touched his own chest, wanting to make certain that he was real. He felt his own heart beating frantically.

"Time simply *is*," the mantis said. "Like space, time has no limits. No beginning, no end."

"We don't know that."

"You have looked up into the sky at night and wondered what was out there," the mantis said. "Do you think that all that emptiness can actually be contained? And once contained, what of the space outside it?"

Juhg had no answer. The question had fascinated him at times, but it was simply too large to properly address. He walked away for a time, trying to assemble his thoughts. "There have been a number of scholars who have addressed that question. I've read several books in the Vault of All Known Knowledge."

"Have you found any solace in their teachings?"

Juhg knew he had not. Everything he'd read had only led to further understanding that when it came to what lay outside the world, he didn't know. Nor did anyone else.

"Some of those scholars have insisted that space is an organic thing," the mantis said. "They say that space grows a little each day, like a plant in a forest, or a pool of water that swells with the rain. But a plant takes nutrients from other sources to put on new foliage, and the rain fills the pool. So where, then, does this new space come from?"

"I don't know."

"How far can it grow? Or is it like a plant or a pool, governed by its own nature or constrained by space?"

Juhg could only shake his head.

"Then how can Time be constrained? Can you just lop off moments like you would pieces of a carrot for a stew?"

"A candle burns," Juhg said, "and is gone."

"A burning candle gives off heat and light and smoke," the mantis said. "If you could gather those things, you could reconstruct the candle, and then burn it yet again. Over and over."

"I don't know what you're trying to tell me," Juhg admitted.

"Time," the mantis said, "was invented for the beings of your world, so that everything didn't happen at once. They spilled out of this world into that one a long time ago."

"You're saying that everyone in my world came from this place?"

"Yes."

"Why?"

The mantis was silent for a moment. Then it folded its upper legs behind its back and started up the mountain. "Walk with me for a while, Librarian Juhg."

"A while," Juhg echoed. "You acknowledge a division of time?"

The mantis smiled. "I talk so that you may understand."

"Well," Juhg said, "I don't. I don't understand at all." Then he realized he was being left behind and hurried to catch up.

"There is another here like myself," the mantis said as they walked.

"Another mantis?"

The mantis looked at Juhg. Bright speculation showed in those deep black eyes. "You see me as a mantis?"

"Are you not?"

"Of course I'm not." The mantis broke into laughter that pealed over the mountainside. "A *mantis*. Indeed!"

Juhg felt a little embarrassed, but he was angry, too. "You look like a mantis."

"That's because your perception sees me as one." The mantis rubbed its chin with one of its forelegs as if in deep thought. "A number of your cultures believe insects to be immortal on your world. Beetles. Grasshoppers. Other crawling things."

"And trees," Juhg added. "As well as rocks."

"Neither of those things could have walked up this mountain with you. But to return to my story, there is another here like me."

"Where is he?"

"Who said the other person was male?"

"No one." Juhg reined in his curiosity. He was leaping to conclusions. The Grandmagister had trained him better than that. "Is the other person female?"

"The other person, like myself, is neither. Perhaps that is another reason why you see me as an insect. Many of them do not immediately reveal their gender. Tell me——" The mantis stopped walking and held its forelegs out. "——am I clothed?"

"No. You're a mantis. Why would you need clothing?"

"If I were a mantis, I wouldn't need clothing. In fact I don't need clothing anyway." The mantis resumed walking. "You're not clothed either."

Juhg felt a sudden intense rush of embarrassment and slowed his gait so that he walked a few steps behind the mantis. He looked down at himself. *I am clothed. I am wearing the robe of a First Level Librarian.* At the same moment, he knew there was no way that robe could be there.

"A joke, Librarian Juhg. Nothing more." The mantis laughed and the sound was harsh. "One thing your kind has invented that I have rather enjoyed is humor. It took me quite a while to get the knack of it, though. Humor is a very delicate thing."

"Humor is out of place," Juhg said sternly. "Laughing at your jokes while my friends face death is . . . is . . . *wrong.*"

"Pity. I thought it was rather funny. The look on your face, I mean. But that's quite all right. Most humor is intended for personal consumption anyway, it seems."

Not caring whether the mantis saw him clothed or unclothed anymore, Juhg ran in front of the creature and blocked its path. "I don't have time for this."

The mantis stopped and stared at him with those oily black eyes. "That is one of the things you will have to come to accept, Librarian Juhg. Here in this place, you have all of Time. You never need fear being late. Not even to go back and chance death with your friends in that rapidly filling basement beneath the sea."

"Send me back."

"There are things that I must tell you first."

"An order of events?" Juhg riposted. "Here in a place where Time doesn't matter?"

"Don't be facetious. It's unbecoming." The mantis stepped around Juhg effortlessly, as if Juhg was standing still, which he was.

Juhg hurried to keep up.

"There have always been two of us here," the mantis said. "At least, that's the way we remember it, know that it is, understand that it will be. Sometimes we have been friends and sometimes we have been strangers. There are many things to experience here." The creature was silent for a moment. "Sometimes we have been, are, and will be enemies. During a period of enmity that was, is, or will be, we fought. Only in this place, neither of us could win. Or we both won. Or it was a draw."

Struggling to accept that, Juhg kept his peace. He couldn't help thinking about Craugh and the others at the mercy of the waters rapidly filling the basement. What if the creature was lying and they were already dead? He couldn't bear that thought.

"In our frustration, I agreed, agree, will agree—"

"Stop doing that," Juhg said.

"What?"

"Talking in that fashion. Stick with the past tense. That's how I can best understand it."

The mantis reflected for a moment. "I will honor your request, since in your world these events have already passed."

"Thank you." Juhg's head hurt with trying to absorb everything. The

nature of space had always plagued him, and even the Grandmagister offered no real understanding of it.

"We . . . *opened* Time and your world was born, as limitless as this
place here, but with different rules. We made Time flow linearly. Like a
river. And we put beings there that had been in this place. They became the
humans, dwarves, elves, goblins, and other creatures. Birds, fish, insects,
and everything else." The mantis shook its head. "So much more than we
expected. But what we had done, are doing, will—" The creature stopped
itself. "Well, it quickly got out of hand."

"Why did you do that?" Juhg asked. "Put all the beings and the creatures into that place?"

"So that we could enjoy our enmity," the mantis replied. "So that the
wars that we fought with these beings could end and there could be a win-
ner declared."

"A game? You created our world as a game?"

The mantis shrugged. They kept walking along the mountain trail but
Juhg hardly paid attention now. "It was unique. Nothing like it had ever
existed before."

"But the beings you put there existed."

"Yes."

"Where did they come from?"

"They were always here."

224

"Then what made you different from them?" Juhg asked.

"That."

"That what?"

"The difference, of course. If we had not always been different, there
would have been no difference, would there?"

Juhg didn't know how to argue with that but he felt compelled to. He
made himself table the subject for the moment. "What am I doing here?"

"I wished to speak to you, to let you know the things you have to deal
with in your world."

"*The Book of Time,* you mean?"

"Yes. You see, when we opened ourselves to that other world so that
we could enjoy our enmity, we left this place open to invasion from the
other side. Until it happened, is happening, and will happen, we had never
before thought anything could disrupt this place. We were wrong."

The wind along the mountain suddenly seemed colder and wetter.

Juhg blinked against the precipitation, starting to feel as cold and as chilled as he had back in the building basement in his sodden clothing.

"Men," the mantis said as if the term were despicable, "found a means to invade this place. They came into this place and stole *The Book of Time,* returning to their world before we could get them."

Craugh, Juhg thought, but he kept the name to himself. "You didn't know this was going to happen?"

The mantis frowned. "I . . . do not like admitting something I don't know. It is . . . uncomfortable."

"It's also," Juhg said, "often the first step in gaining knowledge."

"The concept of learning something that I don't know is . . . well, beyond description, I'm afraid. I have always known everything."

"What am I doing here?" Juhg asked.

The mantis stopped and looked at him. "You have been chosen to find *The Book of Time* and bring it back to this place. People search for it there. Your Grandmagister Edgewick Lamplighter was close to acquiring it, but the fourth section of *The Book of Time* is difficult to acquire. And his enemies struck more swiftly and with more knowledge than he had guessed. Still, he sent you to complete the task, and I will depend on you to accomplish that task as well."

"Why don't you get it?"

"Because I can't enter your world," the mantis said. "I can observe it endlessly, and do. But I can never put a foot in that place. Or a tentacle."

"Tentacle?"

The mantis smiled a little. "Another joke, I'm afraid. They've become somewhat addictive. Of course, I can't remember a time when humor did not exist here. Once something enters this place, it tends to fill it up and become eternal. In all directions of time."

"Does that mean that I—"

"You're not really here, Librarian Juhg. You only perceive yourself to be through the contact I have with you through the piece of *The Book of Time* that you have found."

"So I am back in the basement?"

"Yes."

"Am I drowning?"

"Not yet."

Juhg swallowed hard. "Will I drown?"

"I don't know. Things in your world are so much different there than here. That is why we were able to have our wars in your world: the outcome was never known for certain. Though some of them turned out to be terribly predictable. Then the various races started taking hold of their own destinies and escaped us."

"How?"

"By creating written language and writing books, of course."

"Books?" Juhg was puzzled.

"Yes. With books the various races that learned to read and write, that created means to do so, also created history. They learned how to avoid the situations we sometimes set up to challenge them. We created inhospitable weather, they read their books and found new places to go that they had once been or that explorers had written about. We tried to create war, which was sometimes largely successful, and they consulted books on politics and economics and found that war was not good for either side. They negotiated rather than warred. It all got very boring and we left your world to its own devices. It exists as an aberration, a place apart from this place, but nothing more. Everything that matters is here."

"Except *The Book of Time*," Juhg reminded, angry at the way the mantis could be so smug.

Grudgingly, the creature nodded. "Except for that."

"This is all too much," Juhg said. "I can't do what you ask me to."

The mantis regarded him with its dark eyes. "Do you wish to save Grandmagister Lamplighter?"

A sinking feeling opened in the pit of Juhg's stomach. "Of course."

"To accomplish that, *The Book of Time* must be gathered and returned here."

"I can't even pick up the first part of it in Skull Canal. My hand keeps passing through the gems."

"You have hold of the gems, Librarian Juhg. You do have hold of them. That's how I was able to bring you here. Your decision to feel the pulse of them and be drawn to them instead of attempting to seize them was correct. Gathering the other pieces will be simpler now that you have these."

"Why was *The Book of Time* broken up?"

The mantis hesitated. "There are some things that I can't tell you now. We will talk again. Later." The creature stopped walking. "I weary of trying to stay attuned to your way of thinking. I find it very difficult. You need to go back."

"Wait," Juhg said.

The mantis looked at him.

"Where is the other being? Your peer? Would he or she or it wish to take part in this discussion?"

A troubled look, though terribly abbreviated with the lack of features the mantis had to deal with, fitted itself to the creature's face. "Don't concern yourself with that. Take the gems in your hand and go to the Smoking Marshes. The way will not be easy. There are many challenges, and you have many enemies."

"What enemies?"

"Aldhran Khempus and the other Library. They all seek the portions of *The Book of Time*. They have begun to guess where the pieces are. *The Book of Time* can't be allowed to fall into the hands of humans again."

"Why?"

"Because they have such strong magic."

"You have magic?"

"No." The mantis shook its head. "I don't have magic. I have only the powers that this place gives me. But the humans, and a few beings among the other races, developed magic. It was another unforeseen occurrence that surprised us. If we had known magic would develop, we would never have opened this place and allowed that world to come into existence."

"Beware, because some of those humans who broke into this place and stole *The Book of Time* are still out there. Most of them are dead."

I know, Juhg thought, and he couldn't help thinking of Craugh, wishing he knew if the wizard was helping to save the Grandmagister or merely serving his own dark desires.

"Now go," the mantis said. "Your time grows short." It lifted a foreleg and gestured at Juhg.

The vaporous cloud settled around the mountain suddenly grew thick and closed in on Juhg. Before he could take a breath, the cloud was all that he could see. Dizziness filled his head and he felt himself falling.

14

The Blue Gems

he roaring, rushing, gurgling sound of a waterfall filled Juhg's ears and he realized he was in water up to his neck. Someone was yelling at him. He turned around and saw Raisho and Cobner holding Craugh between them. The wizard was too weak to stand on his own, obviously exhausted by his efforts at keeping his spell in place holding the water back. Cobner and Raisho held up lanterns in their free hands, but their movements and reflection of the light off the roiling water made weird and warped shadows dance around the room.

"Juhg!" Raisho yelled. "Craugh's spell is finished! We've got to get out of here!"

"Where's Jassamyn?" Juhg asked, noticing then that the elven maid was missing.

"She's trying to find a way out," Cobner answered, having to yell over the roar of the rushing water filling the room. "She went up the hallway to see if we could get out that way. I don't know if we can manage it carrying Craugh, though."

At that moment, Jassamyn tumbled back down the hallway stairs, propelled by the incoming sea. Out of control, she slammed up against the wall on the other side of the room and disappeared beneath the waterline.

Juhg kicked upward and swam toward the edge of the circular opening that contained the hiding place for the section of *The Book of Time*. When he reached for the edge of the circle, he realized he had the two blue gems clutched tightly in his left fist. Hurriedly, he thrust the gems into his jacket pocket and clambered from the sunken area.

Standing on the basement's floor, Juhg found that the water there was only up to his hips. The swirling water got much deeper as he approached the area where Jassamyn had disappeared due to the building's tilt.

The miniature draca circled overhead in a panicked frenzy, squalling in its shrill voice. Folding its batwings tight, the creature dove into the water. A moment later, the draca reappeared, clinging tightly to Jassamyn's left ear and fluttering its wings.

Jassamyn staggered to her feet. Blood streamed from cuts at her right temple and chin. Her eyes looked glazed and Juhg could tell her senses were reeling from the impact.

Juhg fought the rising water to get to her side. Before he reached her, the building shook and something grinded beneath the floor.

"Whatever is left of the building's foundation is giving way," Cobner yelled. "It isn't setting on flat ground. It's going to fall, and it's going to take us with it."

Jassamyn brushed the frantic draca from her ear. More blood glinted from the tiny wounds the miniature dragon had inflicted. "We can't go up the hallway," she gasped. "Craugh's magical barrier is still holding some of the water back but it could give way any moment. If it does and we're in the hallway, we won't get out of here alive."

"The hallway's the only way out," Raisho argued. "We have to go that way."

Shaking her head, Jassamyn said, "We'll never make it. The water's building up in that room too fast."

"Carrying Craugh is going to make getting out that way even harder," Cobner growled.

"I can stand," Craugh insisted as he lurched free of Cobner and Raisho. He had lost his hat as he had fallen and his gray hair matted to his head, making him look even frailer. He glared at the rushing water filling the hallway. "We've only got one chance. Gather round."

Craugh's hat floated near Juhg and he grabbed it. The water had now risen to his chest and he had to fight it to cross the room to Craugh.

Looking at Juhg, Craugh asked, "Did you get the blue gemstones?"

"I did," Juhg answered.

"Good," the wizard said. "If you hadn't, getting back down here to get them would be most difficult."

The grinding beneath the building's foundation repeated, sounding louder and more immediate. Juhg felt the floor slide beneath his feet and he lost his balance. For a moment, he floundered in the water and was unable to get his feet under him.

" 'Ere now," Raisho said. "I got ye, scribbler." The young sailor knotted a fist at the back of Juhg's jacket and helped him get his footing.

"Thanks," Juhg said in a choked voice.

"Foller the wizard. I'll watch yer back."

Juhg fought his way through the water, trying desperately to catch up to Craugh. The wizard halted against the wall where the floor tilted down. By the time Juhg reached him, the water had risen past his chin. With the way the water slapped around the room, he found himself choking on it often.

"What are you going to do?" Jassamyn asked.

"I'm going to make an opening for us in this wall." Craugh spoke harsh words that came from deep within his throat. His right forefinger glowed a deep, rich forest green. Working quickly, he inscribed a series of glowing symbols that formed an oval on the wall.

"The wall you're planning on opening up is pointed down toward the sea bottom," Cobner said.

"I know," Craugh said irritably. "Trying to make a hole in the wall facing up would be too hard. The outside sea pressure would prevent the spell's explosion from blowing the wall outward. The air pressure has increased in this room with the water rushing in, and that will aid us as well."

"Explosion?" Juhg repeated, spitting water. The water had gotten too deep for him to stand. He had to tread water to stay in place. "I don't think any kind of explosion in this place would be a good idea right—"

At Craugh's command, lines spread in a circle from the symbols he'd inscribed and filled and the rest of the oval's shape. Satisfied with his work, the wizard turned and fought back against the rising wall of water that was rapidly filling the room. Not even looking, he reached back and caught Juhg's arm, dragging him after.

Stopping in the center of the room, just short of the open circular area, Craugh looked at his companions. Water dappled the wizard's face, running down his cheeks and dripping through his beard.

"This will happen very quickly now," Craugh cautioned. "I will have to divert energy from the spell holding the water back in the upper room to make the spell here strong enough to knock out the wall. Once that upstairs barrier goes down, we will be at the sea's mercy. I will not be able to resurrect that barrier, nor will I have much left to give toward our protection."

Cobner shook his head. "We can't stay here, that's for sure. And I'd rather risk my life on a chance to live than to stay here and drown like a rat slowly." He glanced meaningfully at the dozen or so rat corpses that already floated on the water's surface.

Juhg felt slightly sick, understanding now what the soft bumps that had hit him below the waterline had been. Several other bunches of rats clung together and fought for survival, biting and scratching one another to climb to the top of the flesh and blood islands they created with their bodies.

"Get to it," Raisho said.

Nodding grimly, Craugh turned to the marked wall and raised his staff. He spoke and a glowing green ball formed in the palm of his right hand. Drawing his arm back, he threw, then turned and shielded his eyes.

Juhg took the hint and shielded his own eyes. He'd just closed them when the fiery explosion lit up his lids. As it was, he still saw spots in his vision when he opened his eyes. The building sagged drunkenly, tilting even more toward the sea floor. Juhg couldn't help but wonder how far the drop-off was. Some of the places around Imarish were quite deep. Even now, they might be deeper than they could safely swim up even if they were not fighting for their lives against the pull of the in-rushing water.

Two knots of rats had caught fire from the magical explosion. Green flames lapped at them as they screamed death cries and boiled apart as they sought to save themselves. Beyond them, the wall remained in place although huge cracks now showed on the surface.

"The way isn't open," Raisho said.

"It will be," Craugh responded. "Just stay ready."

With the magical barrier removed from the floor above, the water drained into the basement with ever increasing speed. In seconds, all of them were swimming for their lives and battling frightened rodents that tried to climb up on them.

Craugh kept hold of Juhg and used his staff to push them both above the rising water. Even now, the staff and the wizard's arm were well below the waterline. Although he was wet and bedraggled, Craugh smiled a little with anticipation.

"Don't fret, apprentice," Craugh yelled hoarsely over the rising tide of water. "I didn't come here to die. Neither did you." He spat out a mouthful of water he had inadvertently gulped. "The hallway is filled with water now. There's no air escaping from this room. The air pressure in here is increasing. It has to go someplace, and it will find the weakest source of resistance."

Feeling the increased pressure inside his ears, Juhg fathomed the wizard's desperate ploy. "Munyar's Fifth Principle of Hydraulics: air compresses but water doesn't."

Munyar had been one of the Steelgray Tidal dwarves that lived in the north before the Cataclysm. Interested by hydraulics and how compressed air could be used other than in a forge bellows, Munyar had developed small boats powered by compressed air. Unfortunately, he'd never been able to successfully build an iron container to contain enough air to propel even a small boat more than a few feet.

The dwarven engineer had dreamed of building a ship powered by compressed air that could sail against the wind and allow a decisive military advantage against enemies on the sea. The best that Munyar had been able to develop was a small compressed air tank that hurled a small boat two hundred feet and emitted an obnoxious noise. In his lifetime, Munyar had been known as the dwarven master builder who had invented the flatulent rescue boat that specialized in offshore salvage.

Sadly, no one really knew that Munyar's personal journals yielded some of the first recorded experimentation and understanding of hydraulics. Most of his contemporaries and the generations that later followed only knew about the flatulent rescue boat he'd invented.

Scarcely a foot of space remained above the waterline when the wall gave way with a rumble that could be felt through the water. Cobner swam nearby, dressed only in his underclothes because he had taken off his armor. Curse words had fill the air as he had stripped out of his gear. He had also lost his lantern while undressing and now only the lantern carried by Raisho barely lighted the room.

"Now," Craugh ordered. He looked at Juhg. "You seemed to be affected by something while you were trying to get the gemstones. Can you swim?"

"Yes," Juhg responded, but he worried about the distance they would have to swim.

"All of you," Craugh said as he turned his face up to the ceiling because he no longer had room to hold his head upright, "fill your lungs and swim through the hole in the wall. Once you're in the open sea, stop a moment to get your bearings. You won't be able to see the night's darkness. Your natural buoyancy will pull you toward the surface. Follow that. There may be air bubbles that are forced from this room, but I don't know if you'll be able to see those either."

"Old Ones protect us," Raisho said.

Juhg bumped his head on the ceiling and had to turn his face up as well.

"Go!" Craugh ordered. He took a final breath and submerged, disappearing at once in the murky water.

Cobner went under next.

Jassamyn caught the draca in midair and cupped the miniature dragon in one hand, holding shut its beak and blocking its nostrils. She looked at Juhg and said, "See you soon." She pushed off the ceiling with her free hand, turned upside down, and kicked against the ceiling with her feet to propel herself down and forward.

"Well, looks like it's just ye an' me, scribbler." Raisho held the lantern against the ceiling. Water already lapped at the glass.

"I'll see you soon." Juhg reached his friend, clasped his hand, and let go only when they both started to sink.

"Soon," Raisho agreed.

Feeling as afraid as he ever had in his whole life, even as afraid as he had been in the goblinkin mines, Juhg turned upside down in the water and duplicated Jassamyn's feat of kicking off the ceiling. He went deep at once. Water filled his ears and reminded him that he taken the first step toward drowning.

A moment later, Raisho dropped the lantern into the water and swam after Juhg. The lantern remained lit for just a moment and created a ghostly golden haze against the murky water. Then, just when Juhg spotted the open hole in the wall ahead, the lantern extinguished and darkness claimed the room.

Is the mantis watching from wherever it is? Juhg wondered. *Is it concerned with whether I live or die? Or does it already know the outcome of this?*

Juhg pushed the questions from his head and concentrated on swimming. As the water had filled the room, he had shoved Craugh's pointy hat inside his jacket to keep it safe, but it still created drag as he swam.

In the darkness, he bumped his head and shoulder against the rough edges of the broken rock that framed the hole the wizard had blown through the wall. The sharp pain almost made him cry out, which would have made him take in a breath of water.

Once through the hole, Juhg looked up but could see nothing. Clamping down on the fear that filled him, he forced himself to go limp. At first he thought nothing was going to happen, that Craugh had been wrong and that the sinking building was negating the natural buoyancy he should have been experiencing. Then he felt it; just a slight upward tug.

Heartened, Juhg dug into the water with both hands and kicked his feet. He promptly smashed his head against the building above him. Even the dark mass of the building was invisible in the black water. Using his hands, he negotiated his way around the building. His lungs were near to bursting by the time he reached the corner of the building. When he looked up, though, he could see a faint silvery shine of moonslight against the surface of the sea. Under the circumstances, he had no idea how far the distance was, but he still felt hopeful. He kicked out and swam upward, letting out some of the air in his lungs as he went.

Just when he thought he could go no farther, his hand slid through the sea surface and into air. By the time he realized that, he was already taking his first breath. Treading water, he looked around and saw that Craugh, Cobner, and Jassamyn had made the swim.

"Raisho?" Juhg asked.

"He hasn't come up yet," Jassamyn answered. She released the draca, pushing the miniature dragon into the air. The creature quickly took flight and shrilled with the joy of being alive and once more in its element.

Juhg's own surprise and happiness at surviving the swim from the sinking building was quickly dying with Raisho's continued absence. Taking a few quick deep breaths, Juhg prepared to go back underwater.

"Apprentice," Craugh called in a tired voice. "It's too dark. You would never be able to find him."

"I've got to try."

At the moment, Raisho surfaced only a few feet away. He came up so fast and so hard that he was out of the water to his waist before sinking back down.

Juhg swam to his friend and threw an arm across Raisho's broad shoulders. "I was beginning to think I'd lost you," Juhg said. Craugh and Cobner and Jassamyn were all old traveling companions of the Grandmagister's. They had chosen, for their own reasons, to come along on this adventure. But Juhg knew Raisho had come because of him. Neither of them had family and they had grown close over the last two years.

Breaking away, Raisho shook his head. "Ye won't lose me in the water, scribbler. I'll be able to outswim ye ever' day of yer life. I got turned around 'neath that buildin' fer a moment, is all. I got myself squared away all right."

"Not to be going and disturbing your little reunion," Cobner said, "but mayhap I need to remind you that we aren't in safe waters here."

They swam toward the broken bridge landmark that the Grandmagister had indicated on his map of Skull Canal. When they arrived, they discovered that they were nearly a quarter of the way around the island.

The boat was still tied up where they had left it. They also found out that Dusen and his crew of smugglers had evidently survived the sinking building as well. The smugglers had discovered the boat and were in the process of looting the supplies.

Dusen and his comrades looked worse for the wear. Most of them had lumps on their faces from the spider bites and all of them were drenched to the bone.

Cobner, bereft of his armor and his battle-axe—all of which lay at the bottom of the canal and probably under the sunken building as well—bent down and picked up a large rock in each hand. He showed the smugglers an evil grin.

Craugh clapped his hat onto his head after trying futilely to make it look more proper and stepped forward. He was a little unsteady. Bright green embers flickered at the end of his staff. Jassamyn stepped to the wizard's right and unsheathed her longsword. Moonslight glowed pale blue against the blade. To Cobner's left, Raisho slid free the cutlass sheathed down his back.

"That's our boat," Craugh stated in a cold voice.

Warily, the smuggler leader stared at the wizard. "You cost me a lot tonight. Men and goods. I figure you owe me. I'm willing to spare your lives and let you go." He bared his teeth in a smile and pushed the long hairy tail of a rat skin from his face.

"As I recall," Cobner growled, "we were in the middle of giving you a good thumping." He slammed the rocks in his fists together before him. Sparks jumped. "I'd be glad to go back and get it done right instead of leaving off. I'm not much of one for leaving a task half done."

Juhg swallowed hard, thinking that they had survived the sinking building and the swim to the sea surface only to step back into the fight with the smugglers.

"By the Old Ones," Craugh said in a voice like cold thunder, "but I've had my fill tonight. And I'll not suffer fools gladly." He gestured and a wall of nearly invisible force gusted over Dusen.

The smuggler leader stumbled for a moment, then began to shrink. The other smugglers drew away from Dusen in fear, making signs of warding against evil. Dusen continued shrinking, shrieking out in fear as he dropped down through his clothes and ended up on his hands and knees. His hair slid back and changed, becoming mottled gray skin covered with dark blemishes and warts. Then he vanished entirely within his own clothing. A moment later, a mournful and piteous croak sounded from within the clothes strewn across the naked rock of the island.

A toad sprang out of the clothing and plopped to the ground. Dusen peered up at them with his one good eye and croaked again. By some whim, though Juhg thought it was by Craugh's design, the smuggler leader's eyepatch had shrunk with him, fitting the toad perfectly even now.

"Well then," Craugh said in a mocking voice, "I've increased the toad population of Skull Canal by one. But I'm sure this place could stand a few more toads." He glared happily at the smugglers standing nearby with their mouths hanging open. "Who's next for a steady diet of flies?"

The smugglers dropped the supplies back into the boat and ran to the far end of the island, begging the wizard's forgiveness the whole time. Taking a final last glaring look at the wizard, Dusen the toad bounded off after his fellows.

Cobner tossed his rocks to one side, put his hands on his hips, and arched his back. Vertebrae popped. "I do hate to miss out on a good fight, Craugh, and I would have put one up if I'd had to. But I'm thinking that rowing back to Sharz's house is gonna be all I'm good for until I get a good night's sleep."

They quickly reloaded the supplies into the boat and boarded. Raisho and Cobner pushed the vessel out into the water, then hopped aboard and began rowing.

Craugh sat in the boat facing Juhg. Although the wizard had not asked, Juhg knew Craugh wanted to see the prize they had risked their lives to claim. Suspicion still darkened Juhg's thoughts, though. *The Book of Time* represented power that few who were interested in such things could resist.

It was Raisho who broke the uncomfortable silence. The young sailor kept his oar moving swiftly and steadily through the water as he and Cobner propelled them back through the canals. "Well, scribbler," he said, "are ye gonna keep us in suspense all night?"

Juhg looked at his friend.

Raisho grinned, his teeth white in the darkness. "Let's see the swag."

Reluctantly, but feeling somehow a little safer showing everyone the two blue jewels he had retrieved from hiding place instead of showing them to Craugh alone, Juhg reached inside his jacket and took out the portion of *The Book of Time*. He held them in the palm of his hand.

238

"They're beautiful," Jassamyn said.

"Probably worth a fortune," Raisho agreed.

The others looked at him.

"Not that we're gonna sell 'em."

Everyone's attention reverted back to the two curiously shaped gemstones.

"How do you know those gee-bobs are really part of *The Book of Time?*" Cobner asked. "They could just be part of a treasure that was never found in the building."

"The Grandmagister found the gems," Jassamyn said. "And from the looks of the building, others did, too. But I'm certain they didn't know what it was they had found."

"If they was treasure, I'm sure nobody would have left them behind," Raisho said.

"I've seen Wick walk away from treasure before," Cobner said. "I don't even want to count the times we've up and left a place with treasure laying everywhere just for the picking. Why, the treasure we left in Shengharck's lair in the Broken Forge Mountains would have taken even a dwarf ten lifetimes to spend even if he spent as hard and foolishly as he could." He paused, frowning sadly at the memory. "That day I thought I took me a king's ransom, but I spent it right fast enough. And the dragon was dead! You don't have any problems robbing a dead dragon!" He blew out a breath. "If that volcano hadn't erupted and brought the mountain down, we could have robbed that lair for years."

Raisho dug in with his oar. "Them ain't just gemstones. I tried to get them out of that hidey-hole. I couldn't touch them."

Cobner reached for one of the gems on Juhg's palm. "Looks like you can touch them now."

When the dwarven warrior went to pick one of the gemstones up, his fingers passed through them as if they'd been made of smoke. Frowning, Cobner tried again, but only achieved the same result.

Not believing what he was witnessing, Juhg closed his hand over the strangely shaped gemstones. He still felt them, hard and smooth as glass against his fingers and palm.

"Let me try." Jassamyn leaned in and tried to pick the gemstones up. She had no better luck than Cobner.

"May I?" Craugh asked.

Juhg hesitated, wondering if the gemstones were just an illusion. "Is this a trick of some sort? I mean, there could have been a spell back in that room. Like a mirage spelled into place there. Maybe you are only seeing the visual aspects of it, but I swear I can *feel* them."

Craugh reached for the gems. Even before his fingers touched them, sparks shot up. Stubbornly, because that was the wizard's nature, Craugh continued trying to touch the gems. Then a large eruption of power flared up that knocked the wizard flat.

For a moment, after the horrendous explosion of light and force and sound, Juhg feared that Craugh was dead. Then he saw the wizard's skinny chest rise and fall. Jassamyn inspected Craugh and pronounced him fit enough, saying that there were no wounds and he'd only been dazed.

Cautiously, after a short time had passed, Craugh sat up and glared at the gemstones. He shot Juhg a suspicious look. "Did you do that?"

Juhg shook his head. "No. I didn't know that they would do that." His mind sorted through everything he had learned from the mantis. "The mantis said that magic was anathema to *The Book of Time*. Maybe that's what caused the reaction."

" 'The mantis?' " the wizard repeated.

"The praying mantis I met when I seized hold of the gemstones," Juhg said. He wet his lips, wondering if everything he had experienced had been true or just an illusion. As carefully as he could, trying not leave out any of the details, he began telling his companions of his encounter with the mantis. Before he knew it, his journal and a piece of charcoal were in his hands. While he talked, he drew in the journal, working as best as he could under the moonslight while he captured details in quick sketches.

"Juhg."

Barely awake, Juhg hoped that the voice was only his imagination or the leftover part of a dream. He ached all over from the abuse he had suffered at the hands of the Skull Canal smugglers the day before. He wasn't ready to wake, and he didn't want to face the impossible task of making sense of everything that had happened and putting it into his journal.

Yesterday, while Craugh went in search of supplies and Cobner and Jassamyn inquired down at the docks about buying passage aboard a trade ship bound for the mainland and Raisho watched over him in Sharz's upstairs living quarters, Juhg had worked on updating his journal. Too many things, *important* things had happened that couldn't be forgotten. The conversation he'd had with the mantis was the most important. He had copied the information the mantis had told him into a second journal that he intended to give to Jassamyn. It was insurance, in case something happened to him.

His work on the second journal detailed everything that had happened to him since he and Craugh and *One-Eyed Peggie* had left Greydawn Moors after the attack there. Although he was conflicted about sharing the wizard's personal history, Juhg fully intended to put that into the journal as well. After the mantis's story, Juhg knew that Craugh was tied too tightly to *The Book of Time* not to tell someone. If something happened to him or he got separated from the group, someone else needed to know.

Before going to sleep on the night they returned from Skull Canal, Juhg had made a shorthand list of events he wanted to cover in the journal.

The Grandmagister had always taught him to plan out everything he intended to write. He was organized, had his tasks ordered before him, but he simply didn't have enough time and energy to get them all done.

And now, he again awakened in the midst of his unfinished work on Sharz's private work table. He was beginning to think he'd never again know what a bed and a good night's sleep felt like.

"Are ye awake then?" Raisho asked. "If so, I'll make ye a bite to eat."

As he did every morning, and several times throughout the day, Juhg took the leather pouch from the strap he wore around his neck. Opening the pouch, he poured *The Book of Time* fragments into his palm to examine them.

In the light of day, the two blue gemstones took on an even more incredible luster. During his examination of them once he had returned to Sharz's home, Juhg had discovered the gemstones had tiny slots etched into them that looked like they would allow the pieces to fit together in a tongue-and-groove assembly. However, no matter how he tried them, the pieces would not fit together.

The grooves presented yet another challenge and puzzle. There was no doubt that *something* was supposed to fit onto the pieces, or that the pieces were supposed to fit onto something else.

Feeling a little guilty about his own paranoia, Juhg dumped the gemstones back into the leather pouch. He knew he shouldn't have been worried about anyone else stealing the gemstones because no one else could touch them. He still didn't understand why that was.

Once, when he had left the gemstones in the pouch on the work table, Raisho had tried to move the pouch while he was looking through Juhg's journal, looking at various illustrations to refresh his memory and get ready to add to Juhg's notes as he'd been asked. He hadn't been able to touch the leather pouch either. Further experimentation revealed that anyone could touch the leather pouch when the gems weren't inside it, but not once the gemstones were safely put away. Only Juhg could do that.

"Juhg. C'mon, scribbler, rise an' shine."

"I'm awake," Juhg protested.

"I know, but ye're not up an' about. Ye told me to make sure ye got up." Raisho sounded guilty. "I've already let ye sleep later then ye wanted me to."

Later? That sunk in. Juhg had too much work to do to spend all his time sleeping. He pushed himself up from the work table, checking to make sure he hadn't left an open inkwell nearby. Yesterday morning, he had done that and ended up spilling ink over work he had just finished the night before. The setback had cost him hours of effort in work that had needed to be copied over. He had wanted to give up in frustration, but he hadn't been able to let go the task.

"I capped yer inkwell after I found ye asleep this mornin'," Raisho said.

"Thank you," Juhg said. He felt guilty that he didn't even seem to be able to take care himself when there was so much to be done. Raisho could have helped Craugh get the supplies necessary for the journey to the Smoking Marshes except the wizard asked the young sailor to watch over Juhg.

"What do ye feel up to eatin'?"

"Nothing, really." Over the last two days, Juhg hadn't had much of an appetite. Back at the Vault of All Known Knowledge, he had experienced the same kind of appetite problems when he became truly absorbed by his work. During those times, the Grandmagister had watched over him, taking time out of his day to eat a meal or two with Juhg.

"Well, ye 'ave to eat somethin', elsewise I'll never hear the end of it from Jassamyn."

"A sandwich, then." Juhg squinted at a nearby window. The bright light hurt his eyes. Then he realized the light was on the wrong side of the building for it to be morning. "What time is it?"

242

Raisho walked over to the potbelly stove and took down a heavy iron frying pan. "I'm not feedin' ye a sandwich. Jassamyn wouldn't be happy with that, so I'd end up not bein' happy with that. An' it's afternoon."

"*Afternoon!*" Juhg wheeled on the young sailor. "I told you I needed to be awake this morning."

Raisho turned to face Juhg and crossed his arms over his broad chest. He frowned. "Ye're me friend, scribbler, but I don't remember takin' ye on to raise. An' if'n ye want to get up in the mornin', see to it that ye don't stay up till then. It's 'ard to get up afore ye get yerself to bed."

Shame radiated through Juhg when he realized how right Raisho was. "I apologize. I know it's not your fault. You shouldn't even be involved in this."

Voice softer now, the young sailor said, "Well, ye're wrong about that, scribbler. Ye're me friend, an' ye're smack dab in the middle o' this 'ere mess. That's one reason for me to be 'ere. The second reason is, Greydawn Moors is me home. Leastways, when I ain't on *Windchaser*. The only home I can remember ever havin'. These people that are tryin' to get *The Book o' Time,* why some of 'em are responsible for that attack on me home an' killin' some of me friends. I reckon I owe 'em whatever I can give 'em." Raisho grinned. "Besides that, where else could I get the chance to be a legend by rescuin' *The Book of Time?*"

Juhg looked at his friend and felt afraid for him. Sometimes he felt that the young sailor just didn't recognize danger when it stared him in the face. "Raisho, you do know that most of the legendary heroes you hear about are dead, don't you? And most of them didn't die of old age."

Raisho shrugged and smiled. "Well, I don't plan on bein' one of the dead 'uns. I think it's better to be a legend while ye're alive to enjoy it."

"I don't think you understand what we're up against."

A serious look filled the young sailor's handsome face. "I know what we're up against, scribbler. Mayhap I can't read nor write like ye do, but I listen well enough when ye talk, an' when Cobner talks, an' when Jassamyn talks, an' especially when Craugh talks because he knows enough about things that can kill ye to keep ye hard at listenin' for years." He frowned. "Plus, not listenin' fast enough or hard enough could get me turned into a toad, an' I sure don't want that fer meself." He cleared his throat and went on. "I ain't seen as much of this kind of adventurin' as the rest of ye, but I know when things is bad, an' when the goin' gets dangerous. But I can't see no way to steer clear of any part of this. Unless ye're seein' somethin' I don't?"

"No."

"Well then, there ye have it."

"I apologize again, Raisho, for underestimating you. I just feel so responsible for trying to make sense of all this."

"Ye're a Librarian, Juhg. Makin' sense o' things is part of what ye do. That's in yer nature, just like fightin' an' hagglin' is in mine. It just scares ye that ye don't have all the answers already. Me, I live for the uncertainty. Otherwise life would be borin'. An' I don't want to live bored."

"Not knowing does scare me," Juhg agreed. His hand strayed to the leather pouch that hung around his neck. "The fact that no one else seems able to touch these fragments makes me even more responsible for everything that happens. I just don't want to make a mistake."

"I'm gonna tell ye somethin' that I don't tell a lot of people." Raisho hesitated. "I stay scared a lot."

That surprised Juhg. In the two years that he had known Raisho, he had never seen the young sailor seemingly afraid of anything. If anyone had asked him for a picture of fearlessness, he would have pointed to Raisho. "You?"

"Aye. Me. An' I'll tell ye now, this mornin' just between us two, but don't ever expect me to admit it in front of anyone else."

"But you're not afraid of anything. When we sneaked aboard *Ill Wind* at Kelloch's Harbor, you weren't afraid."

"I was. But I was more afraid that I would fail at the task Cap'n Attikus gave us."

"But aboard *Ill Wind* during our battle with the goblinkin, when Ertonomous Dron captured me, you challenged him."

"I had to. Don't ye see? I was afraid of losin' ye. Ye are me business partner, scribbler. I ain't never had no business partner afore. Nobody I ever really shared anythin' with that mattered." Raisho shook his head, as if surprised at his own honesty. "Ye see, when ye ain't got no family, there ain't no one else to 'elp shoulder whatever mistakes ye make. Each mistake is all yers an' yers alone. All them mistakes, why they just pile up an' strangle ye, they do. With ye, I feel like I'm safe for the first time in me life." He shrugged. "Safe to make mistakes, anyway. This here situation is a mite unsafe all the way around." He paused, looking at Juhg. "Mayhap ye don't understand."

"I think I do," Juhg said. "And even with all the words that I know, with all the books that I have read, I don't think I could have stated those feelings as well."

"I just felt ye should know. I see ye a-workin' on them books way ye are, an' I know ye're not a-wantin' to make a mistake somewheres in there. But we all feel the same way. I'm afraid, Cobner's afraid, Jassamyn's afraid. Even ol' Craugh, though he would probably sooner die then admit it, is afraid."

Juhg knew that Raisho was correct: Craugh would never admit to being afraid. But there was a lot that the wizard would not admit to.

"I think ye've been dealin' with yer fears overlong on yer own," Raisho said. "I think that's why ye left Greydawn Moors to become me partner. An' I think that's why ye never talked to the Grandmagister about feelin' the need to set up schools an' give the books back to the world. Ye were afraid of disappointin' him. What ye keep forgettin' is that the Grandmagister loves ye. Mayhap ye'll disappoint him here an' there, but he ain't gonna quit lovin' ye. Ain't nothin' gonna stop him from doin' that. I've seen him around ye. He takes a lot of pride in how ye've turned out. An' that's why, when he an' Greydawn Moors are hard up against it, that's why he chose to set ye free to finish up this here quest he'd set for himself."

"But what if he was wrong?" Juhg whispered. "What if I fail at figuring everything out? What if I can't help find a way to rescue the Grandmagister?"

Raisho looked solemn. "The only way ye can fail at this is not to give yer best. That's what the Grandmagister expected from ye. Nothin' more. He believes in ye, so ye got to believe in yerself."

Feeling humbled and moved by Raisho's words, Juhg said, "Thank you, Raisho, for being my business partner and my friend."

" 'Tweren't nothin', scribbler. Now ye go an' fetch yerself a bath. Jassamyn told me I was to look out for that today, too." Raisho shrugged. "I think bathin' is overrated, but she seems to put a lot of store by it. Should be plenty of hot water down there, an' fresh towels as well. It'll probably make ye feel better anyway."

Juhg went.

15

A Matter of Trust

Three days later, Juhg stood in the stern of the trade ship *Profit*. The captain, a jocular human in his late twenties, said the name was a hopeful one, but not one that always came true.

With the wind in his face and the sun bearing down on him, Juhg felt like he'd come home. Sailing was a big part of his life although it conflicted with his training as a Librarian. He'd found that out while aboard *Windchaser* serving under Captain Attikus. After spending all those years in the goblinkin mines, never seeing the light of day, never knowing if the sun was up or down, he blamed his wanderlust on those experiences. Yet, as he'd come to know the Grandmagister, he'd discovered that Edgewick Lamplighter had developed the same love for the sea. Neither of them, as it turned out, was entirely cut out for the sedate life of the Vault of All Known Knowledge. Everything they had read had prepared them to explore the regions and histories they had read so much about.

How could a person know about those places, those events, and the people who had lived there and not want to go see? Juhg had wondered on more than one occasion. He knew the Grandmagister felt the same. Maybe most Librarians, and especially those who were dwellers, had their curiosity about the world outside Greydawn Moors (if there existed any such curiosity) sated through the books they read and diligently copied, but he couldn't do that. He wanted to see so that he might bring more experience to the books he worked on in the form of footnotes and monographs.

Raisho stood at Juhg's side, one hand knotted in the rigging and a smile spread across his face.

"I've missed this," Juhg admitted.

"Aye, so have I. There's somethin' about bein' on a small ship with a group ye know ye'll get to know before ye get to where ye're goin'." Raisho shrugged. "'Course, we're not gonna get that chance this trip. In eight days' time, we're gonna be at Ship's Wheel Cove on the mainland."

"I know."

"That's an outlaw town, ye know. I mean, they do enough legitimate business to keep most traders comin' by, but a fair share o' piratin', too. A cap'n known for doin' well, he has to have him a fast ship if he wants to get much out of the harbor."

"I know."

"Gonna be dangerous there."

"We'll be careful." *And as dangerous as Ship's Wheel Cove is, the Smoking Marshes are even worse. That's before we find out what we have to face to get the next section of* The Book of Time.

248

Juhg knew how dangerous the trip was going to be. He had helped Craugh plan the journey and make the maps, pooling what he, the wizard, Cobner, and Jassamyn had seen or heard of the area.

The lack of knowledge bothered Juhg immensely. Although he had the Grandmagister's notes on the area, Juhg missed being at the Vault of All Known Knowledge for the planning stages. He and the Grandmagister had sometimes spent days getting ready to go out.

Of course, the way hadn't always been easy and they'd had to find out more than they knew later, sometimes in the middle of the biggest dangers they faced. But starting out prepared had always lent a certain amount of confidence.

The ship's crew went about their jobs smartly, showing years of experience and commitment. As a trade ship, *Profit* split wages with the crew on a more equal basis than the trade guild ships did. Of course, her young captain also took chances. If the ship was laid up for repairs, he sometimes had to rely on the crew not to have squandered their money and be able to help out.

"Mayhap I'll have me a word with the cap'n," Raisho said, interrupting the comfortable silence that had stretched between them. "See if'n I can't work me way across. If'n that don't work out, mayhap I'll just pitch in for free an' do what I can. Ye're gonna have to take it a little easier, too."

Juhg nodded. While aboard *Profit,* he wouldn't be able to work on his journals as much. The fact that he knew how to read and write, and that books existed, had to be kept secret.

He drew in a deep lungful of air and felt himself relax. *It's a pity this won't last,* he thought. But there was still *The Book of Time* to find in the Smoking Marshes and the Drylands.

And the Grandmagister was still out there somewhere to be rescued. If Hallekk and *One-Eyed Peggie* hadn't already done that.

Raisho nudged Juhg with an elbow. "Want to go up top?"

Looking up at the rigging and the white sails belled with the wind, feeling the ship's deck rock beneath his feet, Juhg said, "Maybe for a little while." He followed Raisho to the nearest ratline, then went aloft. *Just for a little while,* he promised himself. Then he intended to get back to work.

A knock sounded at the door, drawing Juhg's attention from his work. Moving quickly, he raked both journals he was working on into the open cloth bag he had tacked to the underside of the makeshift desk, capped the inkwell and stowed it in a pocket, and stuck his quill in a battered hat he'd bought to disguise them.

The knock sounded again.

Juhg drew the drawstring around the cloth bag, sealing it shut. He walked to the door and unlocked it. The lock was a double-edged sword. If the ship's captain or the crew found out he was using it, they would be curious about what he was doing that he had to hide. On the other hand, if someone didn't know and chose instead to simply barge through the door, the lock would at least give Juhg the chance to hide everything he was working on.

He opened the door just as Craugh was about to knock on the door again.

"I thought maybe you were asleep," the wizard said. He was so tall and the waist of the ship was so short that he had to stand stooped over. Even his staff had to be carried leaned over.

"No." Juhg stepped back, waving the wizard in. "I was working."

Craugh nodded. "Am I interrupting? I could come back."

Having the wizard solicitous of him made Juhg uncomfortable. Since Juhg had been the only one who could handle the gemstones that were part of *The Book of Time,* things between them had changed. Craugh was more respectful, but he was also more distant.

"No," Juhg said. "This is fine." *Not comfortable, though.*

Craugh entered the room with his hat in his hand. It looked only a little worse for the wear since Juhg had rescued it at Skull Canal.

The cabin was small, hardly room enough for Juhg and Raisho to bunk together in the two hammocks with a little room left over for the makeshift desk. Still, Juhg was willing to wager that Craugh had paid a pretty price for the three cabins they had rented for the trip. Raisho had heard some of the crew laughing about the way the mates had been doubled up in their quarters for the duration of the trip to Ship's Wheel Cove to make room for the paying passengers.

Juhg didn't ask where the wizard got the price of the passage and the supplies they'd purchased, including a new set of armor for Cobner which had been tailored to him while they were waiting for the ship.

There was only one chair in the room, and it was tucked in back of the desk.

"I would offer you a chair," Juhg said, feeling even more uncomfortable about the tension between Craugh and him.

"No," Craugh said. "I'll sit in the hammock. That's fine." He took a step, reached the hammock, and sat himself. The hammock hung so close to the ground in the low-ceilinged room that Craugh's knees were nearly up to his ears.

It isn't, Juhg couldn't help thinking, *the most dignified seating for one of the most feared wizards in the whole world.* He sat in the chair. "Are you comfortable?"

Craugh waved the question away. "I'm fine. Really. It's not as bad as it looks."

Juhg was willing to wager that it was actually much worse. But that was all right because it meant Craugh wouldn't be inclined to stay for long.

Craugh looked for a place to hang his hat, then finally gave up and placed it on the floor between his knees and feet. The pointy top bent over like it was tired and depressed.

"I thought perhaps we could talk," Craugh said.

"All right."

"We appear to have reached an impasse of sorts." The wizard frowned. "I must admit, I'm at a loss as to what to do. If we're to accomplish our mission, we need to work together."

"We are working together."

"You don't trust me."

Juhg wanted to deny it, not because he was afraid of the wizard (he was, of course, because he'd finally seen Craugh actually turn someone into a toad and the questions of whether or not he could and whether or not he would had been answered), but because he really didn't want to hurt Craugh's feelings. Despite the gruff and aloof veneer the wizard put on like battle armor, Juhg had gotten to peek at the man beneath it.

"No." Juhg sighed.

Nodding and breaking eye contact, Craugh said, "Given what you know about me, I can understand that. I just hadn't planned on things working out quite this way. The fact that I can't touch those pieces of *The Book of Time* complicates matters."

"Complicates them how?"

"You know I can't touch them, and neither can anyone else."

"I don't see how that complicates things. Since no one can take them from me, I don't have to trust you."

Craugh looked at him. "That's the complication. If I could take them from you, or if I could hire someone else to take them from you and I didn't, then maybe I could win some of your trust back."

"It is a problem."

"An insurmountable one, I fear."

"We can work around it," Juhg suggested. "We already have been."

"But that distrust will still be there."

Juhg couldn't disagree.

"There may come a time that you will need to trust me."

"I hope not," Juhg said.

"Still, there is that possibility."

"Then we'll have to be extra careful."

A tense silence ensued, filled with the creaking of the ship's timbers and the slap of the waves against the ship's hull. Now and again, sailors' raucous voices could be heard up top.

"Was there anything else?" Juhg asked.

"I have some other questions."

"All right."

"Have you read the book you found on the dead man in the trap in Skull Canal?"

"Yes."

"Who was he?"

In quick summation, Juhg relayed all that he knew about the man. Liggon Phares had been a venal man in life, filled with pompous ideas. His journal had detailed the events of his travels from Torvassir, including the insults he'd taken from coach drivers, serving wenches, and innkeepers. When he reached a position of prominence, he planned to have revenge on them all. He'd made a separate list of his intended victims in the back of the journal.

"He had information about the piece of *The Book of Time* at Skull Canal," Juhg finished.

"How did he come by it?"

"Through some of the same sources as the Grandmagister had. He wasn't as thorough in listing his sources as the Grandmagister, but I compared the notes and am satisfied many of them are the same. Some of the books he wrote about were not included in the Grandmagister's references."

"Liggon Phares had access to books Wick did not have," Craugh said.

Juhg nodded. "That was my thought as well. I don't know every book in the Library. Even as good as my memory is and as good as the Grandmagister trained me to make it, I can't remember every book in the Library."

"But Wick could."

"Yes."

"Then this man—"

"Either knew of the other Library you talked about, or he worked for them."

Craugh scratched at his neck. "There was no mention of Aldhran Khempus?"

"No."

"So at present count, we have two other groups pursuing *The Book of Time*," Craugh said. "The other Library and Aldhran Khempus."

"Three groups," Juhg said.

Craugh looked at him. Then understanding lifted the wizard's eyebrows. "Ah, the mantis."

"Yes." Juhg shifted in his chair. "Do you suppose the mantis is the Gatekeeper?"

"The Gatekeeper was human."

"You *saw* him as human. The mantis told me that people who see it see it as they expect to see it."

"The Gatekeeper wasn't as pleasant as you seem to think the mantis was."

"I never claimed the mantis was pleasant."

"He seemed pleasant enough when you talked about him."

Juhg thought perhaps Craugh sounded a little offended and maybe even a trifle jealous. It was funny and sad and pathetic all at the same time. And Juhg felt sympathetic for the wizard.

"I don't know what the mantis wants," Juhg pointed out. "Only that it wants *The Book of Time* back."

"So that the In-Betweenness can be preserved."

"And this world."

"Do you believe it?"

Juhg hesitated. "I think that it wants to preserve its world."

"Do you think it and its missing peer actually created the races that inhabit this world?"

Answering honestly, Juhg said, "I don't know."

"Good." The wizard seemed satisfied.

"Why is that good?"

"Because I don't know either, though I tend to think not. Or that may only be wishful thinking on my part. I believe it's good if we tend toward a little cynicism."

"Except where it interferes with the working relationship you and I have."

Craugh frowned. "Yes." He shook his head. "But I'd rather have you cynical to a degree, apprentice. Were you Wick going through all of this, I would be worried."

"Why?"

"Because Wick enjoys wide-eyed wonderment. Even at this late date, even knowing all the hardships he's undergone and the evils he has faced, he would believe only good would come of this."

"He might not be wrong."

"I'll wait on that account, to see for myself." Craugh hesitated. "Could I see the gemstones again?"

Juhg thought about the request for a moment, then took the leather pouch from around his neck and poured the blue stones onto the table. He kept the pouch on him at all times. It wouldn't do to have a light-fingered crewman going around talking about a magic pouch the dweller had that couldn't be stolen.

The gems lay glittering on the table. Inside, with no windows and only a lantern for light, their color was not as strong.

Craugh put his hand close enough to the gems that sparks spat into the air. "Well, that hasn't changed. We mix about as well as oil and water." He drew his hand back with obvious reluctance. "Have you had any further contact with the mantis?"

"No."

"Have you tried using those stones?"

"How?"

"Just by holding them and calling out to the mantis?"

Juhg was surprised. "I hadn't thought about that."

"Well, of course it might not work."

Picking one of the stones up, Juhg held it in his palm, then closed his fist over it. The stone felt cool against his skin, and the edges were crisp and clean. He closed his eyes and thought about the mantis, calling out to it in his mind.

Nothing happened.

Juhg opened his eyes and looked at Craugh. "It's not working." He sighed. "I wish the Grandmagister were here—"

Without warning, Juhg went blind.

A dark veil swallowed Juhg and he stood in the middle of it. He couldn't even see his hand in front of his face. He took a deep breath and tried to open his eyes aboard the trade ship. He called out Craugh's name but there was no response.

Then a reddish-orange light dawned in the darkness.

"Mantis," Juhg called. He hurried toward the light, not seeing his legs beneath him but feeling his feet shoving against the ground.

In the next moment he burst through the darkness and stood in a dank dungeon. Straw littered the stone hallway floor between two long lines of what he believed were empty cells. Torture equipment hung from the ceiling all the way to the end of the hallway, racks and claws and chains created to do unmentionable damage to a helpless prisoner.

"Juhg."

Swiveling his head, Juhg saw the small, crumpled figure at the end of the hallway. He had missed the man at first glance because he was partially hidden by the brazier that held the reddish-orange light.

Then he recognized the figure.

"Grandmagister." Not caring at the moment how he came to be there, Juhg ran toward his mentor and fell on his knees before him.

Edgewick Lamplighter had been hard used. He was stripped to his waist, and the rest of his clothes were rags. Burns and cuts and whip marks covered his body. Stout chains made up of heavy iron links bound the Grandmagister to the wall.

"Is it really you?" the Grandmagister asked. His tongue was thick with thirst.

Juhg reached for him, his heart feeling as though it was going to break. He had never seen the Grandmagister so beaten before. Only instead of touching his mentor, Juhg's hands passed right through him.

"No!" Juhg cried. He was there with the Grandmagister, but there was nothing he could do to help him.

"It *is* you," the Grandmagister said.

Tears fell from Juhg's eyes. He tried to stop crying because if he didn't he wouldn't be able to see the Grandmagister.

"You found . . . the first piece of . . . *The Book of Time,* didn't you?" the Grandmagister asked.

"Yes," Juhg said hoarsely. He remained kneeling in front of his mentor, helpless when everything in his body screamed out for him to help.

"How did you get here?" the Grandmagister asked. "Did Craugh—"

"Not Craugh," Juhg said. "The gemstones that make up the first section of *The Book of Time.*"

"You're using the stones?" Interest showed in the Grandmagister's beaten face. "So the stories were true. The piece that was given to the humans can see across the present."

Juhg focused on that and walled away his pain. "What? You didn't mention anything of that in the notes you left in Imarish."

The Grandmagister worked his tongue in his mouth, swallowing with great effort. "I didn't . . . know that then. I've found out more since I wrote those journals. Much more." He took a long, shuddering breath. "There are four sections—"

"That was in the journal."

"Kharrion broke *The Book of Time* up into sections and gave them to the humans, dwarves, elves, and goblins that allied with him in the beginning."

"Why?"

"To buy their loyalty. He gave them the power that was in *The Book of Time,* made them stronger so that they could fight his enemies."

"What enemies?"

"The group of wizards that stole into the In-Betweenness and took *The Book of Time* from the Gatekeeper."

Craugh, Juhg thought, but he couldn't mention that to the Grandmagister. Learning of Craugh's part in that would break his mentor's heart. He kept himself still and silent.

"Kharrion used the power to make the armies he'd raised there stronger," the Grandmagister said. "All of the pieces of *The Book of Time* were given so that they would play on the strengths of those who had them." He sucked in greedy breaths.

For the first time, Juhg noticed how hot it was in the dungeon.

"To the humans, Kharrion gave the section that allowed his agents there to see in the present. Human lives are always spent in a hurry, rushing here and there, always thinking about the present. The dwarves got the pieces that allowed them to see into the past. Dwarves base their culture on things made of stone and drawn from the past. Their entire being comes from their history and their legacy; it is how they define themselves. To the elves, Kharrion gave the pieces that allowed glimpses into the future, because elves are forward thinkers and always dreaming, and extremely long-lived. The goblinkin got the pieces that allowed them to see points of randomness, instances in time where action can be taken or not taken to effect change for good or evil."

"Why would the goblinkin get something that sounds so dangerous?" Juhg asked.

"Because the goblinkin were the only ones who could use such power. By nature they are random and capricious, just as fate is." The Grandmagister shifted, trying in vain to find a comfortable position. The chains rattled.

"But wouldn't *The Book of Time* be more powerful all together?" Juhg asked.

"Yes and no. For what Kharrion needed, armies to defeat the wizards that took *The Book of Time* from the Gatekeeper, he had to take the book apart. Disassembling it also prevented his enemies from getting it in case he was defeated. And he was. They all thought Kharrion was dead. No one knew that Kharrion would rise from an unmarked grave a thousand years later to lead the goblinkin in a crusade against the rest of the world."

"To find *The Book of Time*."

"Yes. Kharrion thought his enemies had defeated him and had taken the book."

"Why?"

"Because the strongholds where he had kept the sections of *The Book of Time* had been destroyed, sucked down into the earth as a result of the power they used when Kharrion's armies tried to destroy the group of wizards that pursued him."

"But he should have been able to find the sections of the book in those places."

"Kharrion went and he looked. He did not find them."

"But why?"

"Someone made him not see those pieces."

"The mantis?"

The Grandmagister looked at Juhg. "What mantis?"

Quickly, Juhg explained his experience in seeing the mantis, how he had been called to the In-Betweenness.

"I did not think that creature existed. I thought perhaps the Gatekeeper had found a way to blind Kharrion to the pieces of *The Book of Time*."

"Why couldn't the Gatekeeper bring *The Book of Time* back into the In-Betweenness?"

"He would have to come into this world," the Grandmagister said. "He could never do that. Time itself might end, and that would be the end of everything."

"How did you find out the location of the pieces of *The Book of Time*?"

"I finally translated the last of those books I got from that wizard's sanctum in Hanged Elf's Point." The Grandmagister gave a self-deprecating smile. "It took me long enough. Grandmagister Frollo never let me live down the fact that one of them was past my abilities. Of course, the book was past everyone else's abilities as well, but he wasn't concerned about what others could do. I was always a sore point with him." Despite his pain, the Grandmagister smiled. "Knowing I had that effect on him was rather enjoyable. Even more so when Craugh told Frollo I was going to be the next Grandmagister." He broke out into a coughing fit.

"Grandmagister," Juhg said worriedly, reaching for his mentor only to see his hands fade through him. He had to wait helplessly until the coughing fit passed.

"I didn't figure out the translation until a few months ago," the Grandmagister went on. "I was hurt by your decision to leave Greydawn Moors. I—"

"I didn't mean to leave," Juhg said. "I didn't want to leave."

"Of course you did," the Grandmagister said. "Of course you did. I don't blame you. I admit I was hurt and disappointed. But I knew in my heart why you left. You wanted to set up schools, Juhg. You felt it was time to return the books to the world."

"You knew that?"

The Grandmagister smiled and shook his head. "Of course I knew. You're the best kind of Librarian there is, Juhg: you're a teacher as well as a protector of knowledge. It's one thing to stand guard, but it's another to make something indestructible by giving it freely to everyone who wants it. Teaching people will protect the knowledge so many have worked so long and so hard to accumulate. I know that. But I couldn't allow the books to be taken from the Vault of All Known Knowledge."

"Because you knew about *The Book of Time*."

"Yes. I have suspected for a number of years that *The Book of Time* was not a myth. I knew that it was possible it was one of the books in the Vault of All Known Knowledge, carefully disguised as the book was that opened the trap through. It wasn't until I found out about the other Library—" The Grandmagister stopped. "There is still so much I have to tell you."

"I know about the other Library," Juhg said.

"It wasn't in the notes that I left you in Imarish."

"I found out about it. A lot has happened since your capture."

Footsteps sounded out in the hall.

Turning, Juhg saw Aldhran Khempus approaching. The man looked much the same as he had on the goblinkin ship the night the Grandmagister had been taken from Greydawn Moors. The man was of medium height for a human, with thick brown hair and a matching beard. There was something immediately detestable about Aldhran Khempus but Juhg couldn't quite put his finger on what it was. But it had something to do with his cocky attitude, blatant disregard for the lives of others, and his self-assured smile.

Four heavily armed goblinkin guards followed Aldhran.

"Ah," the man said, "I thought I detected something amiss." He stopped in front of Juhg, who rose to his feet to protect the Grandmagister. "I can't believe you would entertain guests in this place, Grandmagister Lamplighter. I wouldn't keep a farm animal here."

The guards laughed.

Peering more closely at Juhg, Aldhran said, "Ah, you're the apprentice, aren't you? The one who escaped capture back in Greydawn Moors."

Juhg trembled. He didn't know what to do or to say. He was no hero with witty banter or a quick sword. He was only a Librarian who was in a bad situation even a trained warrior would struggle with.

"Did you come here to reacquaint yourself with my hospitality?" Aldhran mocked.

"No," Juhg said fiercely. "I came here to give notice. If you harm the Grandmagister in any way—"

Aldhran stroked his chin as if in deep thought. "Let me see, is there a way I *haven't* harmed the Grandmagister yet?" He shook his head. "No. I can't think of a single one."

Anger surged through Juhg. He stepped toward Aldhran, drawing the attention of the guards at once. Two of them thrust their swords at him. Ignoring them, Juhg stepped through them and looked up at Aldhran.

"If you harm the Grandmagister any further," Juhg said clearly, "I will kill you."

Aldhran laughed in Juhg's face.

More than anything else in the world, Juhg wanted to hit the man, to smash his face and beat him senseless. He'd never had that kind of anger before except toward goblinkin. Amazingly, his fist struck Aldhran's jaw and knocked the man back a few stumbling steps.

Pain exploded in Juhg's fist, then spread up his arm to his elbow. Surprise took precedence over the pain, though. One of the guards swung a sword at him. Juhg tried to get away but couldn't. He closed his eyes, fearing the sharp kiss of the blade. But it passed through him without touching him.

Aldhran cursed hotly and turned back to Juhg. The human's face was a mask of rage. "You'll pay for that, you sniveling halfer!" He threw his hand out and shouted in a language that Juhg couldn't understand.

"Juhg!" the Grandmagister shouted. "Get the rest of the pieces! The last one is here in the Haze Mountains! Get those first! Look out for Craugh—"

Whatever else the Grandmagister said was lost as pain from Aldhran's spell wracked Juhg's body. He hung on for a moment, dropping to his knees there on the dirty straw in the dungeon. He fell, trying desperately to talk to the Grandmagister or hear what he was saying.

Look out for Craugh? What did that mean? Then the world went away as Juhg melted and fell down through the dungeon floor into the waiting blackness.

"Juhg!" The voice belonged to Craugh, but Juhg had never before heard that kind of panic in it. *"Juhg!"*

Weakly, Juhg tried to acknowledge the wizard's impassioned cries, but he couldn't. Then he realized he was lying on the floor of the cabin and he wasn't breathing.

"Juhg! Come back to me! Don't you die on me! Don't you dare die!"

Juhg slitted his eyes. He saw the wizard squatting over him, pulling at his clothing. For a moment Juhg though Craugh might be going for the leather pouch, then he remembered he'd left it on the table.

Fear touched Craugh's haggard face. He leaned over Juhg and pressed his ear to his chest.

Behind the wizard, the door opened and Raisho stepped into the room. The young sailor looked shocked, then drew his cutlass and menaced Craugh with it.

Craugh lifted his head and slapped the cutlass away. "I didn't do this to him. He was using the gemstones to try to contact the mantis. Then he fell to the floor. Help me clear his throat. His heart has stopped."

Trained by saving near-drowned sailors, Raisho quickly knelt and put a hand behind Juhg's neck, lifting slightly so his mouth and throat opened to their best for breathing.

"He's clear," Raisho said. "Nothin' in his throat."

Craugh put a hand over Juhg's chest, pressing flat for a moment, then he spoke and his hand ignited in green flame. A massive jolt ran through Juhg's body, like he'd been hit with a twenty-pound sledge.

"He's still not breathing," Raisho said.

Craugh kept his hand over Juhg's chest. The flames erupted again. This time it felt like the wizard had reached inside Juhg's body and squeezed his heart. He felt his heart come back to life, beating sporadically for a moment, then sprinting into a frantic pace. His lungs came to life next and he took a deep breath.

"Good," Craugh said. "You've come back to us, apprentice." He smiled a little. "I knew you couldn't stay away. We've too much left to do that we need to accomplish."

Maybe Craugh said more, but Juhg didn't know. He'd been putting off sleep and rest for days, and the bill for that all came due at once. He breathed in and out again, then the blackness surrounded him.

261

"Craugh said you died."

Seated up in the rigging, Juhg surreptitiously used a stick of charcoal to sketch in his journal out of sight of *Profit*'s crew.

Jassamyn sat across from him. She wore a light blouse and breeches and went without her leather armor. The draca that accompanied her floated along on the breeze above her and she tossed it grapes from the bunch she'd purchased on the sly from the ship's cook. Apparently everyone aboard was trying to live up to the ship's name.

"Did you?" she asked.

That had been the previous day. Juhg had slept like the dead until this morning, then awoke feeling like he'd been torn apart by trolls and put back together by blind goblinkin that had taken bites out of him at every opportunity.

"I don't know," Juhg said. "I could feel that my heart wasn't beating."

"He said that he saved you."

Juhg nodded. "I think he probably did." Taking the charcoal from the page, he looked at the drawing with a critical eye.

He'd wanted something to keep his hands busy. When he'd wakened, he'd wanted to get back to his journals, but Jassamyn hadn't allowed it, saying that Juhg needed sunlight and a good breakfast. Raisho was just as adamant.

Knowing he'd never get any peace, Juhg had gone along quietly. So far he'd had half a good breakfast and had partially flouted Jassamyn's rules by insisting on climbing up into the rigging to better enjoy the breeze and the fresh air. Jassamyn had accompanied him while Raisho kept watch from below.

"Even though he probably saved your life, even by your own admission," Jassamyn said, "you don't trust him."

Looking at her, feeling the need in her to understand, Juhg shook his head. "I don't."

"But you've already stated that the mantis told you magic doesn't mix with *The Book of Time*. What use would the book be to Craugh?"

"*The Book of Time* is a power unto itself," Juhg said. "You don't have to use magic to use the book. And don't you think that anyone who could control all of time would be perhaps more than a little dangerous?"

Jassamyn tossed the draca another grape. The creature fluttered its wings as it dived in pursuit of the tasty morsel. It caught the grape halfway to the deck forty feet below, then flapped its wings again as it swooped back up with its prize. It sat in the rigging beside Jassamyn and greedily devoured the grape. Juice ran down its face and neck. Its belly protruded from the grapes it had already eaten.

"I do," Jassamyn admitted. She looked out to sea and the wind blew through her hair. "A thing as powerful as *The Book of Time* shouldn't even exist."

"But it does."

"What is going to become of it?"

"You mean after we rescue the Grandmagister?" The images of his mentor tortured and beaten had followed Juhg through nightmarish dreams the whole time he'd slept. "And after we get all four sections? And after we do something with Aldhran?"

"Cobner is going to kill him."

Though he never thought he would ever hear himself say something like that, Juhg said, "I hope so."

"But after all those things are accomplished," Jassamyn said, "what will become of *The Book of Time?*"

Juhg shook his head. "I don't know."

Jassamyn reached for the drawing he'd been working on. It was of her and the draca, just a loose sketch that he would render again later, but it had a finished look about it.

"You have a good hand when it comes to art," Jassamyn said.

"Thank you."

"Cobner thinks you would make a good warrior."

"I'm a halfer. Warriors and halfers. Those things don't go together." Juhg looked down at his arm. Mottled purple and red bruising colored his hand and his arm nearly all the way up to his elbow. He'd woken to find his first two fingers dislocated. When he'd mentioned it to Jassamyn, she'd immediately grabbed his fingers and yanked, popping them back into place. Juhg had screamed, a very unwarriorlike scream of pain because it had hurt very much. He was also certain that if Cobner had heard him the dwarven warrior would set aside his notion of training him.

Below, Cobner strode out onto the deck with his battle-axe. He in-sisted that he wasn't used to the weapon yet and practiced four and five times a day until sweat streamed down his thick body.

The dwarf called out to Raisho, enticing the young sailor into a practice session. In moments, sailors had spread out around the combat-ants, giving them plenty of room to swing their blades. The sound of metal striking metal came to Juhg's ears a split second behind the actual blows because of the wind and the distance. Cobner and Raisho moved in a wicked dance of death, each having learned to trust the other's abil-ities and skill, as well as gaining respect for the other's inventiveness and daring.

"I need to talk to you about something," Juhg said, dreading what he was about to do.

Jassamyn looked at him.

He took the copy of his journal from inside his jacket and handed it to her. "This is why I struggle to trust Craugh," he said, and he proceeded to tell her the stories Craugh had told him aboard *One-Eyed Peggie*.

When he finished, long after Cobner and Raisho had given up in a draw below and gone to soak their heads in buckets of brine pulled fresh from the sea, Jassamyn looked troubled.

"Why did you tell me this?" she asked.

"Partly because I needed someone else to know," Juhg said. "In case something happens to me."

"If Craugh had wanted you dead, all he had to do was not revive you yesterday."

Juhg couldn't argue with that.

"What do you think Wick meant when he told you to watch out for Craugh?" Jassamyn asked.

"I don't know." Juhg had tried to duplicate the contact with the Grandmagister by using the gemstones but had had no success. They were working, though, because he was able to look at Greydawn Moors and see that the island was still under siege, though the defenders had managed to forestall an actual invasion.

He had also looked in on *One-Eyed Peggie*, Hallekk, and the dwarven pirate crew and found them healthy and impatiently sitting at a dock on the Sarkus River that cut through the Haze Mountains. From what he'd gathered, Juhg could only look in on people or places that he was close to. Maybe with time or more practice he could look in on any current event, but at the moment he couldn't. Each of the attempts had left him weaker and weaker, as if the pieces from *The Book of Time* were drawing on him for power.

"Wick could have merely been telling you to look after Craugh," Jassamyn said.

"I know, but after what I told you—knowing that the Grandmagister doesn't even know all that—would you want to trust him?"

A troubled look filled Jassamyn's face. "It is difficult," she admitted.

"Knowing what to do would be best," Juhg said. "I feel . . . like I'm betraying Craugh's friendship."

"By telling me what he told you?"

Juhg shook his head. "By even suspecting him. But I don't know any other safe way to handle it."

Jassamyn sat quietly for a time, then admitted, "Neither do I. But at least now you don't have to bear that burden alone."

"I'm just tired of being afraid," Juhg said, realizing what Raisho had been trying to tell him back in Imarish. "That fear is . . . interfering with my thinking. I've got to let that go and concentrate on getting these pieces of *The Book of Time* so that I can save the Grandmagister."

265

16

The Smoking Marshes

ays later, when they made the landing at Ship's
Wheel Cove (which did resemble a ship's wheel
with all the bridges that led out from the central docking
area where the arriving cargo fed out into warehouses all
around the cove), Juhg's bruised hand was almost healed.
He'd also caught up on his journals, although there was
some ancillary work he wanted to do. There was always
extra work to be done on a writing project if he just
looked for it.

The outlaw nature of Ship's Wheel Cove was immediately apparent from the way goblinkin freely walked
the city's streets. Any city where goblinkin were accepted had at least some of its roots in piracy, caravan
looting, and slavery. Seeing the goblinkin brought some
of the old fears Juhg had had as a child bubbling up to the
surface.

Raisho stayed with Juhg as they made arrangements
for the horses they'd need to pursue the second section
of *The Book of Time* into the Smoking Marshlands. Using
previous experience with horses through actual riding
and from things he'd read in the Library, Juhg chose the

horses and paid for them with one of the gems Craugh carried to make purchases with.

Afterward, feeling a little remiss about the fact that Raisho had gone with him instead of getting some free time in the taverns before embarking on the wilderness journey—something Raisho had never before undertaken—Juhg agreed to a brief stopover.

The tavern was called the Boomarm and even featured one hanging from the front of the building that held up a stuffed narwhal that had seen its best days long ago. There was even a kitchen, and the smell of boiled shrimp and rice reminded Juhg that for the first time in days he was truly hungry.

Inside, the tavern was dingy and mismatched, the kind of place that would be a temporary home to sailors newly in port and a frequent visiting place for cargo handlers waiting to put in a night's work or just getting off after a hard day's work.

The clientele was mostly human, but there were a few elves and dwarves as well. A group of goblinkin sat in the back. They immediately noticed Juhg because he was the only dweller inside the tavern.

"Look, Gronk," one of the goblinkin snarled, pointing a long talon at Juhg, "they's got a halfer in here." The foul creature spat in the sawdust that covered the floor.

268

Gronk was a huge goblinkin, large and big bellied. The top half of one of his ears was sliced off and he wore an eyepatch. His teeth were huge blunt tusks. "Didn't know they served halfers in here," he stated in a deep voice. "Otherwise I'd have ordered me up one."

His companions howled with glee.

Juhg tried to ignore the attention of the goblinkin, hoping that they would see Raisho with him and be dissuaded. He ordered a big plate of rice and boiled shrimp, flavored with sweet lemon curry and minced ginger-nuts, an order of blanched flamesprouts, and a wedge of cinnamon fla-vored tartberry jelly custard pie covered in fresh cream with a trace of sharp mint. Raisho ordered the same thing, but asked for ale instead of the dry cucumber tea that Juhg ordered. They split a basket of corn muffins between them with an extra helping of honey butter.

"Look at the appetite on that one," one of the goblinkin said. "Why, I can't believe he ain't a fat little butterball."

"He sits himself at that table long enough," Gronk said, "an' he will be." He eyed Juhg. "Keep eatin', halfer. Fatten yerself up for when we meet again." He rasped his fork along the edge of his knife.

Seated at one of the tables, Raisho and Juhg dug in. As they ate, the insults offered by the goblinkin—distinctly addressing halfers in general and the one seated in their tavern in particular—increased. Juhg turned a deaf ear to it; he'd heard much worse—and, strangely enough, much more creative—while he'd been a slave in the goblinkin mines.

After a few minutes, Cobner put in an appearance. The goblinkin quietly fell silent for a moment as they eyed the dwarf's keen battle-axe.

"Camping supplies are ready for pickup," Cobner said. He looked at their plates. "Is that edible?"

"Well enough," Raisho answered. He jerked a thumb over his shoulder at the goblinkin. "If'n ye don't mind bad company."

Cobner grinned evilly at the goblinkin, causing all of them to turn their attention back to their plates. "Oh, if they get out of hand, maybe I'll work up an appetite before I eat. Or if they wait, I can work off a big meal. Makes no nevermind to me." He placed his order. In minutes, he was seated with them at their table, digging into their basket of corn muffins.

Both Cobner and Raisho ate faster than Juhg. He savored the meal for a change, knowing the cooking they'd be able to do while out in the Smoking Marshes wouldn't be nearly as good and this would be his last civilized meal for a while. His companions bolted their food as if they were in a competition.

269

Still, Juhg knew the goblinkin couldn't stay quiet forever. Even self-preservation couldn't curb their malicious and malignant natures.

One of the goblinkin tossed an apple onto the table in front of Juhg. Unfortunately, the apple bounced into Cobner's plate. Although the dwarf had eaten his fill, he wasn't much of one for taking insults.

"Here, halfer," the goblinkin said, "why don't you put that in yer mouth an' go lie in the cook's oven for us. Don't bother gettin' out. We'll come get you when you're good an' tender."

Cobner picked up the apple. "It comes to my attention," the dwarf said solemnly, "that I've about had me fill of bad company." He looked at Raisho, who nodded in agreement.

"Short tempers?" Gronk asked, then slapped his thigh and roared with laughter. "I guess it's just because of the company you keep."

With a deceptive flick, Cobner threw the apple and hit Gronk in his good eye. The goblinkin shrieked with pain. In an instant, the goblinkin stood up from their seats and ran at Cobner. The dwarf stood with Raisho at his side, both of them pulling their weapons. They met the goblinkin halfway.

Juhg picked up his plate and glass and made his way outside.

He sat on the steps leading up to the tavern with his plate balanced across his knees. For the most part, he blocked out the sound of fists striking flesh and the piercing screams of goblins in pain and stared out at the curious wheel-shaped docks.

Craugh, coming from the inns where caravan masters often stayed while in Ship's Wheel Cove, spotted Juhg by the time he'd gotten comfortable and came over. The wizard looked around, unavoidably aware that a noisy brawl was taking place inside the tavern, when a tankard sailed through the front door and he had to bat it away with his staff.

"Where's Raisho?" Craugh asked, obviously dissatisfied with the fact that the young sailor had left Juhg unattended.

"Inside," Juhg said.

At that moment, Raisho crashed through the multipaned front window and landed on the wooden porch outside. The impact jarred the wooden steps and Juhg had to make a quick grab to save his glass of tea.

"Well," Juhg said, "he *was* inside."

Cobner stuck his head out the door, grinning happily. "Raisho, are you gonna get back in here or what? This is getting more interesting. Believe it or not, the goblinkin here have friends. Stinky friends."

Smiling, Raisho pushed himself up and started back for the door. "Save the big one for me." He vanished inside the tavern and the sounds of battle increased again.

"He's inside again," Juhg said. He offered Craugh the basket of corn cakes he'd brought out with him. "Corn cake?"

Scowling, Craugh glared at the tavern. "Not right this minute." He rolled up the sleeves of his robe, tilted his pointy hat forward and marched up the steps.

Jassamyn came up as Craugh vanished inside the tavern. She had needed arrows and had arranged for the supplies they needed. "What's going on?" she asked.

"Tavern fight," Juhg said. "Cobner and Raisho are inside."

"Craugh went in after them?"

"Yes."

Leaning forward, Jassamyn picked up a corn cake from the basket. She sat down next to Juhg. "Craugh should leave them alone. They've been cooped up on the ship for days. Everybody's a little on edge. A good fight will loosen those two up and make them more bearable."

Juhg silently agreed. He wanted to be on the road even if it meant braving more dangers to get the next pieces of *The Book of Time*. It would have been better if they could have gone toward the Haze Mountains and prepared to save the Grandmagister.

"I think Craugh's in a hurry to go," Juhg said.

"Wizard!" someone inside the tavern yelled. *"Wizard!"*

"Aw no," Cobner pleaded from inside. "Craugh, you *don't* have to do that. Me and Raisho were just having a bit of fun."

"The fun is over," Craugh declared.

A heartbeat later, a huge explosion sounded inside the tavern. Juhg ducked his head and covered his plate as flying glass and flying goblins sailed by overhead. There were a few humans and dwarves in the mix as well. Evidently the goblinkin had had friends, or the locals had decided strangers to town were better targets than someone who lived in town who might stab them in the back. All of the flying brawlers hit the ground and got up. Alive and untoadified. At least Craugh didn't look like he was going to leave any lasting repercussions.

Craugh came from the tavern rolling down his sleeves. Looking glum and unhappy, Cobner and Raisho followed in the wizard's wake.

"It was just a tavern fight," Cobner protested. "Not anything big."

"An' they were talkin' bad about Juhg," Raisho said. "Ye know we can't stand for that."

"Can't stand for it at all," Cobner agreed. "Not and maintain our sense of integrity and honor."

"It weren't like we killed anybody," Raisho said. Then he looked at Cobner. "Ye didn't kill anybody back there, did ye?"

"No. You?"

"Not me."

"What," Craugh demanded coldly as he wheeled on the two combatants, "happened to the part of the plan where we entered Ship's Wheel Cove quietly, arranged for what we needed, and got out of town without ever being noticed?"

Neither Cobner nor Raisho had an answer.

Craugh looked at Juhg and pointed at the horses tied to the hitching post in front of the tavern. "Are these ours?"

"Yes." Juhg put his empty plate on the glass-strewn porch.

Unhitching the reins of the nearest one, Craugh stepped into the stirrup and pulled himself up. "Then let's be on our way. I've arranged to ride at least part of the way with a trade caravan headed to Torvassir. The woods are reported to be filled with goblinkin bandits."

"All the more reason to thump a few goblinkin skulls afore we head out," Raisho said. "Mayhap their friends will think twice afore jumpin' us out in the woods."

"And maybe," Craugh said, wheeling his mount around to face the young sailor, "they'll come looking for you."

"There is that," Cobner said.

"Oh," Raisho said.

Craugh put his heels to the horse and trotted down the street.

Juhg climbed onto his mount as well, then took off after the wizard. Jassamyn followed him while the draca sailed along overhead. Cobner and Raisho brought up the rear, already arguing about who had gotten the best of the goblinkin and talking about good moves each had seen in the other.

Warriors, Juhg thought. *I will never understand warriors.* They had their hands filled with trying to find the pieces of *The Book of Time,* and Cobner and Raisho went out of their way to take part in a tavern brawl. Remembering the insults the goblinkin had hurled, disparaging comments not only about halfers but the dwarves and humans who took up companionship with them, Juhg amended his thinking. *Well, not* much *out of the way.*

For five days, Juhg and his companions rode along with the trade caravan bound for Torvassir. Even though he was worried about the Grandmagister, his Librarian training kept him busy talking to the merchants, sellswords, and artisans that traveled with the caravan. People on the move tended to gather news and gossip quickly. All of them carried information. Part of the reason for his conversations, Juhg knew, was in preparation for the trip into the Smoking Marshes.

"I've heard the fog that covers that place is filled with ghosts," one young human told Juhg. "My da said there was a battle in that place a long time ago, and that the ghosts of the people that died there got stuck and couldn't go anywhere else because they lost the battle."

There were several other stories, most of them including ghosts and a few of them that held suggestions of treasure to be found somewhere in the marshes.

"It's good that they're not talking about treasure there overmuch," Cobner said later that night around their campfire. "Means we shouldn't be running into anybody in those woods. And if we do, it's likely they aren't supposed to be there."

The travelers usually stayed by themselves in camp so they could talk. The extra horses they brought along carried small tents to keep them dry at night during the frequent showers the area had. Of course, that meant that a lot of times in the morning they had to pack wet tents, which got them soaked. That didn't matter, though; if it was still raining the following morning they were going to get wet anyway. Most of the trip was spent in some sort of misery under the dank, oppressive sky.

At night, Juhg added to his journal. If he lived long enough to return to the Vault of All Known Knowledge, he knew he'd have material to write up concerning the trip. Small things, like two of the ghost stories one of the human children had told him that had bearing in actual history of the place, wouldn't become a book, but they would make nice addenda to some of the histories.

If those histories still survive at the Vault of All Known Knowledge, Juhg thought sadly.

But he didn't feel guilty taking the time to do those things, although Craugh made it apparent that he thought Juhg's investigations were mainly a waste of time. Juhg knew that the Grandmagister would expect him to work even though he was on a mission to rescue him.

On the morning of the fifth day, the caravan was attacked by goblinkin bandits. They came out of the forest just as the rising sun started sweeping the last of the night's thin shadows away.

Howling furiously, obviously hoping to catch the camp before it was truly awake, the goblinkin descended. Unfortunately, they started yelling while still yet too far away.

Juhg hunkered down behind a wagon while Jassamyn and the other archers among the caravan pulled together and loosed a volley that broke the ranks of the goblinkin.

"Hold!" the caravan master yelled. "Archers together!"

Jassamyn bent her bow again. She held the arrow to her cheek, the fletchings lying along her chin.

"Release!" the caravan master yelled.

Jassamyn released along with the other archers. The arrows struck the goblinkin bandits squarely. Several of them dropped dead in their tracks. The survivors quickly turned tail and ran. Unfortunately, they chose to hide in the forest along the trail and prevented the caravan from traveling safely.

For two hours, they fought a holding battle. Occasionally, a goblinkin would stick out an important piece of himself for too long and an archer would put a shaft through it. Jassamyn killed four of them with arrows through the head or heart. It got to the point that Raisho and Cobner were taking bets on which the elven maid would put an arrow through next, and how many goblinkin she would bag before the bandits finally gave up.

Juhg sketched several scenes of the battle, just skeletons that he intended to flesh out later.

 After a while, Cobner complained of being bored. Raisho agreed. Together, they approached the caravan master with a daring plan.

"Let us take a few of the sellswords you've got protectin' the caravan," Cobner said. "We'll go around behind them goblinkin an' take 'em unawares. Should be able to kill a lot of 'em before they notice. They ain't ever been good at countin' noses or watching over one another."

"We haven't lost a man yet," the caravan master said. "The archers can hold them off well enough."

"Maybe," Cobner agreed. "But in the meantime, the horses are drinkin' water an' eatin' feed that you're payin' for. An' how long do you think it'll be before one of them beasties gets the idea to start killin' the horses?"

Juhg knew that was true. Goblinkin were slow thinkers, but deliberate. The horses were more vulnerable than the caravan's travelers.

"All right," the caravan master said, after a brief delay. "But I don't want to take unnecessary chances."

"We'll be discreet," Cobner promised.

Nervous, Juhg watched his friends leave. For the next two hours, he sat beside Jassamyn and Craugh, thinking surely the dwarven warrior and the young human would be discovered with the sellswords they'd taken with them. Instead, the goblinkin started to notice that their numbers were getting whittled away.

"Where's Vallap?" a goblinkin roared.

"Don't know. Pizlat is missin' too."

"So is Vaggas."

Goblinkin began calling out the names of the missing, who did not answer. Finally, unnerved, they fled through the forest. Cobner, Raisho, and the others pursued them for almost a mile. Juhg knew that later because the warriors had left a trail of goblinkin dead in their wake.

That night they camped with the caravan one last time, hunkered down and aware the goblinkin could return without warning. Cobner and Raisho spent time with the sellswords, roaring stories at each other till other members in the caravan yelled at them.

In the morning after they broke camp, they said their good-byes to the caravan and followed the small stream that fed the Smoking Marshes where the fog in the trees got steadily thick and stank of sulfur.

"I can see how this place gets its reputation," Raisho said as he rode beside Juhg. "I ain't seen nothin' but this fog fer miles, seems like."

"It's been less than half a mile," Juhg said.

"Seems longer," Raisho commented.

Out in the wilderness now, Jassamyn took the lead, staying six or seven horse lengths ahead of the group. She kept her bow to hand. Cobner and Raisho took turns riding far enough back to see their back trail.

The trees around the marshes grew straight and tall, adding to the perpetual gloom that seemed to hang over the place. Bobcats, hares, turkeys, and quail moved in the brush, joined by smaller creatures. Twice Juhg saw deer and once he spotted a bear's claw marks on a tree, letting him know that animals in the area still counted the marshland safe enough to come to get food and water. That was heartening. He knew Jassamyn had noted the same things.

The trail they followed was mostly grown over, an old trapper's route that led to the heart of the marshlands where the dwarven city had stood years before *The Book of Time* had caused it and the mountain it had been in to sink into the ground.

The Grandmagister had never traveled the route because he'd discovered the location of the second piece of *The Book of Time* after he'd returned to Greydawn Moors and finally puzzled the location out, but he'd found mention of the trail in some of the books at the Library. Reading in a few other histories of the area confirmed the trail's existence.

Juhg reviewed the Grandmagister's notes. *Juhg, by the time you read this, I don't know if the trail will still be there. Nature already works hard to reclaim it. Elven warders, of course, would tell you that's the expected progression of such things. Still, it doubles as a game trail as well and something should survive of it.*

Before the Cataclysm, this trail was one of the most heavily traveled in the area. Bolts of silk and barrels of fine wines traveled this road, and merchants at both ends got fat with profit. If Lord Kharrion hadn't managed to bring the goblinkin together, the road would have remained open for many more years.

The Grandmagister had also used the stream as a marker, just as the old fur trappers had. In places where the trail had been obscured by underbrush and trees, they only had to stay with the stream and keep heading into the marshes. The only sounds in the forest were the heavy clop of the horses' hooves and the gurgle of the stream. Occasional birdcalls and animal growls punctuated the steady noise.

276

"Where does the fog come from?" Raisho asked.

"There's an active volcano under this area," Juhg answered.

"I remember now," Raisho said. "The Grandmagister writ that the Smokesmith dwarves lived here. The ones what tamed the volcano."

"Exactly." Juhg guided his horse around a fallen tree that crossed the trail. "They operated the Molten Rock Forge, which was also the name by which the mountains became known."

"Armorers, they was."

"Yes."

"An' this is the same place where Fort Yuar was. The place that the Grandmagister taught ye the poem about."

Juhg nodded.

Looking around, Raisho said, "Then ye was kept in a goblinkin mine not far from this place."

"Yes." *And my parents and siblings died somewhere around here, too.*

"Sorry," Raisho said. "Forgettin' meself was what I was doin'."

"It's all right."

They rode in silence for a while, and memories crowded in at Juhg to the point that their weight and all the old guilt felt heavier than the leaden skies that crowded them and seemed held back only by the canopy of trees. He looked in all directions, wondering if he would see a family of dwellers hidden back in the woods, or if he would recognize a place that he had come through with the Grandmagister.

But he didn't. There were no dwellers secreted away in the inhospitable woods, and none of the places looked familiar or they all looked familiar.

"Ye are lucky in some respects, Juhg," Raisho said softly.

Juhg looked at his friend.

"At least ye knew yer ma an' yer da fer a while," the young sailor said. "Me, I was stripped from me ma soon after she'd whelped me. Birthed right into slavery, I was."

"I know," Juhg said.

"Leastways, I got a friend in ye now. An' a good ship in *Windchaser* if I ever get back that way. Ye got a home, too, Juhg. Shouldn't be somethin' you go forgettin' about."

"I won't." *But there's no guarantee any of us will live long enough to return to Greydawn Moors.*

They rode on in silence for a while longer, and Juhg felt certain they were both entertaining the same dark thoughts.

Twilight deepened the shadows of the marshes, making the shadows longer and more sinister, sometimes fading them away entirely for a moment only to allow them to spring back out again. With the coming of the night, the nocturnal creatures had resumed mastery over the marsh. Crickets and bullfrogs sang around the marsh, falling silent now and again when an owl scream or a bobcat yowled to let the world know it was hunting.

Rocking wearily in the horse's saddle, feeling the long days of riding aching throughout his body, Juhg longed for a warm dry place and his bedroll. On occasion, he'd used the blue gemstones to look in on Greydawn Moors and *One-Eyed Peggie*. He hadn't been able to go there as he had with the Grandmagister, but he didn't know if it was because the ties to the Grandmagister were stronger and more intense—as Craugh suggested—or that he was simply afraid to let go too much in case the wizard couldn't restart his heart if it stopped again.

Jassamyn led the way back up from the slow-moving stream, searching for the trail they had once again lost due to the underbrush. She stopped abruptly, her horse shying a little as a heavy-winged owl glided by overhead, and gazed down at the ground.

The elven maid dismounted and kept her horse behind her as she carefully walked along.

"What is it?" Craugh asked. He was grumpy because he'd never sat a horse well and this was the longest time in years that Juhg had seen the wizard ride.

Kneeling, Jassamyn brushed her hand through the tall grass. Her fingers explored the ground. "Hoofprints," she announced in a quiet voice as she stayed low and gazed around the forest and the marshes. "Riders have passed through here not long ago."

"Bandits?" Cobner suggested.

"All of these horses were shod," Jassamyn said. "Whoever these riders were, they were civilized."

"Bandits steal horses from caravans," Cobner said. "Mayhap these are stolen horses."

"Caravan mounts are shod," Jassamyn agreed, "but caravan masters don't always keep them shod well. All of these tracks are cut fresh and deep. And they went in single file through the brush, trying to keep their tracks to a minimum so they wouldn't be as noticeable."

"So somebody else is skulkin' through the woods." Raisho loosened his cutlass in the sheath down his back.

"Or had been," she agreed. "From the looks of these tracks, they were headed into the marshes."

"Same as us," the dwarven warrior said.

"We'll cold camp tonight," Craugh said.

Raisho groaned. He hated cold meals. Over the past few days, with all the rain, he'd gotten his fill of cold meals. That was one thing he'd gotten spoiled to while aboard *Windchaser*: Cook had always kept something hot in the galley, whether it was stew or chowder. And biscuits had been baked fresh.

Juhg had traveled in rough country so much with the Grandmagister that he was accustomed to eating journeycakes for days at a time.

Jassamyn remounted her horse and went on.

Glancing down every so often as they continued circling the heart of the Smoking Marshes, Juhg saw that the hoofprints kept on in the same direction they were. Since there was nothing else out the way they were going, which was one of the main reasons the Grandmagister had headed into the Smoking Marshes all those years ago, he had to believe that the tracks weren't just coincidence.

Suddenly, the marshland forest seemed even more threatening.

They cold camped in the general vicinity of the cave mouth the Grandmagister had indicated on his map. Jassamyn, Cobner, and Juhg all worked to put the tents well back into the hillside under the brush so they couldn't easily be seen. Finding dry ground on which to erect a tent was impossible, but Jassamyn did find an area that was protected by trees.

After a cold meal of journeycakes and jerked meat, they settled in for the night. They drew lots for guard duty and Cobner caught the first shift.

Juhg was assigned one of the dogwatches in the early hours of the morn, but he didn't think he'd be able to sleep when he'd laid down on his bedroll and listened to the misty rain dripping from the pine trees over his tent.

Horrid thoughts kept intruding on the peaceful frame of mind Juhg longed for. Over the years he had seen too much violence. It was too easy to visualize the Grandmagister walking the plank at sword's point into a sea roiling with sharks. Or broken upon a rack. Or dropped into the ocean with an anchor tied around his neck. And there was always the possibility that the Grandmagister would meet his end in a goblinkin stewpot.

Juhg's mind refused to be still, filled with all the thoughts that kept bumping into each other. Most of all, he was worried about the Grandmagister, about whether he was being treated well. Or whether he was dead. Juhg didn't know what he would do if the Grandmagister was killed or died of his injuries.

He thought of the goblinkin buildings bridges along the Shattered Coast to reach Imarish, and what that city and those islands would be like after the arrival of the goblinkin. So much would be lost because a city couldn't simply be uprooted and taken somewhere else.

What he wanted more than anything was to work, to write and draw everything that was inside his head so his thoughts wouldn't be so full. He hadn't gotten to work much since they'd debarked in Ship's Wheel Cove and took up with the trade caravan later that same day. He'd managed a little writing and sketching by taking a few minutes here and there in the woods with Raisho watching over him.

But he wanted—no, he *needed*—to lose himself in the writing.

Dark came earlier in the marshlands than Juhg was used to. On board *Windchaser* or at an inn or at Greydawn Moors, there had always been lanterns or candles or fireplaces to work by. Although the light was not always ideal, it suited his purpose for laying out thoughts and sketches he could turn a better hand to when he had the morning light again.

The pieces of *The Book of Time* lay heavy upon his chest in the leather pouch. A thousand questions hammered his mind about whether they would even find any more of the pieces. He had tried earlier to reach the Grandmagister through the gemstones, but he hadn't been successful. He believed that Aldhran Khempus had erected a magical barrier of some kind around the Grandmagister that the gemstones couldn't penetrate even with their power.

He'd even tried to contact the mantis again.

Looking in on Greydawn Moors and *One-Eyed Peggie* hadn't revealed much. The island was still under siege, though the Blood-Soaked Sea pirates were delivering staggering losses to the goblinkin ships; and Hallekk had sent dwarves out to explore the Haze Mountains.

280

With his mind so busy, Juhg thought he would never sleep, so he was surprised when Jassamyn roused him hours later and told him it was time for his turn at guard duty.

"Are you sure you're up to it?" the elven maid asked.

"Yes."

She hesitated. "You were having nightmares when I woke you."

Juhg had vivid memories of those. He'd been in the dungeon where the Grandmagister was being kept. Aldhran was torturing the Grandmagister, telling Juhg over and over that he hadn't found any new means of torture yet but was revisiting some of his old favorites.

"I thought about letting you sleep," Jassamyn said.

Crawling out of his bedroll, Juhg noticed the chill in the air at once. "No. Sleeping was not time well spent. You save me from a lot worse than a couple hours' turn at sentry duty." He stepped out of the tent and stomped his feet to wake them, not knowing how they had fallen asleep while he had not been able to.

"I've made some persimmon tea," Jassamyn said, pointing to the pot that hung from a tree branch only a few feet away. "It's not the best I've ever made, but maybe it will help you sleep. It's soothing by nature."

"I'll try it." Anything would be preferable to returning to his tent for a few more hours spent with nightmares.

"Wake Craugh when you're finished. And remember, when you wake Craugh out in the wilderness—"

"You want to grab his foot to do it," Juhg said. "I remember."

Craugh woke up irritable anyway when he slept in a bed. After sleeping on the ground, he sometimes came up flailing, bound by nightmares of his own. Now Juhg understood what some of them were.

He walked down to the edge of the water-filled marsh and stared out across the open expanse. His mind painted images of the Ruhrmash dwarves who had followed the Smokesmith dwarves in living in the area after the Molten Forge Mountains had crumbled. He'd never seen any of their great iron ships actually sailing, only bits and pieces of them that he and the Grandmagister had uncovered while hiding from the goblinkin slavers. Later, in the Vault of All Known Knowledge, Juhg had found paintings of the large, fierce ships, all bristling with weapons and spikes and bedecked with moveable shields to protect the crews from enemy attack and the dragon that had lived in the area.

He wished he could have seen that.

Hunkering down, Juhg peered along the shoreline across the great expanse of muddy water. He searched for campfires, as Cobner and Jassamyn had done before him, anything to let them know if the mysterious riders were still in the same area.

To his right, a raccoon climbed down from a tree and crept over to the water carrying a cherry in one paw. Sitting on its haunches, the raccoon washed its prize, then began eating greedily.

A wood mouse exited the treeline and ran over to the raccoon to see if there were any tidbits the raccoon had dropped. Then a heavy *chuff* of air sounded overhead.

Juhg looked up, knowing from experience what he would find.

The great horned owl dove from the steaming, moonskissed silvery fog that hung thick at the treetops. It descended in a rush, trailing its deadly claws behind it as it prepared to strike. The wood mouse froze, and Juhg knew the tiny creature's heart was pounding so hard it was probably ready to explode.

Before the owl could seize its prey, though, Jassamyn's draca zipped through the air with snapping leather wings. The miniature dragon's jaws opened and it took the mouse only inches ahead of the owl. Distracted by the draca's intervention, the owl collided with the ground and rolled, scaring the raccoon back to the trees. After a moment spent wobbly-legged, the owl gathered itself and leapt into the air.

High above in the shifting silvery fog, the draca shrilled in triumph. Then it ate the mouse in one long swallow.

Turning his gaze back to the expanse of trees on the other side of the marsh, Juhg noticed the shadow come up on him from behind. As big as the shadow was, Juhg first thought that Raisho had come up to talk to him because he was having trouble sleeping as well.

Juhg turned, started to speak to Raisho, then caught movement from the corner of his eye as the shadow raised a club high over his head and brought it down.

17

Slither

Kicking out, Juhg hurled himself backward, landing on his rump just as the club slammed into the mud where he'd been standing. The meaty splat of the club meeting the ground echoed over the marsh.

The creature—and Juhg immediately thought of it as a creature even though it was bipedal and intelligence gleamed in its feral yellow eyes—jerked its head around and lifted its club from the mud.

It was at least six and a half feet tall, built gaunt as a wolf, wide across the shoulders and narrow at the hips, and had the protruding muzzle of a wolf. Dark scales covered it, though, instead of fur. The scales looked oily, like gleaming onyx or ebony polished with beeswax. Delicate, shell-like ears framed its head, and they darted and flattened like a cat's. The jaws opened, revealing a double row of teeth. The hands and feet were a combination of human and animal, possessing long digits and curved talons.

"Give me the gemstones," the creature said in a voice that sounded like growling from a deep well. "You are not supposed to have them. They are not for you."

"What?"

"The gemstones." The creature pointed to where the leather pouch containing the blue gemstones hung against Juhg's chest. "I was summoned to protect them from weak things like you."

"By who?" Juhg's instinctive response was a question, and that was his Librarian training taking over when his dweller nature was screaming at him to run. And the second question came with the same speed as the first. "Summoned from where?"

The creature was inhumanly quick, almost quicker than a fear-filled dweller's survival reflexes. It swung the club again, aiming once more at Juhg's head.

Rolling in the mud, Juhg avoided the blow, then avoided two more in quick succession before he was able to get to his feet. From head to toe, a thick layer of mud covered him and his clothing. He found his way clear for the moment, and he found his voice.

"Help! Raisho!" Juhg dodged away, then ran back toward the tents. "Cobner! Craugh! Jassamyn! Help!" As quick as he was, though, he couldn't outrun the creature. Its legs were far longer than his. He delayed the inevitable by dodging around trees and rocks, barely avoiding the massive club twice more.

The creature's splayed feet pounded behind him, growing closer. Taking a look behind, Juhg saw that it was closing on him rapidly. And he was still thirty feet from the tents. He screamed for help again, saw the creature swing the club in a side-to-side strike that was designed to knock his head from his shoulders, and fell to the ground on his hands and knees, locking his hands over his head with his face in the mud to protect himself as best as he could.

The creature's strike took it off balance, dragging it forward. Its momentum pulled it along and its legs struck Juhg's rump and it tripped, falling forward. Landing on the ground, the creature slipped through the mud, twisting and shoving itself up immediately, bracing itself on one hand as it dug its feet in. It stood again, almost twenty feet from where it had fallen.

Before the creature could launch itself at Juhg again, Cobner stepped from his tent with his battle-axe in his hands. Giving vent to a battle cry, the dwarven warrior attacked at once. He swung the axe up and over, clearly intending to split the creature's head open.

The creature blocked the axe blow with its club, then aimed an incredibly quick strike at Cobner's head. Juhg was surprised when the dwarf pulled his head back and down—almost like a turtle—and managed to avoid the blow. Stepping in, Cobner blocked the club to the side with his axe haft, then stomped the creature's foot with his hobnailed boot. When the creature yowled in pain, Cobner bent forward and struck its face with his forehead. Both creature and dwarf fell to the ground.

The creature pushed itself up first, reaching for its club with that amazing speed and drawing the weapon up. Before it could swing, an arrow thudded into its chest, penetrating the black scales where a man's heart would have been.

As if only angered, the creature snapped the arrow off and glared at Jassamyn. Standing in front of her tent only a short distance away, the elven maid was already putting another shaft to string.

"I am Slither!" the creature roared. "Fear me!"

The Slither! Juhg remembered the name from the Grandmagister's journals.

I'm not quite clear on the nature of the Slither, the inhuman being that is supposed to guard the sections of The Book of Time, *the Grandmagister had written.* Haldin insists that the Slither is a discorporate being, a thing wrought totally of fear. That's why it appears in so many shapes. On the other hand, Kannal asserts that the Slither was once a large lizard that was malformed and given a much more intelligent mind. Even more puzzling, the Slither is supposed to be able to travel from each section of The Book of Time *faster than thought.*

Juhg stared at the creature in disbelief. How was it still alive? That had taken place thousands of years ago.

The Slither went on the attack at once, slamming its club into Cobner's axe and knocking the dwarf to one side. The guardian leapt at Jassamyn, who coolly released her arrow. Speeding true, the arrow slammed into the Slither's head, piercing it through, but the wound didn't seem to deflect the creature at all.

Jassamyn dived to one side. Coming to a sudden stop where the elven maid had been, the Slither turned toward her again. That was when Raisho crashed into the guardian from behind, knocking them both to the mud. Used to grappling and wrestling in tavern brawls and contests, Raisho claimed the advantage, grabbing one of the Slither's arms and trapping it behind its back, shouldering the creature's face into the mud as he lay on top of it.

"Hold that thing," Cobner said, getting to his feet again. "I'll put a knot on its knob that it won't be getting over so quicklike." He hefted his battle-axe and ran to Raisho's aid.

Suddenly, the Slither went still, not fighting against Raisho's hold. A black glow spread out from the creature, then it turned to liquid in Raisho's grasp, oozing through the young sailor's arms and legs and escaping his wrestling hold.

Raisho jerked away as if scalded, brushing at his chest to dislodge any remnant of the creature. "That thing burned me! I felt it! Hot as coals, it was!"

"You must have killed it," Cobner said, looking down at the black pool of ooze that was all that was left of the creature.

Incredulous, Juhg stood and watched as the black liquid pool suddenly jerked into motion. It shot across the uneven muddy ground, and though Juhg felt that some part of the pool had to become dislodged or be left behind, it all flowed together, changing shapes as it needed to in order to get around, over, under, or through debris that littered the marshy shore. The black pool gained speed and purpose, twisting and turning—*slithering*, Juhg realized—like a snake.

A few feet away, the black pool flowed upward, forming a column that changed back into the beast-man shape. It stretched its arm out and another club formed there.

286

"I am *Slither!*" it shouted, throwing its hands out to its sides in triumph. "You can't kill me!"

Stumbling over to the others, standing between Jassamyn and Craugh, Juhg studied the creature. No sign of the wounds it had suffered remained. Whatever power it had used to escape Raisho had also healed it.

"I am indestructible!" the Slither roared. "I am made by the guardian of *The Book of Time* by the powerful right hand of Lord Kharrion! Raised up from death and made whole once more!" It stretched out its empty hand. "Give me the gemstones that you have and I will ask Lord Kharrion to allow me to let you pass without taking your lives!"

"If you're the protector of *The Book of Time*, why weren't you in Skull Canal?" Juhg couldn't believe he was drawing attention to himself, but the question wouldn't leave him alone.

"Give me the gemstones!" The Slither came closer, its malevolent yellow eyes fixed solely on Juhg.

"Lord Kharrion is dead," Juhg said. "How can you still serve him if he's dead?"

"I will ask Lord Kharrion if I may spare your life," the Slither bellowed, "if you give me the gemstones now."

"No," Juhg said. Something was wrong. Something didn't ring true. The creature was talking like Lord Kharrion still existed.

"Then you will die!" The Slither raised his club and started forward. "I am Slither, guardian to *The Book of Time!*"

"And I am Craugh!" the wizard roared at Juhg's side. Green embers circled his staff. "This camp is under my protection!" He drew a glowing ward in the air and spoke a single word.

The insignia, looking like a very complicated letter K, spun toward the creature, struck it, and wrapped around it immediately. Once the letter had stretched out to its full size, it bound the Slither's arms and legs together, trapping the creature.

The Slither went rigid again, then he oozed between the magical binding. With nothing left to hold, the glowing trap vanished. Almost immediately, the Slither reformed and ran straight for Juhg.

Craugh threw a hand out toward the creature. Waves of shimmering force hit the Slither and threw it backward thirty feet, sending it sprawling in the mud.

Like a machine, the guardian got to its feet and ran to attack once more.

His face a mask of surprise and anger, Craugh moved forward and threw his hand out again. The shimmering force knocked the Slither from its feet again, propelling it high into the air. Before it had a chance to land, Craugh hit it again with the magical force, knocking it into the air even higher and farther. Then again.

After the fourth blow, the Slither was a shapeless blob that arced out high over the marsh waters. It dropped, still slithering and twisting and twitching, and disappeared into the water.

"Get a lantern," Craugh directed gruffly as he strode to the water's edge.

"What about the other people that might be in the area?" Raisho asked.

"If they didn't hear all that bellowing and roaring," the wizard said, "they're not going to notice a lantern."

Juhg dashed back inside his tent, took a small oil lantern from his kit, and ran back outside. Craugh and the others stood at the water's edge and peered out at the marsh. Kneeling with the lantern on the ground in front of him, Juhg took out his tinderbox, raised the glass on the lantern, and lit the wick. When the flame was going nicely, he lowered the glass and went to the water's edge with the others.

Raising the lantern high, Juhg peered out into the marsh water. The lantern's golden light barely dented the darkness and cast an elongated oval.

"Over there." Jassamyn pointed out to the left.

Craugh took the lantern from Juhg and held it as high as he could reach. Juhg spotted the black mass twisting and squirming through the water and heading for shore at least a hundred yards from their position.

"He's had enough," Raisho crowed. He started jogging around the edge of the marsh with his cutlass in hand.

"He's the guardian," Juhg said. "He's the guardian that the Grandmagister mentioned in his journal. The one who is supposed to protect *The Book of Time*. He was talking like Lord Kharrion is still around."

"I heard him, apprentice," Craugh responded. "I have ears, and it was hard not to hear him yelling." He took a fresh grip on his staff. "But he came after you."

"To get the gemstones that I'm carrying." Juhg watched the dark mass slither up onto the shore. It sat there for a moment, like a fox run to ground and breathing hard. "Craugh, if that *is* the Slither that the Grandmagister researched and found out about, it may know where the second piece of *The Book of Time* is."

"Haring about in the middle of the night in unfamiliar territory is not something I'm wishful of."

On the shore, the dark mass slowly rose up and became something akin to human again. Unsteadily at first, but gaining its balance, the Slither started picking up speed.

"If we're gonna go after it," Cobner said, "now is the time."

Craugh reached up and pulled his pointy hat on more tightly. "Let's go. Leave the horses. They will only slow us down. That thing won't make this chase easy across open ground."

The Slither ran cross-country and took advantage of every bit of cover the land provided. Trees with gnarled roots that stuck up from muddy pools of marshland became hazards. They splashed through other pools, and twice Raisho—who was the fleetest of them—plunged beneath deep water only to come up and pull himself out to take up the chase again while the others avoided the areas. Swamp rats, bobcats, and night boomers—carnivorous lizards that grew up to three feet long—all occupied areas around the marshlands.

Juhg kept up with the others, but just barely. If he hadn't been so fleet afoot and in good shape, they would have left him far behind with their longer legs. His small size helped when they plunged through brush that tore at their exposed flesh and clothing. He went through more than a few barriers that the creature oozed through but his companions had to circumnavigate.

And if the creature had possessed the incredible speed it had shown earlier, he knew that they would never have been able to keep up with it.

More than once, Juhg saw the creature dart around a tree or boulder, or even a few hills, and disappear. He felt certain that it would lose them then, but Jassamyn trailed it without a false step even in the dim moonslight. Her keen elven eyes and knowledge of woodcraft aided her in keeping them apace of their quarry.

Several long, bone-jarring minutes later, Juhg was starting to flag, exhausted by the past few days and the frantic run across broken terrain. Just when he knew he couldn't go any farther, they topped a ridge that looked down over a small valley. Below, not far from the water's edge, the creature vanished into a cave. The hillside contained several other caves as well. If they had not spotted the creature choosing the one it entered, it would have gotten away because they would have spent hours exploring them and Jassamyn would never have found tracks on the hard stone surface of the hill.

Juhg found the strength to stay with the others as they loped down the steep incline. Craugh raised a hand and stopped them at the entrance to the cave.

Breathing harshly, almost done in himself, Craugh grinned mirthlessly. He had always enjoyed the excitement of a hunt. "It occurs to me that this would be a most excellent place for an ambush."

"I'll go first," Cobner offered.

"I'll watch yer back," Raisho said, clapping the dwarven warrior on the shoulder.

Craugh followed the young sailor into the narrow passage of the cave, leaving Juhg and Jassamyn to bring up the rear. At Raisho's request, the wizard passed the lantern up to the young sailor. Raisho kept the lantern high so it would rip away the darkness in front of the dwarven warrior. Moving cautiously, his left foot always ahead of the right so he could brace himself quickly in the event of attack, Cobner went slowly along.

After only a short distance, the narrow cave started a steep incline that twisted and turned down into the earth. Juhg trailed his fingers along the cave's wall. When he examined his fingertips, he found they were coated with gray, powdery ash. He studied the long cylindrical structure of the cave and took note of the jumble of rocks lining the cave floor.

"This is a lava tube," Juhg whispered. One of the first books he truly enjoyed at the Vault of All Known Knowledge had been Tharntin's *A Dwarf's Eye for Caving: A Field Guide for Race Impaired Elves and Humans Who Have Dwarven Natures.* The book had been packed with drawings, black and white as well as full-color plate, of caverns explored by Tharntin and his team.

The Ironpick dwarven author had been truly gifted, not only in his love of caves and exploring but also in his driving narrative style. During the reading of the book, Juhg had felt as though he had crawled, scaled, and nearly drowned in all the caves that had been described in the book. The guide had been the first book Juhg had taken time to make a personal copy of. It saddened him to think that copies of the book, including his own, might no longer exist after the destruction of the Vault of All Known Knowledge. When he had taught young dwellers to read, Tharntin's guide had always been one of the first he started with. Reading the dwarven explorer's exciting accounts had made even the most lackadaisical dweller child dream of exploring unknown underground regions.

Chasing after a murderous creature in the dark through a cave really takes the edge off cave exploration, Juhg thought. And lackadaisical dweller children tended to remain lackadaisical dweller children after they put even exciting books away.

"A lava tube, eh?" Raisho repeated. "I thought it was a cave."

"A lava tube *is* a cave," Juhg said. "But it is a specialized type the cave. Lava tubes are created by erupting volcanoes. That's why ash coats the walls, the tunnel is so smoothly circular, and why so much rock has been deposited along the way. Since the Molten Forge Mountains were rich in iron ore and other metals, the molten liquid cooled and subsided and left the impurities behind. These rocks are the impurities."

"Mayhap we could shelve the geography and spelunking lessons for another time," Cobner whispered with some irritation.

"Sorry," Juhg apologized.

"If you ever decide you're tired of all that open water out at sea, Raisho," Cobner said, "come visit me. I'll take you on a tour of some of the best caves and mines you could ever hope to swing a pickaxe in."

On and on they went, and the way grew steeper and steeper. Juhg found he was soon leaning back so he wouldn't fall forward. Thankfully, the lava tube remained contained and did not branch off into other tunnels to confuse their pursuit. The creature that called itself Slither could only have gone in one direction.

They passed several bat colonies that hung from the ceiling. The stench of guano and sulfur stung Juhg's nose and made him sneeze.

"We're in a live tube," Cobner said. "Feel how warm it's getting? Not getting cold at all. If we were going down into a regular cavern, it would be getting cold by now."

"What does that mean?" Raisho asked.

"Means that this tunnel leads down to at least a section of the volcano. Kind of reminds me when me and Wick fought Shengharck for his treasure hoard in the Broken Forge Mountains."

"Didn't ye mention that that volcano blew up?"

"Yeah, but we got out ahead of the explosion. Usually works out better if you get out ahead of an explosion when it comes to active volcanoes."

"How far down does this thing go?" Raisho sounded a little nervous.

"Why, all the way to the other end, of course." Cobner laughed a little at his own joke.

Raisho didn't seem amused.

Several more minutes passed in silence. The heat grew steadily stronger, till it felt as intense as a baker's oven. Juhg actually started to sweat where he had been almost too cool only moments ago.

Around the next bend of the lava tube, they came upon the first remnants of stone structures that had been carved out of the mountain. Instead of the normal jumble of rocks they had been coming across, Juhg recognize blocks cut with stone axes.

"Wait," Juhg said. He peered at the jumble of stone blocks, then closed in on one in particular.

"This is no time to be a rock hound, apprentice," Craugh said.

Juhg brushed ash from the top of the rock, then from the sides. He felt engravings in the stone surfaces. "This is important. Bring the lantern over here."

Raisho brought the light back to the stone. "What is it, scribbler?"

"It's a cornerstone. He's up and found a dwarven cornerstone." Cobner's voice held a note of reverence and awe. "Used to be, when dwarves knew how to read and write, dwarven architects made cornerstones for important buildings and they wrote on them. Usually gave the name of the clan, the master builder, the name of the building, and the date the cornerstone was set into place. In all my life, I've seen only nine cornerstones."

The cornerstone was written in a dwarven language that Juhg had some familiarity with. He quickly read the inscription, thankful that the words were simple. "This cornerstone was set into place by the Molten Forge dwarves almost three thousand years ago. The master builder's name was Unkor Surehammer. The cornerstone belonged to the clan meetinghouse." He took out a piece of paper from his journal and made a quick rubbing of the stone face that bore the inscription. When he was finished, he folded the rubbing and tucked it back into his journal.

Reverently, Cobner laid his hand upon the cornerstone. "This is a powerful important thing you found, Juhg. When we finish our business with the Slither and we come back this way, I got to take this cornerstone with me. It needs to be set in a place of honor."

"That cornerstone also means we're getting close to where the dwarven city sunk down into the earth with the Molten Forge Mountains," Craugh said. "Let's keep moving."

Excitement flared through Juhg as he continued following his companions down and down into the lava tube. They were seeing whole sections of buildings now that no one had seen in thousands of years.

The heat continued to intensify to the point they were all uncomfortable. More twists and turns followed, and for a time there were no more buildings. An orange glow started to fill the cavern, stripping away the darkness.

That was when they saw the first ghost.

The spectral figure was that of a dwarf dressed in miner's gear. With a pickaxe over one shoulder, the dwarf walked through the lava tube walls while whistling, appearing on one side of the tunnel and disappearing through the wall on the other side.

All of them froze.

"Was that a ghost?" Raisho asked in a whisper.

Ghosts existed. Juhg knew that for a certainty because the Grandmagister had told him stories about the times he had encountered ghosts. However, Juhg had never seen a ghost in the flesh.

Well, Juhg thought ruefully, *a ghost wouldn't have exactly been in the flesh anyway.*

"That wasn't a ghost," Craugh said. "I have seen ghosts and I know that was not a ghost."

"Then what were it?" Raisho asked.

"I don't know."

With some reluctance, the party went forward. It wasn't long before they encountered the second ghost.

The second ghost was a little dwarven boy on his knees working with a pickaxe made for his size. He was cutting blocks and engraving them with letters of the Molten Forge dwarves. The combination exercise taught him how to skillfully use a pickaxe as well as his letters. When he finished, he would be able to work with and cut several different shapes and kinds of stone and recognize all his letters. Learning to spell later with the stones would also make him strong.

After a brief hesitation, Cobner walked straight through the boy and the blocks he was making. The boy never looked up nor gave them any notice.

293

"Ye know," Raisho observed, "mayhap I ain't never seen no ghost, but I bet you can walk right through one just like we walked through that boy."

"Actually," Jassamyn said, "you can't walk through a ghost unless the ghost allows you to. Also, ghosts all have a scent. Whatever these things are, they have no scent."

The frequency of the dwarven "ghosts" increased as they went farther down the tunnel. In short order, there seemed to be a whole community living within the earth.

Finally, they came into the main chamber of the volcano. The cavern was huge, big enough to hold at least ten good-sized trade ships with room for cargo left over. At the other end of the cavern, a boiling molten mass filled the cavern with heat and light. Dozens of the dwarven "ghosts" worked on dozens of "ghostly" projects.

Drawn by the enigma presented before him, Juhg walked unbidden into the cavern. "Something is amiss."

"I'll tell ye what's amiss," Raisho offered. "This place is filled with ghosts an' there ain't no sign of that creature we come in here after."

Juhg walked through several of the "ghosts" and trailed his hands through several others. None of them even seemed to know that he was there among them.

"These . . . these . . ." He gave up trying to find a name for them. "Whatever they are, are from different times. And all of them are dwarves that used to live in this region."

"Mayhap this is a favorite place fer ghosts," Raisho said.

"Juhg," Jassamyn said. "The gemstones of *The Book of Time* are glowing."

When he looked down, Juhg found that the gemstones *were* glowing so strongly that the blue light could be seen through the thick leather. Unconsciously, he closed his hand over the glowing pouch to dim the light. As soon as he put his hand over the gemstones, though, he felt a pull. The physical reaction surprised him greatly.

"What is it, apprentice?" Craugh asked.

Juhg shook his head and looked in the direction of the pull. "I don't know. The gemstones are pulling me in this direction." Curious, he followed the pull, walking through several of the dwarven "ghosts" as they continued about their business.

As he neared the wall to the left, Juhg spotted a grayish gleam buried in the rock.

"Did the Grandmagister's journal specify where the dwarven section of *The Book of Time* would be found?" Craugh asked.

Juhg touched the wall over the grayish gleam. "No, he didn't. He only said that according to the book he translated, the piece had been under the Molten Forge dwarven community."

"We left the last of the buildings sometime back," Jassamyn pointed out. "If that's any indication, then we are under the old Molten Forge dwarven city."

The volcanic rock of the wall should have been hot enough from the lava pool to burn Juhg's hand. Instead, he felt the heat, but none of it was injurious to him. The pull between the gemstones in the leather pouch and the section of the wall continued, getting stronger.

"Something is behind this section of wall," Juhg said. "I don't know how, but I can feel that it is there."

"Well then," Cobner said, "let's just be having a look at it." He took the small pickaxe from his belt that he carried with him at all times. The pickaxe doubled as a weapon and as a tool.

Putting his battle-axe to one side so it would be quick to hand, the dwarven warrior reached out to touch the wall. He drew his hand back at once before it ever made contact with the surface of the stone.

Surprise showed in Cobner's face, made bright by the orange glow from the lava pool. "How did you touch that stone, Juhg? If I was to put my hand on it, it's hot enough to burn the flesh right off of the bone."

"I don't know," Juhg said. The only thing he knew for certain was that he needed to see what was behind the wall. Even if he hadn't been experiencing the pull from the gemstones around his neck, his dweller's curiosity had been fully aroused. On top of that, there was still the mystery of the dwarven "ghosts" walking all over the cavern. He didn't see how the two things could be separate.

Keeping clear of the hot wall, Cobner struck with his pickaxe. Stone chips flew as the sharp tang bit deeply. As he was pulling the pickaxe back for his fourth swing, the creature they had pursued oozed from the ceiling in a long black stream behind the dwarven warrior. Before Juhg or any of the others could shout a warning, and by the time the black stream touched the floor, the Slither stood once more in its man-beast form. The guardian struck Cobner without warning, driving the dwarf to the ground with a double-handed blow to the back of the head.

Wheeling around instantly, the creature focused on Juhg. Looking the Slither in the face, Juhg realized the guardian hadn't overcome Craugh's earlier attacks. The features weren't quite finished and they seemed to have the consistency of pudding. The wizard's spells had affected the creature's ability to hold itself together.

"No!" the Slither shouted. "Stay away! This is not for you! This is for Lord Kharrion!"

Juhg saw Craugh take a step forward and raise a hand.

"Down, apprentice!" Craugh commanded.

Even fast as he was, Juhg barely got out of the way as Craugh's spell smashed into the back of the creature and drove it over his head. He twisted, watching the Slither flail through the air as it flew toward the lava pool.

Groggy and nearly unconscious, Cobner lurched to his feet to do battle, dropping the pickaxe and reaching for his battle-axe.

Juhg picked up the pickaxe and turned to the wall. He lacked the dwarf's skill but not much skill was required to chop a hole in the wall. The gemstones in the leather pouch around his neck continued to glow. Frantically, he drove the pickaxe into the wall six times. At the end of that, the hollow beyond the wall surface was revealed.

Inside the hollow, two more gemstones in the curious shape of a square topped by a mesa floated in a natural formation caused by lava bubbling as it cooled. Those pieces glowed dark brown as brightly as the gemstones around Juhg's neck glowed blue.

"Stay away! Do not touch those! I will kill you!"

In stunned disbelief, Juhg looked back at the lava pool and saw the creature crawling out of the molten rock. Flames clung to the creature as it stumbled toward Juhg. The face and the rest of the body oozed and ran like melting candle wax.

Cobner set himself into a defensive position. He held the battle-axe behind and to one side of his body, ready to swing as soon as the creature came within range.

296

Reaching into the rock formation hollow, Juhg reached for the floating dark brown gemstones. His fingers passed through them but there was a brief cold contact. Concentrating on the task at hand, Juhg tried to find the resonance within the brown gemstones as he had with the blue gemstones. The connection came faster this time, but it also came more powerfully.

Paralyzed, Juhg stood waiting, and was horrified to see all the "ghosts" in the cavern suddenly turn and stare straight at him. Without a word, all of the dwarven "ghosts" approached him.

Craugh and the others sank back to defend him, forming a protective semicircle. They had their weapons raised and green embers swirled like maddened fireflies around the wizard's staff. *It won't do any good,* Juhg thought. *None of us are going to get out of here alive.*

Then blackness filled his head and he was gone.

18

"And This Is the Future, Librarian Juhg!"

h, Librarian Juhg. You have returned."

Cautiously, Juhg glanced around. This time the mantis didn't meet him on the mountaintop. All around him, as far as the eye could see, were beautiful orchards interspersed with artesian wells.

The mantis walked toward him, coming down a brick-laid walkway. Nothing had changed about the mantis. It walked toward him on its four back legs and clasped its upper arms behind its back as if it had been deep in thought.

"I see you have found the second piece of *The Book of Time*," the mantis said. "Congratulations."

"My friends," Juhg said, remembering the situation he had just left them in, "are in a lot of trouble. The creature known as the Slither is attacking them, and so far he's proven unkillable. Also, there are dwarven ghosts—"

"Ghosts, you say." The mantis drew itself up straight and tall in front of Juhg. "And they're dwarves? I guess it's no surprise, really. That whole area used to be overrun with them. Many of them died over the years of old age, sickness, war, and—of course—when Kharrion's spell shattered the mountains they lived in and dragged it into the hollows of the earth."

"Yes," Juhg replied. "But I have never seen a ghost before."

"Nor have I." The mantis smiled. "It would be hard for me to see one, though."

"Why?"

"Because ghosts are always past their expiration dates."

Juhg wanted to groan. The pun was simply awful. Instead, he said nothing at all.

The mantis laughed at his own joke. "I'm sorry. That was uncalled for." It didn't act like it was really apologetic, though. "Actually I can see ghosts. But here I see them as they were before they were ghosts as well as after. And, of course, during the moment of death. Would you like to see a ghost here?"

"No," Juhg said, shuddering at the thought.

"I feel like walking," the mantis said. "Walk with me."

"I really should get back. My friends—"

"Are in trouble again." The mantis nodded. "Yes, I know that. Trust me, you will have plenty of time to get back to them. Now please walk with me. I feel like stretching my legs." It started walking, heading past Juhg.

Having no choice, Juhg fell in slightly behind the creature and started walking. As they walked, he couldn't help but gazing down at the rows of trees. Apples, pears, and oranges all filled the limbs. Flowers grew in wild abandon in the shadows under the trees.

"By now you've found that the first set of gemstones has powers," the mantis said.

" 'By now?' You talk like time has passed here." Juhg was confused.

The mantis looked at him. "You asked me to talk to you like time passes, remember?"

"Yes," Juhg said.

"And you thought I was the one having trouble keeping up with things. All you have to remember is what is in the past and keep up with what is happening now. I, on the other hand, am constantly immersed in all that you perceive, plus what—for you, at any rate—is yet to be."

"I see," Juhg said, though he really didn't see at all.

"That's why we're not meeting upon the mountain."

Juhg looked at the mantis.

"I knew you were wondering," the mantis said.

"We're not meeting on the mountain because why?"

"Because we're already meeting there."

"Oh."

"You doubt me?" the mantis demanded. "I picked this place because it is beautiful—don't you think?"

"Yes," Juhg said, struggling to make sense of everything. It didn't help that he was distracted by thoughts of his friends getting killed by the Slither or the strange dwarven "ghosts" while he was talking to a giant bug.

"You *do* doubt me?" Now the praying mantis looked incensed.

At least, Juhg was fairly certain it looked incensed. Since he'd never seen an angry praying mantis before—or, if he had, he'd never taken notice—he wasn't certain. Before he could tell the mantis that he was only agreeing that the orchard was beautiful and steer the conversation back around to his need to rejoin his friends—as well as secure any help that might be in the offing—the mantis grabbed his wrist.

The strange thing was, the mantis's foreleg *looked* like chitin-covered hide, but it felt like a . . . tentacle?

"Come," the mantis ordered imperiously in a tone that reminded Juhg of Craugh's haughtiness when the wizard was vexed at someone or something.

Pulled stumbling behind the mantis, Juhg took two big steps and turned sharply to the right three times and once to the left. When they stopped, they were standing on the mountain again.

The mantis pointed farther down the narrow trail. "See?"

Turning, Juhg saw that he and the mantis were talking. His past self happened to look up and looked squarely at him.

"That's enough," the mantis said. "Your mind isn't going to be able to handle much of this. And I need your mind working at its best." It took his hand again and walked over the mountain's edge.

Two quick turns to the right, three to the left, and—somehow, though Juhg could not remember seeing steps—two steps *up* took them from the mountain to a river where big brown bears fished for salmon swimming upstream. The bears' claws flashed and they fed with ravenous teeth that tore at the pink flesh.

"But . . . but . . ." Juhg struggled to marshal his thoughts. "That didn't happen."

Lord of the Libraries

The mantis looked at him. "Didn't it? Think back, Librarian Juhg. Think back long and hard."

Juhg did, closing his eyes with the effort. He couldn't believe it when he *could* remember the incident. He *had* looked up the mountain just after seeing his multiple selves, and he *had* seen himself.

He could even remember the mantis telling him that was his future self and he would understand what had happened later.

"I *do* remember," Juhg said hoarsely.

"Of course you do." The mantis folded its arms over its chest and looked satisfied.

"But that's a paradox. I know I didn't remember being there until we went there. And if I didn't see me then till now, how can I remember that my future self was there then?"

The mantis held its arms up and took a step back. "Stop! Now you're confusing me."

"Things can't happen like that," Juhg insisted.

"Okay," the mantis said, "it didn't happen." It stood with crossed arms and waited.

Juhg shook his head. "But it *did* happen."

"Make up your mind."

"How can something like that happen?"

"I thought you said it couldn't."

"It can't, but it did."

The mantis sighed and shook its shining head. "This is why I have seldom, do seldom, and will seldom talk with beings outside of the In-Betweenness. This inability to grasp what is so simple."

"This isn't simple."

"Because you're impaired from living all those years outside the In-Betweenness."

"If I can see into the past, then can't I see into the future?"

"You really shouldn't do that, Librarian Juhg."

"But it's true. Unless this is the last time I visit you here." That possibility scared Juhg. If he never visited the mantis again, after setting a pattern of seeing it after getting two sections of *The Book of Time,* what did that mean? "Am I already dead in the future? Did I not make it out of the dwarven caves in the Molten Forge Mountains?"

"Of course you made it out of the dwarven caves. We talked, you went back, and you saved your friends."

"But *I* haven't done that yet."

"You will."

"How do I know that?"

Sighing again, the mantis took him by the arm and marched past the bears, who barely took notice of them. A few turns later, Juhg couldn't remember how many because he was almost tripping all over himself, they came to a bleak desert covered with rolling sand dunes.

The mantis pointed to where it was talking with yet another Juhg. Instead of being clad in the First Level Librarian robe he had worn last time as well as this time, the other Juhg wore torn breeches and a ripped shirt. A long cut on the side of his face promised a bad scar to come when the wound healed.

"And this is the future, Librarian Juhg," the mantis declared in an exasperated voice. "As you can clearly see, you have some interesting things still coming up."

Appalled, Juhg stared at the other two of them, wondering where he'd been and what he'd gotten into. Whatever it was, it looked bad. Besides the blood from the cut on his face, his other self was covered in smoke and soot.

"That is you," the mantis said. "After you have gotten the third piece of *The Book of Time* in the Drylands. And, oh my, that was, is, will be an exciting time."

At the Oasis of Bleached Bones, Juhg remembered. Fear paralyzed him when he wanted to go talk to his future self and find out everything he was going to know. Most of all, he wanted to know what had happened to himself.

Then his other self looked up at him. Recognition flared in the other Juhg's eyes. He pushed away from the other mantis, breaking its grip on him and running across the dry yellow sand at him.

"No!" the other Juhg yelled. "Don't do it! Don't let Craugh push you into the tunnel in the gemstone room! You don't know what's going to happen! You can't let him—"

The mantis with Juhg grabbed his hand again and marched off with him. The first step raised a blistering sandstorm that obscured the other

Juhg and ripped his words away. Juhg couldn't hear the rest of the other Juhg's warning.

"Wait!" Juhg cried. "I—he—I think there was something that I needed to tell myself!"

The mantis didn't stop walking. "You've seen enough, Librarian Juhg. Most people never get to look into their own futures. In your world, I've found, glimpsing what is yet to come can have dire consequences. You can't really do anything about it, you see, but just knowing something bad is coming makes you so unhappy before the end."

The end? The end is coming? That didn't relax Juhg's mind whatsoever.

"I was trying to warn myself," Juhg said. "There is something that I think I'm not supposed to do. Something that has to do with Craugh and a tunnel." *And I've already got enough problems with believing in Craugh.*

Once more back in the orchards, the mantis released Juhg and looked at him sharply. "Nothing you could tell yourself is going to matter, Librarian Juhg. You're going to do what you're going to do."

"But I can change what I'm going to do," Juhg said. "All I needed to hear was what I was going to say. I just needed to listen to myself a little longer." He looked around, hoping to see himself charging out of a desert. But he didn't. He was the only self he had in the orchard.

The mantis shook its head. "The future can't be changed any more than the past. All of those are anchored in your world. That's why I could never live there."

"But if I knew what it was I wasn't supposed to do, I could not do it," Juhg protested.

"That isn't how Time works," the mantis said. "Time simply *is*."

Juhg thought desperately. "*The Book of Time* is supposed to have the power to change time, to go back and change a moment or a year or a life." He remembered Craugh telling him that aboard *One-Eyed Peggie,* and he had written it himself in his journal and the one he'd given to Jassamyn.

The mantis was quiet for a moment, as if he'd brought up something it had not thought of. "*The Book of Time* has that power in your world, outside of the In-Betweenness," it said finally. "That is one of the reasons it is so dangerous in your world and why it must be brought back here."

"Do I bring it back here?" Juhg asked.

"You are not yet ready to know that answer."

Angry and scared, feeling all the responsibility of what he was doing,

Juhg wouldn't let the question go. He couldn't. "Will I bring *The Book of Time* back here?"

"You have noticed that the pieces of *The Book of Time* possess powers," the mantis said, ignoring him. "You can use the blue gems you got from the human city of Seadevil's Roost to peer into places around the world, to see things that are happening at the same exact minute as you're looking."

"I have done that." Pain sparked inside Juhg's head as he remembered his visit to the Grandmagister in the torture chamber. "Do I bring the book back to you?"

"The brown gemstones allow you to see into the past," the mantis went on. "You can use that power to examine the history of things if you need to."

"What happens if I don't bring *The Book of Time* back to you?" Juhg asked.

The mantis regarded him coldly, and for the first time Juhg felt threatened by the being. "That," it stated clearly, "is not something you want to do."

"You showed me a piece of my future."

"I already regret that," the mantis replied.

Regret? How could the mantis *regret* anything? Especially if it was supposed to know everything that had, was, and will happen?

"It's time for you to go," the mantis said.

"I'm not done yet," Juhg said. "I have questions I want answered."

The mantis pointed into the nearest pool. "Your friends are in danger. Do you really wish to waste time?"

Drawn by the mantis's words, Juhg looked at the pool. He saw himself reaching into the cavity that held the brown gemstones that had been given to the Molten Forge Mountains. The "ghosts" fought with his companions, attacking them savagely. The Slither fought as well, though still not at full strength after Craugh's attacks. The creature had squared off with Cobner, who was giving as good as he was taking.

"They will perish without you," the mantis said. "They can't hope to defeat the Slither or the dwarven memories."

"I don't know how to defeat them," Juhg said. He felt his hold on the In-Betweenness slipping, felt himself being carried away.

"The answer," the mantis said, "lies in the past."

Blackness filled Juhg's vision and he was swept away by it.

———

The sound of ringing steel filled Juhg's ears, and the sound was intensified by the cavern where the battle was taking place. He ignored the sounds and concentrated on the brown gemstones, feeling their weight settle into his hand. Then he closed his hand over them and drew them out of the cavity.

Turning, covered in sweat, Juhg glanced back at his companions. Raisho, Cobner, and Jassamyn fought with naked steel, but their blows did nothing to the mysterious dwarven "ghosts" except knock them backward.

Cobner swung his battle-axe, knocking two "ghosts" from in front of him while he went after the Slither again.

Juhg stayed back, remembering what the mantis said about the answer being in the past. He looked down at the gemstones and felt the power within them. The gemstones had been given to the dwarves because they held so tightly to the past. Just as Cobner had made himself a promise to carry the cornerstone back out of the volcano when they departed.

If we depart, Juhg thought.

But the stones also had power to peer into the past. The mantis had told him that. But what good would that do? How could that help him now when his friends were under attack by foes they could not kill?

Abruptly, the Slither broke past Cobner, slipping under the swing of the big battle-axe and shoving the dwarven warrior to the side. A trio of dwarven "ghosts" immediately swarmed Cobner and bore him to the ground.

304

Uninterrupted, the Slither crossed the distance between itself and Juhg. "Give me the gemstones!" it cried. "They belong to Lord Kharrion!"

Juhg tried to turn and run, but the creature was too fast for him, launching itself at him and knocking him to the ground. He almost dropped the gemstones as the impact against the cavern's stone floor drove the air from his lungs. Stubbornly, too afraid of what would happen if he let go, he tightened his fist around the gemstones.

"Give them to me!" The Slither tried to pry Juhg's hand open.

Why wasn't the creature in Skull Canal? The question floated up into Juhg's consciousness over his screaming fear to survive. If Lord Kharrion had made it the guardian of *The Book of Time,* why hadn't it been there?

The Slither fought with Juhg. Its body shifted and changed, like wine slopping up against the sides of a wineskin, as if it might pour out of itself at any moment.

Was distance the problem? Juhg wondered. Then why make a guardian that couldn't be in all places at the same time? Or was there more than one guardian?

Putting a hand up under Juhg's chin, the creature tried to lever his head back and snap his neck.

Despite the pain and how helpless he felt, Juhg held on. The Grand-magister had mentioned only one guardian of *The Book of Time* but had offered no explanation as to how the creature was supposed to get back and forth. The mantis had mentioned only one guardian. So why this place?

The answer lies in the past, the mantis said.

"The past," Juhg said out loud, his voice straining as he tried to keep his neck from breaking under the Slither's cruel ministrations.

"What?" the creature asked, fixing him with its baleful yellow gaze.

Juhg felt for the power of the gemstones, found it, and pulled it to him.

Suddenly he and the Slither stood on a mountainside bearing a shiny coat of permafrost because they were so high up. The creature halted its struggles and stared around at the mountain. Its misshapen face took on an animalistic look of fear.

"What have you done?" the Slither demanded.

Juhg didn't know. He was just grateful to be alive and his neck in one piece.

Dazed, the Slither released its hold on him and stood.

The cold mountain air washed over Juhg and made his teeth chatter. His clothing was still sweat-soaked from being down inside the buried vol-cano. He shivered and drew in a breath of air, discovering that there didn't seem to be enough of it to breathe even though his lungs filled. He scooted away from the Slither and stood on shaking legs.

"Do you know this place?" Juhg asked.

The Slither still didn't look at him, gazing out in sheer wonder at the beautiful orange mountain coated with the white permafrost. Below the mountain was a lush valley with a stream flowing through it. From where they stood, Juhg could see caves farther down the mountains. Dwarves—men, women, and children—labored in gardens and at stonecutting. Sev-eral ox-drawn wagons were being loaded with cut stone. Out on the stream, other dwarves loaded stones onto small river craft.

"This," the Slither said in a quiet voice, "is my home."

"You lived here?" Juhg was surprised. He had believed the Slither to be a thing, a construct Lord Kharrion had created.

"Yes. I had a wife and children, but they were killed during battles with other dwarven clans. I alone survived." Black tears ran down the Slither's face. "I wanted revenge against our enemies. I wanted to see them broken and driven screaming in fear before me. Lord Kharrion came among us and offered me that chance for vengeance."

"How?"

Turning, the Slither pointed at the gemstones in Juhg's hand. "By becoming the guardian for *The Book of Time*. He changed me into this, made me powerful and strong."

"You were a dwarf?"

The Slither dropped its arm and nodded. "Yes. When I fought in battles against those who tried to take *The Book of Time*, I killed many of my clan's enemies. I was grateful to take my vengeance piecemeal."

"But *The Book of Time* was spread out," Juhg said. "Pieces of it were in four different cities."

"I know that. I was here when Lord Kharrion used the Molten Forge foundry to break *The Book of Time* into four parts. It was intricate work. He labored for months, and he performed his task with a dwarf's skill and cunning and patience."

"Did Lord Kharrion make three other guardians to guard the other sections of the book?"

"No," the Slither said. "I was the only one. He gave me the power to flow along through *The Book of Time*. I knew when his enemies—and mine—got too close to a section of *The Book of Time*. I just had to wish for it and I was there."

"At any one of the four cities?"

"Yes."

"And if two cities were under attack at one time?"

"I could become two," the Slither said. "Or four, if that was what was needed. The power was mine."

"Can you go to the other sections of the book now?" For a moment, Juhg thought he had gone too far.

The creature glared at him. "No. Until I sensed you so nearby, I didn't know if the other sections still existed."

"They do," Juhg said.

"I can't feel them. Only the two that you now possess." The oozing face took on an anthracite appearance. "And I mean to have them back for Lord Kharrion as I promised him I would do when he promised me my chance at vengeance."

Juhg's mind raced. Why couldn't the Slither feel the other sections of *The Book of Time*? That had to be important.

"Wait," Juhg said, backing up across the slippery permafrost.

"No. Tell me how you brought me here. I haven't been able to find this place . . . for a very long time."

"You haven't been able to find it?" Juhg shook his head. "This place doesn't exist anymore."

"You lie!" The creature sprang forward and seized Juhg around the throat, lifting him clear of the ground. "I see this place before me!"

"We're not here," Juhg rasped. "This isn't real." At least, he didn't think it was real. Unless they'd traveled back in time, which the mantis had told him was impossible unless *The Book of Time* was made whole again. Craugh's own testimony led him to believe that as well.

In an eyeblink, they were back in the underground volcano cavern.

Startled, the Slither snarled. "What did you do?"

"Nothing," Juhg said.

His companions still fought for their lives, all of them battered and bloody.

Suddenly, Juhg understood why the Slither still believed Lord Kharrion to be alive, and why all the dwarven "ghosts" wore clothing that stretched across generations. "You're dead," he told the Slither.

"How can I be dead?" the Slither demanded. "I'm holding you by your throat. One squeeze, halfer, and it's you who are dead."

"You're a memory," Juhg gasped. "Just a memory inadvertently kept alive by this section of *The Book of Time*." That had to be the answer. It was the only one he could come up with, the only idea that fit all the existing circumstances.

The gemstones pulsed in Juhg's hand.

Suddenly, the cavern faded away and they were once more standing outside on the mountain. Juhg glanced around for the others, wondering if he had returned to the cavern. But he hadn't. He still stood on the mountain. Without warning, the mountain shook beneath them. Almost immediately afterward, the volcano broke free from its prison of earth and spewed high into the sky, filling the air with soot and ash and burning lava stone.

In the next few minutes, the horrendous thunder of the volcano exploding washed away every other sound. The Slither screamed at Juhg and looked like he was tightening his grip around his neck. But Juhg already felt the strength of the creature's grip fading.

Cracks opened up in the mountain as well as the surrounding land. Dwarves ran for cover but there was no safe harbor in the lands that had been theirs for generations. Sheets of flame fell from the sky. Smoke and ash poisoned the air and filled lungs, causing suffocation if the victims weren't burned to death outright. The stream that had provided drinking water as well as a resource for their forges had become a boiling death. Chasms opened in the valley and swallowed down dwarves, animals, and equipment in fiery gulps.

"I . . . I remember," the Slither mouthed, and Juhg read his muzzle instead of hearing him because the rolling thunder continued. "Old Ones preserve me!"

The ground fell away from the Slither, and he fell with it. Juhg fell as well, rushing down into the yawning mouth of the volcano. He screamed, but he didn't even hear himself. He flailed his arms and legs, dodging huge boulders that fell with him.

Below, the Slither changed from the creature's form to that of a dwarf. He seemed almost at peace as he dropped into the bubbling molten lava.

Juhg closed his eyes, not wanting to see the end coming, knowing that somehow the mantis was wrong or had lied, because there was no way he was going to visit the In-Betweenness again.

Juhg felt a hand on his shoulder.

"Scribbler," Raisho asked in a quiet voice. "Juhg. Are ye all right?"

Gasping for air, still feeling the heat of the volcano all around him, Juhg opened his eyes. He was on the stone floor of the cavern, not falling into the open mouth of a raging volcano. He held the brown gemstones tightly in his fist.

Slowly, Juhg looked around. The cavern was empty except for his companions.

"They're gone," Jassamyn said. She looked worse for the wear. Blood stained her face. "Do you know why?"

With Raisho's help, Juhg rose to his feet. His knees still trembled and he had trouble believing he was still alive.

"They were memories," Juhg croaked. His throat felt raw and bruised from the Slither's grip. "Just memories."

"What do you mean?" Craugh asked.

Juhg held up the brown gemstones in his hand. "They were just memories, held trapped here by the power in these gemstones. This section of *The Book of Time* holds the power to look into the past. Lord Kharrion broke *The Book of Time* into pieces here. When the Slither attacked me, I saw his memories of where he had lived."

"He lived here?" Cobner asked.

"Once upon a time, he was a dwarf. Lord Kharrion altered his form and gave him powers to become *The Book of Time*'s guardian. He also gave him the ability to walk to the different sections of the book without crossing the space in between."

"What happened to the Slither?" Jassamyn asked. She held her hand up and the fluttering draca landed there. "And to the . . . 'ghosts'? I suppose they were memories as well."

"They had to be," Juhg said. "Just memories of dwarves who had lived here and left their lives marked on the stones of this chamber." He took a deep breath. "While I was in the Slither's memory—I don't think we were actually back in the past—"

"You never left this room, Apprentice," Craugh said. "You remained on the floor fighting the Slither. Till it, and the others, disappeared."

"I helped him remember and I believe that was what took him away from here," Juhg said. "I was with him when the Molten Forge Mountains exploded and killed everyone here." Tears slid down his face as he remembered the dwarven men, women, and children who had perished in that onslaught. "And, Old Ones help me, now I don't think I'll ever be able to forget."

"Did you sleep much?"

Crawling from his tent, Juhg saw that Jassamyn tended the morning campfire. Dawn had come for a time, but the shadows of the trees still stretched long and tall over them. The impenetrable fog that lingered over the Smoking Marshes was only a little less so this morning, but it was the brightest day Juhg had seen since arriving there.

"Some," Juhg answered. He tried to work the aches and pains from his body, but the task proved too painful to complete or even pursue with much enthusiasm or vigor.

"You didn't sound like you rested."

"Not overmuch." Juhg peered around the campsite and saw Cobner and Raisho readying the horses.

"I'm afraid it's going to be a breakfast in the saddle," the elven maid said. "Craugh is in a hurry to go."

"I'm in no mood to linger here either," Juhg said. But it would have been good to rest for a little while.

After they had made their way back out of the caves last night, with Cobner carrying the cornerstone which he swore he would see to a safe place, they had returned to camp. Craugh and Juhg had examined the gemstones till they could no longer keep their eyes open. As with the blue gemstones, no one else could touch the brown gemstones. The wizard had tried touching them, but at the sight of sparks, he'd given up his efforts and accepted that he could only examine them visually.

Further experimentation with the brown gemstones revealed that Juhg could indeed look back into the past. He saw himself and the Grandmagister stealing through the marshes all those years ago, and he visited parts of his friends' past—but that had seemed somehow wrong and he'd quickly given it up.

Craugh, whose past Juhg would have liked to explore, could not be reached. Every time Juhg tried, and he'd tried again only moments ago, he'd gotten a splitting headache. Coupled with the aches that already filled him, he'd allowed himself to be quickly dissuaded.

Juhg had also tried to visit the mantis's past and had failed at that. Since the In-Betweenness insisted on being past, present, and future all rolled into one, Juhg supposed he couldn't see into the mantis's past because the creature really didn't have one.

Jassamyn handed Juhg a cup of stew she'd made from crayfish she'd taken from the marsh, and wild vegetables and greens and herbs she'd found in the forest. She'd also picked a bag full of fresh blackberries that were ripe and sweet.

They broke camp within minutes and began retracing their path out of the Smoking Marshes.

Seated on his horse, leaving the reins wrapped around the saddle pommel and trusting the animal to simply follow Craugh's horse ahead of it, Juhg worked in his journal. Over the years of traveling with the Grandmagister, he'd learned to work almost anywhere, and the metronomic measure of the horse's movements was not much worse than working aboardship.

Hours passed but he scarcely noticed them, drawn deeply into his work and knowing that still so much work remained ahead of him. Finally, though, he was done. He put away his charcoal and waited till Craugh finally, mercifully, called a break to rest the horses and to prepare a brief meal.

Raisho cared for the horses, leading them to water and holding onto the reins. Closer to the outer perimeter of the marshlands now, the sun shone through in places. They'd stopped at one of those places.

The young sailor stood with his face turned up to the sun, just enjoying the warm heat for a moment. Juhg walked over to him but was afraid to interrupt.

"Ye're too polite, scribbler," Raisho said. "Ye stay quiet like that, like ye don't want nobody to know ye're there, why ye're like to be waitin' a powerful long time."

"Can I talk to you for a moment?" Juhg had struggled with how best to approach his friend with the news that he had.

Raisho gazed at him and shook his head. "Of course ye can."

Juhg hesitated.

"Out with it. Ye take too long to spit it out an' Craugh'll be ditherin' about needin' to mount up an' get movin' again."

"I looked back into your past last night," Juhg confessed.

Raisho laughed and shook his head. "I expect ye were properly mortified at what ye saw. I done some things here an' there that I don't even want to remember."

"It's about your parents, Raisho," Juhg said.

Raisho looked at him, clearly not understanding.

"I found them," Juhg said. "I looked back into your past and saw when you were taken from your mother's bosom."

That was another memory he thought he would never forget. Early in the morning when he'd found that twist of past, he'd been alone. Seeing the baby taken from his mother had hurt. Even now he felt the beginnings of tears.

"Ye saw me parents?" Raisho whispered hoarsely.

"I did." Juhg opened his journal to display the two people he had labored to draw that morning.

Raisho took the journal in shaking hands. He stared at the people, then touched the faces ever so lightly.

Juhg started to tell him that the drawings were in charcoal and fragile, but he didn't. If he needed to, he knew he could recreate the drawings from memory. "Your da's name is Tranth. Your ma's name is Machia."

Tears streaked Raisho's cheeks. Embarrassed, he wiped them away. " 'Is'? Ye said, 'Is'?"

Nodding, Juhg said, "They're *alive,* Raisho. You have two brothers and a sister as well. They were born after your parents escaped slavery. Your da is a fisherman—"

"That's why I have the sea in me blood," Raisho said excitedly. "I come by it honest. An' me ma? What about her?"

"She's a healer."

"They're alive," Raisho whispered.

"Not only that," Juhg said. "I know where they are. I can tell you how to find them. I know the place and the village and the house. I've seen them."

Raisho stared at the drawings. "I want to see them. I want to see what I come from."

"I know. That's why I wanted to tell you." Juhg paused, knowing Craugh wouldn't be happy with what he was about to say. "No one would blame you if you decided to leave us and go there."

For a long time, Raisho stared at the drawings. "I can't, scribbler. Not until we finish this. I started this with ye, I'll finish it the same way. When I go to see them, I'll take ye with me." He grinned under his tears. "Ain't no other way they're gonna believe me."

Juhg smiled back at his friend, but he hoped they only lived so long.

"What about yer own da an' ma an' siblin's?" Raisho asked. "Did ye find them as well?"

"I did," Juhg replied, feeling the cold pain ache deep within him. The memories he'd found had tortured him all during the night, giving birth to the nightmares that had followed him into his sleep.

"Where are they?"

Juhg had to force his words through his tight throat. "They're dead. They all died in the mines. Before the Grandmagister rescued me." He paused. "I have no family."

Releasing the horses' reins, Raisho dropped to his knees and hugged Juhg fiercely. "Ye do, Juhg. Ye got me. I swear as long as I live that ye'll always have family. Ye are me brother. Me heart an' yers, we beat together."

Juhg hugged his friend—his brother—back and hoped that they lived long enough for Raisho to see his family. They were heading into the Drylands, and that was one of the most dangerous places Juhg had ever been.

315

19

Red Sails

For nine days, Juhg traveled by horseback with his companions. They pushed as fast and as hard as they dared for the Drylands and the third piece of *The Book of Time* that was supposed to be in the Oasis of Bleached Bones.

On the morning of the tenth day, they reached Fringe.

The town seemed proud of its reputation as the last town on the west side of the Drylands. Part of the municipal décor consisted of skulls of every type hanging on the shops and public buildings. Not a few of them were goblinkin skulls (and most of those were gathered at the taverns and inns). All of the skulls served as a grim reminder that hospitality and comfort of any kind ended at Fringe.

After spending so much time in the wilderness and seated on horses, Craugh relented and allowed them to spend a night at a proper inn, which he paid for. Raisho and Juhg roomed together, while Cobner and Craugh took a room. Jassamyn got a room of her own between them to ensure her safety.

In addition to being known as the last chance for supplies and comfort, Fringe was also known as being a lawless place. Smugglers and thieves tended to stay in town when trouble was looking for them elsewhere. Of course, they usually started trouble in Fringe before leaving. The Peacekeepers in Fringe took a harsh line with lawbreakers and three or four of them could usually be found hanging around town, literally, in various stages of decomposition.

Craugh got them up early the next morning, drawing groans and protests from all. Over breakfast, the wizard gave them assignments.

"Cobner," Craugh said, "you and I will see about transportation."

"Horses won't carry us across that desert," Cobner said. "We'll have to use sandsails."

"Sandsails?" Raisho looked up. "A ship or a boat?"

"Something like that," Cobner said. "You'll see soon enough."

"I could go with ye," Raisho volunteered, obviously curious about the craft.

"You're going to be arranging for supplies," Craugh said. "You'll get the food."

Raisho scowled and turned his attention to his breakfast plate piled high with sausages and fruits.

"Jassamyn," Craugh went on, "we'll need more arrows for your bow. And get whatever else you think we'll need in the way of weapons. We're facing inhospitable land as well as ferocious beasts and goblinkin." He dropped a bag of gold into her hand.

"What about me?" Juhg asked, realizing the wizard wasn't about to assign him a task.

"Get your journals caught up, apprentice," Craugh said. "And see if you can get those gemstones to impart any further knowledge regarding Wick or what we'll be facing in the next few days. Our race is nearly run, but the way hasn't gotten any easier."

Silently, Juhg nodded. He wished that using the gemstones was as easy as the wizard made it sound.

During the course of the day as he worked on his journals, Juhg also used the gemstones. With the blue gemstones, he looked in on Greydawn Moors and found that the island defenders had actually made headway against the goblinkin.

During his survey of Greydawn Moors, Juhg's attention was caught by a young dweller working among the ruins of the Library. All of the repair work on the Vault of All Known Knowledge had ground to a halt with the arrival of the goblinkin siege forces. Caught for a moment by the jarring image of the dweller working on a journal next to the broken heap of rock that had been the main Library tower, Juhg studied the figure.

The white Novice robes marked the dweller as a Librarian. Then the features registered and Juhg knew he was watching Dockett Butterblender, one of the more promising of the new Librarians. In fact, the Grandmagister had been on the verge of promoting Dockett to Third Level Librarian and placing him under Juhg's tutelage when Juhg had decided to leave the island.

Peering more closely through the magic of the gemstone, Juhg saw that Dockett was working on a sketch of a nighttime battle off the coast of Greydawn Moors. Varrowyn was easily recognizeable.

He's doing his duty, Juhg thought. A pang of guilt twinged inside him. Dockett had only a few years in at the Library, but already he knew the importance of the mission they'd undertaken to preserve knowledge—*all knowledge, including the current events happening at Greydawn Moors.*

Watching the young dweller work, Juhg remembered how important the Grandmagister had held those two jobs of the Librarian: taking care of history by protecting the books, and keeping history current by adding new books and writings to the Library on a regular basis. Someone had to keep records of everything important that happened, and it was history even though it was but a moment ago.

Good job, Dockett, he thought, and wished that he was there to recognize the young dweller's efforts in person. If he survived, he intended to do that very thing. Reluctantly, hating to leave his observation of such a common task, he turned his attention to other activity on the island.

Some of the island's trade ships ran the goblinkin blockade and brought back necessary supplies and medicines to help stretch the island's meager resources. Juhg also ascertained that Hallekk and *One-Eyed Peggie* maintained their position at the bottom of the Haze Mountains.

He attempted to use the brown gemstones to investigate more of the mysteries surrounding Lord Kharrion, but those were locked away behind some impenetrable veil. He had no contact with the mantis, although he had tried.

How was the Grandmagister faring? Juhg desperately wished to know. Once they reached the Oasis of Bleached Bones, they were only seven days away from the Haze Mountains. The first two days would be spent again on a horse, followed by five days of travel by river barge along the Dragon's Tongue River, so named for the peculiar small fish that filled the waters there.

But that was only if they survived the trek across the Drylands.

What weighed most heavily on Juhg's mind was Craugh and the uncertainty the wizard represented. Craugh's part in the theft of *The Book of Time,* the Grandmagister's attempted warning, and even the warning from Juhg's future self made trusting the wizard a difficult choice.

Juhg had spoken to Jassamyn about the matter when he had given her the updated version of the journal he had made for her. The elven maid had listened attentively and been sympathetic, but she had no advice. Watching her, Juhg knew that she was torn as well because she had been a friend to Craugh even more years than he had. He felt guilty again for having brought the matter to her attention. The Grandmagister would be better at handling the situation Juhg faced, and he couldn't wait to let the Grandmagister deal with it.

Raisho was to bed hours before Juhg finally went to sleep at the makeshift desk he'd fixed between the beds. Waking only a little after falling over, Juhg roused himself enough to blow out the candle and go to bed.

"Have ye ever traveled by one of these contraptions afore?" Raisho asked early the next morning. He scowled at the vehicle Craugh had secured to cross the desert.

"Yes," Juhg answered. "A few times with the Grandmagister when we had to go to Shimmerpool to the north."

The vehicle looked very much like a small, two-masted sailboat equipped with sled runners. Only the craft did not have a proper hull, possessing only canvas seats and a storage area made of small dowel rods instead of solid wood to keep the weight light.

"What's it called?" Raisho asked.

"A sandsail," Juhg answered.

"Ye're sure that it will get us across the Drylands?"

"Travelers use them all the time. If you tried to take a horse across the Drylands, you and the horse would die. As we go out there, you'll see not a few who perished out there on the sand."

Raisho shook his head. "I have to tell ye, scribbler, I ain't looking forward to none of this."

Juhg silently agreed. But there was no way around the need to go, and no other way to get there.

The human who had sold Craugh the two sandsails delivered them with his son. They both rode mules and pulled a sandsail behind. Both were taciturn, burned beet-red from constant exposure to the hot sun.

"When you get out there on the sand and far from Fringe," the man said, "you want to be careful. Goblinkin have been reported out there more often than normal."

"Goblinkin?" Craugh repeated. "Why would goblinkin spend time out in the Drylands? Mayhap they don't die as easily as men, elves, and dwarves, but the desert kills them, too."

"Nobody knows," the man said. "But travelers have been disappearing out that way for months."

Craugh thanked the man and paid the balance due. The man wished them good luck and left.

Working quickly, the companions loaded the two sandsails with supplies. Most of the supplies consisted of water because, as far as anyone knew, there was no water to be had in the Drylands after leaving Fringe.

 319

Cobner and Craugh took one of the sandsails, leaving the second for Jassamyn, Raisho, and Juhg. The wizard believed the weight was as equally divided as possible.

Jassamyn had limited experience with sandsails, so Juhg took the driver's seat. Luckily, the wind was with them. Juhg let out the sails and watched in satisfaction as the canvas captured the wind. Slowly, at first, the sandsail started forward and the skis shushed through the sand.

Once clear of the city, Juhg added more and more sails, building primarily to the forward mast since it was the tallest. Both masts had specially constructed yardarms that telescoped out so additional sails could be easily added. In no time in all, the sandsail sped across the great expanse of the Drylands faster than a racehorse could run. And unlike a racehorse, the sandsail could keep up to speed as long as the wind blew.

Satisfied with the arrangement of the sails, Juhg stepped back into the driver's seat and belted in. Raisho sat next to him, while Jassamyn rode behind him. Her little draca clung to one of the yardarms on the rear mast.

"It goes fast," Raisho said. "I will give it that."

"As long as the wind blows," Juhg agreed.

"An' if the wind stops blowin'?"

"Then we're becalmed, just like *Windchaser* when the wind goes away."

Raisho regarded the distant horizon and rubbed his chin. "Ain't much different than sailin', then is it?"

"No," Juhg replied.

"Except when a ship's becalmed, you don't get out and pull it," Jassamyn said. "I've been on trips before when I had to pull a sandsail for miles before we caught another breeze."

"Goes to show that ye never spent much time on a real workin' ship," Raisho said. "I've manned many a longboat with oars to pull a ship a few miles in hopes of catchin' a wind."

At Raisho's request, Juhg began teaching the young sailor how to steer the sandsail with the reins that controlled the different sail panels. In less than an hour, Raisho could handle the sandsail as if born to it. Jassamyn laughed and clapped at the young sailor's exuberance.

320

For a moment, Juhg was caught up in the levity, then the weight of the gemstones in the leather pouch around his neck brought back the reality of their situation. With the sandsail in good hands, he turned his attention back to his translation of the Grandmagister's journal.

Looking out over the rolling mountains of sand, it was hard to imagine that once a great forest had lived there, much less a river and one of the greatest elven cities ever. Juhg wondered how Lord Kharrion had presented his case to the elves to get them agree to join his cause.

Demonstrating his newfound skill, Raisho shifted some of the sail panels to lose speed, let Cobner and Craugh's sandsail slide past him, then swooped behind them, briefly stole their wind to slow them down, and charged ahead once more. Raucous comments flew between the dwarven warrior and the young sailor.

Though he intended to refamiliarize himself with the Grandmagister's notes, the sibilant shushing of the sand skis, the warmth of the sun, and the wind in his face all lulled Juhg to sleep before he knew it.

The goblinkin slavers struck just before sunset.

Jassamyn spotted them first, shaking Juhg awake even as she yelled for Craugh's attention.

Groggy, Juhg looked up at the elven maid. "What's wrong?" He looked back to the west, in the direction she was looking, but the setting sun made it hard to see.

"Sails," Jassamyn replied, taking up her bow and putting an arrow to string. "Red sails."

"In the sunset?" Juhg sat up straighter and squinted. His eyes burned from dryness and fatigue, but he thought he saw what had caught Jassamyn's attention.

A collection of red sails sailed in the sunset. Coming out of a sky that looked like a dying sun had burst over the horizon and stained everything red and purple, the sails were hard to spot.

"How many, do ye think?" Raisho asked.

"Six. Maybe seven."

Juhg silently agreed. "Maybe it's a trade caravan."

"A trade caravan out here?" Jassamyn asked.

"A few run through here," Juhg said, but he felt that the sandsails he was staring at weren't a trade caravan either.

321

"Not this late at night. We were looking for a place to put down for the night ourselves."

"At least we got the wind," Raisho said. "Can we put up any more sail?"

"That's all of it," Juhg said. Sailcloth was hard to get in Fringe. The materials to make the canvas weren't indigenous to a stingy land that bore few crops, and packing sailcloth out by trade caravan was only done by special order for an expensive price.

"Then we've got a problem," Jassamyn said grimly. "Because they've put up more sails than we have. They're overtaking us."

The sun continued to sink and the unidentified sandsails sped closer and closer, throwing out great clouds of dust behind them. Juhg reached into his pack and took out his spyglass. He steadied the glass and peered at their pursuers as Raisho jockeyed the sandsail across the barren expanse of the Drylands.

Through the spyglass, Juhg spotted the creatures that manned the other craft. Although one of them was a fat human male, the rest were goblinkin. He recognized the odd-shaped heads that looked like upside-down triangles, the broad shoulders that rivaled a dwarf's, and the splotchy gray-green skin. Their spiky black hair waved in the breeze, as did their long, wilted ears that hung down much like a dog's ears and framed their ugly features. They wore red cloth, too, making it harder to distinguish them from the sunset.

"Goblinkin," Juhg announced.

Jassamyn shouted the news to Craugh.

Watching the speeding sandsails close on them, Juhg's throat grew dry. He remembered well the long hard years he'd spent in the goblinkin mines. And the images of his parents and siblings' deaths at the hands of goblinkin were fresh, raw wounds.

"All the desert to go," Raisho lamented, "an' nowhere to run."

"They'll pay dearly," Jassamyn said as she rose to her knees and drew an arrow back. She released a measured half-breath and released the string.

The arrow left the bow and smashed into the prow of the lead sandsail, quivering when it stuck.

Immediately, as though they had practiced the maneuver for years, the goblins split up. Three sandsails went to the left and three to the right. Like wolves taking a helpless doe, they closed in.

Jassamyn rose again. This time when she released the arrow, it sped true and slammed into the face of one of the goblinkin. The stricken creature jumped in its seat for a moment, bleeding and shrieking, then quickly went still. The other goblinkin sitting up front took over the vehicle's reins while the two in the back dragged their dead comrade out of his seat and tossed him out into the desert.

The body hit the sand and skidded and rolled several feet before coming to rest like a child's broken doll.

Lightening the load, Juhg realized.

Then Jassamyn's hand was on his head and she pushed him down into his seat. "Duck!" she ordered.

Propelled by her sudden move, Juhg went down into the seat. He ended up looking up out of the seat.

Goblinkin arrows slapped the canvas overhead and dug into the sand just below his rump and ahead of his feet. When Jassamyn's hand was removed, he sat up cautiously. Gazing up at the sails, he saw that several of the arrows had found a new home in their sailcloth.

Jassamyn raised and shot again, putting an arrow through the new driver of the same sandsail she'd targeted before. The arrow pierced the goblin's neck and he reached up to tear the missile from his flesh. Unfortunately, handling a sandsail at top speed with a vigorous wind lying full on it was tricky business.

The sandsail with the dead man in it turned sharply and rammed the one next to it. Both craft—tangled by their rigging, masts, and sails—suddenly spilled over and rolled, breaking up and scattering across the desert.

Craugh stood in the craft next to Cobner and drew his hand back. A whirling green fireball filled the wizard's hand and it threw it at the lead craft closing in on them from thirty feet out.

The fireball flew through the air, expanding in size as it went, and burst across the sandsail. The goblinkin craft came to a stop as if it had slammed into an invisible wall. Green flames covered the sandsail, stretching back and coating the goblinkin aboard. Then the green flames became fire. Burning figures leaped from the fiery craft and went sprawling across the desert floor. Out of control, the burning sandsail caught a banked sand dune, went airborne and came crashing back down, spreading across the desert.

Expertly, the surviving sandsail that chased the craft Juhg was in swooped in behind them and stole their wind in a move that was reminiscent of what Raisho had done to Craugh earlier. The sandsail's canvas started to sag immediately. Juhg felt the craft slowing in response.

The goblinkin driver cut to the right quickly, narrowly avoiding a collision. The goblinkin warriors hooted and jeered and screamed, rising from their seats with axes. The one in the back lifted a shield to block Jassamyn's shot, then threw a hand-axe at her.

Moving quickly, the elven maid blocked the flying hand-axe with her bow, sending the weapon ricocheting behind them. The goblinkin in the front seat whirled a grappling hook around its head, then let fly.

The grappling hook shot forward and tangled in the sandsail's rigging. Cheering their success, the goblinkin veered away. The triumph of one of them was cut immediately short as one of Jassamyn's violet-and-white-fletched arrows pierced his heart while it stood to bare its haunches and shake its rump at them. The goblinkin grabbed the arrow in its heart and dropped over the side.

Rope paid out from the goblinkin sandsail to the grappling hook tangled in Juhg's sandsail's rigging. One of the surviving goblinkin in the back tossed out a curiously shaped three-bladed device. When it struck the sand and immediately dug in, Juhg knew what it was.

"Anchor!" Raisho warned, recognizing what it was as well.

When we hit the end of that rope, Juhg thought, *we're going to tear our mast and rigging to pieces.* He pushed himself up out of his seat and walked along the sandsail's center beam. He grabbed the rope with one hand to steady himself and slipped free his boot knife with the other. He sawed frantically at the rope, knowing he could never hope to untangle the grappling hook.

The rope jerked in Juhg's hand as the anchor skipped sand in their wake. Then he felt the hardness inside the rope and knew that the goblinkin had used rope with wire core too think to cut with his knife. At that moment, the sand anchor dug deep and the line went tight for just an instant before the grappling hook snapped the main mast in half and collapsed the front sails and rigging.

Juhg got caught up in the tangle as the rigging snared his foot and yanked him free of the sandsail. A moment of disorientation ended when he smacked into the unforgiving surface of the desert sand. All the air went out of him and blinding pain ripped through his body.

Caught around the ankle, the broken rigging dragged Juhg nearly a hundred yards before the sand anchor—torn free of its hold by the same violence that had ripped the sandsail's mast to pieces—found a new purchase and dug in again. This time the rigging ripped free of the sandsail.

"Juhg!" Raisho's agonized cry sounded far away in the steepening darkness of the approaching night.

Out of breath and hurting, his right ankle feeling like it was on fire, Juhg tried to get up. It took three attempts. During that time, Raisho and Jassamyn drew ever farther away, pushed by the surviving rear sail and unable to control their craft.

Juhg tried to run and his ankle buckled and he fell down again. He struggled to get back up immediately, feeling a little hope when Cobner brought the other sandsail back, but he had to tack ferociously to come back around to Juhg's position.

A whirring *shush* stirred behind Juhg. Knowing what made the sound but hoping that he was wrong, he turned and saw two more goblinkin craft bearing down on him. Evidently they'd followed in waves, planning for the first wave to disable the target vehicles but knowing those craft wouldn't be able to take advantage of their success very quickly.

Crying out from the pain in his ankle, Juhg hobbled as quickly as he was able. The *shush*ing of the approaching sandsail came closer. Although he didn't want to, he turned around to face the goblinkin, thinking he could throw himself to the side to avoid getting hit by the craft.

But it was already too late. One of the goblinkin hung a big arm outside the sandsail and caught Juhg around the middle. He tried to fight his captor, wedging his good leg against the sandsail's frame to keep from getting dragged in.

Then one of the goblinkin in the back seats leaned forward with a maniacal smile and smashed a club against Juhg's head. Pain flooded his face and head, but Juhg barely had time to acknowledge it before his senses fled.

"—not dead," someone was saying in a sullen tone. "I didn't hit him that hard. An' if he is dead, why, then it's his own fault for him having such a thin head. Can't blame me for not knowin' that ain' ever' dweller got himself a thick head."

"Our deal was for you to bring the dweller back alive," a cultured voice said. At least, it sounded cultured in tone because it spoke goblinkin fluently.

Juhg had learned the language down in the goblinkin mines, starting out with swear words and insults. He remained quiet, knowing he was strung up by his wrists by iron manacles from the feel of them, and listened. All he had to do was stay quiet and learn what he could. For sure, he was going to learn he was in a lot of trouble.

"He ain't dead," another voice protested. "He's still breathin'."

"I'm talking about his mind, you moron," the cultured voice said, sounding a little less cultured now. "If you've killed his mind with that blow, why, then it would be the same as him not breathing." He cursed vehemently. "Would you look at the cut on the side of his face? That's going to take a lot of stitches to fix."

Cut? The announcement caught Juhg by surprise, triggering images of seeing his future self in the In-Betweenness, and he breathed in sharply.

The voices stopped bickering. Someone put a hand under his chin and pulled up. Even that slight pressure made the pain in the side of his face excruciating.

"You're awake, aren't you, Juhg?"

That came as a surprise, too. How did the goblinkin know his name? Had he said it while he was unconscious? He immediately doubted that. Judging from the pain in the side of his face and the throbbing in his skull that made even his teeth ache, he'd been quite unconscious.

"Come, come," the cultured voice said. "Open your eyes and let's have a look at you."

Stubbornly, Juhg refused to give up the unconscious ruse.

Petulance entered the cultured voice. "If you don't acknowledge me, I'll allow Nhass to slice off one of your ears for his collection."

Slowly, Juhg opened his eyes. Well, he opened one of them anyway. The other was swollen shut. He swallowed and tasted blood. A brief exploration with his tongue revealed that he had three loose teeth and that touching them sent new explosions of pain cracking through his head.

The fat human he'd seen in the sandsail out on the desert stood before him. His greasy black hair lay tightly against his skull. He wore a thin mustache and a wispy goatee that would have suited a rat better. His clothing indicated wealth, or a predisposition to wearing fashionable attire, although a cape for a shirt and breeches seemed a little overmuch. For a human, he looked to be in his middle years.

Four goblinkin stood behind him. All of the goblinkin carried clubs or swords.

"I am Orgon Tuhl," the fat man said. "Perhaps you've heard of me."

Juhg started to shake his head and instantly regretted it. He said, "No."

That put the fat man off. "No? Well, surely the Grandmagister mentioned me."

"No," Juhg repeated. Then he recognized the man. "I've seen you before."

Tuhl preened. "I see my fame precedes me."

"You were in Fringe this morning," Juhg said, knowing it was true. "When Craugh had the sandsails delivered." Thinking about that reminded him of his friends. He looked around the room where he was being held.

The stone room was twenty feet square and seven feet tall. Just tall enough to hang a dweller by his wrists and keep him on his tiptoes. Evidently he wasn't in the desert any more.

Thankfully, Craugh, Raisho, Cobner, and Jassamyn were not there.

"Your friends got away," Tuhl said. He waved a perfumed hand. "But that was only because I didn't tell Nhass to bring them in. We only wanted you, you see."

"Why?"

"Because you're Juhg, the handpicked apprentice to the Grandmagister of the Vault of All Known Knowledge."

Juhg felt shock radiate through him and he knew it must have shown on his face.

"Oh yes, we know about your little secret," Tuhl crowed. "We'd known about it for years, actually. And thanks to the trap that we set up, we learned where your precious hiding place was. We would never have thought to look in the Blood-Soaked Sea. None of our maps showed an island out there. Just the monsters."

Juhg kept quiet, trying to figure out what to do. The pain inside his skull made it hard to think.

"We are contemporaries, you and I," Tuhl said. "I am also a Librarian of renown."

"I've never heard of you," Juhg said, and saying that gave him a certain sense of satisfaction. He just hoped, on further reflection, that it didn't cost him an ear.

Tuhl breathed out as if he'd been slapped. "You will."

Juhg remained quiet and still.

"You see, I was the one who figured out the mystery of *The Book of Time*." Tuhl approached Juhg and tried to touch the leather pouch that still hung around his neck. His fingers passed through, and though he'd doubtless tried to take the gemstones several times while Juhg was unconscious, the fat man frowned unpleasantly. "How did you get these?"

"I found them."

The fat man's face darkened. "Mayhap I'll tell Nhass he can have both ears. You obviously don't listen."

The biggest, ugliest goblinkin in the room grinned. "If I get a pair, I always eat one. Have a hard time stoppin' with just one, though."

"Do you know where you are?" Tuhl asked.

"No."

"At the excavation site of Sweetdew, the famed city of the Crown Canopy elves." Tuhl grinned, obviously relishing Juhg's surprise.

"Excavation site?" Juhg asked.

Tuhl shrugged. "A relatively new endeavor. My Library was grateful to learn that I had uncovered the lost secret of *The Book of Time*. Unfortunately, we lacked the manpower to manage the excavation here. So I made a deal with Nhass. He and his goblinkin get to raid the ruins of the city—taking whatever gold and silver and gems they find—and they help me find the piece of *The Book of Time* that I knew was here."

Juhg looked around. "The elves never built anything of stone."

"Wood doesn't last forever. Especially after it's dead. During the excavation, Nhass and his goblinkin had to . . . ah, recruit workers to handle the physical effort required."

"Slaves," Nhass growled. He smiled again. "Lots and lots of slaves."

"The partnership has worked out quite well," Tuhl said. "Nhass and the goblinkin have gotten quite wealthy conducting their enterprise—and getting richer every day. *And* they found the section of *The Book of Time* for me." He paused. "Unfortunately, I can't get to it. No one can." He smiled. "When I saw you and recognized your face from drawings other Librarians have done from past engagements we narrowly avoided with the Grand-magister, I was elated. I knew you could only be here for the section of *The Book of Time*. You can imagine my surprise when you were brought here at my insistence and I found that pouch around your neck. Since I can't touch it, I knew that you had at least one other piece in there."

Juhg said nothing.

"I suppose you got them in order?" Tuhl asked. "We hadn't yet learned the order, and we didn't know where the section was that Lord Kharrion gave to the dwarves he had aligned himself with during his first bid to take over the world. Since we didn't know the location of all the pieces, it was hard to know in which order to even begin. Since you are here, and since you have been successful in your endeavors, I have to presume that the section here is next."

Juhg just watched the man without making a reply.

Turning to Nhass, Tuhl said, "Release him and bring him."

"Release him?" Nhass didn't like the idea. "He is a Librarian." He stopped, then hastily added, "*Enemy* Librarian."

Tuhl shook his head. "He's a *dweller*. Bring him." He walked to the door and stood waiting.

Unable to stop himself, Juhg groaned as Nhass had two of the goblinkin release his manacles. Unable to stand, he dropped to the stone floor and lay there.

Nhass kicked him. "Get up."

Knowing it would be pointless to argue with the goblinkin, Juhg made himself stand, then he hobbled after Tuhl. A brief examination of his ankle showed him that it was swollen to twice its size. Fortunately, though, nothing looked broken.

Outside the room, Tuhl walked down a narrow tunnel lined with wooden panels and lit by pitchblende torches. Sand seeped down between the cracks in the panels but they appeared to be holding.

They walked for a long time, and Juhg got the feeling that he was traveling through an anthill. Everywhere he looked, wood panels and timbers held back the desert sand. Goblinkin overseers abused slaves—primarily dwellers, though there were some elves and dwarves in the mix.

The tunnels in most places were narrow, scarcely more than enough room for a full-grown goblinkin to go through. Farther down, he saw a room with a large artesian well that had evidently tapped an underground river. He'd been wondering how the goblinkin could care for so many slaves. Not that they would have worried about it, but going out and constantly getting new ones would be a waste.

329

They walked by one dig site where dwellers passed back buckets of sand that were poured onto a big wagon that was then pulled up the steep incline to be empted elsewhere. As they worked, a section of the roof over their heads fell. For a few moments, a dozen dwellers lay trapped under a huge pile of sand. None of the goblinkin ventured into the unsafe tunnel. Other dwellers and a few dwarves rushed in to save them.

Nhass put a spear to Juhg's back and kept him moving. Everywhere Juhg looked served to remind him of the goblinkin mines he'd almost died in—the goblinkin mines that his family *had* died in.

Farther on, a dwarf found a cache of gold coins and gems. Goblinkin rushed over to take the loot away, cursing and slapping the dwarf and the other slaves to work faster now that they had found part of the riches again.

The goblinkin had built another stone room around the area that held the elves' section of *The Book of Time*. Even across the room in the dim light, Juhg saw the bright green glow of the gemstones.

Tuhl walked over to the gemstones where they floated in midair. "I think they were kept cached in a tree," the fat man said. "After the forest was killed and the desert formed, the wood rotted and disappeared. For a while the sand hid them." He waved his hand through the gemstones, showing that he could not touch them. "Come over here."

Juhg didn't want to. Nhass gave him a sharp poke with the spear in his already sore ribs. Crossing over to the gemstones, Juhg stood still.

"Touch them," Tuhl commanded.

Reluctantly, Juhg put his palm against the gemstones and began feeling for the resonance that told him he could pick them up. They felt cold and smooth, and—except for being green—they were a match to the four gemstones he'd already found and now carried in the leather pouch. He felt the link beginning to take place.

Just then, Tuhl pushed him back. "How do you do that?" the fat man asked.

"I don't know," Juhg said. At a sharp poke from Nhass, he went on. "I just feel for the resonance of the gemstone's movements. After a bit, I can feel it. Then I take it out."

"Who told you how to do it?"

"No one."

Tuhl studied Juhg as if looking for the truth. The fat man let out a sigh. "Do you know why no one else can touch the gemstones?"

Juhg shook his head, which immediately throbbed in response. He didn't know which hurt worse: his head, his ankle, or his eye.

"Do you recall the story of the two princes of the In-Betweenness?"

"No." Juhg's curiosity was raised in spite of the pain he felt.

"I'm surprised at you, Librarian Juhg. The story of the two princes of the In-Betweenness is very important to understanding *The Book of Time*." Tuhl cleared his throat and began. "You see, they were once two brothers back near the very beginning of time. These brothers had wondrous powers, but they were jealous because they did not have control over everything. Nor were they gods. With all the power that they had, they decided that they should be gods. All they had to do, they thought, was find the Old Ones and convince them of their worth."

Juhg stood still as Tuhl walked behind the floating gemstones and waved his hand through them one more time, as if not believing he could not touch them.

"The brothers searched for many years and finally found the bridge that led to the place of the Old Ones," Tuhl continued. "Never before had anyone done such a thing. Of course, the Old Ones punished the two princes for their audacity. Both princes were made to serve in the In-Betweenness. However, living in that place, where time has no meaning, drove them both quite insane. With only each other to interact with, they battled incessantly. But when they weren't battling, they were planning their escape."

Sharp cries of pain sounded outside, followed immediately by the familiar lash of a whip. Both sounds sent shudders through Juhg.

Tuhl went on. "One day, the brothers came up with a plan. They would entice wizards in our world to come across and try to steal the Gatekeeper of Time's great book that he had kept about the things he had done."

The story sounded eerily familiar.

"Now, the brothers had been forbidden to ever touch *The Book of Time* or have anything to do with the Gatekeeper. They plotted for one thousand years before they were able to find a group of wizards strong enough to break the barrier between this world and the In-Betweenness."

Juhg listened intently. Things that happened so long ago, could Craugh have forgotten some of the things that happened? Or could the wizard have been fooled by the two brothers?

"One of the brothers, however, had a plan that he did not tell his brother about. He had figured out a way to get back into this world. So he did. And he took *The Book of Time* from the wizards who had found a way into the In-Betweenness. The other brother, once he found that had he'd been tricked, flew into a frenzy. Using the same means that they had used to bring the group of wizards over into the In-Betweenness, he brought forth a champion of his own and equipped him with powers to defeat his brother. The champion defeated the brother and broke up *The Book of Time*."

"Why did he destroy *The Book of Time*?"

"It was not destroyed."

"But why break it apart?"

"The story goes that if *The Book of Time* was left together, the other mad

Lord of the Libraries

brother would have come through into this world." Tuhl shrugged. "But that's just a story. Since you are a Librarian, you should know that most stories about an object with infinite power always have some repercussions."

"Then why are you searching for *The Book of Time*? Juhg asked.

"Because however that book arrived in this world, it has power. Mayhap it even has the power to change the past." He frowned. "As to the reason why only you can touch the sections of the book, the story goes on that the brother who was left in the In-Betweenness is the only one who can select a champion to once more gather the book's pieces and make it whole again."

"So it can be a gateway to this world again?"

"Yes. Tell me, Librarian Juhg, were you chosen to be the champion?" Tuhl's tone was mocking.

Juhg shook his head. The only person who had chosen him to do anything in this matter had been the Grandmagister, and that assignment had come late and now appeared unwise because he hadn't been able to complete it.

Tuhl laughed out loud. "I was only joking, of course. No one would choose a dweller to do something that was important." He looked at the floating gemstones. "The only reason you're able to touch the gemstones is because you figured out the trick with the first one by accident. All the myths I've read about *The Book of Time* indicate that it can only be assembled by one person who is attuned to the pieces. The first person to recover the first piece will then be able to use the other pieces as long as they are gathered in order." He smiled. "As it stands at the moment, you are that person. The fact that I cannot touch the gemstones and you can bears witness to that."

A chill of dread skated up Juhg's spine.

"However, it occurs to me that if you were no longer alive, perhaps I would be able to retrieve the gemstones."

At Tuhl's order, Nhass and his goblinkin warriors herded Juhg from the room, guiding him down several tunnels till they came to a deep pit filled with carrion beetles. The familiar black carapaces with the crimson underbelly made them immediately recognizable. All of them were nearly as big as Juhg's head.

Juhg tried to fight against the guards, but there were three of them in good shape and himself who was not. After only a brief struggle, they threw him into the pit. He landed hard upon the ground, rolling over a few of the carrion beetles with sickening crunches. Unfortunately, the sound didn't signal the fact that he had crushed them. They were much hardier than that and the crunches came from the breaking bones of earlier victims that all looked dweller-sized, telling him what the goblinkin did with the slaves who perished.

He pushed himself up with his hands and stumbled away from the predatory insects. They scented him at once, coming after him. Inside the circular pit, there was no place to go. He pressed back against the wall and tried to sink into it.

I'm sorry, Grandmagister, Juhg thought. *I tried my best. Truly, I did.* Then he waited for the beetles because there was nothing else to do.

20

"Finish Your Task, Librarian!"

With the goblinkin's unkind and anticipatory jeering ringing in his ears, Juhg hunkered against the wall, dreading the bite of the carrion beetles' mandibles. His death would not be slow, but Tuhl was right in saying that there would be nothing left of him. Would that break the spell that linked him to the gemstones? Juhg didn't know, but he believed that if anything would, the gruesome death that awaited him would.

A lit pitchblende torch suddenly dropped into the midst of the pit in front of the first line of beetles. The loathsome creatures reared up on their back legs as they came to a stop. Their mandibles clacked together in frustration and green ichor dripped to the sandy bottom of the pit. Some of the beetles took refuge under the broken bones left from previous victims.

Then one of the goblinkin dropped into the pit as well. A familiar violet-and-white-fletched arrow stood out between his shoulder blades. The carrion beetles crawled over their newest victim and began tearing hungrily at the goblinkin flesh.

As Juhg looked up, meaty impacts filled the cavern above him. Two more guards tumbled into the pit as

well, another with an arrow through his head and the second disemboweled. A dwarven war cry rang out and Juhg recognized Cobner's ebullient
bull-like voice at once.

Raisho, looking disheveled, dropped into the pit beside Juhg. "Well
then, scribbler, as rescues go, I guess this is a close one."

Juhg couldn't speak.

Raisho grabbed him around the waist and threw him out of the pit.
Juhg landed facedown in the sand, catching a glimpse of Cobner battling
Nhass and driving the big goblinkin back against the cavern wall. Nhass
never truly had a chance against the dwarven warrior's wrath. Craugh was
upon Tuhl like a cat upon a mouse. The wizard's hand gripped the fat
man's throat and he held him up off his feet almost effortlessly.

Before Juhg could get to his feet, Raisho hauled himself out of the pit
and nearly landed on him. Then the young sailor pulled him to his feet and
pushed him toward the door.

"Let's go, scribbler. There's a lot of tunnels between here and the
exit."

Juhg ran, limping as best he could. As he passed Craugh, he heard
Tuhl's neck snap in the wizard's grasp. Almost casually, the wizard tossed
the fat man into the pit.

"How . . . how did you find me?" Juhg asked as they reached the tunnel outside.

"Craugh," Raisho replied. "He had an enchantment placed on ye. Allowed him to track you durin' them few times Jassamyn wasn't able to find
her way 'cross them shiftin' sands."

An enchantment? The thought didn't sit happily in Juhg's mind. Why
would Craugh create such an enchantment and place it on him?

In the tunnel, Jassamyn started to head in the opposite direction than
the way Juhg had been brought. She fired her bow twice more as warning
cries from goblins raced through the tunnels.

"Not that way," Juhg said.

"That way is out," the elven maid replied. "I carefully memorized the
turns."

"Back this way," Juhg said. "The third section of *The Book of Time* lies
back in this direction."

Craugh joined them, summoning a green ball of light that hovered

336

near him and lit up the tunnel. He shook his head. "We can't come this far without taking the gemstones there. Lead on, apprentice."

We can't? Juhg wondered. *Or you can't?* Either way, he took off as best as he could. With the adrenaline surging through his body and his survival instinct hitting him hard, some of the pain left him and he ran back the way they'd come.

He dodged beneath a goblinkin axe as the creature stepped out of a tunnel ahead, slid briefly through the sand, and pushed himself up on the other side. Raisho engaged the goblinkin slaver with his cutlass, batting aside the other's futile attempts to defend himself, then cutting the creature's throat and shoving his foe from his path.

Juhg ran on. Two goblinkin slavers went down in front of him as the tunnel straightened and Jassamyn had more room to use her bow. He repeated the turns out loud as he ran, hoping that he'd made no mistakes in his counting.

He paused in an intersection, momentarily confused because goblinkin seemed to be everywhere and everything looked the same. Farther back the way he'd come, Cobner stopped at a line of chained slaves and brought his battle-axe down. Sparks flew and the chain lay in pieces, vanished before good dwarven steel.

The dwarven slaves among the dwellers cried out in hope and anger, swiftly pulling the chain through their manacles to earn their freedom. They picked up weapons from the fallen goblinkin and followed Cobner as he ran to catch up to the companions.

Getting his directions right, Juhg took off at a hobbling gait again.

Almost immediately, they were confronted by a superior force of goblinkin. He halted and stepped back.

"This way," Cobner roared, pulling on Juhg's arm.

Turning, Juhg followed the dwarf. The wound in his face hurt terribly and he could tell it was bleeding again because he felt wetness running down his neck. His mouth tasted of sand and his breath came in strained, dry gasps.

"Back!" Cobner roared to the newly freed slaves as they rounded a bend in the tunnel. Dwarves led the dwellers, but they all had weapons. Cobner waved them into a tunnel opposite the one they took, leaving the intersection clear.

Cobner led the way around the tunnel and came to a dead end in a storeroom filled with supplies. He cursed. "I made a mistake," he growled. "We'll have to go back."

Back in the tunnel, he pushed them back against the wall just as the sound of goblinkin voices and thudding feet filled the tunnel.

The goblinkin came at the run and raced down the tunnel that had not been taken, evidently discounting the tunnel to the supply room because they knew it was a dead end.

Juhg breathed raggedly and hoped that the goblinkin didn't stop going.

"Now," Cobner whispered. "Quickly." Holding his battle-axe in both hands, he ran back into the tunnel they'd just quit, taking the path back toward the gemstones. They'd just started around the corner when a cry went up from the goblinkin.

Glancing over his shoulder, Juhg saw that the goblinkin had caught on to their mistake and had started back to the intersection. Juhg's leg throbbed and he knew he wouldn't be able to outrun them.

Craugh moved forward, the green ball of light staying close to him. "Go," he commanded, pushing Juhg into motion. "I'll hold them here."

"Ye can't hold them," Raisho said. "There's too many of 'em."

Craugh turned on the young sailor. "I said I would hold them. Now get moving before you lose this chance." The wizard strode into the tunnel to face their enemies.

338

"Let's go," Jassamyn said. "Craugh can fend for himself. He always has."

Reluctantly, Juhg started forward, but he kept watch behind.

Wind whipped up around Craugh, lifting sand from the tunnel floor and whirling it into tiny dust devils. His robe flapped and his beard fluttered. Even the green ball of light rolled and changed with the force of the gathering winds.

Too late, Juhg saw the streams of sand open up all along the ceiling of the tunnel. He stopped, fought his way through Jassamyn and Raisho, and tried to get back to the wizard.

"Craugh, no!" he yelled. "The tunnel is going to collapse!" That was what his future self had been talking about. He saw that now. "Craugh, get out of there!"

But it was already too late.

"You've got to keep going, apprentice. Our fate is already written."

Craugh threw his hand forward and the winds that had gathered beside him rushed like maddened bulls into the ranks of his enemies. The wind blew the goblinkin down as the wizard had evidently desired, but it also tore away the flimsy supports that held up the wooden ceiling panel above him.

The sand became a rushing river, opening up and pouring down into the tunnel. Craugh went down under the onslaught, never having a chance at all. He sprawled, flat on the ground, as he was buried by a ton of sand that kept spilling down until the tunnel was choked with it.

In disbelief, Juhg stumbled and fell. His knees landed on the outer edges of the sand pile. Only then did he realize how close the rest of them had come to being buried alive along with the wizard.

Somehow, the green ball of light remained lit in the tons of sand. Its green glow filtered through the sand.

Frenzied, Juhg started digging into the sand with his bare hands. He tore his nails in his haste. Shock slammed into him as he struggled to comprehend what he had seen happen.

I should have known. I did know. I told myself. Juhg scooped at the sand, barely making a dent in the raw tonnage of it that choked the tunnel. For every handful he managed to scoop out, two more handfuls slid from the gaping hole in the ceiling.

A gentle hand fell on Juhg's shoulder and pulled at him.

"Juhg," Raisho said softly. "Give it up. He's gone."

"No," Juhg cried stubbornly. "He's not gone. He's still in there. We can save him. We can." He never stopped digging. "Help me, Raisho. Please. Help me."

Jassamyn came around to the other side of him and looked at him. "Juhg, Craugh would want you to finish this." Dust-smeared tears tracked her face as well and Juhg saw that she had to work to make herself speak. "He was my friend, too."

"I was wrong about him." Juhg couldn't stop digging. He concentrated on the green glow that emanated from the pile of sand. "Don't you see, Jassamyn? I was wrong about him and he died saving me."

"Saving *us,* Juhg," Jassamyn said. "He saved us so we could see to the Grandmagister's safety." She captured his hands. "That's what we have to concentrate on now."

Juhg struggled to take his hands from her, but her strength was too great for him. Then, without warning, the green glow beneath the sand melted away. Some of the darkness filled the tunnel again, kept at bay only by the torches on the tunnel walls. Giving in to his guilt, Juhg fell forward and wept unashamedly on Jassamyn's shoulder.

"Juhg," Raisho said gently, "we've got to go."

Numb from everything he'd experienced, Juhg stood and walked back down the tunnel. There was no chance of pursuit from the goblinkin in that direction now. Craugh's sacrifice had at least brought them that.

Inside the stone room where Tuhl had shown him the green gemstones, Juhg clasped them, felt them grow more physical in his hand, then he had them only a moment before the blackness pulled him in.

The mantis stood alone out in the great desert as Juhg had seen on his last visit. He stood his ground, refusing to go over to the creature. He didn't want to talk with it. The pain inside him felt too raw, too big, for his body or his mind to contain.

"Librarian Juhg," the mantis greeted.

Juhg said nothing.

"Don't be angry at me," the mantis said. "Or yourself."

"Craugh is dead," Juhg said.

The mantis walked over to him, barely leaving a trail in the sand. "I know."

"You knew he was going to die."

"Yes."

"You should have told me."

"If I had told you," the mantis said as it stopped in front of him, "you might have tried to warn him."

"I would have. I've been suspicious of Craugh for the last days that we were together."

"You were right to be suspicious of him," the mantis said. "He was one of those who brought *The Book of Time* into your world and allowed Lord Kharrion to use the book's power for his own evil purposes."

"How long have you known that?" Juhg asked.

The mantis regarded him with its placid eyes. "Always. As I have known everything else in this place."

Juhg trembled with barely suppressed rage. "How many more are going to die?"

"None," the mantis said.

The answer came too quickly and triggered instant resentment within Juhg. He asked another question that immediately came to mind. "Will I save the Grandmagister?"

Again, the answer came too quickly. "Yes."

Juhg could constrain his emotions no longer. "You're lying."

Taking no offense, the mantis asked, "Why would I lie?"

"To keep me from giving up and quitting."

"I already know if you give up or quit."

Juhg turned away from the creature, no longer able to bear the sight of it.

"Even if I did not know that," the mantis said, "I have learned much about you during our talks. You are not one who gives up easily, Librarian Juhg. When you see a path through a problem, no matter how treacherous or hurtful, you see it through to its conclusion. That is your nature. You can't avoid or change that."

"This has cost too much," Juhg said. "I'm tired and I'm hurting. I can't do this."

The mantis let the silence between them stretch out for a time. "You have been chosen, Librarian Juhg."

"By you?"

"No. Fate chose you. I only accepted you and offered what help I could."

"Allowing my friend to die," Juhg said, turning around with tears in his eyes, "is not what I would define as help."

"Not today, perhaps," the mantis agreed, "but in time you will come to recognize that Craugh did the only thing he could do: risk his life for the lives of his friends. You have done the same for your friends, when circumstances have called for it."

Looking back over his years with the Grandmagister, Juhg knew that he had done exactly that dozens of times. He had been scared most of those times, and uncertain of the eventual outcome of his risk many of those times. He had never stinted, never held back. He wasn't brave, he knew that, but he loved his friends fiercely and felt the responsibilities of the tasks he'd taken on.

"Don't casually dismiss the sacrifice Craugh has made for you," the mantis said. "If you forsake the mission your Grandmagister has given you, that is exactly what you'll be doing. Here, at the end of this thing, Craugh has redeemed himself. Allow him that moment of nobility."

Stung by the mantis's soft words, Juhg couldn't speak.

Then, from the corner of his eye, he saw his past self suddenly walking across the desert with the other mantis. Unable to stop himself, Juhg ran to his past self, shouting the same warning that he had heard only days ago in the Smoking Marshes.

His other self looked shocked and troubled for just an instant, then the other mantis took him by the hand and led him away as a blinding sandstorm rose up and blew over him.

Choking on the dust and grit, Juhg dropped to his knees. He knew he wouldn't listen and he wouldn't understand. He knew that his past self would suspect Craugh even more intently.

He could do nothing now just as surely as he could do nothing then. For a time, he remained there in the desert on his knees, baking in the sun and feeling the terrible weight of grief and loss. And even through that, he didn't know if he would survive to rescue the Grandmagister.

Or even if the Grandmagister was still alive.

He was surprised at how long the mantis left him alone with his thoughts. Then again, in a place where time had no meaning, maybe it wasn't long at all. The sun never moved from high overhead.

342

Finally, because he didn't know how much time was passing in his world and he didn't want to put any of the others in jeopardy, Juhg pushed himself to his feet and turned to the mantis.

"Is there anything else?"

The mantis looked at him. "I will tell you this: when you finally learn how to put the pieces of *The Book of Time* together, you will be in immediate danger."

"Because *The Book of Time* opens a gateway to this place," Juhg said.

"Yes. Tuhl told you that."

"How do you know that?"

"You told me."

"No, I didn't," Juhg said.

The mantis smiled a little. "Then you will tell me when we next meet again."

"Then I will live?" Juhg asked. "I will be successful? Will I save the Grandmagister?"

"I can't answer those questions."

"But you already have. Didn't you hear what you just said?"

In a louder voice, the mantis said, "Time grows short in your world. Finish your task, Librarian!" It raised an arm.

Before Juhg could say another word, the blackness overwhelmed him and swept him away.

When Juhg returned to his body in the stone room, in the Oasis of Bleached Bones, where the green gemstones were kept, the pain and raw emotion raging within him seemed even stronger. He rose to his feet with Raisho's help and they went out into the tunnel.

Cobner and Raisho led the way, striding side by side through the tunnels. Goblinkin met them before they'd gone three paces from the doorway.

The dwarf swung his battle-axe, giving vent to loud battle cries. Beside him, Raisho swung his cutlass and knife in a flurry of blows. From the way they moved together, an onlooker would have sworn they'd fought together for years. And in between their cruel blows, meted out with vengeance in their hearts and designed to kill or incapacitate their enemies, Jassamyn bent her bow, sending arrow after arrow into the backs of fleeing goblinkin that sought to avoid the certain death that was the dwarven warrior and young sailor.

Two more turns through the tunnels led them to where a slave group was huddled against the wall. Goblinkin slavers stood over them, cutting them bloody with their vicious whips as they sought to maintain order.

The goblinkin turned at once and knew that the group bearing down on them was not their comrades. Eleven of them stood in a ragged line that filled the tunnel.

"Lay down yer weapons," one of the goblinkin roared. "Lay down yer weapons an' we'll let ye live."

"Jassamyn," Cobner growled, "he's makin' my ears tired."

The elven maid put a shaft through the speaker's right eye, then another through the neck of a second man, and a third through the open mouth of a goblinkin seeking to yell out in warning or in anger. Before the first goblinkin dropped dead to the ground, the third was already falling.

Cobner and Raisho rushed the remaining goblinkin. Juhg stood in awe as they fought and slew. The goblinkin put up a brave defense for a moment or two, but in the end their fates were plain for all to see. The last two turned to flee for their lives. Jassamyn slew them both before they'd gone a dozen paces.

"Help us!" one of the slaves cried out. "Free us and we will fight with you!"

Without a word, Cobner and Raisho struck free the chains that bound the slaves. Slowly and painfully, the slaves stood on uncertain legs and took up weapons dropped by the dead goblinkin. Then Cobner led them forward, striking out once more for the exit.

The freed slaves were vengeful and bloodthirsty. No goblinkin they encountered was spared, and many of them died horrible deaths at the hands of those they had beaten and mistreated.

Juhg found no spark of remorse in his heart for the savaged bodies of the goblinkin they found, nor for the ones that his companions left behind. He didn't try to find one either. From the things he had endured at the hands of their kind and what he had seen of the slaves around him now, he had no pity left to him.

At length, they all climbed up from the buried remains of the elven city. Morning stained the eastern skies lavender and rose, with a hint of the golden dawn that was yet to come.

They took one of the sandsails and some waterskins, and left the other craft to the escaped slaves. The goblinkin didn't have enough sandsails to transport all the captives back to Fringe, which was the closest city, but the dwarves who had formed the leadership of the freed slaves—over the protests of the dwellers who had regained some sense of their selfishness now that they knew they would live to see another day—promised that arrangements would be made for all who survived.

Juhg lay back and had his face wound tended by Jassamyn, who had insisted on caring for it before they left the Oasis of Bleached Bones because fresh water would be hard to come by out in the desert if they became becalmed. She also didn't want to risk infection.

She used catgut she winnowed from one of her extra bowstrings to make the sutures, then a curved needle that was actually a little too large for the task to sew his face back together. They had nothing for pain, but Juhg was already in so much pain that a little more made no difference at all.

"I'm no healer," Jassamyn said as she tied a suture to pull the wound closed.

"It's all right," Juhg replied. "Thank you for taking care of me." He kept seeing Craugh going down under the mountain of sand.

"And I've no hand for this kind of fine work," the elven maid apologized. "My mother never saw fit to have me trained in this other than to make do."

Tseralyn, although a queen of her own trading empire now, remained a mercenary at heart. Her daughter had taken up the sword and the bow as well, learning horsemanship instead of sewing.

"This is going to leave a scar," she said softly. "Quite a terrible one, I'm afraid."

"It doesn't matter," Juhg told her. And it didn't. Once Jassamyn had finished the last suture and fussed over him for a little longer, she left him alone in the shade of the small tent Raisho had put up for him.

Lying on the small hill, Juhg looked out over the Oasis of Bleached Bones and found the place was aptly named. Hundreds of bones—dwarven, human, elven, dweller, goblinkin, and others—lay strewn across the golden sand. Some said that it was from the battles that had been fought there. Others claimed that the bones came from the elven forest below, rejecting the bones of the dead as it gathered strength to grow once more, after it had gotten strong enough to break the magical destruction Lord Kharrion's spell had wrought.

He hoped that was so, because Craugh deserved a beautiful resting place. Bringing the Grandmagister there to that sea of barrenness was too hurtful to think about. Juhg thought it would have been better if they could come to an elven forest where everything grew healthy and beautiful.

Before he knew it, the pain subsided enough that fatigue and wear claimed him and he slept.

That afternoon, when Cobner declared them squared away and Jassamyn finally relented and said that Juhg had slept enough, they readied the sandsail. Several of the dwarves had already taken off for Fringe, intent on making rescue arrangements as soon as possible.

Raisho took the sandsail's reins and Cobner occupied the navigator's seat. The wind didn't favor them when they departed, though. It came from the east, the direction they needed to travel, so Raisho had to tack into it, heading mainly to the south to achieve any speed at all. Several times gusts rose up that caught the sandsail broadside and nearly over-turned it.

Once he'd gotten comfortable in the sandsail, Juhg slept again. He kept his hands on the book Tuhl had brought with him. The book detailed Tuhl's efforts to find *The Book of Time*. The bandage over the side of his face was hot and heavy, and he sweated profusely beneath it.

During the night, Raisho gave the reins over to Cobner, who had bet-ter night vision, and slept. They ran through the desert all night with Cob-ner at the helm. By morning, the wind changed directions, once more coming from the west so that they could run full ahead of it. But they couldn't run ahead of the summer storm that unleashed heavy rain that soaked them to the skin for more than an hour before the storm broke up and let the sun out again.

By afternoon, they were at Grass's Edge, the first eastern city on the other side of the Drylands. The division between the magically corrupted land of the desert and the city was immediately noticeable. It was as though a master draftsman had laid down a line of demarcation between the desert and the Sighing Forest.

Fever burned through Juhg when they arrived.

"You're too sick to ride," Jassamyn told him.

"I'll ride," Juhg said. "We're only three days from Minter's Stream. We can take a barge there down to the Dragon's Tongue River."

"Dying is not going to save the Grandmagister," the elven maid in-formed him.

"Neither is delaying the journey."

Grass's Edge was more friendly than Fringe. The population was more mixed, the largest population being human, but it was waystation to sev-eral elves who liked trading. Several of the elves also acted as guides through the Sighing Forest to the caravans that wended their way to the Dragon's Tongue River and the interior of the mainland. The elves didn't do that for the money the caravan masters paid, but to protect the forests from the thoughtless ways of those who didn't care for it.

Feeling the heavy giddiness of the fever, Juhg walked the city with Raisho to buy supplies. By the time they had what they needed, Cobner and Jassamyn had traded the sandsail and a few gems they had taken from the elven treasure found in the Oasis of Bleached Bones for horses.

They stopped long enough for the midday meal at a hostelry that offered venison—which Jassamyn insisted was necessary to help Juhg get his strength back—and were on their way through the Sighing Forest by midafternoon.

An elven warder met them at the beginning of the trail through the forest. He was young and proud, with a shock of amber-colored hair and haughty purple eyes. He wore a tunic of patterned green that would allow him to disappear into the forest if he chose. A longbow hung over his shoulder and a longsword was belted at his waist. A red-tailed hawk sat on his horse's saddle. He stood beside the small, quick forest animal.

"Would you like a guide, Lady?" the elven warder asked.

Other elves occupied a treehouse campsite farther back in the forest. Only Juhg's trained eyes allowed him to pick out the resting place the elves had built thirty feet off the ground in the towering trees.

"I would," Jassamyn answered in the elven tongue. She spoke a formal version of it, which surprised the elven warder. "If we can arrange a suitable price."

The elf smiled a little. "I'm sure that we can find one, lady."

Jassamyn dickered for the price as if she were spending the last of her gold, and the elven warder battled with the attitude that she could never make the trip without him and that he had any number of other paying clients waiting. In only a few minutes, they agreed upon a price.

Juhg swayed in his saddle and might have fallen off if Raisho had not reached over to steady him.

"Is he sick?" the elven warder asked.

"He suffers from a wound gotten while fighting goblinkin out in the Drylands," Jassamyn answered. "I found no poultices I wanted to use in Grass's Edge."

"The Drylands have gotten to be a bad place," the elf said as he walked to his horse and rummaged through his saddlebags. "Many goblinkin roam the sands out there."

"Less so than before," Cobner said.

The elf raised an eyebrow.

The dwarven warrior grinned. "It's quite a tale. One meant for the sharing on the road between men what's been through a scrape or two and know the how and why of putting your life on the line."

"Then that shall be the price for the medicine I have to offer." The elf brought a poultice over to Juhg. "My name is Ashkar. My people are the Woodwind elves."

"The reason the Sighing Forest is so named," Juhg remembered, and found he was talking before he knew he was going to. "Your people have music that sounds like the wind through the trees."

Ashkar seemed surprised. "You've been through the Sighing Forest before?" He pressed the fragrant poultice under Juhg's bandage.

"Yes. With my mentor."

"And who is your mentor?"

"Edgewick Lamplighter," Juhg said.

Ashkar looked at him in surprise. "The Grandmagister of the Vault of All Known Knowledge?"

The old fear hit Juhg like a fist blow. He couldn't answer.

"How do you know about the Library?" Jassamyn asked.

"Lady," Ashkar said, "all of the mainland is talking about Greydawn Moors and the Library that is said to be there that holds all the books in the world. Word has spread. The defenders who sail the Blood-Soaked Sea have spread the word that the Library is in danger." He shrugged. "A few have gone there, but so many don't believe the tales."

"They're true, right enough," Cobner growled.

"Then why are you here instead of there? I've been told that even though some few have gone to help those who live in Greydawn Moors that the goblinkin are massing anew."

"The Grandmagister was taken by a man named Aldhran Khempus," Jassamyn said.

Juhg couldn't believe that his companions were telling everything they knew. The Library was supposed to be kept secret. *But the secret is out, isn't it? It was gone the day smoke from the burning buildings along Yondering Docks touched the sky. Like most secrets, it will never be secret again.*

"We ride to the Haze Mountains now to rescue him," Jassamyn said.

"Is it true? What they say? That the Vault of All Known Knowledge contains books on all the races of the world?"

"Yes," Juhg croaked. "There are Librarians there, Ashkar, who can teach you the old ways of your people. They can help you find out who your ancestors were, what cities they lived in, what works they left behind. All those things are there."

"How do I know what you say is true?"

Shaking from the fever and from the trepidation about what he was about to reveal, Juhg climbed down from his mount. He walked to the elven warder and took his journal from his jacket. He opened the book and flipped through it, showing the pictures and the writing he had done.

"This is a book," Juhg said. "Just the book of our travels. Of my travels. Since I left Greydawn Moors." He stopped on a page that held a drawing he'd done of the city, another of the Library before it had fallen, and other of the Grandmagister. He showed the elven warder pictures of Raisho and Cobner and Jassamyn. And Craugh. And he wept unashamedly when he told the warder of the wizard's death in the tunnels of fallen Sweetdew.

As he went on, unable to stop himself, Juhg watched Ashkar call out to the other elves, who dropped from their lofty retreat and joined them. And still Juhg talked, telling them all of the things the Grandmagister had done, the risks he had taken, and the things that Juhg had read about.

He talked for hours and didn't know it. So much was bunched up inside of him that once it started to come out it couldn't be stopped. He talked in spite of his dry throat and his pounding head and the pain he felt over the loss of Craugh and his trembling knees.

He showed Ashkar how to write his name in his tongue, taking out his quill and ink and writing it in his journal, then taught the young elven warder—at his request—to write his own name in the dirt at their feet with a twig. Other elves asked that their names be written as well. And Juhg showed them.

He taught them their names and told them stories about their ancestors. He gave them back parts of themselves that they had never known they had lost. Some of the names of heroes and warriors were known to the warders, and some of them found families in the past that they had never known they had.

Toward evening, when Juhg finally realized how long he had talked, he was surprised to find that his audience had increased from a dozen or so elven warders to more than a hundred humans, dwarves, and elves, all drawn from the forest or the city to hear the wondrous tales told by the dweller who claimed to be a Librarian from the Vault of All Known Knowledge where all the books in the world had been stored.

Juhg found that instead of being weakened by the constant barrage of questions and challenges the people before him brought up, that he was invigorated by it. He was a teacher, not just a repository of knowledge that he couldn't tell anyone. He was giving back more than he had ever known he could give. The career of Librarian had now come full circle; he was giving back everything he had protected and kept secret for so long.

When people in the back complained that they could not see him properly, a caravan master pulled up a cart and helped Juhg stand on it. Lanterns were hung from the trees and food was provided for those who were hungry.

Children—human, dwarven, elven, and dweller—gathered at the wheels of the wagon, watching in astonishment as the dweller told of battles past and heroic deeds, and the bravery of the Unity army and the Builders who had caused Greydawn Moors to be torn from the sea floor.

The talk continued until the morning, though Jassamyn tried to stop it so that Juhg could rest. He couldn't remember when the fever had left him. Nor could he believe how strong he felt after not sleeping all night. But with the dawning sun, he knew they had to go.

And when they rode east to the Dragon's Tongue River, elves and humans and dwarves rode with them.

"You know what you just done back there, don't you?" Cobner asked with a wide grin.

Juhg couldn't speak, but he was certain the Grandmagister would never approve of what he had done.

"What you done," Cobner said, turning in his saddle to gaze back at the long line of riders behind them, "is raise us an army." He reached over and fiercely hugged Juhg. "By the Old Ones, Juhg, I am proud of you. And the Grandmagister will be too, never you fear."

Juhg sincerely hoped so, but they didn't even know if the Grandmagister was still alive.

21

Aldhran Khempus's Power

By the time they had reached the Dragon's Tongue River, more riders had massed for the trip down to the Haze Mountains. Trailtown, the city located on the river that thrived on caravan trade, was overwhelmed with new arrivals looking to see the dweller Librarian they had heard about.

Ashkar had sent elven warders scrambling through the forest in all directions to notify everyone within hailing distance and to spread the news that the talk they had heard of the mysterious Library and the island where it was hid was all true.

All during the day as the river barges were prepared, Juhg met with leaders of the different clans and groups in the largest hostelry available, letting them go back to their followers to relay what he had said. The groups had to be scheduled.

"By the Old Ones," Raisho said during one of the lulls between meetings, "I've never seen so many people in all me life."

"Neither have I," Juhg admitted. In truth, seeing so many people together scared him. Usually bad things happened when so many people got together.

"One lamentable thing about it, though," Cobner said, "we're not gonna be able to sneak up on Aldhran Khempus. Likely he's got spies out and about to watch things for him."

Jassamyn smiled as she fed the draca. "Aldhran Khempus *did* have spies out. Men he employed to keep their eyes and ears sharp."

"Did, did ye say?" Raisho asked.

"Did," Jassamyn repeated. "Ashkar and the Woodwind elves knew most of those men. The rest of them they found out about. If there is an Aldhran spy about between here and the Haze Mountains, it's one that knows nothing of what's going on here."

Cobner grinned a rogue's grin. "And you won't find many goblinkin along the river either. After the dwarves we freed in the Drylands got back with their stories about how the goblinkin were enslaving them to dig in the sands for elven treasure, why, the dwarves took it upon themselves to go goblinkin hunting, claiming they was taking vengeance for what went on in the Drylands." He rubbed his hands. "Aldhran Khempus won't know we're coming, Juhg. Just like Greydawn Moors didn't know he was coming. Vengeance is gonna rain down on him when we get there."

That made Juhg uncomfortable. He walked over to the second-floor window of the rooms they'd been given to do their meetings in and looked out. Since Ashkar had started taking care of his wounds, he'd nearly fully recovered.

"The Grandmagister is still in the middle of Khempus's keep," Juhg said. "If things start to go badly for Khempus, he won't hesitate to kill the Grandmagister to seek out his own revenge."

"When he looks down into the valley before the Haze Mountains," Raisho said, "he's gonna know things are going to go badly for him."

"There is other news, too," Jassamyn said. "Some of the elves from down near the Haze Mountains are talking about the things that are going on there."

"What things?" Juhg asked.

"The goblinkin had been talking about a mysterious red crystal that Aldhran Khempus has been working with. It's supposed to be very powerful."

"A red crystal?" Juhg asked. "The fourth section of *The Book of Time* is supposed to be red gemstones."

"This one is cut in the shape of a square. Aldhran Khempus uses it for a power source."

Juhg reached into his jacket. "Last night, I finally had the chance to read through Tuhl's journal." They had recovered the Librarian's personal effects from the beetle room. The beetles wouldn't eat paper even when it was covered in blood.

"Last night?" Jassamyn asked. "You were supposed to be sleeping."

"I tried," Juhg said. She had posted Raisho and Cobner on his door for six hours and not allowed anyone in to see him.

Jassamyn looked accusingly at the young sailor and the dwarven warrior.

"Don't look at me," Cobner protested. "I didn't see no light in his room."

"I climbed up onto the roof and read by candlelight," Juhg said. He'd found a small space, just dweller-sized, next to the hostelry's big chimney. It had provided protection for the candle as well as obscuring him from sight of the people gathered and talking in the streets about the story of the dweller Librarian and the Grandmagister held by goblinkin in the Haze Mountains.

Jassamyn sighed and looked exasperated. She'd only that day removed the sutures from his face. She'd been right: the scar left by the goblinkin club was going to be a frightful one. For now, the flesh was still puffy and pink, showing signs of having been freshly healed.

"Tuhl's journal was encrypted, too," Juhg said, "but the code wasn't nearly as specific as the one the Grandmagister used. Tuhl used a simple exchange method that I've seen several times before. I found out that Aldhran Khempus had been working with the other Library for a while."

"He was a Librarian?" Cobner asked.

"No. He's a wizard. At least, that's what the people at the other Library believed him to be. From all accounts, he came from nowhere. He had no history. But he knew about the Library. About both Libraries, actually. But he didn't know where the Vault of All Known Knowledge or Greydawn Moors was." Juhg shook his head. "Khempus was the one who spelled the book that Ertonomous Dron carried in Kelloch's Harbor."

"The one that opened the gate in the Vault of All Known Knowledge that allowed the Blazebulls, Dread Riders, and Grymmlings in?" Cobner asked.

"Yes. There were forty-seven other books that Khempus took the time to trap in a like manner. All of them were sent out to different locations."

"Bait for a trap," Raisho said.

"And I found it," Juhg said.

"Herby found it," Raisho corrected. "Ye an' me an' Capt'n Attikus an' *Windchaser,* why we just brought it back to Greydawn Moors. That was what we was supposed to do."

"I know. And Khempus knew that, too. When the trap was sprung, he was prepared to sail from the mainland, not knowing he was much closer than he'd thought."

"But you said Khempus wasn't working for the other Library," Jassamyn said.

"He wasn't. As soon as the trap was sprung, Khempus left the other Library. According to Tuhl's journal, the Librarians believed that Khempus suspected the Grandmagister knew where the pieces of *The Book of Time* were."

"How?"

Juhg shook his head. "We'll have to ask the Grandmagister. I suspect, though, that their paths crossed. From when I was taken captive aboard the goblinkin ship, I gathered that they had a history together."

"So as soon as Khempus knew where Greydawn Moors was," Raisho said, "he quit the Library cold an' met up with his goblinkin chums."

"Yes." Juhg took out Tuhl's blood-stained journal. "What Khempus may not know is that Tuhl spent time in the Haze Mountains with the goblinkin there. He spoke their language and often used them to search for *The Book of Time.* Gave them information for treasure hunts and looting in exchange for murder and kidnapping."

"Like he was doing in the Drylands," Cobner growled.

"Yes. Tuhl suspected that the fourth section of *The Book of Time,* the red gemstones—or *stone,* if the elves are correct—was located in the goblinkin keep."

"Ye keep sayin' it's a goblinkin keep," Raisho said, "but I didn't know goblinkin built keeps."

"They don't," Juhg agreed. "Before the goblinkin took it over, before the Cataclysm, the keep belonged to humans. A group of traders that specialized in hauling goods up and down the mountains on both sides. They called the place the Eagle's Nest because it was so high. They were not always honest with everyone they traded with, though, and had many enemies. Some they were jealous of and some they just didn't like. All of their chosen enemies were powerful, though. That was why they carved escape routes into the mountain."

"How do you know that?" Cobner asked.

"Because Tuhl found the journals written by one of the family members years ago," Juhg said, flipping through the pages of the blood-stained journal. "Tuhl had thought *The Book of Time* might have been hidden in one of them, so he explored them. Without the goblinkin knowing."

"He wrote about that in his journal?" Jassamyn asked.

"Yes." Juhg tapped one of the pages. "Here."

"Does Khempus know about them?" the elven maid asked.

"According to Tuhl, no. The Library planned, if they could find a thief or band of thieves brave enough, to hire him or them to steal *The Book of Time* from Khempus in the event that he found it."

"I don't see what good that does any of us," Cobner complained.

Jassamyn sat forward in her chair and grinned at Juhg. "Because Tuhl left a map, didn't he?"

Smiling himself, crookedly because the wound at the side of his face hurt terribly, Juhg flipped the page and revealed the first of the diagrams Tuhl had recorded in his journal. He touched part of the map. "This one," he said, "goes to the dungeon where I saw the Grandmagister."

The barge trip down the Dragon's Tongue took five days. The army held up the on the fourth day and camped out in the Sighing Forest so they could travel the last leg of their journey by night and not be detected.

Past midnight, Juhg arrived in the basin where *One-Eyed Peggie* was tied up. The port city that occupied the stretch of land around Spit Basin at the end of the Dragon's Tongue—the derogatory name of the place earned by the cutthroats, smugglers, thieves, and brigands who called the city home—was still in full swing and had a reputation for indulging in sinful delights until dawn.

High above the city on a rocky shelf of land nearly eight thousand feet above, putting it almost fifteen thousand feet above sea level, the blunt lines of the goblinkeep sat in the craggy crown of the Haze Mountains.

The wispy clouds that circled the mountain range earned their name in the bright moonslight.

Stealing through the alleys between the well-lighted taverns festooned with festive colored lanterns, Juhg and his companions made their way to the docks without drawing attention to themselves. They were surprised to see Hallekk standing out on deck awaiting them.

The big dwarf stood with his arms folded over his broad chest. "Juhg," he said, looking at the scar on the dweller's face. "It's good to see ye. Ye've had a hard time of it from what I seen." When Juhg stepped onto the deck, Hallekk took him in a fierce embrace and held him tight for a moment.

For a moment, Juhg was nonplussed. Then he reasoned out Hallekk's seeming precognitive ability. "The monster's eye," he said.

Hallekk greeted the others and welcomed them aboard. "Since we put down anchor here an' been waitin' on ye, there ain't been much else to do."

With *One-Eyed Peggie* slowly rolling a little to allow for the river current spilling into the basin, Juhg almost felt like he'd come home. Only one thing—one *person*—was missing.

"What of the Grandmagister?" Juhg asked in a small voice.

"He's alive," Hallekk said. "Khempus has done hard for him, Juhg, but he's managed to stay alive."

Juhg let out a tense breath. After losing Craugh, hearing bad news about the Grandmagister would have emptied him.

"Ye've got an army a-waitin' out in them woods," Hallekk said. "That surprised me."

"It surprised me, too," Juhg admitted. "But talk of what is happening out in Greydawn Moors has already reached this far."

"It's them caravans," Hallekk said. "Ye'll never meet a busier bunch of busybodies tellin' stories an' news and stuff."

"So I see. Though I'd never before suspected they could get news out this quickly."

"It's important news," Jassamyn said. "It's not every day that you find out a Library exists. I can still remember when the Grandmagister told me."

"Most of these morons around here don't believe it," Hallekk said. "They talk about it an' such, but they don't believe it. All they think is that the island is gonna become a goblinkin lodestone an' get ever'body there kilt."

"It almost did that."

Hallekk looked at Juhg. "Me an' my crew, we're about fed up to the gills with sittin' around an' makin' nice with people we'd rather be deep-sixin'. What are ye gonna do with that army ye raised up?"

"We're going to climb that mountain," Juhg said, "and we're going to free the Grandmagister and finish putting *The Book of Time* back together."

It was eight thousand feet, give or take, from the basin at the foot of the Haze Mountains to the keep. If it had been on level ground, it would only have taken a man thirty minutes or so to walk. Climbing that distance, even though they were able to negotiate the distance without resorting to climbing ropes and pitons, took hours.

Finding the secret entrance that had been disclosed in Tuhl's journal took almost another hour. Dawn had started to streak the eastern side of the Haze Mountains by that time, and Juhg worried that the day would come before they were in place.

He, Raisho, Cobner, Jassamyn, and thirty warriors culled from the ranks of the humans, dwarves, and elves—all of them trained and experienced warriors, guaranteed by their peers—made the climb.

At the top where the air was thin, Juhg had to stand for a moment to try to catch his breath. His head spun and his knees felt weak.

Raisho came up beside him and put a hand on his shoulder. "Are ye okay, scribbler?"

Juhg nodded. For a moment, he couldn't speak.

"Don't want to put any more pressure on ye than ye already got," the young sailor said, "but ye're leadin' these men. They're goin' on faith with ye. If'n ye take a nosedive in here, it might not go over so good with the troops."

"It's the height," Juhg said. "It always affects me like this. I'll be all right. Just give me a minute." He looked up at his friend and saw the worry in Raisho's eyes. "I'll get this done. Craugh gave his life to get us this far, and the Grandmagister has held out this long waiting on us. I'm not going to stop now." He took another breath and straightened, squaring his shoulders.

Another three hundred feet above, the rocky ledge where the goblinkin keep perched looked barren and alone. The goblinkin didn't even bother to patrol above, knowing that no army could encamp in the broken terrain on that side of the keep and certain that the long, winding road leading up to the keep's massive front gates was well guarded.

Juhg crossed to the boulder where Tuhl had indicated the secret door was hidden. The scrubby trees protected the area from being seen from above. Grabbing the boulder and finding it delicately balanced, Juhg rocked it in the manner Tuhl had written about, listening for the clicks that signaled the tumblers were closing inside the lock.

At the fourth click, the boulder leaned over and brought up the hidden door, revealing a square tunnel cut into the earth. Iron rungs mounted on the wall offered handholds down into the waiting darkness.

Cobner, dressed in armor he'd insisted on packing up the mountain, volunteered to go first. He swung down and started stepping down. When he reached the floor below, he called for a lantern.

Juhg lit the lantern and passed it down on a small rope. Then he swung down, followed by Raisho, who was assigned to stay with him no matter what happened.

The air inside the tunnel was musty and old. With thirty-four people standing in the narrow confines, most of them wearing armor and some more than others, bristling with weapons, the available space filled up quickly.

Cobner took the lead when they were all down and the hidden door was again hidden. Juhg trotted at the dwarven warrior's side, just two steps behind.

No directions were necessary. The tunnel ran straight for a hundred yards, till it was up under the center of the keep.

Juhg felt tense and nervous. His stomach fluttered and he wanted to throw up. *That wouldn't show much leadership,* he told himself glumly as he fought the urge.

By now Ashkar, Hallekk, and the other leaders who had been picked from the groups of humans, elves, and dwarves that had come to rescue the Grandmagister, who had protected the Vault of All Known Knowledge, were outside. They hid in the last of the night's shadows on the western side of the Haze Mountains, well below the hundred-yard area the goblinkin kept cleared in the unlikely event they were ever attacked.

The pieces of *The Book of Time* felt hot against Juhg's chest. Looking down, he saw that they glowed strongly enough to show through the leather. He reasoned that it had to be because they were in close proximity to the final piece.

Does that mean that the goblinkin piece is reacting, too? He didn't know and it was far too late to do anything about that. Not too late to worry about it, though.

At the end of the tunnel, another set of handholds led up.

Cobner shined his lantern up, splashing the light against the iron door. "Where does this come out?"

"In the dungeon. Evidently the man who designed this thought it was possible he could get locked in his own dungeon."

"Optimistic sort, wasn't he?" The dwarven warrior grinned. "Me, I figure if they catch us and get they chance, the goblinkin will kill us outright. I know I'm planning the same for them." He moved the lantern light over to the tunnel cut into the wall beside the door. "And where does that one go?"

"To the lord's private chambers."

"Be interesting to find out if we could catch Aldhran Khempus abed, now wouldn't it? Would make short work of this attack. Aside from killing a lot of goblinkin, of course. But that's something you can develop a liking for."

"We get the Grandmagister first," Juhg said. "Then we try to find the final piece of *The Book of Time* and shut down whatever power Aldhran Khempus is siphoning off of it."

Cobner grabbed the first rung on the wall and started up. "Whereat does this come out in the dungeon? 'Cause if it's at the front door, I want to know if I'm going to have goblinkin trying to thump my knob soon as I stick it up."

"At the back," Juhg answered, and hoped that was right. Tuhl's drawings hadn't been to any specific scale and that had bothered him. Details mattered.

Crowded in behind Cobner, Juhg waited till the dwarf raised the iron door a little and peered through. Then Cobner went slow and stealthy, with the grace and ease of a cat in spite of the armor he wore.

Juhg went up into the room after the dwarf, feeling his injured ankle twinge a little with the strain. He breathed slow and easy, which was hard because his lungs still felt like they were starved for air.

Cobner squatted behind a corner of the dungeon cell they'd come out into. Juhg took up a position behind him and looked over his armored shoulder.

The Grandmagister hung limply in the same manacles Juhg had seen him in when he'd managed to visit him briefly through the blue gemstones. Some of the cuts on the Grandmagister's back and arms had healed a little only to be broken open by new violence.

Unconsciously, Juhg started to get up. Cobner laid a big hand in the middle of his chest and sat him back down again. The dwarven warrior pointed to Jassamyn and the elven archers in the group, then at the six goblinkin that stood guard in the dungeon. Three of the goblinkin were asleep, sitting and standing in their assigned positions along the hallway. One of them was pulling nits. And the other two passed the time talking to each other about meals they'd made of dwellers.

Cobner lifted a hand, held it, then dropped it.

Elven-made arrows leapt from elven-made bows. All of them pierced their targets through the throat, making it impossible for the goblinkin to yell a warning to anyone posted outside the dungeon. Two of the goblinkin dropped dead on the spot because the arrows had caught them with their heads leaned back and the arrowpoints had driven deeply into their brains as well. The other four stumbled around in shocked surprise, but Juhg was certain they would get around to remembering the door any moment.

They didn't get a moment, though, because Cobner jumped out of hiding and lunged for the goblinkin. His axe swung twice, eviscerating one

goblinkin and splitting the skull of another. More elven arrows accounted for the other two.

Juhg ran to the Grandmagister's side, his heart torn at the bloody sight of his mentor.

"Juhg," the Grandmagister whispered in his hoarse voice. "Is it really you?"

"Yes," Juhg said. He took out the lockpick he'd brought to deal with the manacles and quickly unlocked them.

Once free of the iron bands, the Grandmagister would have slumped to the floor if Juhg had not caught him. Tears burned Juhg's eyes but he refused to shed them. *Don't be weak now,* he told himself. *The Grandmagister isn't safe yet.*

Ashkar knelt beside the Grandmagister. "Is this him? The Grandmagister?"

"Yes," Juhg answered.

The Grandmagister's eyes opened.

"They already knew," Juhg told him. "Since the attack on Greydawn Moors, they knew."

Weakly, the Grandmagister nodded. It was the most bedraggled Juhg had ever seen his mentor look, even after they had spent weeks on the run along the mainland. Open sores wept infection. He stank terribly.

"Grandmagister Lamplighter," Ashkar said politely as he took a small stopper vial from the kit that hung at his belt, "I've got a potion here that should help you regain some of your strength and stave off the pain for a while. Afterwards, you'll sleep for a day or two. Do you understand?"

"Yes," the Grandmagister said. He looked at the elven warder. "You're a Woodwind elf, from the Sighing Forest."

"Yes." Ashkar smiled. "Once of the Silverglen elves before Lord Kharrion destroyed our homes. We had all but forgotten what Silverglen was like until your apprentice told us."

"It was," the Grandmagister said in his weak voice, "beautiful. You should see it."

"Juhg tells me that I can if I come to the Library."

"Of course."

"Now, if you'll drink this we'll see how you feel."

Juhg held the Grandmagister as Ashkar poured the contents of the potion down his throat. Weakly, the Grandmagister lay back on Juhg and breathed deeply and evenly for a moment. Juhg thought he saw a faint shimmer around the Grandmagister's body. The potion didn't heal the Grandmagister's wounds, only time and rest would do that, but it would give him strength. The potion helped when necessary, but it had drawbacks to its use.

"We'll get you out of here," Juhg said.

"Do you have the pieces of *The Book of Time?*"

"Yes. They were where you said they would be in your journal."

Looking up, his eyes already more alert and filled with less pain, the Grandmagister touched Juhg's wounded face. "Someone has hurt you. I am so sorry, Juhg, for having to send you after those things."

Tears ran down Juhg's face. "We've both been hurt, Grandmagister. We will get better. Just wait and see. We will get better." He fumbled the leather pouch from around his neck as the Grandmagister sat up.

Cobner and the rest of the warriors held the dungeon, waiting to see what the Grandmagister wanted to do.

Pouring the pieces of *The Book of Time* into his palm, Juhg showed them to the Grandmagister.

"Well, I have to say it doesn't look like what I had figured. I had envisioned something with more—more—"

"Pages?" Juhg supplied.

"Frankly, yes. Though I know I should realize by now that not all books are made of paper. Still, they are more comforting and handy when they come in that fashion." The Grandmagister tried to pick one of the pieces up between his forefinger and thumb. His fingers slid through the green gemstone. "And *that's* certainly surprising."

"I know," Juhg said.

"They look like they go together," the Grandmagister mused. "Have you tried putting them together?"

"Yes," Juhg answered. He folded the pieces in both his hands, trying combinations. "They're slotted, and it looks like they should slide together, but—"

One of the blue gemstones slid into a green gemstone and locked into place.

"That's never happened before," Juhg said.

"How long have they been glowing like that?"

"Since we climbed to the top of the mountain."

"Then proximity to the fourth section does have an effect on them." The Grandmagister frowned. "Which could well mean that Aldhran Khempus knows the other three pieces are here. Give me your hand."

Standing quickly, Juhg helped his mentor to his feet. The Grandmagister looked at Ashkar. "I do feel much better. Thank you."

"Of course, Grandmagister," Ashkar replied respectfully.

The Grandmagister looked at the elven warder. "Well, that's something new, too."

"What?" Ashkar asked.

"Respect. That's not something I've seen a lot of."

"But you're the Grandmagister," Ashkar replied. "You have read the books and histories of many people. How can anyone not respect everything you've done?"

"Believe me," the Grandmagister assured him, "it's far easier than you think." He turned his attention back to the gemstones. "Let's have another look at these."

Together, solving another puzzle together, Juhg and the Grandmagister put *The Book of Time* together. Juhg was surprised at how easily everything seemed to fit when he had spent frustrated days with them.

"It's a tesseract," the Grandmagister announced when all the pieces were formed.

Amazed, Juhg looked at the device. All the pieces were hinged together and could be swung open for viewing. He'd learned about tesseracts in books on geometry written by dwarves, who had the best heads for imagining spatial alignments. When the tesseract was fully opened, it could lay flat, then closed and opened again another way.

"A four-dimensional equivalent of a cube," the Grandmagister said. "I suppose it was selected because the fourth dimension, after height, length, and width is—"

"Time," Juhg whispered, making the connection as well. "But where does the four gemstone go? The one that Aldhran Khempus has?"

"I'll show you. Fold the tesseract back into a cube."

Juhg did.

"Now, what do you see in the center of the cube?"

"An empty cube space."

"That is *exactly* the same size as the gemstone Aldhran Khempus taunted me with when he brought me here."

"He showed it to you?"

The Grandmagister nodded. "Of course. He's a big gloater, Aldhran Khempus is."

"Then the fourth section of *The Book of Time* goes in there."

Nodding, the Grandmagister said, "One would have to think so."

Juhg turned the cube, feeling the power pulsing through the thing now. Lights gleamed along the cube's surfaces. As he studied them, he realized that the light wasn't a reflection of the lanterns the warriors carried or the pitchblende torches on the walls.

"Do you know how this works?" Juhg asked.

"Not exactly. The book I read wasn't a manual on *The Book of Time.* More a general history."

"Oh," Juhg said.

The Grandmagister clapped him on the shoulder. "Nothing to worry about. We'll figure it out."

Nothing to worry about? Juhg wanted to scream. *We'll figure it out?*

"There's really nothing else we can do," the Grandmagister went on as if sensing Juhg's reservations. "This thing was let loose in the world and Lord Kharrion has already used it, managing to destroy four cities and thousands of lives. It has got to be stopped." He looked around. "Where's Craugh? Didn't he come with you? He usually has an opinion on these things."

"Grandmagister," Juhg said, not wanting to deliver the bad news. "There is something—"

"Beg your pardon, Wick," Cobner interrupted, "but maybe I need to remind you that we happen to be in a somewhat delicate situation at the moment. This is Aldhran Khempus's keep right now, and he's apt to be purely vexed when he figures out we've come and freed you."

"You're right, Cobner." Stronger and obviously feeling less pain, the Grandmagister said, "And he's going to be even more vexed when we take the last piece of *The Book of Time* from beneath his nose."

Cobner didn't appear pleased. He looked the way that Juhg felt.

"Mayhap that isn't such a good idea," the dwarven warrior said.

"Cobner," the Grandmagister said, walking over to the dwarf and looking up at him, "if this were not necessary, I wouldn't ask you. Aldhran Khempus has learned how to tap into the power of the red gemstone Lord Kharrion gave to the goblinkin all those years ago. That stone represents the vagaries of Time, the whims that seem to come out of nowhere and topple empires and make heroes of the village idiot. The humans had the power to see into the present, the dwarves the power to see into the past, and the elves the power to see into the future. But those powers pale beside what can be unleashed from that final piece of *The Book of Time*."

Looking at the other warriors, Cobner asked the question without saying a word. The assent was mutual.

"All right then, Wick," Cobner said with a crooked grin. "I never figured on living forever, and dying in bed doesn't appeal to me." He took up his battle-axe. "Lead on. I'll follow you wherever you go."

"It's not far," the Grandmagister said, and took off toward the door.

Cobner ran at the Grandmagister's side, like they had done for years.

And, like he had done for years no matter what they'd been up against, Juhg ran after him. Raisho trotted beside him. Running through the keep wasn't a happy thought, but if the attack had gone according to plan, the warriors massed in the forest would have attacked by now.

At least Aldhran Khempus's attention, and his goblinkin forces, would be divided.

22

Deadtime

Outside the dungeon proper, the Grandmagister trotted up long curving stairs toward the door at the top. Only two pitchblende torches lit the way, so the group moved through patches of lights, leaving darkness at their heels just before their vision failed them.

Juhg couldn't believe how fast the Grandmagister was moving. For himself, Juhg rediscovered all the aches and pains he'd collected since *One-Eyed Peggie* had dropped Craugh and him off at Imarish. Thinking of Craugh brought the newest pain thundering into his mind and struck him through the heart. He could only imagine how the Grandmagister would feel when he found out the friend he'd shared untold adventures and all those long years with was no more.

Pushing the thoughts from his mind, Juhg concentrated on surviving the coming engagement. Bearding Aldhran Khempus in his lair was daring. The man had nearly conquered Greydawn Moors with his surprise attack, and he had certainly crippled the navy and destroyed much of the town.

The Grandmagister paused at the door at the top of

the stairs, allowed the warriors who followed him to catch their breath, and listened.

Beyond the door, Juhg could hear the squalls of goblinkin. Evidently the assault on the front gate had started—and had caught the goblinkin by surprise.

At a nod from Cobner, the Grandmagister shoved wide the door and stepped out into a large room. Armor and swords filled shelves and stands, testifying to the nature of the room. At least ten goblinkin were in the room trying to grab weapons and armor. They went down like wheat before a thresher as Cobner led the attack with a dwarven war cry.

Juhg walked through the spilled blood and over the dead goblinkin that the warriors left behind them. The stark violence was not new to him, but it was jarring. He steeled himself to it, knowing it was only the first to come.

The Grandmagister continued to lead the way, turning outside the armory to the right and heading for wide stone stairs that led to the great room on the floor below. Evidently the front half of the keep was built lower on the western side of the mountains.

Without warning, the multicolored cube in Juhg's hands yanked violently. He held on to it, not believing when he was yanked from his feet over the stairway railing. He landed hard enough to knock the breath from his lungs and was hauled across the stone floor by an invisible force toward the wide doorway behind the curving staircase that the Grandmagister and the warriors followed.

"Juhg!" Raisho yelled, vaulting over the railing after him.

Spinning and kicking on the stone floor, feeling that his arms would surely be yanked from their sockets, Juhg clung fiercely to *The Book of Time*. He called out for the Grandmagister, but he feared his voice was lost in the sudden squawking of the goblinkin warriors that stepped through the doorway ahead of him.

Too late, Juhg saw that dozens of goblinkin stepped out of hiding places around the great room. Then he saw Aldhran Khempus standing at the center of the doorway, one hand raised imperiously as he called *The Book of Time* to him through the power of the square-cut red gemstone that floated in the palm of his hand. Maybe he couldn't physically touch the gemstone, but his magic evidently held sway over it.

It was a trap! Juhg realized then. Somehow Aldhran Khempus had known they were coming. Perhaps one of the man's goblinkin spies had gotten through the elves and the dwarves after all.

Juhg came to a halt in front of the man, straining to hold *The Book of Time* from leaping out of his hands to Aldhran Khempus.

The man stood straight and terrible, dark with fury in his wrath and confidence. Lean and in his middle years, cruelly handsome, he wore short-cropped brown hair that matched his chin beard and mustache. He dressed in a mail shirt with long waist.

He grinned down at Juhg and said, "Hello, witling." Then he glanced up at the Grandmagister leading the warriors down the staircase. "And hello to you, Grandmagister Lamplighter. Do you see how this has worked out? I have *The Book of Time* after all, and you have lost your good friend, Craugh."

The warriors kept coming, following Raisho as the young sailor rushed toward Juhg.

Moving his other hand, Aldhran freed his gleaming sword in a canny move and put the blade to Juhg's neck. "Hold them back, Lamplighter, or I swear by every darkly evil thing that I will kill your apprentice and feed him to the goblinkin."

The Grandmagister held up his arms, stopping the tide of warriors. The elves, dwarves, and humans circled, eyeing the overwhelming odds with angry pride. Even Raisho obeyed the Grandmagister's authority.

Everything in the room balanced on a single heartbeat, Juhg realized, and that heartbeat was his.

"What do you want, Aldhran Khempus?" the Grandmagister demanded.

"Nothing." Aldhran lifted the red gemstone Lord Kharrion had given the goblinkin with his power. "I have what you caused to be brought to me. You thought by letting your apprentice escape that night in the ship that you would buy yourself time, sell your pain and maybe your life to keep me from getting *The Book of Time*. Instead, your lackey has delivered it to me." He paused. "As *I* had planned after he escaped that night."

The Grandmagister said, "You can't have that book."

"I already have it. And I wouldn't have for a lot more years if you hadn't found Vios Thrault's hidden sanctum in that cemetery in Hanged Elf's Point all those years ago. Only he had known what Lord Kharrion had done with the pieces of *The Book of Time*. Thrault had it in mind to go after the book himself, but he lacked the nerve both to do the deed and to share his information with anyone else."

"I can see how trusting you might promote grave doubt," the Grandmagister said.

Aldhran seemed to take no offense and laughed uproariously. "Then you and I shall not enter into a bargain of trust, Grandmagister. You had my best offer years ago when I asked you to tell me where *The Book of Time* was."

"I didn't know then," the Grandmagister said. "Only your constant questions led me to believe the answer was somewhere within the Library. That was how I found Vios Thrault's old journal, which I hadn't been able to decipher. And why I spent so much time on it."

"You did well. I give you my compliments. But now I choose to reap my reward." Aldhran looked down at Juhg. "Now, dweller, open *The Book of Time* that I may complete it."

"No," Juhg said fiercely. "I will not."

"You will." Aldhran gestured and Juhg felt his will begin to evaporate like sand castles before an incoming tide.

Juhg watched in horror as his hands moved and laid open the gleaming tesseract that was *The Book of Time*. The bright lights danced even more quickly inside the gemstones, becoming a whirling concoction of colors.

Aldhran gestured again and the square-cut crimson gemstone floated toward the cavity inside the tesseract that had been designed for it. Sparks flew as the final piece neared the opening.

A familiar voice floated into Juhg's head. *It is time, Librarian Juhg. Now our goals can meet.*

Recognizing the voice of the mantis, Juhg was confused.

Let me through. I can handle him. This is what I was made for, what I waited all these years for.

Trusting the voice, Juhg relaxed and *The Book of Time* clicked shut on the final gemstone and became complete. The cube flashed, but Juhg continued to hold on to it, reluctant to let Aldhran have it.

In the next moment, a beam of light opened a hole in the empty space between the goblinkin and the warriors who stood with the Grandmagister. The mantis stood on the other side of the opening, on the mountain trail where Juhg had first seen it.

Aldhran didn't seem surprised to see the creature.

Too late, the suspicion that had scratched at Juhg's mind blossomed into realization. He'd been tricked. The mantis hadn't lived in the In-Betweenness all its life. Little things it had said, the way it had become casual with conversation and made references to time. More important than that, the mantis had insisted on cracking jokes and making sharp rejoinders, all of which depended solely on a sense of timing.

Remembering Tuhl's story in the sandy graveyard that was all that remained of Sweetdew in the Oasis of Bleached Bones, Juhg wasn't surprised at all when Aldhran Khempus said, "Hello, brother. It has been a long time since I have seen you."

"Truly a long time," the mantis agreed. As it stepped forward, the top half of the thing started changing, becoming the twin of Aldhran Khempus.

They are the two brothers Tuhl spoke of, Juhg realized. Knowing that two of them in the same world would be far more than the world could bear, Juhg spun to avoid Aldhran Khempus's sword and kicked the man in the shins. When the man's concentration lapsed, so did the spell that controlled *The Book of Time.*

Freed from the paralysis that gripped him, Juhg got his feet under him and ran, digging at the multicolored cube as Aldhran yelled for the goblinkin to seize him. He worked at the pieces of *The Book of Time,* willing the gemstones to come apart so that he could free the red one at the heart of the cube.

A goblinkin threw a spear at him and Juhg leaped to avoid the missile. Still, the heavy wooden haft tangled in his legs and tripped him as he came down. Even then, though, his hands managed to separate *The Book of Time.* As he hit the floor, he struck out at the red gemstone in the center. When the gemstone dislodged, the beam from the cube ended.

Rolling over, sprawling across the stone floor of the great room and trying to recapture the tumbling red gemstone with one hand and hold on to *The Book of Time* with the other, Juhg saw the opening to the In-Betweenness wink out of existence with half of Aldhran Khempus's brother inside the great room and the other half still in the other place.

Sliced in two—and several other pieces, as was the case because he hadn't stepped evenly through the gateway—the twin fell to the floor in bloody ruin. His head bounced against the stone floor, eyes wide and staring in shocked disbelief.

"Nooooo!" Aldhran Khempus howled. His eyes locked onto Juhg's. "By the Darkness, halfer, you will die for what you have done here this day." He brought his hand back and threw it forward as if he were throwing a spear. Crackling lightning shot from his hand.

On his knees, fumbling for the red gemstone, Juhg didn't have a chance. He watched the lightning bolt come straight for his chest and knew that he was about to die.

Then a gnarled wooden staff materialized out of thin air, interposed itself in front of Juhg, and smacked down smartly on the stone floor.

The lightning struck the wooden staff and a concussive blast blew back the lines of goblinkin and the warriors standing with the Grandmagister. Redirected by the staff, the lightning blast flew from the end of the staff and blasted a huge chunk out of the stone ceiling high above. Black scorch marks scarred the stone floor and the area around the gaping hole that had been ripped into the ceiling.

All other sounds went away, leaving Juhg deaf and sitting on his knees. The huge force waves that had sent goblinkin and warriors tumbling over each other like leaves in the fall never touched him. He looked up at the robed figure that had protected him, recognizing the staff and the pointy hat and that impossibly tall, gaunt frame all at one time.

"Craugh," Juhg croaked.

Craugh showed him a wintry smile. "Surely you didn't think a little falling sand could kill me, apprentice."

"No," Juhg said, throwing his arms around the wizard's legs.

"Apprentice," Craugh said sternly.

Juhg immediately released the wizard.

Striding to the center of the room, his eyes never leaving those of Aldhran Khempus, Craugh roared out in rage, "I am Craugh, called often the Unruly and the Unholy. I am a warrior born and a wizard trained. I have killed and warred and built empires and destroyed them. I am father to the greatest evil this world has ever known."

Juhg couldn't believe what he was hearing.

"I have known pride and shame, tasted victory and defeat, spilled the blood of my enemies and shed my own," Craugh continued, coming to a stop in the center of the room with his staff across his knees. "I have fought for passion and I have fought because I lacked anything else to do."

Juhg hugged *The Book of Time* close to him, feeling the power within the thing.

"I have known many things in my long life, but I have known the friendship of only one who gave that friendship in spite of all the faults he knew I had, though he did not know them all." Green fire blazed from Craugh's eyes. Wind whirled through the room, circling the wizard. "And I know you, Aldhran Khempus, as I knew your dead brother lying here in pieces before you, as men that rode into the In-Betweenness to steal *The Book of Time*. I have come here today to kill you, for past transgressions as well as the harm you have given to my friend." He took a deep breath and went on in a cold voice. "I am going to kill you, Aldhran Khempus, so protect yourself as best you may."

Aldhran shouted words and a massive wind rose up from the throat of the hallway behind him and blew goblinkin and warriors before it, rolling them into piles that became bloody fights. Arrows flew for just a moment, then the combatants were far too close to deal with each other with anything more than edged steel.

Raisho was immediately in his element, coming over to guard Juhg just as Cobner wove a net of deadly steel around the Grandmagister. Jassamyn sprinted up the stairwell, her bow in her hand as she shot goblinkin archers who stood at the balcony and tried to shoot the human, dwarven, and elven warriors below. Her draca fought at her side, spitting flame and raking eyes out with its talons.

After the wind subsided, Aldhran screamed in rage and ran at Craugh with his sword raised over his head, obviously intending to halve the wizard. Moving with speed and economy, Craugh blocked the sword blow and returned a blow of his own that Aldhran riposted.

Then Aldhran threw his hand out. Magical force rippled between them and Craugh left his feet, flying back against the large double doors that led out into the main courtyard.

Bright sunlight shone down on Craugh as he crawled to his feet. He set his pointy hat aright, then gestured. Immediately Aldhran was lifted from his feet and yanked out into the courtyard as well.

Unwilling to miss the fight, and having precious little room to maneuver inside the overcrowded great room, Juhg lunged around combatants. He picked up a mace that one of the goblinkin had dropped and used it for great effect, smashing goblinkin toes and kneecaps—and, once, a goblinkin noggin, when one came down close enough for him to manage it. He left a ragged line of victims behind him, helping the outnumbered human, elven, and dwarven warriors.

Craugh and Aldhran continued their battle under the morning sun that reached rosy fingers of dawn over the Haze Mountains. Their shadows reached long and lean behind them.

Every time the staff and sword met, sparks flared out several feet in all directions.

Looking toward the front gates, Juhg saw that the massive doors had not opened. The goblinkin so far were able to defend against their attackers, and now some of them were starting to pull back from their posts along the massive wall to help with the small group already within their walls.

"Raisho," Juhg called. "Jassamyn. They haven't gotten the gate doors open yet." He took off, running across the horse-tramped earth. He shoved *The Book of Time* deep into his jacket pocket and pulled the drawstrings.

The inner courtyard formed a great rectangle that held a drill yard and combat exercise equipment to the left and low horse stalls to the right. Choosing discretion over certain destruction, Juhg ran to the right, climbing over the side of the corral that held the horses.

Arrows whipped past him for an instant, then one of the brighter goblinkin commanders realized that the archers endangered the animals more than Juhg because hitting a horse was much simpler than hitting a fleet-footed dweller. He ran, shooing the horses by flailing his arms, causing them to charge into the goblinkin that tried to intercept him.

Raisho was at his heels, forcing the goblinkin to turn immediately to face the threat of the young sailor's flashing and deadly cutlass. Jassamyn didn't even pause as she nocked arrow after arrow, sending shafts into the goblinkin that managed to get in front of Juhg.

A trio of goblinkin got ahead of Juhg and he managed to avoid them by sliding between the feet of a mare, then leaping back up on the other side. He grabbed a pitchfork and threw it into the face of the first goblinkin that came around the horse. Still on the move, Juhg ran behind another trotting mare, grabbed her tail, and swarmed up onto her rump. He was up on her rump before she kicked and planted a hoof into the second goblinkin's face.

Juhg ran across the horse's back as it broke into a trot, then leaped to the roof of the low shed that offered the horse shelter from the elements. The third goblinkin drew back its sword to swing on him, but Jassamyn put an arrow through its head.

At the end of the shed, Juhg leaped to the ground again, crying out as pain racked his injured ankle. Goblinkin archers atop the wall turned and fired at him, but he ducked in close to the wall and ran toward the gates. Jassamyn brought down two more goblinkin archers as he moved. Then Raisho was there, covering his back as they streaked for the windlasses that held the drawbridge up and that raised the metal gate behind it.

Juhg drew his knife as Raisho stepped in front of him and engaged two of the goblinkin guards protecting the windlasses. The young sailor cleaved the head of one of his two opponents, then found himself momentarily fighting for his life against the second.

Passing by the goblinkin, Juhg kicked out with his leg and stomped the creature's foot as hard as he could. During the moment of distraction and dropped guard, Raisho slit its throat with the cutlass. In the next moment, Jassamyn put an arrow through the heart of a goblinkin along the wall.

Then Juhg was at the drawbridge windlass. His knife scraped across the rope and the strands parted like butter. The drawbridge fell open with a massive thump.

Moving on to the windlass that raised the huge iron gate, Juhg started tugging but found that he lacked the strength to move it more than an inch at a time. "Raisho. Help."

Coming over to join him, the young sailor leaned into the task. His muscles rippled and the windlass turned rapidly. The human, elven, and dwarven warriors waiting outside the gate rushed forward at once, screaming war cries.

In seconds, the inner courtyard was a bloody battleground. The goblinkin held for just a moment, then crumpled and gave way like a beaver's dam during a high flood. They fell and fell again.

In the center of the courtyard, Craugh blocked Aldhran Khempus's sword thrust and reversed his staff, catching his opponent's neck in the forked end of the staff. Mercilessly, Craugh twisted the staff and broke Aldhran's neck with an audible snap. Then he held high the savage trophy he'd claimed, showing the rest of the goblinkin that their master was no more.

Almost immediately, the fight left the goblinkin. No quarter was offered, though; the human, elves, and dwarves wouldn't allow it. The few
goblinkin that weren't killed or tossed off the mountain ended up chased
down the mountainside till they managed to escape into the forest. Not
many of them made the escape.

Juhg stood there in the middle of it all, knowing that he stood at a piv-
otal period in history. In his mind, words were already connecting that
would tell of the day, the men, and the battle.

Lord of the Libraries

uhg climbed the stairs that led to the Grandmagister's office. It was strange going there because he had been so used to going to the Grandmagister's old office. But so much building was going on now to restore the Vault of All Known Knowledge that he knew it would take a long time to get used to it.

In addition to the renovation, the dwarven architects had also designed new wings for the addition of the books they were even now bringing in from the Library Tuhl had served at. A lot of the materials that Library had gathered had been dark and evil and malignant, but they had a number of books as well that replaced all and more of what the Vault of All Known Knowledge had lost in the attack triggered by the trap Aldhran Khempus had set. As soon as books were copied at one Library, they were quickly sent to the other. Copies would soon be on hand at both sites.

Farther down the Knucklebones Mountains, in the shadows of the Ogre's Fingers, the newest buildings were being added. Those were Juhg's pride and joy, a surprise gift from the Grandmagister and the dwarven construction board. Four schoolhouses had been designed to train teachers who wanted to go out to the mainland to establish schools there. Or to train people from the mainland who wanted to learn to read and write, learn the histories of their people, and return home to share everything they had learned.

Five months had passed since the battle up in the Haze Mountains. Everyone who had lived had healed, though there were a number who had fallen in battle. Their names lived on in tales told by warriors, and in the book that Juhg had written about all that had led up to the battle that morning.

It was the first time Juhg had ever felt strange about writing about things he had done and participated in, primarily because he had had such a dramatic impact on the outcome of things.

But the Grandmagister had insisted that no one else could write the tale. However, the Grandmagister had relented and agreed to edit the work when it was finished, as well as add articles and monographs and an appendix on things that needed to be better fleshed out that Juhg judged himself not capable of doing.

They had worked on the book back and forth for nearly all of those five months while handling increased visits to Greydawn Moors, helping make decisions about the renovations to the Library, and agreeing on the schoolhouses as well as the curriculum that would be taught.

Imarish *was* going to be the center for the first mainland school. Armies of humans, elves, and dwarves were already gathering to drive the bridge-building goblinkin from Imarish within the next year, long before the goblinkin could reach the Canal City.

At the door, Juhg waited politely for a moment, enjoying watching the Grandmagister reading, something he had seldom gotten to do during the past five months. It was, Juhg saw, an old favorite of the Grandmagister's from Hralbomm's Wing. A little tattered, perhaps, but still readable. Juhg was also certain that the copy wasn't the only one that existed. The Grandmagister had also gotten the Librarians producing copies at a never-before-seen rate. Some of the dwellers who had left the service of the Library came back of their own volition, feeling perhaps a little threatened by the newcomers arriving at the Yondering Docks on a daily basis.

The title of the work was *Taurak Bleiyz and the Bleak Pits of Darkhearted Vormoral*.

"Will he save her?" Juhg asked. "The mighty dweller hero, Taurak Bleiyz, I mean? Will he save the fair Gylesse?"

Looking up from the book, the Grandmagister marked his place with a forefinger and smiled. "Of course Taurak Bleiyz will save the fair Gylesse from the Bleak Pits of Darkhearted Vormoral. Doesn't he always?"

"In the best stories, yes."

"And don't forget, he has his magical war club, Toadthumper, at his side."

Juhg smiled and felt the scar still pulling at the side of his face.

"Come in," the Grandmagister invited.

Juhg went in and sat. They talked for a few minutes about the construction going on, then about the book. The Grandmagister had finished the final reading only the night before and found it a very good read. He'd put it into production that morning and there was already a long line of people who wanted to read the books as fast as they could be put out.

"I've asked you here to tell you something," the Grandmagister said after they'd drifted into a comfortable silence.

"What?" Juhg asked.

"Well, I've asked you here to tell you good-bye, Juhg."

"Are you going somewhere?"

"Yes, yes I am."

That bothered Juhg. "But the Library—"

"Will be fine in your hands," the Grandmagister told him. "Both of them."

"Both of them?" Juhg replied.

"Yes. We now control both Libraries, that which we've managed to save from the Vault as well as Tuhl's collection. You are now Lord of the Libraries and it is up to you to manage the collections as you see fit."

"Couldn't I go with you?"

The Grandmagister shook his head. "Not on this trip. Nor do I think you would want to go. Your work is here, Juhg. You're a teacher, and I think you're going to be the finest teacher ever."

"But you're a teacher, too. You taught me."

"There's a difference between you and me," the Grandmagister said. "At the very heart of you, you want to teach. You love showing people new skills and watching them make them their own. You love helping people understand things they'd never even truly wondered about before. As Lord of the Libraries, you will teach others to do the same. It is no longer the time for books and knowledge to be kept in a vault. It should be loaned out for all." He paused. "But the heart of me, my heart, is something else."

"What?"

"I'm a rover, Juhg. That's why I kept going back to the mainland all these years."

"You were searching for books."

"The search for books was important," the Grandmagister allowed, "but that was the excuse, not the reason. I love seeing new places these days, Juhg. Meeting new people. Having new experiences." He smiled. "I suppose it's Hallekk's fault in a way. I mean, he is the one who shanghaied me and first brought me aboard *One-Eyed Peggie*. But it's not his fault. He's a pirate at heart, and probably always will be."

"Where are you going?" Juhg thought the trip sounded permanent, and that worried him.

Reaching into his desk, the Grandmagister pulled out *The Book of Time*. It looked more like a book these days, journal-sized and filled with pages, though it still had gemstone covers and gemstone color plates inside.

As Juhg had kept it, he found that gradually it adjusted to the Grandmagister. One day he'd gotten up and found out he wasn't able to pick it up anymore. But the Grandmagister had been able to.

From that day forward, the Grandmagister kept it. Juhg wasn't sad to see it go. It was only a short time after that custodial change that *The Book of Time* began to have pages.

Craugh, over dinner down at Carason's Eatery, which still existed and was still the Grandmagister's favorite place to eat, had voiced the opinion that *The Book of Time* had found a kindred spirit in the Grandmagister and had started changing itself to suit the Grandmagister's tastes. Neither Juhg nor the Grandmagister had another opinion.

The Grandmagister tapped the book. "I'm going here," he said.

"Into the In-Betweenness?"

"Yes," the Grandmagister said. "Into the In-Betweenness . . . and beyond."

"How will you get there?"

"The book will take me. I've been reading it every chance I get. Every time I open it, I find something new, something I've never thought about or a new way of thinking about something I've done or seen for a very long time."

"But why would you want to go there?"

"Because it exists, Juhg, and because I can. If you don't understand that, you never will. I just love the idea of going there."

"But you're the Grandmagister. You've got a lot of work to do here."

The Grandmagister shook his head. "All the work that needs doing here can be done by you. Or at least overseen by you. You've been doing more of the day-to-day decision-making than I have for the last month. And you've never even noticed." He paused. "You're ready for this, Juhg. Just as I am ready to begin my journeys among the worlds that lie beyond the In-Betweenness."

"When are you leaving?"

The Grandmagister reached under the desk and took out his old traveling pack. "Now."

"You can't leave *now*," Juhg protested.

"If I don't," the Grandmagister said, "it will only prolong the sadness. We'll both dread it." His voice thickened. "I love you, Juhg. Very much. Part of me doesn't want to go."

"Then don't." Juhg's eyes felt hot with tears.

"I thought about that, but *The Book of Time* simply opens up too many possibilities. I can't pass them up. And somewhere, somehow, something that I learn could be important to what you're doing here. We've already had troubles walk in on us from other places. Maybe we need to know more about those places." He stood and walked around the desk. "Now come on and give me a farewell hug. I've got to be going. I really do or I fear that I'll never go at all and I'll always wonder what might have been."

Hugging the Grandmagister, Juhg thought about all the adventures they had shared and all the things the Grandmagister had taught him.

"I'll miss you," Juhg said in a tight voice. He felt defeated and wanted to cry all at the same time. He remembered when he'd left Greydawn Moors, so certain that he and the Grandmagister had finally ended up along different paths. But that had been his decision and it had been easier to live with.

Now . . . now he couldn't imagine a time when the Grandmagister would not be in this place. It wasn't fair. And at the same time, he knew that he couldn't ask the Grandmagister to give up his grand adventure.

"And I'll miss you." With effort and a deep sigh, the Grandmagister released him and stood back.

"Does Craugh know?"

"Yes. He isn't happy about it, either. And I've written letters for the ones that I didn't get to say personal good-byes to. I would appreciate it if you would take care of that for me."

"I will."

"And take care of Craugh, would you? He's not much for making friends, but I know that he respects you a lot."

"I'll take care of that, too." In fact, Craugh had been around more the last five months than he ever had. He'd even taken dinners with Juhg and talked long into the night.

"Then I guess it's time for me to go." The Grandmagister took out *The Book of Time* and opened it.

"Before you go," Juhg said, "will you tell me how everything we're doing here is going to work out? With the schools and the teaching? Are we truly going to make a big difference with what we're doing?"

"There are some things," the Grandmagister said, "that you're not supposed to know ahead of time." And with that, he faded away like he'd never been.

For a long time, Juhg sat in the Grandmagister's office and felt lost and alone. Finally, knowing there were things that needed doing and that he could not begrudge his mentor his adventure because he loved him, he got up and went out of the building.

Outside, he was surprised to see Craugh sitting in a cart inside the Library courtyard.

The wizard looked at him, and there was sadness in his green eyes. "Is he gone then, apprentice?"

"Yes," Juhg said in a hollow voice.

A single tear slid down Craugh's face, but Juhg knew he was not going to mention it. After all, he'd seen Craugh turn a man into a toad in Skull Canal.

"I'm going to miss the little rascal," Craugh said. "He was forever getting me into some mischief that I had no business being involved in."

"I know."

The wizard wiped away his tear with a forefinger and acted as if he didn't know what it was. "That little rover has all the secrets of the universe now. Well, I guess that's the way it's supposed to be."

Juhg hesitated. Despite how everything had ended, there were still questions. "Did you ever ask him what happened to your son?"

Craugh shook his head. "That's all in the past. We're not supposed to worry about that now."

"No," Juhg agreed, "we have other jobs to do." But still, his uncertainty worried over the mystery of Lord Kharrion. *Was the Goblin Lord truly gone forever? Or did Kharrion yet have a trick to play?*

mel odom

Soon after they returned to the Grandmagister's office, a knock sounded at the door.

Glancing up, Juhg saw Dockett Butterblender standing there in his new Third Level Librarian robes. After reviewing the writing he'd done on the siege of Greydawn Moors, as well as the destruction of the Library, the Grandmagister had given Dockett an immediate promotion. Of course, the Grandmagister being the Grandmagister, he'd also asked for some revisions on the manuscript.

"Yes, Third Level Librarian Dockett," Juhg said.

Dockett looked a little uncertain. "I was expecting to find the Grandmagister here."

"You have," Craugh said. He waved eloquently to Juhg. "Grandmagister Juhg. Chosen by Grandmagister Lamplighter before he took leave of the Vault of All Known Knowledge."

For the first time, Juhg realized just where the Grandmagister had left him. And Craugh was a willing accomplice in the feat. The floor seemed to spin beneath him.

Grandmagister Juhg. Grandmagister Juhg, indeed.

"Then I can leave this book with you," Dockett said, lifting the book he'd worked so hard on.

"Yes." Juhg's voice was dry and raspy. "Of course. I'll attend to it in short order, Dockett."

The young dweller smiled. "Thank you, Grandmagister." He turned to go.

A thought seized Juhg's mind. "Dockett, a moment before you go."

Dockett turned. "Yes, Grandmagister?"

"It comes to my attention that I'll need someone to help me carry out my duties," Juhg said. "There will be a number of things to accomplish if we're to put both Libraries back into working order."

Hesitantly, Dockett nodded.

"Take the rest of the day off," Juhg instructed. "Be here at eight in the morning. You and I have a lot to discuss."

Smiling, Dockett said, "I won't let you down, Grandmagister." He turned and made to flee down the hall. Unfortunately, his foot caught in the stiff folds of his new robe and he fell head over heels. Embarrassed, he got up again, nodded to Juhg, and left hurriedly.

"Not exactly the most graceful of dwellers, is he?" Craugh commented.

"He's dedicated," Juhg said. "And wise. I'll take that." He flipped open Dockett's book, amazed by the depth of detail and the fine, steady hand that had rendered the drawings.

"Ah yes," Craugh said, "another book that will probably not be read."

"Wrong," Juhg said with fire in his voice. "This book *will* be read. Just as all the books about these struggles will be read. The world can no longer cloak itself in ignorance and an abdication of responsibility. People throughout the mainland will have to learn to read again, and they will have to learn their histories. The ones who don't will be left behind by those who do." He held up the book, remembering all who had shed blood to save the Library, and all of the dangers all of them had faced. "Choosing to remain uneducated will no longer be acceptable. Not by me. Not by any Librarian who serves under me. We will provide schools and lessons and reasons to learn."

Craugh smiled and gave a slight bow. "Yes, Lord of the Libraries."

Juhg felt slightly embarrassed. "That does sound a little over the top, doesn't it?"

"Perhaps a little."

"But I mean what I say, Craugh."

"I know that you do. It won't be easy."

Juhg sighed. "No. But we'll get it done. Somehow." Suddenly, the enormity of what he was about to embark on hit him. He felt alone and overwhelmed.

An uncomfortable silence hung in the air for a moment, dragging out through the sounds of the rebuilding effort and the outdoor classes where the new arrivals were being given tours and training.

"I was thinking," Craugh said, "that we're both going to need a friend. Especially one who shared as much of Wick as each of us did."

"I was thinking the same thing."

Craugh looked out at the blue sky. "I've got a jug of old wine I've been saving for a special occasion. And a wheel of cheese that I'm sure I paid way too much for on a day I was feeling overly generous. We could go for a ride, if you've the time and you're of a mind to. I could tell you stories about Wick that you've never heard."

And Juhg was certain the wizard could do that. "I'd like that," he said. "I'd like that very much."